CIRCUIT OF HEAVEN

CIRCUIT
OF
HEAVEN

Dennis Danvers

AVON · EOS

Excerpts from *Rebecca* by Daphne du Maurier, copyright © 1938 by Daphne du Maurier Browning.

AVON BOOKS
A division of
The Hearst Corporation
1350 Avenue of the Americas
New York, New York 10019

Copyright © 1998 by Dennis Danvers
Interior design by Kellan Peck
Visit our website at **http://www.AvonBooks.com/Eos**
ISBN: 1-56865-683-1

First Avon Eos Printing: February 1998

AVON EOS TRADEMARK REG. U.S. PAT. OFF. AND IN OTHER COUNTRIES, MARCA REGISTRADA, HECHO EN U.S.A.

Printed in the U.S.A.

For my mom, who dreamed of being a singer,
and my dad, who dreamed of being a writer.

The world was all before them, where to choose
Their place of rest, and Providence their guide.
They, hand in hand with wand'ring steps and slow,
Through Eden took their solitary way.

Milton, *Paradise Lost*

Prologue

NEWMAN ROGERS HAD BEEN ERRATIC LATELY, DE-spondent, flying into a rage over nothing, working into the wee hours of the morning. His coworkers would often find him sleeping on the sofa in the waiting room when they came into work in the morning, or even slumped over his computer. He was brilliant, a genius perhaps, but he was only one member of a team working to develop artificial intelligence and was not thought to be indispensable. Whatever he was working on so compulsively—he didn't share it with the rest of the team—soon prompted him to cease work altogether on the job he was hired to do. Management was concerned.

And then, on a mid-December afternoon in 2020, he was fired for calling his supervisor an idiot. He was thirty-nine, well thought of until recently, but under the terms of his contract he couldn't work on artificial intelligence research for any other firm for a period of two years, even though every other firm would only be interested in him for such research.

None of this seemed to concern him, however. He holed up in his apartment and continued to work, hacking his former employer's system late at night. A few months after his dismissal, he published an obscure paper demonstrating, with a string of elegant proofs, that artificial intelligence was impossible. He added, however, in a modest concluding paragraph, that it might be possible to digitize human personality and, building on techniques already in use in medicine and virtual reality simulations, transfer the personality to another organism, or even to another, more durable, medium altogether.

While competing theorists flung themselves at his proofs like a pack of skilled dogs, a small group of wealthy and aging businessmen contacted him and offered to finance his research. Suddenly he found himself in charge of a team of researchers with almost limitless resources. In 2030, the first practical application of his work, the transfer of the identity of a ninety-seven-year-old owner of a large insurance company into the quick-grown clone of a healthy young man, was performed with complete success. Even young men eventually die, however, and Newman was encouraged to continue developing a more durable medium for human intelligence.

To help finance this venture, his backers, over his objections, marketed Constructs—humans made from portions of several different personalities implanted into a cloned body—as servants and laborers. To overcome customers' uneasiness with what some described as the new slavery, the clones, with increasingly clever, even entertaining gene splices, were made to look as if they weren't human. Unfortunately (and as Newman had predicted) the partial personalities that made up each Construct reconstituted themselves over the years, remembering their former lives and identities.

In 2040, Rogers succeeded in designing the Alternative Life Medium Assembly, ALMA for short, a vast network of silicon crystals in which any number of human personalities might dwell in a world they would experience as indistinguishable from the real world. The operating system could be programmed to eliminate disease, violence, and death—and it would last forever. He had invented paradise.

The new world government, shakily formed in 2036, sold the former site of the Pentagon for the construction of ALMA, dubbed "the Bin" by the media, a nickname that stuck. In 2050 it went on-line, and some half a million souls who could afford it entered their new world. In 2060, after ten years of mounting pressure from residents of the real world, ALMA was opened up to everyone eighteen years or older who did not scan as criminally insane. By 2074, the Supreme Court (the majority of whom now resided in the Bin) lifted the ban against minors, so that anyone, young and old alike, might enter the Bin and live forever.

After a few years, the only people left in the real world were members of religious sects who believed the Bin to be in violation of God's laws; the criminally insane; and a handful of persons who, for one reason or another, stubbornly distrusted paradise. By 2080, the remaining population of the real world, not counting Constructs, was about 2.5 million, though reliable figures were hard to come by. The population of the Bin was over 12 billion.

As for Newman Rogers, the patron saint of ALMA, no one knew where he was or what he was doing, though rumors were plentiful.

1

JUSTINE WAS DREAMING SHE WAS SOMEONE ELSE: She was in the real world, a long time ago, before she was born—there were people everywhere and cars moving up and down the streets like huge schools of brightly colored fish. All the shop windows were intact, lit up with fluorescent and neon, full of cheap jewelry and boom boxes and skimpy clothes stretched over chipped mannequins. She hurried past them, a light drizzle falling, the streets black and slick, glistening with reflected light. The ozone smell of the rain hovered over the stench of exhaust fumes and urine and rotting food.

She was seventeen, sneaking out at night, hurrying to meet a boy around the corner, at the end of the next block. His name was Steve, and she remembered his face—maybe twenty, thin, a sharp nose, a closely trimmed goatee, hungry eyes. She had his address on a slip of paper wadded up in her hand, and when she thought about him, her hand tightened around the lump of paper, and she walked even faster. She was crazy for him. She hardly knew him, and Alice, a girlfriend, said he was bad news, but she was crazy for him anyway.

She started up the narrow stairs to his apartment, when

a door opened above her, and he stepped onto the landing, light blazing at his back. He must've had a dozen floods in there. Music blared in the cavernous stairwell.

"Hey Angelina," he shouted, and she followed him into his room, cluttered with electronic equipment and wires snaking across the floor. The lights were on stands, all aimed at the bed in the middle of the room. He circled around her, taking her jacket, wrapping his arms around her, stripping off her shirt. He seemed to be everywhere at once. He pushed her onto the bed and looked down at her. She could hardly see him for the glare of the lights. "Put this on," he said, pulling something over her head like a bathing cap. He pinned her arms and pushed himself into her, hammering away at her. He came in a matter of minutes and rolled off of her. She opened her hand and there was his address, wadded to a pulp in her hand. He yanked the cap off her head, and she woke up.

Her heart was racing. Her stomach was in a knot. Her fist was clenched around the sheet. Slowly, she opened it. There was no slip of paper there. It was just a dream. I'm still me, she thought, still Justine, twenty years old, in the Bin six weeks—and I've never seen a car in the real world except rusted out junkers, never walked down a city street without feeling the grit of glass under my shoes.

The girl in her dream was named Angelina, and it'd been 2002. She had no idea how she knew that, but there it was, like a memory. Justine was born in 2061.

In the present, she was in her hotel room with a man's naked arm across her chest. He wore a fat gold ring with an onyx pentagon on his middle finger, a heavy gold chain around his wrist. His fingers were fat and stubby, his nails buffed and polished to a shine. Downy white hair covered his arm, the back of his hand, like moss. He was sound asleep, his face half-buried in the pillow. He'd said he was a senator, she remembered. He looked the part—silver hair, strong jaw, square shoulders, just enough crow's feet to make him seem wise and fatherly. Old enough to be her father. She couldn't remember how she'd ended up in bed with him. I must've been tying one on, she thought. Watching him sleep, there was something she didn't like about him, though apparently there'd been something she'd liked well enough the night before.

She looked around the room, moving her head carefully to make sure she didn't wake him. A narrow shaft of light, where the curtains weren't quite drawn, cut across the room. It was a nice room, a tasteful room, with delicate furniture and a vaseful of jonquils on the dresser. Not the sort of room to wake up in with a stranger. His clothes and hers, tangled and inside out, were scattered around the rose-colored carpet. She didn't remember that either.

She remembered fucking him. She remembered that too clearly, tortured herself with the memory for a while, thinking, Justine, you're too damn lonely.

She carefully lifted his arm off her and slid out of bed, placing his arm on her pillow as if it were a sleeping kitten. She gathered up her clothes and went into the bathroom, locking the door behind her. As she took a shower she tried to remember the man in her bed. His name was W something—William or Waylon or—Winston, that was it. She was almost sure. Winston.

But when it came to what kind of person this Winston was, all she could remember was lewd, cartoonish sex like something out of a porno. God, she thought, that wasn't me. I must've been worse than drunk.

She took a long shower, fiddling with the massage, lathering herself up till she looked like a marshmallow. She wanted to put off for as long as possible talking to the stranger in her bed. But then, she asked herself, who else are you going to talk to? She didn't know anyone in D.C., not a fucking soul. She rinsed herself off, watching the

7

huge gobs of suds pile up around the drain. She stepped out of the shower, wiped the steamed-up mirror with the side of her arm, and grimaced at herself, thinking, I don't even know the guy I just fucked.

But then, she thought as she dried off, if I wasn't myself, maybe he wasn't himself either. By the time she'd finished blow-drying her hair, she'd decided to at least give the guy a chance. Maybe have breakfast with someone for a change. She shut off the dryer and stuck it into its little cubby hole. The whine of the thing echoing off the tiles still rang in her ears. She picked up the wad of clothes and disentangled them. They were surprisingly fresh for the night she'd spent. She had started turning them right-side out when she realized there were voices coming from her room.

She put her ear to the door, but couldn't make out what was being said, though the tone and cadence came through. There were two male voices, one deep and rich, the senator's voice, but talking too fast, making excuses she would guess, and the other voice, cutting through the senator's like a nun bringing a young sinner to his knees, with a few unhurried phrases as resonant as a bowed cello. She listened until they seemed to be done, but couldn't make out a word, listened hard for someone opening and closing the door to the room, but there wasn't a sound.

She dressed quickly and quietly and came back into the room. There was only Winston sitting on the edge of the bed, fully dressed, his hair neatly combed. He rose to his feet and bowed slightly. He was wearing a turn-of-the-century Italian suit, charcoal, almost black, with faint pin-stripes. It hung perfectly, showing no signs of having spent the night in a heap on the floor. "Good morning, Justine," he said. His smile was almost paternal. He's as embarrassed as I am, she thought.

"Good morning. Would you like some coffee or something?" She went to the room service pad set into the wall beside the bed.

"No thanks," he said quickly. "I really must be going." He smiled apologetically. "An important committee meeting."

"Hope you don't mind, but I need some." She pressed the little picture of a black cup of coffee, steam lines rising out of it in neat squiggles. A panel slid open, and there was coffee. Like *Star Trek,* she thought. She looked around the room, but there was no one else there, no sign anyone had been there. The room door was right by the bathroom. If someone had left, she would've heard him. She blew on the coffee until it was drinking temperature, then drank half of it. "Was somebody here? Were you talking to somebody just now?"

"Talking?"

"Just now. I thought I heard you talking to somebody in here."

He shook his head more emphatically. "No, I wasn't talking to anyone." He squared his shoulders and shrugged with his hands. The chain around his wrist made a clicking noise. "I'm afraid I sometimes discuss things out loud with myself. A silly habit. Actually, I was wondering if you might join me for a dinner party this evening at my sister's house in Front Royal. It's my nephew's birthday. I believe you told me last night that you would be free this evening."

She laughed. "I'll have to take your word for what I said last night. I don't remember much of it. What else did I say?"

The question seemed to make him nervous. He spoke as if reciting— "You said you were a singer, that you were only in town for a week and didn't know anyone here, not even the musicians you'll be performing with. I thought, under the circumstances, you might like to meet some people." He added sympathetically, "It's a bit disorienting at first."

"Disorienting?"

"The Bin. You're only just in."

She nodded. "Six weeks. But I suppose I told you that already last night."

"Yes."

She sat down on the edge of the bed and motioned for him to sit down, but he remained standing. "Do you have strange dreams when you're first in?"

He furrowed his brow and shook his head. "Dreams? No, I've never heard of that."

"To tell you the truth, Winston—it's Winston, isn't it?— I don't remember how we met."

"I bought you a drink in the bar."

She nodded, contemplating the tangle of rumpled sheets. She couldn't even remember going into the bar. "I apparently didn't need it."

"Maybe we can make a fresh start," he said hopefully. "Just forget about last night."

"That's easy." She laughed. "I've already forgotten it." She'd been afraid he'd be all over her, but now he was polite, almost formal. I must've laid on the lonely-little-girl bit a little thick last night, she thought, and now he feels sorry for me. Truth was, she felt sorry for herself. The last six weeks was a series of hotel rooms. No friends to speak of. Even her old band had quit or wandered away. She wasn't sure what had become of them.

"So what do you say? Seven-thirty? I'll meet you in the lobby."

"Sure," she said. "I'd like to meet some people."

"Wonderful!" He bowed again, excusing himself and letting himself out before she even had the chance to stand up. Maybe my instincts about him were wrong, she told herself. Maybe he's okay.

She finished her coffee, pushed the icon for another cup, and was reminded again of *Star Trek*. But this time it struck her—she'd never seen *Star Trek*. It was an old TV show, she knew that, but there hadn't been any TV since before she was born. The only TV she could've seen was playing in the corner in some period virtual. But there it was, this memory of some guy in a funny uniform—Captain Kirk, his name was—taking a cup of coffee out of the wall just as she had done. Who the hell is Captain Kirk? she wondered. How do I know this? She shook her head, figuring she was just hungover, still spooked by her dream.

SHE NEEDED TO GET OUT, DO SOMETHING. SHE HUNTED through her bag and found a letter from her agent listing her dates for the next several weeks. In the letter was the number of the hotel where her new band was staying. She called and got John, the bass player. He had the visual turned off, so she didn't get a look at him, and his voice was low and muffled. She told him she wanted to meet the band at the club in the morning so they could rehearse before tomorrow night.

"No problem," he said.

"How's eleven?"

"No problem."

"So what're you doing today?"

"Sleeping."

"See you tomorrow morning, then."

She hung up the phone and pulled her address book out of her bag. She looked through it. It was mostly empty, nobody in it she could really call a good friend, just acquaintances—other musicians, her agent, some club owners, little more than voiceless faces in her memory and some of them not even that. She finished her coffee and went down to the lobby.

* * *

HER HOTEL WAS ONE OF THE "RESTORED" ONES OFF DU-pont Circle. In the real world, the place was a ruin. But in the Bin, the lobby was done up turn-of-the-century with lots of brass and etched glass and fiber-optic light fixtures sprouting out of sconces.

She went into the restaurant, sat in the corner chewing on a bagel and drinking another cup of coffee, watching all the tourists and their families planning their days with maps and brochures. She imagined herself one of the little girls, crawling on her daddy's lap as he pointed out the pictures of the places they would go. Behind her, a table burst into laughter, and she rose from her chair and left without looking back.

I'll be a tourist myself, she thought—the monuments today, galleries tomorrow, the White House and the Capitol the next day. I've only seen pictures of those places. Maybe I'll even meet somebody. You couldn't tell. They said it was easy in here. They said everything was easy in here.

She spent most of the day going to the monuments— Washington, Lincoln, Jefferson, Rogers—the famous dead. But it was the living she watched. Thousands of them. A few were by themselves—busy people on their way to someplace, or drugged-out zombies who didn't care where they were going. But most were with somebody— a friend, a child, a lover. She watched their faces, their hands gesturing, the way they leaned this way and that as they spoke to each other. The way they sometimes touched.

All the while she kept thinking about Angelina and her dream. The crowded streets. The bright windows. She'd been inside a world she'd only read about in books or seen in a virtual. She could still smell the cars and the wet streets. She wondered if she might be cracking up. There were scare stories about people going into the Bin and breaking up like a virtual in a thunderstorm, that there were flaws in the crystalline structure of the Bin, and you could find yourself in nightmarish worlds that made no sense, completely alone. But in my dream, she thought, I wasn't alone. I was inside Angelina.

BY MIDAFTERNOON, SHE WAS WANDERING THROUGH THE largest and most crowded monument, the Rogers Memorial. There were exhibits covering every aspect of Newman Rogers' life, detailing his every achievement, but the center of attention was an enormous holograph of him, towering over the central hall, delivering his last speech—the day ALMA went on-line—over and over again.

He was a tiny man, blown up to be forty feet tall. The Savior of Mankind. The podium came to his chest so that those who stood too close in front couldn't see his face and had to content themselves with his baggy pants. His soft, reedy voice echoed through the hall, and though people were jammed in on every side, the only sounds were shuffling feet, and here and there, someone crying.

Justine worked her way up the escalators to the third-floor balcony. She wanted to see his face. By the time she squeezed into a place at the rail, he was coming to the end of his speech. He took off his glasses and laid them on the podium, rubbed his enormous eyes. When he opened them, he was looking directly at Justine—

> I have only one more thing to say before we change the world, forever—for that's what we're doing, you know. I'd hoped that one of the other speakers, more qualified than myself, would've said it first, and let me off the hook. But it's only fair that it should be me, since I'm the one who got us here.

There are those who have said that by ending death, by eating from the tree of Life, we sin by presuming to be gods. I confess I sympathize with their views. I can only pray that God grants us a godlike wisdom to match our cleverness.

There are more—like the other speakers here today—who seem to think that with the end of death, the human task is finished; that with the end of death, comes the easy life of Olympians; that with the end of death, comes the end of God—for who needs Him anymore, now that we've built our own heaven? To these people, I would like to quote from the Book of Job—

> *Is not God in the height of heaven?*
> *And behold the height of the stars, how high they are!*
> *And thou sayest, How doth God know?*
> *Can he judge through the dark cloud?*
> *Thick clouds are a covering to him, that he seeth not;*
> *and he walketh in the circuit of heaven.*

The story goes that he muttered, "Turn the damn thing on," as he left the podium, but if he did, it wasn't recorded on this holograph. It flickered and began again: Newman Rogers noisily spreading his notes on the podium, his hair blowing across his face, waiting for the applause to die down so that he might speak, looking, Justine decided, sadder than any man she'd ever seen.

She searched the faces of the crowd, one by one, not sure what she hoped to find there. There were others, like her, who were crying, but she couldn't tell whether they were crying for him or for his sentiments. She lowered her head and pushed through the crowd, brushing tears from her eyes.

14

*   *   *

SHE SET OUT IN NO PARTICULAR DIRECTION, HURRYING AT first, then slowing her pace. She was here now. This was home. She should take in the spring, enjoy walking down streets free of wild dogs and wild men. She didn't remember much of her life before she came in. That must be part of the disorientation Winston mentioned. *It's probably not anything I want to remember,* she thought.

It was still hours before she was to meet Winston at the hotel. She took one side street, then another, trying to get away from the buzz of so many people. Pretty soon, she was wandering through a residential neighborhood of nineteenth-century rowhouses, neatly trimmed hedges, and flower beds lining the sidewalk. She imagined herself opening one of the little iron gates and mounting the steps to knock on one of the heavy wooden doors framed in stained glass. *Hi, my name's Justine,* she'd say, *I'm new here.*

And they would say, *Why come in, dear, and have a cup of tea.*

She closed her eyes and let the daydream dissolve. When she opened them, she noticed a wooden sign hanging over a narrow brick stairway that descended to a basement shop:

> WARREN G. MENSO
> *Books on All Subjects*
> *Ancient and Modern*

She didn't know how she'd missed the sign before. She looked up and down the street. It was the only shop visible in either direction. *Maybe what I need is a book,* she thought. *Prop myself up in bed and lose myself in a novel.* She descended the moss-stained steps, breathing in the smell of damp stone. She pushed open the door, and a brass bell rang above her head, but no one appeared to greet her, and no one sat at the rolltop desk beside the door. A maze of pine shelving radiated from the doorway in all directions. Yellowing, hand-lettered index cards were thumbtacked here and there—*History, Romance, Horror, Art, Classics, Science Fiction, Mystery.* Each sign had an arrow like this ➡ to show the way. She chose *Classics* and walked down the narrow aisle, running her fingers along the spines of old, jacketless hardbacks.

She took one down, read a sentence or two, put it back, got another one. The old book smell of the place filled her with contentment. She loved to read. She hesitated as she started to take another book from the shelf. What have I read? she asked herself. Her head was full of authors and titles; she even knew something about them. *Wuthering Heights* was by Emily Bronte. It was the story of Cathy and Heathcliff. But when it came to whether she'd read a particular book or not, she couldn't be sure.

She scanned the shelves for a familiar title, and a faded green book with gold on the spine caught her eye. She tilted her head to read the title—*Rebecca* by Daphne du Maurier. She took it down. It was familiar, but she couldn't remember ever reading it. She opened it and read the beginning—

> *Last night I dreamt I went to Manderley again. It seemed to me I stood by the iron gate leading to the drive, and for a while I could not enter for the way was barred to me. There was a padlock and a chain upon the gate. I called in my dream to the lodge-keeper, and had no answer, and peering closer through the rusted spokes of the gate I saw that the lodge was uninhabited.*

She took it as a sign that the story began with a dream, just as her day had. She clutched the book to her chest and decided to spend the rest of the afternoon at Manderley with Rebecca—whoever she might turn out to be.

She heard someone clearing his throat and turned to find a little old man standing at the end of the aisle, a dreamy smile on his face. His body was slightly stooped, and he leaned on a cane, grasping it with bony hands. His hair was as white as paper. His wrinkled skin looked like cracked glaze on an ancient vase.

"It's a wonderful book, isn't it?" he said. Even his fluting voice was old and worn.

She blushed and looked down at the book she still clutched to her chest like a life preserver. "I don't know. I don't think I've read it."

He nodded, still smiling. "You've never seen anyone who looks so old, have you?"

"I'm sorry—"

He waved his cane a few inches above the floor and settled back onto it. "Don't be ridiculous. I know I'm a curiosity. Why would a sane man look like this in here?" He chuckled to himself. "But I don't want to forget I'm getting old, goddamnit. Be a hundred, week from today." He winked at her. "I want to look the part."

"I think you look wonderful," she said, and she meant it. There was something endearing about him, even noble. "I was just surprised."

He studied her for a moment, his head nodding almost imperceptibly. She didn't know if this nodding was another symptom of his age or something else—approval, she guessed from the light in his eyes. "Thank you," he said. "But for me there is no beauty like a young woman's in all the world, and you are a most beautiful young woman."

She blushed again. "Thank you. You must be Mr. Menso."

"That's me." He bowed over his cane and righted himself.

"I'm Justine Ingham," she said, and stuck out her right hand. He took it in his left, holding onto his cane with his right. He had a gentle touch, turning her hand over as if examining it, admiring it. There was nothing lecherous about it. Her hand in his looked young and beautiful. But his is beautiful too, she thought.

"I am most pleased to meet you, Justine. Most pleased." He squeezed her hand and let it go.

"I love your shop," she said.

"Thank you, my dear."

"How much do I owe you for this book?"

He waved his cane again. "Nothing. Don't use money. Damned nuisance. Why do we need money in here? I know people don't want to give it up, don't want to change a thing, want everything to be precisely what they were used to. Hell with that. Change is exactly what this place needs, don't you think?" He swept his arm to take in the whole Bin.

A pair of legs in dark brown trousers walked past the windows that ran along the ceiling at street level. "I certainly wanted a change this morning," she said. "But I really don't know what the Bin needs. I haven't been in that long."

"Well, I don't know what it needs either—though God knows I've tried to figure it out—and I've been in here since we cranked it up." He cocked his head to one side. "You don't sound too happy about being in here."

"No, it's fine. I just don't know anyone."

"Well, now you know me. You need to get out. Meet people."

"I'm going to a dinner party tonight."

He studied her again, nodding his head. She liked him and hoped they might become friends. She smiled back at him, and neither one of them said anything, until it was his turn to blush. "Forgive my staring," he said, bowing again, this time in apology. "You see, you remind me of someone I knew a very long time ago. You have a certain quality she had, a special something." He looked at her with his sad, wrinkled eyes. "We were sweethearts."

She was touched by the old-fashioned word, and his great, sad eyes, but she didn't know what to say, though he didn't seem to expect her to say anything.

He cleared his throat and pointed at *Rebecca*. "It's a swell book. You'll love it. Sure you don't want anything else? Got everything here. Like the sign says—all subjects, ancient and modern."

He wants to find me another book, Justine thought, give another gift to someone who reminds him of his sweetheart. "Do you have anything on dreams?" she asked.

"Follow me." He led her through several twists and turns to a dead end where a dozen shelves of books about dreams filled the wall. She stared at them stupidly, no idea what to look for.

"What aspect of dreams were you interested in?" Mr. Menso asked.

"Interpretation, I guess. I had an unusual dream this morning, and I want to figure it out. I can't seem to get it out of my head."

"How unusual?" he asked.

"It was so real," she said, and ended up telling him her dream from beginning to end. She felt comfortable with Mr. Menso, snug inside his labyrinth of books. He listened intently the whole while.

He plucked a book off the shelf and handed it to her. "This is what you need."

Lucid Dreaming: The Gateway to Your Hidden Selves, it said. By Gwenna R. Morse. It was a slim paperback. On the cover a woman was holding a door open, about to step across the threshold into a moonlit landscape of tree-covered hills, fields, and flowers. In the distance were the spires and towers of a magnificent city. Beneath the trees a circle of women danced. Justine turned it over in her hands. "This will help me interpret my dream?"

He dismissed the thought with a wave of his cane. "Interpretation. Freudian mumbo jumbo. Waste of time. No, this book will teach you how to enter into your dreams and take charge of them." He rapped the floor with his cane to punctuate his words.

Justine laughed nervously. "Why would I want to do that?"

He leaned toward her confidentially. "To understand the dreamer, Justine. Dreams are mere shadows. Only the dreamer is real."

"But that's just it. Angelina doesn't seem like some shadow to me. She seems real."

He danced his eyebrows and grinned at her. "Maybe she's dreaming of you, my dear."

She rocked her head from side to side in exaggerated confusion. "Mr. Menso, you're making my brain hurt."

He chuckled, bobbing his head up and down. "You're right. You're right. You are beautiful. You are young. It is spring. You shouldn't be cooped up in here with a dotty old man." He turned and led her back to the front door. "I am most delighted you came to see me today, Justine."

"This has been the very best part of my day," she said, hugging him hard. She kissed his cheek, and his skin on her lips was as dry as paper. He held open the door, and with some difficulty, followed her up the steps to the street. She promised to come see him again before she left D.C.

A block away she looked back, and he was still standing there, watching her. She waved, and he raised his hand to his lips and blew her a kiss. What a sweet man, she thought. What a dear, sweet man.

SHE WAS STILL ELATED WHEN SHE GOT BACK TO HER HOTEL. She'd made her first friend in the Bin. She stretched out on the bed with a cup of hot cocoa and read far enough in *Rebecca* to find out that Rebecca wasn't the heroine, but her new husband's dead wife—whose presence hung over the new bride's life like a cloud. Justine liked the heroine. She reminded her of herself—or at least the way she wanted to see herself—a little bit afraid of everything, but brave nonetheless. Brave enough to love her husband against the odds. She found her elation bleeding away, however, as she read of the young girl's seemingly hopeless love for a man who'd already had the perfect wife.

She grew drowsy from reading and set *Rebecca* aside. She picked up the dream book, thinking she'd nap and use whatever secrets it might give her. She opened it up and read the first paragraph:

> *Each of us possesses a myriad of identities: who we are, who we were, who we wish we were, who we've dreaded becoming. These selves live side by side in the world of our dreams. When, in the midst of a vivid dream, you become aware that you are dreaming, seize the power this moment has granted you: Interrogate the denizens of your dreamworld, shape this world to your desires, enter into the world you have created, and take possession of the boundless domains of your Self.*

This all sounded like pretty silly stuff to Justine. She flipped back to the publication date: copyright 1997. No wonder. The heyday of claptrap. All of a sudden she didn't feel like sleeping anymore. She didn't feel up to interrogating any dream denizens. She tossed the dream book aside. I still feel lonely, she thought. Hanging out with my Selves isn't likely to change that, no matter how many are lurking in there.

She had more time than she needed to get ready for dinner, but she couldn't think of anything else to do. She got out of bed and tried on all the dresses in her closet, spent an hour fussing with her hair. She wanted to look beautiful, like Mr. Menso said. She was young, and it was spring.

She was sitting in the lobby, waiting for Winston, by seven o'clock.

2

IT WAS NEMO'S TWENTY-FIRST BIRTHDAY, AND HE was on his way to visit his parents in the Bin, riding the Metro from Richmond to D.C. It'd been Christmas since he'd seen them last. Twice a year was about all he could handle.

Most of the time, it didn't bother him much anymore—it'd been eleven years, after all. But every time he went to see them he'd watch the world slide by outside the window, listen to the clatter of the wheels on the rails, and remember when they went into the Bin. Then he'd get mad all over, just as if he were ten years old again.

He'd figured for a long time that his parents were going in. It was only a matter of when. They talked over dinner about people they knew who'd already gone or were about to go, their voices thick with envy they thought Nemo was too young to notice. Then they'd cut him a guilty look and ask how things were going at school.

He knew he was the snag—the only reason they weren't in already. Mom wasn't sure she could leave her baby boy, and Dad wasn't sure he could put up with her weeping and wailing once he talked her into it. But there'd never been any doubt they'd go sooner or later. Often these friends they talked about had a kid, and Dad would say, "They placed him in a fine school," and Mom would add brightly, "He visits them several times a week."

Of course, Nemo knew the "fine school" was one of the dozens of half-ass boarding schools that'd sprung up like fungus on a rotting log so that parents with an itch to jump into the Bin would have someplace to ditch their kids, and that junior could only "visit" for twelve hours at a stretch before his autonomic nervous system started wacking out. But he didn't say anything. He just chewed on his meat and told them everything was fine at his school, too.

So he wasn't surprised when he came home one afternoon to find his parents sitting around the kitchen table with a Construct who looked like Lawrence the Dragon from the kids' virtual. He was obviously a Caretaker, a Construct made to look after rich kids. Dad had found a way around Mom's guilt.

"Look, Nemo!" Dad said like somebody out of a commercial. "It's Lawrence the Dragon!" As if, at ten, he gave a shit about a virtual for four-year-olds.

The Construct looked pretty much like the cartoon character. His eyes were the same bottle green, the same color as the scales that covered his body. But the Construct's eyes, as they looked into Nemo's, weren't bright with the maniacal cheer his namesake's exuded. They were kind and penetrating and apologetic. The Construct could see that Nemo knew why he was there. He rose to his feet like Jack's beanstalk—seven feet tall at least. "Pleased to meet you, Nemo," he said in a lilting British accent, nothing like the cartoon character's nasal bleat.

Nemo took the scaly hand and squeezed it. The scales weren't hard as he'd expected. They felt like thin pieces of leather. "Hi," he said back. Nemo didn't mind that

Lawrence looked like a giant lizard. He knew it was only a gene splice.

"Why don't you show Lawrence your room?" Dad said with his usual subtlety. Mom looked like she was sitting in the middle of one of her virtual soaps, at one of the weekly crises in the plot.

Lawrence and Nemo went up to his room in silence. Lawrence had to duck at the landing to keep from hitting his head. Nemo could almost hear his parents holding their breath, waiting for him to be out of earshot, so they could talk about how it went. What did they expect? "Oh goody! You're going to abandon me"?

Nemo flipped on the lights and shoved some books off his bed to give Lawrence someplace to sit down. Nemo stretched out on the three-legged sofa he'd hauled down from the attic and propped up on a cinder block. Most of his room was furnished with stuff he'd gotten from the attic—his grandmother's stuff. He never really knew her. She died when he was only five. She could've saved herself by going into the Bin, but she hadn't wanted to. Nemo's mom always got upset when she talked about her mother, so they hardly ever talked about her. Nemo had gotten to know her through her stuff in the attic—the CDs and videos and photographs and scrapbooks. There was even a stack of her diaries. He read them late at night, keeping them a secret from his mom and dad. When he was little, she was his secret friend. When he got a little older, she seemed like his secret lover.

Lawrence had made himself comfortable on the bed, stretching out, his huge feet dangling over the edge of the bed, his hands—the size of baseball gloves—behind his head.

"They're going into the Bin, right?" Nemo asked.

Lawrence nodded. "Bet you're pretty P.O.'d," he said in a thick Texas accent.

"It's no big deal," Nemo lied, imagining the years ahead of him, rotting in some dorm until he was eighteen or the law changed, whichever came first. Then they'd expect him to join dear old Mum and Dad in the Bin forever. They could stuff that idea. He was never going in.

Lawrence was watching him from the bed, letting him feel sorry for himself. "What're your real names?" Nemo asked him, trying to be smart.

"Lawrence."

"I mean your *real* names. Aren't you made up of bits and pieces of a bunch of different people, who used to be real, with their own names?"

Nemo thought Lawrence smiled, but he couldn't be sure. "That's right. But our name's Lawrence, now."

Nemo figured Lawrence was just holding out on him. "My science teacher says that when they started making you guys, you weren't supposed to remember who you used to be, but no matter what they did, you remembered anyway, because self-consciousness reconstitutes itself from any significant portion of the whole person." Nemo was quite good in science and, at ten, quite proud of the fact.

This time he was sure it was a smile, but he didn't know what was so damn funny, and he wasn't about to let that slow him down. "He said that when all those self-consciousnesses wake up stuck inside some lizard body or something weird, taking care of kids or being policemen or some other crap job, they must be pretty pissed off. He said a Construct has three or four names at least—but the one he tells you isn't real. It's like a brand name or something."

Lawrence bobbed his head up and down slowly. The smile was gone. His voice had an edge to it no cartoon dragon's ever had. "Your science teacher's about half right and half stupid. We don't use those other names anymore.

Those people are dead, you understand? Name's Lawrence, if that's okay with you and your science teacher."

Nemo finally realized he was being a jerk. "I'm sorry, Lawrence," he said, and he meant it.

Lawrence shrugged. "No offense taken. You got a right to know who you're dealing with."

"I thought you guys were illegal," he said, but he'd taken the smart out of his voice

"We're one of the last ones made. Your parents pulled some strings to get us."

"Uncle Winston?" Uncle Winston was Mom's brother, a senator, the family hot shit. The family visited him every Sunday in the Bin, had tea in the garden, or in front of a roaring fire.

"That's the man," Lawrence said.

"What an asshole."

Lawrence laughed. "We couldn't possibly comment," he said in the British voice.

"So what're you supposed to be?" Nemo asked. "My butler or babysitter or something?"

"Caretaker. We'll take care of you."

"If I'm being stuck in boarding school, what do I need you for?"

"Plenty," Lawrence said, and laughed again with several different jerks and gestures that Nemo figured was the whole gang of self-consciousnesses in there whooping it up.

Nemo asked Lawrence if he wanted to listen to some music, and he shrugged and said sure, but when he got a glimpse of Nemo's grandmother's CD player, his face lit up, and he got up off the bed quicker than Nemo would've thought possible.

"That's quite an antique," he said, looking down at the player as if it were a baby in a cradle.

Nemo hit Play and Bob Dylan singing "Frankie and

Albert" came through the speakers, but the machine was acting up again, and the song sounded as if it were being chopped up into little pieces. Nemo started to hit it—that sometimes worked—but Lawrence laid a huge hand on his arm. "Let us," he said.

He took a screwdriver out of a pouch he wore at his waist and opened up the machine. His fingers poked delicately among the wires and circuits. He made a few adjustments—wiggling this and that, tightening a screw—and closed the case. He started it up again. Dylan's voice came out whole, in all its fierce glory. "That'll do till we've got a soldering iron."

"Cool," Nemo said. "How'd you know what to do?"

"One of us used to take these things apart and put them back together again, took damn near everything apart and put it back together again. That was back in Texas."

"So how many of you are there? I mean . . ."

"Good a way to put it as any. Three."

"The Texan and the Englishman, and somebody else?"

"English woman. She was what they used to call a nanny."

"So who's the third one?"

Lawrence's hands fluttered in the air in a quick series of mysterious gestures. "He was a mute," the Texan said quietly. "We talk for him now. He lived in Nagasaki. We're honored to meet you."

Nemo tried to imagine what it would be like to be three different people from three different countries, living their lives inside one strange body. "Could you teach me sign language?" he asked.

"Sure enough," Lawrence said, moving his hand slowly so Nemo could watch what he was doing.

"What does that mean?"

"*I would be honored,*" he said.

Nemo practiced it over and over, following Lawrence

around the room as he examined the CD player, the VCR, the ancient TV. "We all liked old things," he said.

"I hate virtuals," Nemo told him. "I just want to listen to the music. I don't want the whole damn band in my bedroom, you know what I mean?"

"Indeed," Lawrence said, and laid one of his huge hands on Nemo's shoulder and gave it a squeeze.

THEY'D LISTENED TO A COUPLE OF CDs, AND LAWRENCE had the back of the TV off, explaining to Nemo how it worked, when Nemo's folks called them downstairs and led them into the living room. It was all done up in white—white carpet, white furniture, white drapes. Even the fireplace, a virtual fire blazing, was white. Nemo was never invited there unless there was trouble. It was part of the mid-twentieth style of the house, Nemo figured, that there be a room set aside to receive strangers and to discuss serious family matters.

"How do you like Lawrence?" Dad asked Nemo, as if Lawrence weren't sitting right across the room. Nemo just nodded his head and looked over at Lawrence, who was studying them all with his big green eyes, not missing a thing. Dad seemed to think Nemo didn't know what was going on, but he had most of it figured out. He only wondered what sort of spineless excuse he was going to give for dumping him.

"Lawrence is going to be looking after you for a little while," Mom said.

"For quite a while," Dad corrected her.

They glared at each other and forgot about Nemo momentarily so they could bicker.

Mom said, "Do you always have to make things so difficult? Winston says the law will change any time now."

"I don't give a damn what Winston says!"

"Do you always have to be right, Todd? Is that all you care about? If it makes you happier to think you won't see your son for eight years, then go ahead and think it—just so long as you're right!"

"For godsakes, Elizabeth, I've told you a million times—you can see him every damn day if you want to—he just won't be living with us!"

Mom didn't say another word. She just glared at him, until he turned to Nemo, his smile back in place.

"We're confusing the boy," he said.

"The boy isn't confused," Nemo said, and everything got real quiet. "You're going into the Bin, right?"

Dad didn't even bother to tell him not to call it the Bin. His dad didn't have to fight with him anymore. Mom started crying and telling Nemo everything was going to be all right, and Dad launched into his prepared text. "It's very simple, really," he said several times, telling Nemo about the Bin as if Nemo were visiting from another planet, a stupid planet: They were going to be uploaded into the Bin, shed their bodies, and live forever. But, unfortunately, children couldn't go because the law still foolishly said they were too young to make such a decision. Nemo had heard it all before.

"Why now?" Nemo asked.

Dad stopped talking. He could see Nemo wasn't fooled. "My doctor's advised me that it's time for me to go in." He paused dramatically. "I have a heart murmur."

"A heart murmur," Nemo said. "That's it? A heart murmur?" He turned to Mom, now sitting on the edge of her chair with a tissue to her face, trying to be brave. "What about you?" he asked her, more gently than he'd intended. "Do you have a heart murmur, too?"

Fresh tears sprang to her eyes. "I'm going in to be with your father, dear."

"We don't want to die, son," Dad said.

Nemo stood up and glared at them both. "Go ahead and kill yourselves," he said. "But you're wrong about one thing. You'll *never* see me in there! *Never!*" He hit the back door, opening the screen door wide so it'd slam shut with a crack like a rifle shot. They wouldn't follow him; they never did. They said that was because they respected his need for privacy. Nemo figured it was because they didn't give a shit.

By the time he'd gotten to the end of the driveway, Lawrence was walking alongside him, taking one long, easy stride for two of Nemo's. Lawrence was looking down the street like some hero in a twentieth-century movie.

"You don't have to follow me," Nemo said. "I'm all right."

"We know that," Lawrence said.

They were walking by a FOR SALE BY OWNER sign, the paint peeling away. The house had been empty for as long as Nemo could remember. "How could they do this?" he asked, chunking a rock at the sign and wiping away his tears with the palm of his hand.

"They don't want to die," Lawrence said.

"But they won't be real."

"There's two schools of thought on that."

"Not to me," Nemo said.

"There's two schools of thought to most everything. We're used to having at least three most of the time."

"So when are they going in?"

"Tomorrow morning. We're to take you to your new school."

"You spending the night at my house?"

"If you like."

I'd be honored, Nemo signed.

*　　*　　*

IF HIS PARENTS HADN'T GONE IN, NEMO ALWAYS REMINDED himself, he never would've met Lawrence. And Lawrence had been right. He'd needed him for plenty. Four years of boarding school, crammed to overflowing with pissed-off kids, stuck in a world that was falling apart, went a lot easier with a seven-foot companion who, among other talents, was a martial arts expert. And then, when Nemo was fourteen and the law'd finally changed so that he could've gone into the Bin if he'd wanted, Lawrence had stayed with him when he ran away from school and moved back into the house his parents had abandoned, helped him fix the place up so they could live in it again, taught him everything he knew. Lawrence took care of him all right.

As it turned out, Nemo didn't make good on the threat he'd shouted at his father. He had been in the Bin many times, visiting his parents. But he hadn't gone in for good. Maybe that was because he could still get pissed off twice a year, though he'd convinced himself he had good reasons for what he was doing, but as Lawrence had taught him, there were two schools of thought on that.

Over the years, Nemo had whittled down his parental visits to his birthday and Christmas. So twice a year he visited the Bin and remembered when they went in, and twice a year he let himself get pissed off about it. The rest of the time, he lived his own life and didn't give the Bin much thought—until he was on this train going to visit Mom and Dad again. Merry Christmas—Happy Birthday—Merry Christmas—Happy Birthday—Clickety-clack—Clickety-clack.

"What time is it?" he asked Lawrence in the seat beside him. Lawrence had that look he took on when he was talking to himself in his head. The scales over his eyes fanned out like a peacock's tail, and his eyes had a faraway, glassy stare.

He pointed patiently to the digital clock at the end of the car, ticking off the seconds. It read 7:43:32.

"What time are we supposed to be there?"

"Eight o'clock," Lawrence said in his nanny voice.

They could've just gone into the Bin at Richmond and taken the Metro in the Bin, but Nemo always insisted on going as far as they could on the real train. He didn't want to spend any more time in the Bin than he had to.

"We'll be late," he said.

"No doubt that will please you," Lawrence said.

Nemo sat watching the clock tick off the seconds, listening to the wheels on the rails. At 7:49 he looked over at Lawrence, swaying back and forth in his seat, his eyes already closed in one of his catnaps. He never slept more than an hour at a time. He'd told Nemo it was something the Texan had taught himself to do as a little boy after reading a book about Thomas Edison—so that he too would have more time to make things.

Nemo rested his forehead on the glass and watched the Metro fly past rows of drooping metal buildings, past weed-grown highways scattered with rusted-out cars, past a housing project covered up in green mounds of kudzu, making it look like elves lived inside. Probably only rats and roaches. They finally had the place to themselves.

The former residents had all gone into the Bin, except for the handful who'd squatted in the abandoned homes of surgeons or stockbrokers. But most of them didn't last long when they figured out they couldn't burn enough wood to heat those big barns, and that, if they wanted water, they'd have to dig a well with a pick and shovel, and if they wanted electricity, they'd have to rig up a generator—and then find or make fuel to run it. Sooner or later, most everybody went into the Bin. It was just too easy, too hard not to. Too hard to turn down paradise.

The doors at the end of the car slid open and a fundie

came down the aisle. She was fifteen or sixteen, her long hair braided and wound into a bun. She wore a camouflage print dress, a flaming cross stitched above her left breast. The tracts in her hand read *ONWARD CHRISTIAN SOLDIERS! SATAN IS WINNING THE WAR!* She halfheartedly offered Nemo a tract, and he shook his head. She slumped against a pole, looking toward the two remaining cars of the train, both empty, then sat down across the aisle. "There's six people on this whole train," she said to no one in particular. The train dove into a tunnel near Fredericksburg, making the fluorescent lights inside the car seem brighter. She turned toward the window, looking at her reflection, or at the tiled walls of the tunnel, scrawled with graffiti going by too fast to read.

There wasn't anyone left for her to save anymore. She absentmindedly riffled the tracts in her hands like a deck of cards, her pretty face reflected in the window, her eyes wet with tears. Nemo figured pretty soon she'd go into the Bin, defect to the winning side. Let the real world go down the tubes—leave it the wackos and creeps with their God or their scams or their paranoia. It'd never worked out anyway. About the only things still working were these trains. They were built by Constructs in the late thirties and early forties. They still kept them running for reasons known only to themselves, though the trains pretty much ran on their own, connecting every major city. They were operated by computers, powered by some geothermal plant somewhere, built before they figured out they didn't have to make a bunch of machines, they could just climb inside one enormous one.

The train stopped in Alexandria and a lone old man got on the car behind them. He was lugging two car batteries with a harness that went over his shoulders. He dropped the batteries down in the aisle and sat on them. The fundie girl glanced back at him but didn't bother to get up and offer him a tract.

When the train started slowing down for Pentagon Station, she got up and stood in front of the door, leaving her tracts on the seat. "You want these?" Nemo called after her and pointed at them. She shook her head and turned back to the door.

Nemo nudged Lawrence awake. "We're here," he said.

Lawrence blinked his eyes and rose to his feet, immediately awake. They stood behind the fundie girl as the doors slid open and followed her up the escalators. She smelled like chamomile. At the top, she turned right toward Receiving. Lawrence and Nemo turned left toward Visitors. She looked back over her shoulder and gave Nemo a small, sad smile.

He wondered where she was from. You could visit the Bin from almost anywhere. There were at least a couple of VIMs at all the Metro stations. But if you wanted to go in for good, you had to go to one of a dozen Receiving Points throughout the globe, but most people came in here. Over the years, it'd become the thing to do to come in at D.C., make a pilgrimage to the Rogers Memorial to thank him for eternity.

"Mighty pretty girl," Lawrence said in his Texan voice.

"She's going into the Bin," Nemo said.

"She's still mighty pretty."

THE VISITOR'S CENTER WAS PRACTICALLY DESERTED. IT looked exactly the same as it always did. The same powder-blue carpet with sensory enhancers so that it felt as if you were walking on blue marshmallows, even though, if you looked down at your feet, they weren't really sinking at all. The same murals of farmlands that glowed just after a rain, mountains that pierced the clouds, and cities that looked like a fleet of rocket ships ready to blast off. The waiting room for heaven.

The only person there was Victor, the same security guard who was always there—a Construct with feline features whose skin glowed like neon. He nodded at Lawrence as he passed, loping back and forth year after year like an animal in a pen.

They stepped into the two closest VIMs—Visitor Interface Modules, called coffins since they looked like streamlined caskets—and settled back into the soft cushions as the lids whirred closed automatically and the coffins slowly rotated to a horizontal position. The orientation tape droned the same assurances of safety and warnings about visiting too long that it'd been droning for thirty-one years, and then everything vibrated like a tuning fork. Nemo felt as if he'd fallen a mile in three seconds. The coffin rotated to a vertical position, and the lid swung open, and there he was, in the Bin, though it looked as if he hadn't gone anywhere. The same carpet, the same murals, the same everything. He got out, knowing his body, his real body, hadn't moved at all.

Not that you could tell the difference. There were people who claimed they could tell—detect a blur if they moved too fast, or taste the difference between a real steak and a virtual one. They were kidding themselves. That was exactly what was wrong with the Bin—you couldn't tell the difference. You were so many electrons blissfully bashing around inside of acres of silicon, and you didn't know the difference.

From Pentagon Station in the Bin, they caught a train to Front Royal. There wasn't a real train to Front Royal. It was an invention of the Bin—time marching on and all that. Nemo had always figured they could just zap people around in the Bin anywhere they wanted without the fiction of trains or planes. But that wouldn't be real, and reality was what the Bin was all about—reality, only better. They'd found that people needed space and time and the illusion of a body moving through both, or they'd often go crazy. It was only death they wanted to do without, death and the many forms of dying. Physical death, at least.

The Metro in the Bin was exactly like the real one, but free of graffiti and packed with people. They were all talking and laughing without a care in the world. Everyone had a place in the Bin. They could work or not. Travel, stay put. Eat, sleep, make love. Watching their smug faces, Nemo wanted to tear their hearts out. But he couldn't have, even if he'd been the type. You couldn't murder anyone in the Bin. The only true violence allowed was suicide. Everyone, Nemo's government teacher had intoned, has the right to die, if they so chose.

The couple in front of him, young and pretty and tanned, were planning a vacation to the Rockies. Nothing had changed in here. Try going to the Rockies in the real world, Nemo wanted to say to them. Highways shot to hell. No gas anyway. The mountains full of gun-toting survivalist crazies training for an invasion from space or something. But these people didn't have to worry about that. They had the world they'd been used to—consensual reality, they called it—but all fixed up with no crime or disease or death. You'd have to a be a fool to turn down a deal like that, wouldn't you? That's what everybody said. Every fucking body. By the time he reached his parents' house, Nemo had gotten himself so worked up he wanted to turn around and go back home.

"I CAN'T DO THIS, LAWRENCE." THEY WERE STANDING AT the end of his parents' front walk—a winding stone pathway through lush vegetation that might've been the yellow brick road, only it was slate. The house, set off by weeping willows and wisteria, was a Tudorbethan monstrosity, complete with window boxes and a thatch roof. His parents had ordered it out of a catalogue. It was called "The Shakespeare." It had edged out "The Cleopatra" and, Dad's favorite, "The Donna Reed."

"What, precisely, is 'this'?" Lawrence asked, his hands on his hips.

Nemo winced. He was up against the nanny.

"You know damn well what I mean—'precisely.' I know what they're going to say before they do."

"That's what families are for, Nemo. Now, come along. Let's not keep them waiting, shall we? If you don't see them, they'll only beseech us to persuade you to come at some future date, and frankly, we're weary of being beseeched." Lawrence and his parents still maintained the fiction that Lawrence was their employee, and Lawrence reported to them on their son's progress from time to time.

"Tell them to bugger off."

"A spirited suggestion, but rather your responsibility, don't you think? Perhaps you can offer it to them over dinner." He made a sweeping gesture like a maître d'.

"If they start nagging me to come into the Bin, I'll walk."

"They have promised not to breathe a word on the subject."

THE DOOR WAS A MASSIVE, DEEPLY SCARRED AFFAIR, AS IF a batallion of crazed soldiers had flung themselves against it in full armor to lend an appropriately ancient ambiance. The doorway was wreathed with English ivy that never changed. The line Nemo had traced with a black marker seven years before around one of the tendrils was still visible as if he'd only just done it. His mom had explained that they could've ordered growing ivy, but that struck her as an unnecessary bother. She had her hands full, she said, with the yard and the garden. The door knocker was a roaring lion's head, the tarnish worn away where countless visitors would grasp it to a shine—on the snout, the fangs, and the fringes of the mane—but dark everywhere else. Its eyes and mouth and ears were dull black pits. Nemo stuck his forefinger down the thing's throat, lifted, and let it fall with an impressive clunk.

Uncle Winston answered the door, drink in hand. He was tall, but not too tall, and good-looking in a states-manlike way, with silver hair and broad shoulders and a posture like a pine tree. He smiled as if for a camera, holding it even as he spoke. "Newman!" he exclaimed, clapping his hand on Nemo's shoulder. "Happy Birthday!"

"Nemo," Nemo said, shrugging off Winston's hand. "Don't call me Newman."

Uncle Winston looked vaguely hurt for a moment, but recovered himself after two beats, wagging his head with the exaggerated tolerance of a politician. "You young people have such notions. You should be proud of your name. You are named after a Great Man."

Nemo loathed it. Millions of boys were named after Newman Rogers, Inventor of the Bin. His picture was everywhere—a short dweeby guy with owllike eyes and ears that stuck out like stubby wings. "I'm proud of Nemo," he said.

"A crazed character in some old science fiction movie, your mother tells me. What sort of model is that for a young man?" He sighed, setting aside his superior wisdom. "But this is your party. I'll call you whatever you wish." He held up his glass. "Have a drink? Everyone's out in the garden." He gave his regular-guy, good-natured chuckle. "I'm afraid we're a couple ahead of you."

"I'll have scotch, and since you asked, Lawrence will have bourbon."

Winston gave Lawrence a thin smile. "Certainly. And how are you this evening, Lawrence?"

"Very well, Senator, thank you. Nemo, by the way, was originally a character in a Jules Verne novel of the late nineteenth century. The film adaptation came much later, of course. He commanded a submarine, waging a one-man war against the evils of his day."

"How interesting," Uncle Winston said, his smile thinner still, so that he looked like he was about to bare fangs—one of the senator's faces that never made it into the news. Nemo wished he were a paparazzi. But Uncle Winston recovered quickly and spread his arms wide to take in the beautiful house—all the beautiful houses throughout the Bin—and smiled his best heartfelt smile. "We have no wars here!" he said.

"But you sure as hell have evil," Lawrence drawled, and walked past Winston to the bar to make their drinks.

THEY FOLLOWED WINSTON OUT INTO THE GARDEN, DRINKS in hand. It smelled of fresh-mown grass and cherry blossoms. A thunderstorm was piling up on the horizon, but it wouldn't be here for hours. Nemo's parents were in front of the grape arbor talking to a tall, slender woman in a black knit dress. Her almost-white blond hair blew across her face, and she reached up and pulled it back from her eyes just as she caught sight of Nemo. She smiled, and without thinking where he was, he smiled back. "Hi," she said.

"Hi," he said, and for a moment it was as if they were the only two there. Her features were in sharp focus, while everything else dissolved into the background.

Uncle Winston's hand clapped down on Nemo's shoul-

der. "Nemo, I'd like you to meet Justine. She's my . . .
uh . . . dinner companion for the evening."

Nemo saw her cut a look at his uncle as he was trying
to figure out what to call her. She didn't look like the
bimbos he usually had on his arm. She was younger, about
Nemo's age, and she looked intelligent. He stuck out his
hand. "Glad to meet you."

She smiled at him again and took his hand. Nemo gestured to Lawrence with a toss of his head as he shook her
hand. "This is my . . . uh . . . dinner companion,
Lawrence."

She laughed, her eyes crinkling almost shut, and
squeezed Nemo's hand before letting it go. It was a warm,
infectious laugh. Nemo found himself beaming like an
idiot.

She shook Lawrence's hand firmly, apparently not
minding that it was covered with scales. Lawrence's lipless
smile was like a crescent moon.

"Mighty pleased to meet you, ma'am," he said.

Her eyes brightened. "You're from Texas!"

Lawrence laughed, the slow Texas chuckle. "You might
say that. You too?"

She smiled and nodded. "Dallas."

Mom and Dad had been standing back, watching the
introductions, their faces long and worried. Nemo's visits
always made them nervous. They're trying to do the right
thing, Lawrence often told him. We all are, Nemo
thought.

"Son!" Mom gushed and lurched toward Nemo, as he
knew she would, already in tears, her arms outspread, a
handkerchief waving in one hand. He put his arms around
her and let her cry against his chest. It always got to him,
to hold her again, like he was a little kid and nothing had
changed. She felt the same, soft and slightly pudgy. Her
tiny hand clutching the handkerchief might've been a little

girl's. She hadn't aged in ten years. At least she hadn't gotten "plastic surgery" so she could live out eternity in her twenties. He was the one who'd changed.

"Happy Birthday!" Dad said with forced joviality, bobbing up and down nervously. "You can see you need to visit your mother more often."

"Maybe so," Nemo mumbled, holding her tight. "Too bad she can't visit me."

Mom started crying even harder, and Dad gave Nemo a murderous look. "What a thoughtless thing to say."

"I didn't mean anything by it. It just came out."

" 'It just came out,' " Winston mimicked, shaking his head.

"It's the truth, isn't it?" Justine said, and they all turned to stare at her. "It is too bad, isn't it?" She blushed and gave them all an apologetic smile. "I'm sorry. It's none of my business." She looked down at the ground, then up at Nemo with a steady, friendly gaze.

Mom raised her head from Nemo's chest and stared at this strange young woman in her garden, then up at Nemo, a stunned look in her eyes. "I'm sorry, Mom," he said quietly, and for a moment there was silence.

"Let's go into dinner, shall we?" Uncle Winston announced, taking his sister by the shoulders, pulling her out of Nemo's arms, and guiding her back toward the house as if she were on wheels.

"Perhaps I misunderstood you," Dad said, and followed them toward the house, each foot landing precisely on the flagstones. Unaccountably, Lawrence followed after him without a word, leaving Justine and Nemo standing in the empty garden.

"I'm sorry for butting in," she said.

"You weren't," he said, and shrugged. "Well, maybe you were, but I didn't mind."

He knew they should go into the house, but he just

wanted to stand there with her a little longer. Listen to the fountain. Smell the cherry blossoms. Look at her. But he didn't know what to say. She looked at him as if she knew what he was thinking anyway. It probably wasn't too hard to figure out the way he kept staring at her. Her dress was cut low in front, the wind still tossed her hair around, her green eyes were clear and bright. He wanted to run his hands up and down her bare arms and shoulders, hold her in his arms, kiss her where the fabric stopped, just above her breasts. He stuck his hands in his back pockets.

"You ever meet a Construct like Lawrence before?" he asked abruptly, as if he were accusing her of something.

"No," she said. "He seems nice."

"He is. Most people won't touch him, treat him like he's not human, but he is. The scales are just a gene splice. He's cloned from an athlete, his personalities are human— all of them better than most people I know. It's him who should be treating us like we've got the plague instead of the other way around. He's the best friend I've ever had."

"You're lucky to have such a good friend," she said. He sensed in her tone that she had no such friends.

A bird started singing close by, and they both looked off toward the sound, trying to catch sight of it. Everything had been uploaded. Nemo wondered what it was like to be a bird or a rat or a butterfly and find yourself living forever. He wondered if any of them ever killed themselves. "Your folks live in Dallas?" he asked her.

She listened to the bird singing, her mouth turned up at the corners in a sad smile. "I guess they did once," she said. "I don't really know." She looked back to him. "I never knew them. They didn't keep me. They dumped me in an orphanage when I was born. It wasn't so bad really."

"You're an orphan?"

She shook her head. "That's what people will call you,

but I looked it up when I was little. An orphan's parents are dead. My parents didn't die. They just didn't want me."

"They go in the Bin?"

"I guess so."

"You never tried to find them?"

"It's them who should be trying to find me." She spoke quietly. He knew the tone. It was old, quiet anger, like a block of stone, a cornerstone, something to build on.

He nodded sympathetically. "I'm sorry."

She shrugged her shoulders. "That was twenty years ago."

They stood there for a moment. The bird had moved on. "Do you mind if I ask you something?"

She shook her head.

"What's somebody like you doing being Senator Bozo's . . . uh . . . dinner companion?"

He thought she might be mad, but the question seemed to amuse her. "What do you mean 'somebody like me'? You don't even know me."

"I can tell you're smarter than he is. He wouldn't like that."

She laughed. "Thanks, I think."

"And you're nice, too. You didn't have to say anything when my parents and I got into it, but you were paying attention, you cared about what was going on, and you don't even know us."

"Maybe I'm just nosy."

"Most people in here don't pay any attention to anybody but themselves. Why should they? Everybody's okay. Everybody's got what they want. You're different."

She looked down, as if ashamed. "I haven't been in here very long. Maybe I'll change."

"I don't think so," he said, though he couldn't have said why.

She looked up at him and took his hand. "We should go in," she said. "Show me the way?"

He offered his arm like he'd seen in old videos. She smiled and wrapped her arms around his and walked close beside him as they moved slowly toward the house. He could smell her perfume, feel each place where her body touched his. He didn't care whether she was real or not. He liked her. He liked her a lot.

At the back door, she said. "I never answered your question."

He couldn't remember asking a question she hadn't answered. He wondered whether she knew some of the ones he hadn't asked.

She looked up at him, leaned forward confidentially. "I haven't the faintest idea what I'm doing here with Senator Bozo," she said, making a face. "He's not my type."

"So what's your type?" he heard himself asking.

"Sweet nephews," she said, and kissed his cheek.

No one seemed to mind they'd taken so long. The food was on the table. The four of them sat there with their hands in their laps. Nemo expected Dad to make some remark about keeping people waiting and consideration to others, Winston to have that snooty look he got when he was pissed, Mom to be working on a second hankie because her son didn't appreciate the marvelous dinner she'd worked all day to prepare from scratch. But they all sat there smiling and happy as you please, like some family from a hundred years ago about to say grace.

Nemo seated Justine beside Winson and took the seat opposite her, next to Lawrence. Mom and Dad sat at either end, Mom closest to the kitchen. Everything was done in mid-twentieth century. It could've been Ozzie and Harriet's house. A big drop-leaf table in the style they used to

45

call Early American, a sideboard with coffee mugs hanging on pegs, saying things like MOM'S COFFEE and I NEVER MAKE MISTEAKS. Some of them had pictures of bunnies or kittens on them. The food was laid out "family style," as Mom called it. Some family, Nemo thought, their son laid out like a dead man, and they can't even see it. The whole damn world laid out.

Uncle Winston raised his wineglass. "To the birthday boy!" he said, and they all joined in, looking so damn happy it was weird. Nemo looked across the table at Justine, her eyes crinkled up in laughter, her glass held high, and he did feel happy. Maybe I should try to lighten up like Lawrence said, he thought. What the hell, it's only for tonight.

Mom had made lasagne, Nemo's favorite when he was ten. She'd made it every birthday for the last eleven years. The smell of Italian sausage and cheese made his mouth water. He took a swallow of wine, and then another. While he was here, he figured he'd eat and drink too much. When he got back to the real world, he'd be sober and hungry. He and Lawrence planned to cook up a rabbit later, maybe have a few drinks from the still Lawrence had built to fuel the generator he'd rigged up. Maybe they'd watch *Harold & Maude* or *Harvey* again on the antique VCR.

"The lasagne's great, Mom," he said, and she beamed at him. At his fourteenth birthday party, when the law had just changed, and Mom and Dad were ecstatic, figuring he was coming into the Bin, he'd refused to eat a bite, pointing out the absurdity of virtual people eating virtual food. Mom had sniffled throughout dinner while Nemo and his dad yelled at each other. He'd tried to hurt them, make Mom cry and Dad clench his jaws till the veins stood out on his neck. But venting his rage hadn't made him feel any better. It hadn't changed anything. He used to think anger was something you could use up, purge from your system, but now he knew it just fed on itself and made you feel worse. Just let it go, he'd decided. They had their world. He had his. They saw each other twice a year. Surely, he could be cool twice a year.

Justine was talking to his parents. They asked her about Dallas. She talked to them easily, smiling, but she didn't give out much. Nemo was the only one who knew she didn't have a family to talk about. Mom and Dad, by the route of their stereotypical ideas about Texas, turned the conversation to stories about Nemo playing cowboy when he was little, a pair of sixguns strapped round his waist, ridiculously cute. Nemo couldn't believe it. Usually the subject of his childhood—when they all lived together as a family—was strictly off limits.

Justine smiled slightly, her eyes bright as she listened to the stories Nemo already knew. She seemed interested in hearing about him. The wall behind her was covered with photographs, half of them Little Nemo in the real world: A guitar as big as he was hung around his neck. Riding a bicycle—slightly out of focus. Standing on a huge rock waving at the camera, Dad beside him looking down. Turn around, he wanted to say. I'm right behind you. Virtual Nemo was there, too—a scattering of posed pictures in this house, usually on his birthday, a forced smile on his face, his never-aging parents smiling desperately at the camera as Lawrence took their photograph.

Directly above Justine's head was his parents' wedding portrait, the shoulders of Dad's tuxedo so heavily padded in the style of the time that he looked like an inverted pyramid. This was flanked by travel pictures: A sunset somewhere where there were saguaro cactus. Mom in front of the Taj Majal. A polar bear on an ice floe. And a new one, Mom and Dad at the rail of a cruise ship. The life preserver beside them read *FANTASIA*. They always looked the same, but they had changed. The Bin had changed them. They didn't have a care in the world.

Justine laughed out loud at the punch line of one of the cute-little-Nemo stories and looked at Nemo, her eyes crinkled up. He liked her laugh. It was low and sexy and full of life. Too bad she wasn't real. Too bad he couldn't take her home, ride on the graffiti-scrawled Metro, talk all night, drink some of Lawrence's brew and make love on the sleeping porch under the stars. The real stars. Blazing now that all the factories were shut down, and the cities were as dark as tombs at night. He tried to smile back, but couldn't manage it.

He looked down at his plate, the food still steaming. He didn't feel hungry anymore, but he ate anyway. Fresh romano, ricotta, and mozarella. Sausage with red pepper and fennel. Just get through this meal, he told himself, and then I can go home. He drank off his wine and poured another glass. Out of the corner of his eye he could see Lawrence watching him, knowing exactly how he felt. She'd said, *You're lucky to have such a good friend.*

He was indeed.

NEMO GOT THROUGH THE MEAL ON AUTOMATIC PILOT. HE'D say a few words if somebody said something to him, tried to look interested in what everybody else was saying, but he was really just floating there, the way he'd heard you did when you died: You float up above everything and watch yourself dying, with everybody gathered around your body trying to bring you back. Then you turn to this white light, and that's it, and you're gone for good. Nemo wondered if he turned around, if he just quit watching his family, whether there'd be that great white light at his back. But in those stories, people come to meet you, people who died before you, people who loved you and looked after you. Who'd meet me? he thought. He didn't know anybody who'd died. Except his grandmother, who seemed more like words on a page than a real person.

By the time they were sitting around in the den after the cake and the birthday card with a deposit receipt and a bit of doggerel inside, nobody expected Nemo to say much of anything. He was working on another Scotch. He was almost enjoying himself, tuning in and out of their talk about this and that. He listened every time the conversation turned to Justine, but every time she turned it back again, never giving anything away. He knew more about her from their five minutes in the garden than the rest of them did from talking to her all night.

He couldn't take his eyes off her. Every once in a while, she'd catch him looking at her and smile, look into his eyes. He wondered what she was doing here, how she'd ended up coming to his birthday party, who she was, and what she cared about, but he couldn't really talk to her with everybody else around. He had to content himself with watching her, studying the contours of her face. He imagined kissing her, holding her in his arms.

Such thoughts would get him nowhere. Sparks, his mom's cat, had also taken a fancy to Justine. He curled up in her lap and purred loudly as Justine scratched his head. Like many cats in the Bin, he was a little odd. He was thirty-one years old and hadn't eaten in five years, somehow knowing he didn't have to. Every once in a while, he'd snack on the patch of catnip in the garden and go tearing around the house, but mostly he lay in the sun or enlisted some human to pet him, and seemed perfectly content. As Justine listened to Lawrence telling a story about a black lab he'd had in Texas, Sparks stood up and burrowed his head into Justine's chest. Nemo couldn't watch anymore.

He shifted in the squishy leather chair he was sprawled

in and turned toward his Mom. She was talking about the plight of some friends of hers, asking Uncle Winston if something couldn't be done for them. She wrung her hands and looked at her big brother as if he were Solomon, and she just knew he could fix anything. Dad also looked at Uncle Winston as if he could fix anything, but he didn't look so happy about it.

It seemed this couple Mom knew wanted a kid, but it was getting too hard to adopt from outside—meaning the real world was getting low on breeders to meet the demand—and this couple hadn't made provisions for in vitro before they'd come in.

That was the way it worked ever since kids were allowed in the Bin. Couples going in who didn't have any kids usually left a few fertilized eggs in the deep freeze in case they ever decided to clutter up their perfect lives with children. Just give the word, and the eggs would be thawed out and brought to term, delivered for uploading and cremation nine months later, no muss, no fuss, no labor pains. Even his mom and dad had stashed away a few ovum for a rainy day, though he knew from many late-night fights that he'd been an accident that had kept them from going into the Bin for years—till they found a way around their consciences. These friends of theirs must've gone in a long time back, or they'd been pretty sure they wouldn't want kids. But that's the way it was a lot of times—they'd get in here and find out they were bored and thought they needed a kid to play with. Nemo's heart bled for them.

Uncle Winston was nodding and *hmhm*-ing his concern for his little sister and these people he didn't even know. This was the routine that got him elected term after term. "Your friends shouldn't have long to wait," he said. "Virtual birth will pass this session. I'm sure of it."

Nemo rolled his eyes, and tried to shut out the drone

of Uncle Winston's campaigning in his sister's den. Even Justine and Lawrence had dropped their own conversation to listen to the Senator. Nemo had heard it all before. Virtual birth would eliminate having to deal with reality at all. The parents' genetic uploads would be matched up, and a virtual child was born. A child who never existed in the real world at all, no embryo to mess with, no body to burn. It'd been possible ever since they cranked up the Bin, but it'd been illegal because even all these silicon dwellers weren't so sure about legalizing a bunch of little tykes who'd never met a hydrocarbon. But this session, everybody said, it'd be legalized. Uncle Winston was leading the good fight for the as-yet-unborn silicon babes.

Everybody quit talking, and Nemo looked around the room. Without realizing it, he must've made some sort of grunt of disapproval—it was a bad habit of his when he'd had too much to drink—and everyone was looking at him. He shifted in his chair, and the leather made a noise like a giant wadding up a saddle. He tried to look pleasant, harmless, and attentive. Uncle Winston had this tight-lipped little smile. Dad looked tired. Mom was afraid Nemo was going to spoil another dinner party. Lawrence just watched. He wouldn't give Nemo any trouble no matter what he said. *You and your folks—that's none of our damn business,* he often said.

Justine's eyes looked sad. Nemo couldn't help looking into them, and he thought he knew what she was feeling. This conversation—talking about some couple who wanted kids, virtual or not—must make her feel awful. She had no parents, would never have any. No laws could change that. Sparks jumped down from her lap and padded off upstairs to sleep on one of the beds. He always avoided unpleasantness.

When the silence had settled in, Uncle Winston asked

Nemo, "Did you have something you wanted to say?"
There was an edge to his voice that added *you little shit.*
"No," he said quietly. "I don't think so."
Winston's surprise was monumental. "But certainly you
must have an opinion, Newman. You've always been such
a thoughtful young man. We'd all love to hear what you
think about the most important issue of the day. You've
been so quiet all evening." Uncle Winston looked around
at the rest of them as if they were there for one of his town
meetings, and Nemo was some heckler from the back row.

Nemo looked at them, too—his family. And at this
beautiful woman whose eyes, blazing with anger, were
trained on Uncle Winston. Maybe she knows what's really
going on, he thought, that Winston is calling me out to
put me in my place, show me who's in charge here, make
me look like some hothead jerk. Nemo looked back to
Winston and shrugged his shoulders. "You know what I
think, Uncle Winston. I don't have to say it and upset
everybody, spoil my birthday party. It's getting late anyway. Why don't Lawrence and I just head on home."

The leather chair made a smacking sound as he peeled
himself off of it and stood up. Lawrence rose silently to
his feet.

Uncle Winston feigned surprise and patted his hands on
the air in front of him. "Don't be ridiculous, Newman.
Sit down. Sit down. We're just having a friendly discussion here. We're all open to a wide range of reasonable
opinions."

As Winston looked around at everybody again to see
their nods of approval, Justine scowled and stood to her
feet. "Nemo, if you're leaving, would you mind taking me
back to my hotel? If it's not too much out of your way."

The smile left Winston's face like a picture falling off a
wall. "I will take you home, Justine, whenever you like."
He'd lurched to his feet and was standing up tall, his

shoulders thrown back, but Lawrence towering beside him spoiled the effect. Mom and Dad sat looking up at the four of them as if they were a trapeze act, and one of them was about to fall.

Justine looked Uncle Winston up and down from his silver dome of hair to his black, glistening shoes, and didn't see a thing she liked. "I'd rather go with Nemo," she said. Uncle Winston tucked in his chin and didn't say a word. She offered Nemo her arm, and he took it.

Nemo looked over at Lawrence. The scales around his left eye fluttered in a wink. "Reckon we'll stay and help your mother clean up," he drawled. "We'll catch up with you later." Nemo didn't know whether to be glad or terrified that he was going to be alone with Justine.

"Thank you for a wonderful evening," Justine said to Nemo's mom and dad, who now rose to their feet, nodding and smiling and saying their goodnights in a daze. She stayed right beside Nemo as they worked their way to the door where Nemo hugged Mom and shook Dad's hand and went out into the moonlight and cicadas. She took his arm again, and they walked the three blocks to the Metro station before either one of them said anything.

"Why'd you do that?" he asked.

"Because they were pissing me off. That pompous ass baiting you, and your mom and dad letting him."

Their train rolled into the station, and they got on a car with a few dozen people on it. They sat down close together, side by side. As the train pulled out of the station, he said, "You didn't have to do that."

She laughed. "You just don't get it, do you?" She took his hand and squeezed it. "I like you. I wanted you to take me home."

They rode through the night, the moon high and full and bright, holding hands all the way to D.C. He thought, I must be dreaming, and in a way, he was.

3

THOUGH NEMO DIDN'T SAY TWO WORDS TO JUStine on the train, he held her hand, stared at her when he thought she wouldn't notice. Just as she was doing to him now, studying his profile as he gazed out the window, apparently deep in thought. He's attracted to me, she thought. That's clear enough. But she hoped it was more than that. She liked him. His dark, deepset eyes had frightened her at first; his intensity had made her uneasy. But there was a fundamental kindness beneath all that thoughtfulness. She'd liked him immediately, instinctively. When she first laid eyes on him, she wanted to know him. And he wanted to know her—she was sure of it—in spite of his silence now.

She couldn't help noting the irony. She'd met someone in the Bin, but he was only here twice a year, as rare as a solstice. He'd chosen to live outside for seven years. She didn't know why, though she'd been searching for clues all evening. Before he arrived, his parents cautioned her that their son held "radical views," but they hadn't elaborated, and she'd just nodded and smiled, not knowing it would matter to her. Her own reasons for staying out were vague and insubstantial, but his feelings must be stronger than that to keep him out for seven years. Stronger than any attraction he might have for me, she thought. But we're just spending the evening together. What can be the harm in that?

He turned from the window and caught her staring at him. They looked into each other's eyes, and she held nothing back from his intense gaze, even though her heart was racing. He looked away, and she realized that she frightened him as well.

SHE TOOK HIS ARM AS THEY GOT OFF THE TRAIN AT DUPONT Circle, and they took a long escalator ride up to the street. He was even more somber now than he'd been on the train. The silence had become unbearable. "What're you thinking?" she asked.

He said, "I was thinking this escalator probably doesn't work half the time in the real world."

The way he said it, she almost felt ashamed for being in here, and immediately resented it. Was it bad that things worked in here? Was it her fault his life was hard out there? She looked down the steep, silver incline they'd just ascended effortlessly. "I guess we're lucky we're in here then, huh? I'd hate to have to walk up that."

He started to say something, but stopped himself. "How far's the hotel?" he asked.

"A couple of blocks," she said, and he lengthened his stride. She held onto his arm and matched him stride for stride, then she started pushing it, picking up the pace, hamming it up with long, exaggerated strides. He smiled in spite of himself and slowed to a pace more suitable for walking his sweetheart home. He still didn't say anything, but when, at her prompting, they stopped to look in a shop window, it was her reflection he looked at, and not the merchandise.

She figured that once they got to the hotel, he planned to bolt. But she didn't intend to let him leave without an explanation. If he couldn't trust her with the truth, then maybe it was better he left. That prospect hurt more than she would've thought. You've just met the guy, she reminded herself. It's not a big deal. But she knew she was lying. She remembered Angelina in her dream. She was crazy for a guy, too, and look where that got her. But she wasn't Angelina, and Nemo certainly wasn't any Steve. Not that she'd mind if he was a little more assertive. She felt like she was doing all the work.

Nothing ventured, nothing gained, she thought, like a voice in her head. She couldn't remember where she'd heard the expression before, but she liked the old-fashioned sound of it. She took it to mean she would have to get in his face.

EVEN THOUGH IT WAS ALMOST ELEVEN O'CLOCK, THE LOBBY was still full of people. By the front desk computer was a group of Indians, their luggage piled around them, checking in. They stood around chatting except for a little man in a white linen suit, probably the tour guide, who scurried around counting everybody.

"Buy you a drink?" Justine asked Nemo and nodded toward the bar.

The entrance to the bar was off to her right, a rock archway with *The Grotto* writing itself repeatedly in blue glowing script across the top. It was about half full of couples having drinks, huddled over hurricane lamps. Way back in the darkness someone played drippy piano non-stop. She wondered if anyone else in there was like Nemo, just visiting, having a drink, his real body in a coffin. Maybe Nemo was wondering the same thing.

"I can't," he said. "I have to go. Lawrence and I have

some stuff planned." He stuck his hands in his pockets and looked over at the Indian tourists as if something interesting were happening over there.

She didn't say anything. She didn't want to talk to the side of his head. When he finally turned back to her, she looked him in the eye. "What's going on, Nemo?"

"What do you mean?" He started to look back at the Indians, but settled for the floor between them. Part of her just wanted to drop it. If he wanted to go, let him go. But she at least had to know why. She liked him a lot, still believed he liked her in spite of the way he was acting.

"What I mean is, you act like you're interested in me all evening—in a sweet, shy sort of way. You don't say a word on the train, but you sit close to me, hold my hand, look at me all dreamy-eyed. And now, all of a sudden, you've got 'stuff' to do? Did I miss something?"

He shook his head and spoke to the floor. "I'm sorry. It's late. I'm tired. Thanks for coming to my birthday party."

"Fine. Don't tell me. And by the way, your father was right. What you said was thoughtless. I spoke up to get you off the hook. I guess I should've kept my mouth shut."

He raised his head and looked at her, his brow creased with worry and concern. "I'm sorry, Justine."

"Sorry for what? Just tell me, Nemo. What is it? Does it bother you I came with your Uncle?"

"No. That has nothing to do with it."

"He asked me out. He seemed nice. He wasn't. You never made a mistake like that?"

He shook his head and looked into her eyes. "That's not it at all."

"Then what is 'it'? There is an 'it.' You just said so."

"Look Justine, I really like you. I'm glad I got to meet you. But now I've got to go home, get something to eat."

That was too much. "It's because I'm in the Bin, isn't it? Why is that such a problem for you, Nemo? Most people are. It's not catching, you know. I won't steal your body while you're not looking."

His mouth opened and closed a few times before he spoke. "I'm sorry. I just need to get home."

"Okay. I'll figure out my own story. You think you're better than me—because you still live out there in the *real* world? Maybe you're a Christian—waiting for the Rapture—while I'm a hellbound sinner."

He put up his hands as if she held a gun on him. "No, I'm not Christian. I'm not anything. I just don't like the Bin, okay? I don't think I'm better than you. I think you're absolutely wonderful. I've never met anyone like you. You're . . . I just don't think it'd be such a good idea."

She couldn't help smiling at his upraised hands. "I'm what, Nemo?" she prompted.

He lowered his hands. "You're beautiful," he said. "I like you very much. But I can't . . . I should go."

"I'm not proposing, Nemo. I'm just asking you to have a drink with me."

He hesitated, and she reached out and took his hands. "I know you want to," she said, tugging at him, and he let himself smile. "We can argue sitting down?" she added hopefully, and he laughed—the first time she'd heard him laugh. "See? You're having fun already." She slipped her arm around his waist and squeezed. He put his arm around her shoulders, and they walked into the *Grotto*.

THEY FOUND A TABLE AS FAR AWAY FROM THE PIANO player as they could get. He was playing a medley of themes from old romantic virtuals with elaborate arpeggios thrown in every other measure. Justine imagined the actors about to embrace, distracted and foolish in the swirl of notes, imagined she knew exactly how they felt.

They selected their drinks by touching icons on the tabletop. The hurricane lamp slid over to one side, and the drinks rose out of the middle of the table on a little elevator, the glasses wet with condensation. When they picked up their drinks, the elevator descended, and the hurricane lamp slid back into place.

He laughed again, not a happy laugh this time, but an ironic little chuckle, as dark as the bar they were sitting in.

"What's funny?" she asked.

He pointed at the hurricane lamp where the drinks had been. "It's such a Bin thing—these silly gizmos like that. Seems like you could do anything in here—the drinks could appear floating in the air or something—but instead it's just hokey shit like that."

"Is that what you don't like about the Bin—the silly gizmos?"

He ran his thumb along the rim of his glass. "It's more complicated than that."

"I can do complicated," she said. "You said I was smart, remember? In your parents' garden? You haven't changed your mind since then, have you?"

He smiled at the thought. "No, you're even smarter than I figured."

"And why is that?"

"Well for one thing, you talked me into coming into this bar."

"That wasn't hard. You wanted to come."

He nodded. "Yes I did, very much. How did you know that?"

She smiled and pointed at the hurricane lamp. "My little secret. So tell me what's funny."

He tapped on the hurricane lamp. "Okay, take this business. It's supposed to look like a machine—everybody understands machines. If the drinks just floated in the air like I said before, people couldn't process that as real, so they made up this thing. Everything's supposed to seem real in here. Now, I could build one of these on the outside without too much trouble, but the important difference between this one and the one I'd build, is that mine would change. I'd have to keep it working—replace parts, lubricate it, adjust it. It'd still break down sometimes no matter what I did. No one ever works on this one. It's just there, somebody's idea of a neat way to get a drink. It never wears out. There are no moving parts. No parts at all in here. Ideas don't have parts."

"Sure they do."

"I mean moving parts, parts that wear out."

"You don't think ideas wear out?"

He started to answer, and she burst out laughing. "Are you always this serious? Talking so solemnly about 'moving parts' without cracking a smile?" He smiled then. He could have a good time. It was possible.

"Not always. Sure you don't want to change the 'solemnly' to 'pompously'?"

"I'll keep it in reserve. So what do you do on the outside?"

"Salvage. Old electronics mostly. CD players, VCRs, stuff like that. Lawrence and I find them, fix them up, trade them for stuff we need. I like digging up old CDs. You never know what you might find."

She pictured him digging through landfills looking for old rock and roll. "Your mom told me you like music."

"When did she tell you that?"

"She talked quite a bit about her boy before you got there."

"That must've been something." He took a drink, swirled the ice cubes around.

"Maybe you're too hard on her."

"Maybe." His voice was grim.

Justine had liked Nemo's mom. She did tend to rattle on, but that was okay. Anybody'd be nervous with a son like Nemo coming to dinner. He probably deconstructed the lasagne. "So was she right about the music, or is she just wrong about everything?"

There wasn't a trace of a smile now. "I'd rather not talk about my parents."

She started to just let it go. She hardly knew him. It wasn't any of her business. Then thought, what the hell. "I don't think your parents are so bad, Nemo. How do you know you wouldn't have done exactly what they did? You might see it differently thirty or forty years from now. Besides, they didn't mean it to be permanent. Seems to me, you're the one who's made that decision."

"Is that how you feel about your parents? Forgive and forget?"

She thought about it. She remembered many nights, lying in her bed thinking about her parents, wondering who they were. "Sometimes. I can't really forget them— I don't know who they are. I make up different ones. Sometimes, they're shits. Sometimes they have no other choice. I forgive the nice ones—that's easy. I'm working on the shits."

He finished his drink and set it down. "I better be going," he said.

"Come on, Nemo. Don't run off. I promise to change the subject." She reached out and touched the *Scotch* icon, held up her glass—still half full. "Keep me company till I finish my drink?"

The hurricane lamp slid to one side, and another scotch rose out of the table. He didn't laugh this time, but stared at the glass for a moment before he finally took it and the lamp slid back into place. He took a deep swallow.

"So what kind of music do you like?" she asked him.

He shook his head. "You're really something, you know that? Lawrence has been trying to get me to talk about my parents for years, and it only took you five minutes."

"I thought we were talking about music."

"I'm changing the subject. To tell you the truth, Justine, sometimes I think that I'm staying out of the Bin just to prove my folks wrong. To prove they didn't have to go in. Is that childish or what?"

She laid her hands on his. "What do you think the rest of the time?"

He looked around the room as if he were trying to memorize it. "That's the hard part. Every time I see them in here I think they've made a terrible mistake. When I try to put my finger on it, to put it into words, I can't. But it's like they're dying in here without even knowing it. They're like people pretending to be my parents, but they're really not."

She squeezed his hands. "Sounds like my folks."

He smiled. "I'm sorry," he said. "I always get a little morbid when I visit my parents."

"What about when you meet girls?"

"I don't meet many girls."

She laughed and gave his hands a shake. "I would've guessed that. Now tell me what kind of music you like before I resort to torture."

He laughed with her, loosening up a little.

"What kind of torture?"

She arched an eyebrow, pretended to think about it. "How about I tie you up and never let you go?"

He looked into her eyes. "I could take a lot of that."

She blushed, imagining it. "Music, Nemo."

"Okay. I'm pretty boring actually. I like everything. Whatever I can get my hands on. It's silly, but when I dig around in some old basement and turn up a hundred-year-old CD of what's-his-name's greatest hits, and fix up an old clunker to play it on, I feel like I'm keeping the music alive. Nobody sings much out there, except the fundies and their hymns. There aren't enough people to listen."

She nodded in agreement. "It's better if someone's listening. I'm a singer."

He did a double-take. "You're kidding."

"That's why I keep turning the conversation to music, while all you want to talk about is your parents." He laughed again. If you could just distract his brain, he had a sense of humor.

"So what kind of stuff do you do?" he asked.

"Old covers mostly—pop and country. I like old songs nobody's heard of. Sort of like you and your basement CDs."

"Who's your favorite singer?"

"You probably never heard of her. Aimee Mann. Had a band called Til Tuesday, late 1980s, did solo albums in the nineties."

His eyes widened, and he grinned from ear to ear. "Hear of her? I love her stuff. I found her CDs in my grandmother's collection. I played them all the time at boarding school, still listen to them. I've never met anyone else who's even *heard* of her." He paused and studied her as if she were a photograph. It was an odd sensation. "You know, you look just like her."

She started to object, but then she thought about it. She did look a lot like her. She wondered why she'd never realized it before. "Thanks," she said. "She was very pretty."

"Yes, she was," he said, but when she returned his gaze, he lost his nerve again and looked around at the crowd.

"Come on, lighten up, Nemo. Relax, have a drink with me. Then you can go home to your girlfriend in the real world. That's it, isn't it? You've got somebody on the outside."

He shook his head, took a deep swallow from his drink. "Had a girlfriend," he said. "She's in here now."

She imagined the whole story. "I'm sorry," she said.

He shrugged it off, but he wasn't very convincing. "Why should you be sorry? Shouldn't I just upload myself and join her—live happily ever after like a normal person?"

She put her hand on his arm. "But you didn't want to upload yourself. You wanted her to stay with you. She probably told you she would, but she didn't, and now you feel betrayed and abandoned—just like your parents made you feel. That's why I'm sorry."

He studied her, a half smile on his face. "I told you you were smart."

"It wasn't hard to figure out. You get attached, don't you, Nemo?"

"Yeah, I guess I do."

"What was her name?"

"Rosalind. We'd been together a couple of years. I've got a friend named Jonathan, a fundie. She's his cousin." He sighed. "She left a note taped to the mantel."

"Have you seen her since she's been in here?"

He shook his head. "Don't want to." He looked around again at all the couples. "She'll find somebody in here."

"You make it sound like a shopping expedition."

"Maybe it is."

"Maybe it isn't."

"You mean like destiny and all that?" he asked skeptically.

She laughed and shook her head. "I don't know what I mean. Stephanie, a friend of mine at the orphanage, used to call me a 'terminal romantic.' I guess I haven't changed much."

"So how long you been in the Bin?"

"Six weeks."

"How's it been?"

She rocked her head from side to side. "Okay, I guess. My band just broke up, just as we were starting to get somewhere. I don't even know these guys I'm playing with tomorrow night. My agent found them. He says they know all the tunes. We'll see."

"I don't mean that," he said, his voice low and serious. "Is it different? Are you happier here?"

She really didn't know what to say. The question scared her a little. "I don't know. I'm still getting used to it."

"How come you waited so long to come in?"

"I don't know." She looked into the flame of the hurricane lamp, ran her fingertips lightly across the glass. "I didn't know anybody in here."

"What changed?"

She wanted to change the subject. She didn't want to talk about herself any more than he wanted to talk about his parents. "Nothing changed. I just didn't have anyplace else to go. I had to go somewhere, do something." She shrugged. "I was lonely. I didn't know anybody outside either."

"You must've known somebody."

She desperately tried to remember, but there was no one. "There were girls at the orphanage, but I lost track of them."

"Any regrets?"

She looked up from the flame, at the light flickering in his eyes. "Sure. I'm still lonely in here."

That hung in the air for a moment. Great, Justine, tell him how lonely you are. She wanted to crawl under the table. "Let's talk about you again. Why've you stayed out? It's not all about your parents, is it?"

It was his turn to look into the flame. The piano player was finally winding down, banging out chords with ponderous intensity. There was a small ripple of applause.

Nemo looked up from the flame, a crooked smile on his face.

He took her hands. "You know those old pictures of the Earth from space—a big blue ball? I have one of those up in my room. It was my grandmother's. Must be over a hundred years old. I go out walking sometimes and look around at everything abandoned and falling apart, thinking about that picture and how it wouldn't be the same now to float out there in space like the astronauts and look at the Earth, knowing most of the people are gone. Used to be you could look at it and say, 'That's where I live. That's my home.' People used to say we were bad for the Earth, and I guess we were, but I don't think it'll be the same place without us." He looked into her eyes. "Do you know what I mean?"

"I think so." She looked down at their clasped hands. "I wish I didn't."

"How come?"

"Because I like you. And I'd like to see you again. But everything you're telling me says that's not going to happen, is it?"

His voice was leaden and sad. "I don't think that'd be such a good idea."

"Because I'm not real? Don't I feel real to you, Nemo?"

He squeezed her hands. "Too real."

"We could just be friends."

They looked into each other's eyes, gave each other the same sad smile. "I guess not," she said.

"I'm sorry—"

She released his hands and put her fingers to his lips. "Don't be. I'm glad you think we couldn't be just friends." She slid back her chair and tried to sound cheerful. "I guess we should call it a night then. Show me to my room?"

4

NEMO NODDED AND ROSE TO HIS FEET, FEELING hollow and empty inside. I'm doing the right thing, he kept saying to myself. I'm doing the right thing. So why do I feel so awful? He followed her to the elevator. She didn't take his arm this time. They stood waiting a few feet apart, watching the numbers light up. They rode up in silence, avoiding each other's eyes. Her room was in the back corner of the hotel, as far away from the elevator as you could get. They padded down the long, carpeted hallway, stood in front of her door, their heads hung down, not saying anything. Finally she stuck out her hand. "I'm glad I got to meet you, Nemo."

"Me too," he mumbled, and took her hand. It was beautiful, her fingers long and delicate. He couldn't let it go. He pressed her palm to his lips and kissed it.

She ran her fingertips over his cheek. He closed his eyes, and she whispered, "Don't be afraid of me."

He pulled her into his arms and kissed her. Her lips were soft and warm. She held him close and pressed her body against him. He'd never felt so alive. He didn't care if it was real. His feelings were real enough. Not even he could doubt them. She clung to him as if she felt it too, as if she never wanted to let him go.

They kissed for a long time, passionate and then tender. Then they stood there, just holding each other, afraid to let go. He didn't know what to do, didn't want to think about it. He just wanted the feeling to last. Finally, she whispered against his cheek, "Come hear me sing tomorrow night?"

He pressed his cheek against hers, breathed in her scent, knowing what he should do, but knowing he wasn't going to do it. "I want to."

"Please?" she whispered.

He kissed her hair, her ear. "Yes," he said.

She drew back and looked into his eyes. "Promise?"

"Promise."

Her face shone. Nothing he'd ever said in his life had ever made anyone so happy. "The club's called Black Dog," she said in a rush. "It's on K between 11th and 12th. First set's ten o'clock."

He just nodded stupidly. He could still feel her kiss on his lips, feel her body in his arms, see the joy in her eyes. He was sure his must have shone as well.

"I guess we both need to get some sleep," she said, and he let her go. She turned and opened the door to her room. "Good night."

"Good night," he said, still in a daze. She caressed his cheek and disappeared into her room, the door closing behind her with a click. He stared at it. He could undo it all with a quick rap at her door. He looked down at his hands that'd just held her and knew he could no more ball them into fists and knock on her door than he could rise from his coffin and walk. He turned on his heel and took off toward the elevator, hit the down button with the side of his fist.

By the time he'd reached the lobby, he was in a rage.

He cursed himself as he hurried down the street to the Metro. It'd started raining, a strong spring shower. He passed a couple dancing in the puddles, singing an old love song off-key. "One kiss and you're fucking Jell-O," he muttered to himself as he boarded the packed train to Pentagon Station, swaying against strangers who paid no attention as he cursed their paradise, who chattered on, making their plans.

Knowing they'd never die.

He went to the row of coffins, found his, and got in. More Bin nonsense. Place was meaningless in here, but the fiction of reality had to be scrupulously maintained. This is where he came in, so this is where he left, as if it were a doorway. He hit Download, and the lid closed. It took a few seconds to rotate to the horizontal position, and then there was the falling sensation, and he was back in his own body. He usually felt a sense of relief being back home in the real world. But not tonight.

THE REAL WORLD WAS DESERTED. IT WAS RAINING THERE, too. He boarded an empty train, leaned against a pole and watched the buildings slide by in the darkness. No lights anywhere. No signs of life. He couldn't believe he'd promised to go back into the Bin the next night. Then he thought about Justine, the look in her eyes, and he believed it.

The train passed through Quantico about thirty miles south of D.C., and he caught sight of the stacks from the crematorium glowing in the distance, the only light for miles, except the lightning. He thought about Jonathan and what he'd say if he knew he was falling for a Bin girl. Probably not much unless he asked him. That wasn't Jonathan's style. He witnessed, but he never preached.

Knowing Jonathan, Nemo had come to appreciate the difference.

Nemo first met Jonathan when he ran away from school and came back to his parents' house, or what was left of it. Most of the furniture was gone or busted up for kindling. The banister was gone, the interior door facings, the columns in the hall—most anything that would burn without bringing the house down. Somebody'd left a rat-chewed sleeping bag in front of the fireplace, and a stack of books next to the fireplace for starting fires. On top was a Bible. The pages from Genesis to Judges were torn out.

What his parents had called the "breakfast nook" was ankle deep in shattered dishes, thrown against the wall that had been papered with a photomural of an idyllic mountain lake in springtime. All that was left of the mural was a smear of faded blue where a young couple sat blissfully in a canoe. A chef's knife had been buried in the middle of it, a good two or three inches.

Lawrence and Nemo were hauling junk into the yard, making two piles—everything that'd burn and everything that wouldn't. Jonathan came up and stood on what was left of the sidewalk, a hard place under the knee-high grass. He was about Nemo's age, tall and thin with dark, thick hair cut like somebody'd put a bowl over his head. His eyes were large and dark with long black lashes like a girl's. His face was pale and earnest, but not weak. He had the sort of calmness required to stroll into a lion's den or chat with Pilate.

"Are you moving in?" Jonathan asked, polite and friendly in a world where caution was the accepted etiquette.

Nemo threw down what was left of one of the metal kitchen chairs, watched the seat and back slap together like closing a vinyl book. "This is my house," he said. "I'm moving back in."

Jonathan gave him no argument. "My name's Jonathan," he said. "We'll be neighbors." He pointed down the street. "We live in that big white house with the black shutters." Nemo looked past an old pickup truck sitting in the middle of the road, stripped of its wheels and doors and windows, the hood open, the engine gone. All the houses looked pretty much like Nemo's—weather-beaten, scarred, the porches choked with vines, shattered glass scattered around like confetti. One of them had a corner burned away.

Then there was Jonathan's house, three houses down, on the other side of the street, the place where the Proxmires used to live. It had glass in all the windows. The paint gleamed. The grass was cut and edged, the hedges precisely trimmed. A blue flag with a white cross and red pentacostal flames waved gently from a flagpole mounted above the front steps.

"Who's 'we'?" Nemo asked.

"My mom and dad, my little brother, and me." Jonathan shrugged. "We take in people sometimes. If you need a place to sleep until you get your house fixed up, you can stay with us."

"No thanks," Nemo said. "We'll be okay." Lawrence had come up behind Nemo, his shadow stretching across the road.

"Come on down if you change your mind. Dinner's at sundown. We've got plenty." Jonathan raised his eyes to Lawrence's. "My name's Jonathan."

Nemo watched Lawrence's shadow nod, heard his Texan voice rumble, "Lawrence. Pleased to meet you."

They both watched Jonathan stroll down the middle of the road and into the big white house. "If we were you," Lawrence said, holding up a battered can of creamed corn, "we wouldn't turn down dinner. Unless you got a can opener on you. This here's the only food we could find."

They ended up spending a couple of weeks with Jonathan's family. They fed them, gave them a place to sleep, even gave them paint and brushes and helped them paint, helped them dig a well, gave them rabbits to raise and seeds to plant. Even when their place was all fixed up, Nemo spent as much time at Jonathan's house as he did his own.

Jonathan's father, Harold, a stockier, muscular version of Jonathan, explained to Nemo one night at their kitchen table, his face lit by candlelight, just why he and his family didn't go into the Bin. "The Lord will come for us one day," he'd said as if he were talking about the sun coming up or the rain falling out of the sky. "And I want to be here when He does." The whole family—Jonathan, his little brother Matthew, Constance, their mother—had nodded in agreement, and Nemo had wished that he'd grown up with them, had their faith. But he knew he didn't, knew he never would. And then Rosalind came.

It was a few years later. He'd just turned eighteen. Rosalind and her father Peter, Harold's little brother, came to live at Jonathan's house because Rosalind's mother, Peter's wife of seventeen years, had gone into the Bin.

Rosalind didn't say much of anything to anybody. Everyone thought she was broken-hearted and afraid, except Nemo. He watched her, and he could see it in her eyes, in the way she moved from room to room never staying put for too long, in the way she speared her food with her fork with a quick brutal movement, in the way she'd hacked off her dark hair in sharp angular lines with a razor. It wasn't grief. It was anger. She was burning up with it.

But three weeks after she'd moved in, Jonathan and Nemo invited her to sing with them on Jonathan's front porch, and to their surprise, she joined them. Jonathan played an old Gibson guitar with a crack in the front and strung with piano strings. Unlike a lot of fundies, he played something besides "Amazing Grace" and "Old Time Religion." He liked the blues, and Rosalind had a strong, bluesy voice. She closed her eyes when she sang, pouring her rage into old songs about no-good men who'd done her wrong, even though she was only sixteen years old.

When they quit singing, she fixed Jonathan and Nemo in her harsh gaze and told them she was going to check out the main crematorium in Quantico. She didn't believe all that crap about piles of bodies on a conveyor moving through fire in an endless stream. She was going to see for herself. And if Jonathan and Nemo had any guts, they'd go with her. Nemo could usually pass up a dare, but he couldn't pass on this one. And once he'd agreed, Jonathan wouldn't let him go alone. They sat on the porch and listened for an hour, as Rosalind, who hadn't spoken more than a dozen words in the three weeks since her arrival, told them her plan.

THEY RODE OUT AT DAWN ON THE TRAIN TO D.C. NEMO was on the aisle on the left, Rosalind across the aisle from him, Jonathan in the seat behind her. Rosalind had a pair of wire cutters stuck in the back pocket of her jeans. Jonathan had a tiny pair of binoculars around his neck. Nemo kept his eyes on Rosalind. The sky behind her—gray clouds streaked with red and purple—might've been her anger. Her dark eyes were intent on the horizon, waiting to catch sight of the smoke stacks in the morning light. Nemo had no doubt people were being burned out here. He didn't have to see the bodies. She was the reason he came. He had plenty of his own anger, but hers wasn't deadening and pointless like his. Hers put her on this train at dawn, tracking it down, stalking it, ready to spit in its face. He wanted to be there when she caught up with it.

"Any time," she said, and he followed her gaze and saw the stacks and the line of smoke stretching toward the sun. She reached up slowly and yanked the emergency cord, lurched to her feet and into the aisle as the train started braking, letting the momentum carry her to the door at the front of the car. Jonathan and Nemo fell against the seats in front of them and scurried after her when the train rocked back. She shoved open the doors with her shoulder and leapt into the air. Nemo jumped after her, hitting the ground hard, running into the high grass and dropping flat when Rosalind did, about twenty yards from the train.

Rosalind said she'd checked it out, yanked the emergency cords on four different trains, and every time the train would take exactly three minutes to run through its security program, and then it would take off. Nemo lay in the grass, the ground cold and muddy. Fortunately, it hadn't rained in weeks, or this place would be a swamp. Rosalind was just ahead of him. The legs of her tight black jeans made a V in the grass. The soles of her hiking boots were an arm's length away. He heard Jonathan shifting in the grass behind him and knew he'd jumped, too.

The train's motors started their whine, and the train sped away, leaving them in silence. Nemo pulled out his contribution to the expedition, a periscope he'd made from a plastic pipe, a roll of duct tape, and a pair of hand mirrors. It took him a moment to get his bearings, and then he saw them on the horizon, the smoke stacks, directly in front of where they lay. Rosalind had timed it perfectly. All they had to do now was crawl on their bellies for a mile or so.

"They're straight ahead," Nemo said, and they all started crawling.

The night before, when he'd lain in bed thinking about
what they were going to do, Nemo had imagined crawling
endlessly through the mud, had prepared himself for an
ordeal that would push him to the limits of his endurance.
But as he moved through the mud like a snake, he didn't
tire. His blood was racing, and his senses were alive. He
was surprised each time he stopped to check their position
that the smokestacks were bigger, closer than he'd expected them to be. It seemed to him they'd been crawling
maybe five minutes when he ran into Rosalind, stopped
at the fence. And there, about a hundred yards away, was
the crematorium.

She pointed wordlessly at a place a few yards off to
their left where the land was eroded away from beneath
the chain-link fence. They could crawl under it without
even cutting it. Jonathan came up beside them and shook
his head as Rosalind pointed toward the opening. "We
should look first," he whispered, holding up the
binoculars.

They didn't know what kind of security there was.
Crawling through high grass to the perimeter was one
thing, but between them and the low, featureless concrete
building was nothing but packed dirt and gravel. If anyone
was watching, they'd be seen. "It'll be robots," Rosalind
had argued. "Who in the fuck's going to work in there?
Robots can't kill people. Worst that can happen is we get
tossed out."

Jonathan studied the place with his binoculars. Nemo
didn't figure he could see much more than he could. It was
a big concrete box that joined up with a round building at
one end. From the air it would've looked like a big rectan-
gle joined to a circle, like a keyhole. The smokestacks rose
out of the round building. On the opposite end from the
stacks, a pair of railroad tracks came out the end of the
building and then through a wide gate in the fence, around

the corner to their left. The tracks disappeared into the distance, headed for D.C. to the north.

All of a sudden the smokestacks roared and belched smoke hundreds of feet into the air, and the ground vibrated like a drumhead. When the sound stopped, it still seemed to hang in the air, changing everything—making the colors brighter, the edge of each blade of grass more precisely defined—as if the blast had compressed everything into a more substantial reality.

"What the hell was that?" Nemo said.

"Souls," whispered Jonathan.

Rosalind turned on him with a sneer, but whatever she was going to say was forgotten when a train rolled out of the building and came to a stop at the fence. It looked like a Metro train, only it had no windows. It was three cars long, all flat black with a small silver pentagon on the side where the big M would've been on Metro cars. There was something that looked like an air conditioner perched on top of each car. The train was stopped only a moment when the gates slid to one side, and the train sped away, the gates closing behind it.

"I say we go in," Rosalind said.

"There's cameras covering the grounds," Jonathan said. "But that's about it. No people anywhere."

And then they all heard it at the same time, jerking their heads around like startled deer: the sound of an approaching train. Rosalind didn't hesitate. She broke into a crablike run toward the gates. Nemo knew immediately what she intended to do. He went running after her, not sure whether he was going to stop her or go with her. By the time he caught up with her, she'd already crawled up to the tracks and rolled into them, lying on her back between the rails, hoping to hitch a ride with the dead.

Nemo looked down the tracks. He couldn't see the train yet, but he could feel it under his feet. He didn't have time to crawl. He ran toward the tracks and dove between the rails, skidding on his belly through the ballast. He rolled over on his back and looked down the tracks in time to see Jonathan lie down between the rails a few yards away, just as the train came into view. Nemo snapped his head back, flattening himself into the ties. The brakes squealed, the sound ringing through the rails and inside his head as if he were inside a shrieking bell.

The sky disappeared and the train covered him. The undersides of the cars were braced with steel girders in an X pattern. He reached up and grabbed the top branches of the X above him, hooked one foot, and then the other, onto the bottom branches. Staring at the underside of the car, the same flat black as the top, he couldn't see Rosalind or Jonathan, couldn't hear them. The muscles in his arms were already aching, sweat burning his eyes. Then the train lurched into motion, and the ground sped by at his back. He tightened his grasp on the steel, now slippery with his sweat. Then the light suddenly dimmed, and everything smelled like wet concrete. The train stopped, and he half lowered himself to the concrete floor beneath him. It was bitterly cold, maybe ten degrees. His breath came out in clouds, and his nostrils felt brittle. He was glad he'd worn a heavy jacket. He stuck his periscope sideways from underneath the car and saw Rosalind crouched in the shadows, Jonathan beside her, beckoning to him, about ten yards away.

He ran over to them, hoping he wouldn't fall over anything in the darkness. The only light came from maintenance robots, white metal cylinders bristling with appendages, moving up and down along the track, plugging their sensors into the train. If the robots had taken any notice of them, they gave no sign of it. Nemo crouched beside Rosalind and looked around. He could make out the curved wall of the round building at the front of the train. There was only one track going into it. There was a switch a few yards behind the train where the tracks forked in two before heading out the massive doors that'd apparently opened to admit them.

A quiet whirring sound brought his attention back to the train. The sides of the cars were rising slowly like birds opening their wings. The robots were all in a row shining their spotlights inside where bodies were stacked from floor to ceiling. One of the arms was dangling down, a woman's, maybe twenty-five or thirty years old, fully dressed, looking like she'd just lain down for a nap. She was on her side, perched precariously, facing Nemo. She looked like she might roll out onto the concrete any moment. One of the robots reached out with a shovel-like extension and pushed her back into place.

There was a low rumble, all the robots glided back, and a tunnel opened in the side of the round building. The train rolled through the opening, and the tunnel closed behind it. A few seconds later there was a loud roar that rumbled on and on like thunder in the summertime, only louder, as if they were up in the clouds, in the middle of it. When it stopped, the round wall opened itself up again, and the train emerged, radiating an intense heat Nemo could feel on his face even through the bitter cold.

The cars were completely empty. Not even any ashes. Their sides slowly closed, and the switch in front of the doors threw. The train started moving. The doors parted just as it reached them and closed immediately behind the last car.

For some minutes, nobody said anything. The air still smelled like hot metal. The robots sat in a silent row alongside the track, their limbs at rest.

Finally, Nemo said, "How are we going to get out of here?"

Rosalind was still staring at the concrete cylinder, completely quiet now. She gave no sign she'd even heard him. Jonathan was looking at the doors that led outside. "We could make a dash for it when the next train comes," he said.

"It'd run you down," Rosalind said in a dead, flat voice, not taking her eyes off the curved wall where the tunnel had appeared.

"Then we run for it when the next train leaves," Jonathan said.

They all knew what that meant. They'd have to stay in here with another trainload of bodies. "There's not enough time," Rosalind said.

The switch threw again, and the doors opened, blinding them for a second. A new train rolled in, and they watched the whole thing again.

When the train disappeared into the tunnel, Rosalind said in the same flat voice, "We have to ride out on it like we came in."

"It'll burn your hands off," Nemo said.

She turned slowly toward him as the roar started up again inside the cylinder. Even if she'd tried to say anything else, he wouldn't have been able to hear her. She took off her jacket and peeled off her sweatshirt, cut it apart with the wirecutters. She put her jacket back on and wrapped her hands with the pieces of her sweatshirt. Nemo followed her example, but the zipper on his jacket had broken, and he couldn't get it closed. He gave up and let it hang open, then wound his hands in his shirt. Jonathan had silently followed their examples.

They lay down beneath the rails in front of the doors. When the train covered him, Nemo clenched his teeth and seized hold of the X. He could smell his shirt scorching. The flesh between his thumb and forefinger on his right hand seared with pain as he got too close to the metal, and he tried to adjust his grip to distribute the pain. The heat blasted his face and chest, his eyes filling with sweat, blinding him. He hooked one foot over the metal, then the other, but the first one slipped off as the rubber heel of his boot melted just as the switch threw and the train started moving. He held his leg stiff, bobbing up and down only a foot above the ties. His hands felt as if he were clutching hot coals. With a lurch, the train stopped at the gates, and he wanted to let go. His leg cramped, and he watched it dip inevitably toward the roadbed. "God," he prayed. "Please, God."

The train jerked into motion, and he almost lost his grip. He counted to ten slowly and deliberately to make sure he'd cleared the fence, then let go, hitting his head hard, skidding on the ballast. He opened his eyes and stared into the deep blue sky, holding his blistered palms up into the air, knowing he'd never be the same.

THAT NIGHT ROSALIND CAME TO HIS HOUSE AND UP TO HIS room with bandages and ointment. She dressed the cuts on his back and the burns on his hands. His face and chest and stomach were bright red, starting to blister. She dabbed on ointment and rubbed it in, said, "I'm sorry," each time he flinched. Her own face was red, and there was a cut on her left hand, but she was relatively un- scathed, on the outside at least.

They made love standing in the middle of the room, wincing with pain when they grazed each other's wounds.

They never talked about her moving in. She just stayed there. Her father didn't seem to mind. Everybody, even Nemo himself, seemed happy for them. But Rosalind, even though she'd made it all happen, never seemed any hap- pier except for brief moments like that first time they made love, or sometimes singing in the shower, her voice ringing off the tiles.

She'd been changed, too, her anger transformed into something darker, but she never would talk about it. After twenty-three months, she left Nemo a letter saying she was going into the Bin to find her mother. When Nemo went to tell Peter that his daughter was gone, he'd said, "She's not my daughter anymore."

She'd kept her mother's picture on the mantel in their bedroom. He'd wake up and find her sitting up in bed staring at it in the flickering light. The note she left him was taped to the mantelpiece. The ashes of her mother's photograph fluttered on the coals. He laid the one page letter over them and watched it burst into flames, then moved all his stuff to the bedroom down the hall.

Like he'd told Justine, he didn't want to find Rosalind. He knew where she was, exactly how she'd gotten there, still had nightmares where he saw her in the flames. He knew the precise path to take if he wanted to follow her. It was the same path that led to Justine. He looked out at the dark night. The glow of the crematorium was long behind him. Flashes of lightning glowed and died. Barely audible over the sound of the train was the rumble of distant thunder. Rain hissed against the glass. It was as if he could still hear the roar of the incinerator, Jonathan whispering, "Souls."

NORTHSIDE STATION WAS ONLY FOUR BLOCKS FROM NEMO'S house, but he had to cut around a pack of wild dogs and ended up going ten blocks to get home. He was in no hurry. The rain had stopped, and the sky was clearing, the moon hanging overhead. He wasn't ready to go home, but there was no place else to go.

Justine hadn't had it quite right about him and Rosalind. They were never really that close. They'd seen death together, and they were both terrified. But they'd made different things of their visions. Hers led her into the Bin, just as Nemo's seemed to keep him out.

Whenever he thought of going in, which he did more often than he admitted to anyone, he heard the roar of that fire, and it felt like a warning, a cryptic message from the gods. It was like the story of Oedipus Lawrence had told him. Like Oedipus, he didn't know enough to understand what he should do, or even to understand what he was being warned against. He knew that every one of those people he saw consumed lived on in the Bin, never having to face death again, that in a sense they hadn't really died at all, and it made perfect sense to follow them. And he knew that if he didn't, he could very well live his whole life out here and die, and still not understand the roar of that fire, still not understand what the gods were trying to say to him—because maybe there weren't any gods to be understood. But if there weren't, what was the point of conquering death? What was the point of anything?

As HE CAME UP HIS FRONT STEPS, HE WAS LOST IN THESE thoughts. Otherwise he would've noticed the squeak of the porch swing or the shadow of a man in the moonlight.

He bent over the front door lock and fumbled with his keys in the darkness. He'd just found the keyhole when an unfamiliar voice said, "Good evening, Nemo," and he jumped, his keys falling to the porch with a clatter.

He peered into the darkness and made out the shape of a tall, rail-thin man, his long legs stretched out in front of him, swinging back and forth in the swing as if the wind blew him. "Do I know you?" Nemo asked.

"I'm a friend of Peter's," he said. "Rosalind's father. He said you were a young man of strong convictions and feelings, particularly about the evils of the Bin."

Nemo had sounded off to Peter the night Rosalind had gone in. Nemo'd been about halfway crazy, and Peter had been there for years. No telling what he'd told this guy. "So who're you? And why're you on my porch in the middle of the night?"

"Call me Gabriel. I was waiting for you."

"Did you talk to Lawrence? Did he tell you to wait?"

"Lawrence. That would be your Construct."

Nemo caught the superior sneer in his tone. "Caretaker. Now why don't you tell me what the fuck you're doing here, so I can go to bed."

"Fair enough." The man stood up. He seemed nearly as tall as Lawrence, but he couldn't have weighed more than a hundred and thirty pounds. "Peter said you might be someone I should meet."

"And then what?"

"You are something of a mystery, Nemo. You are of sound mind, with no apparent religious affiliation to prevent you from going into the Bin, and yet you stay out. Why is that Nemo?"

"Well, it's not so I can stand here in the middle of the night talking to you. I'm going to bed now. Why don't you take a hike?"

Just then the front door opened and Lawrence ducked through it holding a lantern. He held it up high, and Nemo saw Gabriel in the glare, his long silver hair was swept back, hanging down past his shoulders, his beard reaching his belt. His eyes were large and deep-set, unblinking in the light. He smiled humorlessly, a thin line in the mass of hair. "Good evening," he said to Lawrence, who didn't say a thing. Gabriel vaulted the porch rail, his hair streaming behind him, and dropped to the ground. "We'll be in touch, Mr. Nemo," he called from the darkness. "We'll be in touch."

Lawrence was still peering after him. Lawrence had incredible night vision. His borrowed genes had come from a nocturnal lizard.

"Where's he headed?" Nemo asked.

"He's going in the side door of Jonathan's house. Peter's room, we believe. He did say it was Peter who recommended he make your acquaintance."

"You were listening at the door?"

"We heard your keys fall. We were merely performing our duties."

"I can pick up my own keys, Lawrence."

Lawrence wagged his head at Nemo's ingratitude. "That is not the task to which we were referring. We've been observing our visitor for perhaps ten minutes when you arrived."

"How did he know I was coming home? Who the hell was that guy?"

"We would hazard a guess that he is a member of the underground."

Nemo knew such a thing existed, of course. Everybody did. But he'd never actually met anyone on the inside. A bunch of crazies hellbent on destroying the Bin—might as well try to destroy Everest. "What could he want from me?"

"Your anger, of course. Revolutions always require a great deal of anger."

"I'm not *that* angry."

"We would say our visitor quite disagrees and has plans for you." Lawrence gestured with the lantern toward the open door. "At present, however, it's time for a proper meal, and then on to beddies. We've had quite the birthday, haven't we, Nemo?"

"Screw you, Lawrence."

"There, there. Now you see? That's the very anger of which we were speaking."

5

Justine was dreaming again.

She was an old woman, moving through her house with a feather duster, doing some last minute tidying up. She'd sent the nurse to the market, wanting the house to herself. She was expecting a caller, a young man from the college, who'd looked and sounded so nice over the phone, though she couldn't quite remember his name. She never had visitors anymore. Her daughter used to come see her, but now there was only this hateful woman showing up in her place.

She took a list out of her pocket. She checked off the items one by one: She had made cookies. She had made coffee. The tea things were ready. She had even, with much effort (all that stooping and lifting) cleaned the cat box, though now she caught the inevitable scent of fresh cat shit in the air. They queued up when she changed the litter, all three of them, to christen it.

Who are you? Justine asked.

But the old woman paid her no mind, shuffling down the hall to the utility room, now reeking of catshit. The cats lay sprawled on the dryer, no doubt exhausted from their efforts. She opened the cabinet above their heads, but they didn't stir. She took out a new box of plastic bags. She'd used the last one in the old box changing the litter. Shoving Ishmael, a big black tom, to one side with her elbow, she set the box down on top of the dryer. With her thumb, she pushed as hard as she could on the perforated line, but the E-Z Open Flap wouldn't budge.

She shuffled back into the kitchen and returned with a steak knife. She positioned the box against the dryer controls to hold it in place and, placing the knife blade on the perforation, leaned her weight against it. The blade broke through and plunged into the bags. She almost lost her balance, but managed to steady herself on the dryer. The cats flopped over, repositioning themselves. She pulled the box to her by tugging on the knife handle. When she had it in her grasp, she pulled the knife loose from the bags and sawed at the cardboard until she had a hole big enough for her fingers. She groped around, and finally snared one. Her fingers ached with the effort. She started tugging at it, and at first she thought it wasn't going to come loose, then it popped out, the box spinning across the top of the dryer, as she stumbled backwards, the plastic bag in her hand, flailing the air to keep her balance. Her back hit the wall, and she managed to right herself, just as one of the cats, a Siamese named Sasha, stretched out his hind legs and kicked the box of plastic bags over the edge of the dryer, so that it fell between the wall and the dryer.

It might as well have fallen to Siberia. Clutching the bag in one hand, she made her way to the sink. The cat box sat underneath it. She shook open the plastic bag as best she could by waving her arm about. Steadying herself on the sink with the other hand, she lowered herself to one knee in front of the cat box. She laid the bag on the floor and picked up the scoop she kept on the trap.

They'd all three shit in the very back of the box, of

course. She'd have to lean way over to get the three discreet piles, unless she repositioned herself and dragged the box out, but the thought wore her out. No, she could reach it just fine. She'd done it before. She stretched out her arm and had just snared the first lump of shit, when the doorbell rang, and she tried to get up too fast, grazing her shoulder on the sink. She got upright, but felt herself spinning like the last revolution of a top and flung out her arm, striking the wall with the scoop, which snapped in half like a twig.

She teetered there for a moment, balanced on the broken plastic handle, and then she started forward. She reached out desperately with her free hand and managed to grab one of the triangle braces that secured a shelf overhead. A can of paint, empty from the sound of it, fell off the shelf and bounced on the floor, rolling to a stop on the threshold to the kitchen.

The doorbell rang again. Slowly, carefully, she centered her weight and pushed herself away from the wall, dropping the broken scoop to the floor. She let go of the brace, and stood for a moment, then started shuffling toward the front door at the other end of the house, her hands throbbing with pain, wishing she could remember the young man's name. She smelled something burning and sniffed the air. Cookies. She clucked her tongue. What a shame.

At the large mirror in the foyer, she turned and looked at herself, patting her hair into place. She was nearly as old as Mr. Menso. Her hands were twisted with arthritis. The face in the mirror smiled. "Hello, Justine," she said.

JUSTINE SAT UP IN BED, HER HEART RACING.

It was morning. The curtains were open, and the room was filled with sunshine. There'd been thunder in the night, and the rain had beaten against the windows, but now the city looked bright and new, washed clean. Justine swung her legs over the side of the bed and was surprised they moved so easily, were so young and firm. She'd had arthritis. In her dream, she corrected herself, she'd had arthritis. With a shaking hand, she pressed the *Coffee* icon on the room service pad. A panel slid open, and there was the coffee. As she picked it up, she thought, it's the old woman, the one in my dream. She's the one who watched reruns of Captain Kirk.

She started, splashing herself with hot coffee, wincing as the cup slipped from her grasp and fell to the floor, rolling into the corner. The coffee oozed into the beige carpet in a neat, brown crescent. Stop it, she told herself. Just stop it. Get out of the damn dream. She wiped her hands on the sheets and punched the *Coffee* icon and the *Maid* icon. She took a swallow of the fresh coffee, burning her throat and tongue. She rubbed her burned tongue against her teeth and winced, thinking, I know something because somebody in my *dreams* knows it? Justine, get a grip.

She went into the bathroom and turned on the shower. She stood in the water, remembering her dream. I even knew the cats' names, she thought. What was the third one's name? Timothy. Named after *Timothy the Tiger,* a children's book about a cub looking for his mother. The boy from the college, his name was Bill something. Or Tom.

But she didn't know the woman's name. She didn't know what year it was, where she lived. She thought the old woman was a widow, but she didn't know her husband's name. Of course, you don't, she told herself. Because she's not real. She's a woman in a dream.

Wade. Her husband's name was Wade.

She sank to the floor of the shower and let the water

beat down on her head. Why am I having these dreams? Why do they frighten me so much? Nothing horrible happens in them. I'm in no danger—I'm not in them at all. They're like somebody else's dreams.

She froze. Maybe that was it. Maybe they were somebody else's dreams, some kind of screwup when she was uploaded. She tried to remember when she came in—who was there and what was going on—but she couldn't remember a thing. That must be part of it, too—somebody else was probably walking around in here with her memories.

She slid up the wall, thrust her face into the water, and held it there. Fine. They were welcome to them, but she wanted to dream her own damn dreams. She let the water play across her body, remembering Nemo holding her, kissing her. She imagined them lying in his bed, making love, the poster of the Earth on the wall above his bed. She felt weak in the knees, and leaned back against the cold tile.

It was impossible. He lived in another world. She imagined herself floating in space, looking down at the Earth, knowing he was down there somewhere, but she could never go to him. But he'd come in tonight. He'd promised her. And if he didn't, well then, he obviously wasn't worth worrying about.

She got out of the shower and wrapped herself in a warm towel, opened the door to let the steam escape. She took a deep swallow of her coffee and wiped the mirror dry, studying her reflection for clues. In my dreams, she thought, I have a life—friends, neighbors, relatives, lovers. Why is my own life so empty? She looked deep into her eyes, trying to find the women in her dreams, but felt foolish and hurried off to get dressed, studiously avoiding the dresser mirror.

The maid program had run while she was in the bathroom. The bed was made. The coffee cup and the stain were gone from the carpet. She looked around the room. Everything was perfect. She ran her tongue over her teeth; the burn was gone. She took off the towel and tossed it on the bed. Her thigh, where she'd just spilled a cup of hot coffee, didn't have a mark on it. She was in the Bin now. Dreams or no dreams, she was just going to have to get used to it.

SHE TOOK THE METRO DOWN TO THE CLUB, HOLDING HER guitar case between her knees, her arms wrapped around the neck, her chin resting on top of it. She could understand if Nemo didn't come see her tonight. It was stupid, really. Pointless. She could also understand what he meant about the Bin. Things were different in here, or maybe they just weren't different enough. She stared out the window, watching the tunnel slide by, waiting for her station to come into view.

But still, he'd promised. Right. Men promised a lot of things. What would she do if he didn't show up? She couldn't even mail him a postcard.

As she came out of the station into the sunlight, she wondered if she stared directly at the sun in here, whether she'd go blind. She decided not to try it. She didn't want to push her luck. She had the feeling she was going to need all she could get. At least she got to sing, she reminded herself. Nemo or no Nemo. At least she got to sing.

The club was only a couple of blocks from the station. The front was painted with a huge black dog's face, the door set in the lolling tongue. The red door was unlocked, and Justine stepped into the darkness. It smelled of beer and cigarettes. The only light came from a hologram of a miniature Budweiser wagon driving around the perimeter of the place near the ceiling. When it passed over her head she could hear the *clip-clop* of the Clydesdales, heard them snort, heard the crack of a tiny whip.

Somebody was sitting on the dark stage playing bass runs. When her eyes adjusted to the darkness, she could see he was tall and skinny with brown hair past his shoulders. His T-shirt and jeans hung from him, grazing his bones. She walked to the front of the stage. "You must be John," she said.

He stopped playing and raised his head slowly. "That's right," he said. "And you must be Justine." He reached over beside him and flipped a switch. The stage lights came up slowly, and he blinked a few times in the light, a lazy smile spreading across his face. "And this must be the place." His voice was deep and unhurried. His drooping lids made him look like a drowsy cat.

"Where're the other guys?"

John shrugged long and slow, like a cat stretching. "Beats me. I told them about it. *Busy* night last night." He winked.

"You mean women?"

"Most definitely," John said, bobbing his head up and down. He set his bass down and lit a cigarette, holding it in a V of skeletal fingers, watching the smoke drift into the air. "Don't sweat it," he said. "We know all the tunes backwards and forwards and sideways."

"It's not that easy," she said. "Knowing the tunes isn't the same as being tight. We've never played together."

John laughed, a rumbling sound deep in his throat. "Sure we have. You just weren't there. Your agent Lenny gave us virtuals of you and those clowns you used to play with. Edited those turkeys out and stepped right in. We are into it. We are strictly twentieth century. A blast from the blasted past. We are the band of your dreams."

Justine couldn't remember recording any virtuals, but

she let that go. She couldn't remember a lot of things. "Are you high, John?"

He laughed again. "Always, Justine. Always."

She sat down at the nearest table, pushed the *Coffee* icon, and picked up the cup that rose to the table's surface. The tables were painted with the same dog's face that was out front. "You want any coffee, John?"

He winced and shook his head. "No, man, that shit'll keep you awake."

She laughed. "So tell me about yourself."

He shrugged again, studied his cigarette. "Nothing much to tell. I play the bass, this band and that. It don't matter to me."

"You ever play outside?"

He made a face as if he'd smelled something rancid. "Shit no. Outside. Man. Don't even talk to me about outside. Couldn't wait to leave that place behind." He took another drag, held it in his lungs.

"How long you been inside?"

"Ten years."

"You're twenty-eight?"

"You got it." He perched his cigarette on top of his amp and picked up his bass. He started playing the intro to "That's Just What You Are," soft and clean, just like it was supposed to be. "So what's your story?" he asked, still playing. "You fresh?"

"Six weeks."

He nodded sagely, paused to take off in the music for a few bars, his eyes closed, his head bobbing up and down. "Holdout," he said, his eyes still closed.

"That's right."

He raised his heavy lids and looked at her. "You'll get into it. You'll see." He grinned again, and she thought of the Cheshire Cat. "Haven't you heard? The Bin is the fucking Salvation of Mankind." His rumbling laugh stretched on for a few bars, then it was forgotten.

He'd kept playing the whole time without missing a beat. He was off on another tune now, playing flawlessly. Maybe Lenny hadn't done so badly. If only the other two would show up. "When you were first in the Bin, did you have weird dreams?" she asked.

He smiled to himself. "I always have weird dreams."

"I mean, dreams where you're somebody else altogether, like an old man or something?"

He shook his head, tilting it back, closing his eyes as his bony fingers glided up and down the neck of his bass. "I am always me. Always."

THE OTHER TWO, RICK AND IAN, WERE FORTY-FIVE MINUTES late. They both looked as if they'd just crawled through several bars to get there. Ian, the drummer, was a small, freckled, bald man with a shock of red hair ringing his scalp in frizzy curls, and a chinstrap beard flecked with gray. Rick, the lead player, scowled as he moved. He was probably handsome, but Justine couldn't get past his repertoire of grimaces. His black hair was slicked back into ducktails. He wore a white ruffled shirt unbuttoned to his navel, tucked into leather pants two sizes too small. He tottered around the stage on high-heeled boots as he tuned up.

"You guys always this prompt?" Justine asked them, sipping her third cup of coffee.

The sound of her voice seemed to add to the burden of Rick's pain. Ian chuckled as if she were joking. John said, "Why don't we just play the tunes, Justine? You'll see. Band of your fucking dreams." Rick scowled and positioned himself in front of a mike, looking as if he and his guitar were facing execution. Ian started warming up with tight little riffs.

"I don't like to be kept waiting," she said.

Rick rolled his eyes. "You got something *else* to do?" he sneered. "Is time ticking away?" He glared at her. "I figured you from the virtuals as some kind of uptight b—"

John's laugh erupted suddenly, cutting Rick off. He looked at them all, still laughing. "You know what they used to say outside? Get this. 'Relax, you'll live longer.'" He laughed again, like boulders rolling through the room. "Is that hysterical or what? 'Relax, you'll live longer.' I love it."

John finally quit laughing and stood there smiling at Justine. I'm supposed to drop it, she thought. John's letting me know I can argue with Rick all day if I want to, and nothing will change. Meanwhile, Rick was glaring into the corner like a boxer waiting out the mandatory count.

She laid her guitar case on the table and took out her guitar. Just drop it, she told herself. Either they can play the tunes or they can't. If they can play, I don't care what kind of assholes they are. If I walk, what the hell do I do then? What else am I going to do but sing?

She slammed the case closed, strapped her guitar on. "Give me a D," she said to John, and he obliged. As she tuned, she said in a hard voice, "We do the first set straight through, no breaks, just like this dump was packed to the rafters, you got it?"

John and Ian nodded. She waited, and finally Rick turned his head and give her a thin, wicked smile. "Sure, boss lady," he said. "Anything you say."

THEY PLAYED THE FIRST SET PERFECTLY. IAN DIDN'T BANG on the drums; he played them. His touch was flawless. He seemed to know the quirks of her phrasing and played off them. Rick, though he still looked haggard and sullen, seemed capable of playing anything. He never looked at her, but when she missed a cue and failed to come in with the verse, he covered for her effortlessly. John bobbed around the stage, a smile on his face, stitching the whole thing together with his bass. She found herself singing better than she thought she could. They kicked the last tune so hard, she wanted to shout with joy, but the only sound was the tiny Clydesdales passing over Ian's head. Her new band was incredible.

"Second set?" Rick asked deadpan.

"I don't think we need to," she said. "You guys are really fantastic—the band of my dreams, like John said." She smiled at John, and he smiled back.

"Does that mean we can leave now?" Rick asked.

She met his hard, level stare. "Look, I'm sorry about being uptight, okay? I'll try to lighten up if you will. We're going to be spending a lot of time together, and it might help if we got along."

"No problem," he said in the same flat voice.

"How about I take you guys to lunch?" she asked them all. Only John nodded.

"Ian and I already ate," Rick said.

"Then I'll buy you a beer."

Rick put his guitar in its case. He snapped it shut and turned around, the case under his arm. Ian stood up behind him, waiting. "Like you said, Justine, we're going to be spending a lot of time together." The two of them left. Ian turned and gave her a friendly wave as they cleared the door.

Justine stared after them. "What the fuck is his problem?"

"Rick's okay. You just got to understand him."

She shook her head. "No, I don't have to understand him, but go ahead, enlighten me."

John shrugged. "If you want. It's like this: The man wants to fuck you. When we were playing with your virtuals, he used to stand behind you and watch your butt moving with the music. But you're in the band now. In his face all the time. Better to fuck the bar babes. Then leave town. He knows this. Believes it. But he still wants to fuck you. Pisses him off. You understand?"

"What in the hell makes him think I'd want to fuck *him?*"

John laughed. "They all do." He lit up another cigarette.

"So what's Ian's problem? I suppose he wants to fuck me, too."

"He goes where Rick goes. Like I say, all the girls go for Rick. Ian's there for the runner-ups." He picked up his guitar case. "So, Justine, where you taking me for lunch?"

They went to a Burger King, all done to period, including holographic counter girls that took your order. It was John's favorite place. She watched him devour two double-double Cheese Whoppers, a jumbo fries, and a large shake. She had another cup of coffee and a fried apple pie. She tried to talk to him, tell him about her weird dreams, but it was like talking to the holographic counter girls.

"They're just dreams," he said, his mouth full of whopper.

"But I'm all different people in them. I know different people. Everything looks like it's before I was even born. Nothing is from my life, nothing."

"So what's the problem, Justine? Sounds pretty cool."

She gave up, looked past him to the street outside, the

beautiful spring day shining through the glass. "So what's there to do in this town, John? I've never been here before."

He pondered this as he chewed. "Go see the Bin," he said and stuffed the last of the hamburgers in his mouth.

"We're in the Bin."

"I mean the facility. They've got tours and shit." He had trouble getting the word *facility* past his burger.

He meant the machine itself—the virtual representation of where they all resided, like a camera filming itself.

"I don't know. I'm not sure I want to see it."

"Why not? It's cool."

"I don't even know what I'm doing here. Seems to me it'd be like visiting your own grave."

John groaned and shook his head. "No, man. Don't get weird about being in here. Trust me. You've done the right thing. I knew this girl once, got to thinking too much about stuff, just like you're doing? Went and had herself *downloaded* into somebody's body that was coming in. Can you believe that shit?"

"Is that possible?"

John snorted. "Stupid, but possible, if you got the connections. They rip off the body before it gets fried. Point is, she's *dead* now. Pneumonia or some shit. Is that stupid or what?"

She didn't answer him. She just shook her head. "I still don't want to go see the Bin."

He shrugged. "There's always museums and shit." He popped the last fry in his mouth, took one last noisy slurp at his shake, and stood up. "See you tonight, Justine. Thanks for lunch."

"Would you like to take in a few museums with me?"

"Thanks Justine, but this is when I sleep." He stood up and started laughing to himself. "You know what they used to say? *Ars longa, vita brevis.* I love that. Now every-

thing's *longa*. Think I'll take a *longa* nap." He shambled
out the door, still laughing at his own joke.

She sat there for about twenty minutes, her elbows resting on the orange formica tabletop, nursing her cold coffee. "Hell with it," she said. She went out into the street
and looked up and down. She went to a tourist information kiosk a half block away and waited for a couple to
finish using the console. Their baby sat in a stroller behind
them fast asleep, bundled up for the arctic, even though it
was in the sixties. She watched him sleep, listened to the
sound of his tiny deep breathing that seemed to fill his
whole body.

He was wheeled away, and she stepped up to the console. She started to push the museum icon, but she wanted
something to take her mind off things. She was afraid
she'd just roam through the museums and mope. And then
it came to her. What she really wanted to do, more than
anything, was go to a play. She pressed the theatre icon,
and a dozen plays came up on the screen. She knew immediately which one she wanted to see. *Romeo and Juliet* was
playing at the Shakespeare Theatre at two o'clock. A map
to the theatre by Metro and by foot flashed on the screen.
A pleasant voice asked if she'd like a printed map. She
said no and took off on foot for the theatre.

There was a line at the box office, and the lobby was
packed with people. She didn't hold out much hope of
getting in. But most everyone else wanted seats in pairs,
and she was by herself. There was a lone seat available in
a box practically on the stage. She hurried in as the lights
dimmed and took her seat just as the chorus began to
speak.

She'd read the play in English class. Her teacher, Sister
Gertrude, had tried her best to bleed the passion from the
play and leave only the carcass of Great Literature for her
students' dissection, but she hadn't quite succeeded, at

least not with Justine. Alone in her room, reading the play aloud, she'd imagined herself as Juliet, in love with Romeo.

And here on the stage was a Juliet whose passion matched the one she'd conjured as a girl. The actress looked young, as if she actually were the not-quite-fourteen Juliet was supposed to be. But she also had a low, sensual voice, and her slender body moved, in the presence of Romeo, not like a gangly teenager's, but with the erotic sway of a passionate woman. Justine leaned toward her and was swept away. By the time the play was not yet half over, Justine felt the emotions the actress feigned, and Juliet's words seemed to come from Justine herself:

> Come, night; come, Romeo; come, thou day in night;
> For thou wilt lie upon the wings of night
> Whiter than new snow upon a raven's back.
> Come, gentle night; come, loving, black-browed night;
> Give me my Romeo; and, when he shall die,
> Take him and cut him out in little stars,
> And he will make the face of heaven so fine
> That all the world will be in love with night
> And pay no worship to the garish sun.
> O, I have bought the mansion of a love,
> But not possess'd it; and though I am sold,
> Not yet enjoy'd. So tedious is this day
> As is the night before some festival
> To an impatient child that hath new robes
> And may not wear them—

Justine couldn't bear to listen as the nurse brought the news of Romeo's banishment that would blight Juliet's hopes. She watched numbly, knowing the lovers were doomed. Sister Gertrude had implied that Romeo and Juliet brought death upon themselves through their reckless passion. But Justine believed their passion was the single good in a world that refused to change. Little older than Juliet, all Justine could manage to say to Sister Gertrude in defense of the lovers was "But they loved each other—" before the sister's smirk and the laughter of the other girls cut her off.

She'd never seen the play before, only read it. As words only, Romeo and Juliet had broken her heart. Now here they were, standing before her. The tears flowed down her cheeks as Juliet spoke the last words Romeo would ever hear from her, spoken, as her first vows of love, from her balcony. Behind her blazed a star-filled night, the faint light of dawn in the east. Romeo stood below, in the shadows:

> O God, I have an ill-divining soul!
> Methinks I see thee, now thou art below,
> As one dead in the bottom of a tomb.
> Either my eyesight fails, or thou look'st pale.

By the time the play was over, Justine had cried herself out. Her crying had caught the attention of the man sitting next to her who'd patted her hand as Juliet died, and said, "It's just a play, dear. No need to get so upset." She bit her tongue and nodded politely, though she couldn't imagine that Shakespeare would've shared the man's sentiments.

Now she sat in her seat and watched everyone leave. She was glad to see there were a few others sniffling and drying their eyes. As she was watching the last stragglers disappear out the exits, Justine was startled to see Mr. Menso in the middle of the front row, his chin resting on his cane, smiling at her. He gave her a little wave and rose to his feet.

"Wonderful play, isn't it?" he said as she joined him in the aisle.

"Mr. Menso, I can hardly believe you're here. You're almost the only person I know in this town, and I looked up, and there you were."

"A pleasant surprise, I hope. I never miss *Romeo and Juliet*. It's my favorite play by my favorite playwright."

"Mine too." She took his arm. She was at least a head taller than he was. They walked up the aisle and out into the day, still bright though the sun hung low in the sky. He headed west, toward his shop, and she walked beside him. It was hours before she had to be at the club.

"Did you ever see it with your sweetheart?"

He stopped and peered at her a moment. "As a matter of fact, I did. That was . . . let me see . . . seventy-five years ago. The idea was, you see, that the play would kindle a passion for me, but of course it didn't work. She cried as you did today, and I comforted her. I asked her to marry me that night, and she said no."

"I'm sorry."

He chuckled. "Don't be. She said no many times."

"Whatever happened to her?"

He shrugged. "She married someone else."

"I'm sorry. Is she still . . ."

"Married? Alive? No. She died out there." He tossed his head over his shoulder to mean the real world. "I lost track of her for years after I came in here, but then I had news from a mutual friend. She lived to be eighty out there." He shook his head and leaned on his cane. "Her husband died the year after I came in here. She never remarried. Lived for fourteen years with nobody to keep her company but her cats." He smiled ruefully. "Guess I should've stayed." He started walking again. "How are the dreams, by the way?" He'd picked up the pace, fleeing her sympathy, turning the subject away from himself. Poor, sweet man, she thought.

"I dreamed I was an old woman with arthritis. I could even feel the pain in my hands."

"Did you read the Morse book?"

"No. I started it, but I'm afraid it seemed pretty silly to me."

He smiled as if pleased that she didn't like the book he'd given her. He was an odd little man. "Yes, I suppose it is. Perhaps your dreams are of a higher order than Ms. Morse is speaking of. Have another look at it. You may find something of value yet."

"Well, actually, I did follow its advice in a way. I asked the woman who she was."

"Well, what happened?"

"She spoke to me. The woman in my dream, that is. She looked into a mirror and said, 'Hello, Justine.' "

"And what did you say?"

"Nothing. I woke up."

He smiled. "Don't wake up next time."

"That's easy enough for you to say. It was very spooky."

"And what was her name?"

"I don't know."

They'd come to a small park. In the middle was a fountain with a pair of holographic dolphins leaping together as if in play. Mr. Menso had stopped again and stood staring at the fountain, as if he hadn't heard her, nodding his head. She wondered if he was all right. "Mr. Menso?"

He turned back to her, cheerful again, but his eyes were sad. "I'm sorry, my dear. My mind wanders sometimes. So, tell me, how was your dinner party?"

"It was wonderful. I met someone."

"Ah! A young man, no doubt."

"Yes."

"I'm delighted for you." He leaned forward on his cane, looking up into her eyes. "But you don't seem so delighted yourself."

"It's nothing. We just met."

"Doesn't sound like nothing." He gestured with his cane to a bench beside the fountain, and they sat down. He propped his cane against the bench and leaned back, stretching out his legs. "I'm all ears," he said.

She told him about Nemo, from the moment she first saw him until they kissed good night. Off and on all day, she'd tried to put her feelings in perspective: You're just lonely, Justine, infatuated. You can't trust this sudden passion. But as she talked to Mr. Menso, she was soon caught up in her own story, just as the play had carried her along, and she felt everything she'd felt the night before all over again. Especially the hopelessness of it all. She was afraid she might start crying again.

"Why so upset, Justine? It sounds to me as if you've fallen in love with an exceptional young man."

"He lives in another world, Mr. Menso. This morning I imagined going to see him there. It was wonderful. I wanted it more than anything, but I can't. It's impossible. The whole thing's impossible. He probably won't even come tonight."

Mr. Menso shook his head back and forth and sat up straight, taking his cane in hand. "You are so young. First of all, I'll wager he comes to see you tonight, and that he's every bit as bewitched by you as you are by him— more so if he's got any sense. And as for visiting his world, try this." He handed her a card: *Real World Tours—We Never Close.* There was a phone number and an address. "Friends of mine. Tell them Warren sent you. And tell this Nemo that Mr. Menso says to take you home and show you where he lives—if his intentions are honorable."

She smiled at him. "You're very sweet, Mr. Menso, but Nemo doesn't want to get involved with me."

He snorted. "Since when does a young man's feelings have anything to do with what he wants? Sounds to me like he's already 'involved,' as you so unromantically put it. Whatever happened to falling in love? 'Get Involved.' Bah! Is that what happened to Romeo and Juliet—they Got Involved?"

"But Mr. Menso, that's a play."

He danced his eyebrows and made an arc around them with a sweep of his cane. "Haven't you heard? It's all a play. We make it up as we go along." He winked at her. "So we might as well make it beautiful, don't you think?"

"What if Nemo doesn't see it that way?"

Mr. Menso chuckled and put his hand on hers. "You are the east, my dear. You are the sun. Whatever he sees from now on is bathed in your light." He patted her hand and rose to his feet. "I must be going. I'm meeting a customer at my shop. He's looking for a copy of *Anna Karenina* for his wife's birthday, and I have a beauty. Odd present, it seems to me, for a husband to give, but perhaps he hasn't read it. Don't worry, Justine. Things will go splendidly this evening. Lovers find a way."

After he'd gone, Justine watched the dolphins in the fountain, thinking about what Mr. Menso had said. The dolphins' play didn't seem to be random, she noticed after a while. They went through a cycle of about ten minutes duration. She watched them perform their dance three times, then walked slowly back to her hotel.

WHEN SHE GOT BACK TO HER ROOM SHE TRIED ALL THE NUM-bers in her address book, but still no one answered. She left a message for her agent to call her, though she wasn't sure why. Just to have somebody to talk to, she guessed.

She thought back to the orphanage, all the girls she knew there. Surely one of them was in here now, probably most of them. That seemed to be the only time in her life she remembered with any clarity. She took out a sheet of stationery and made a list of the names she could remember. She punched the info icon on the phone and accessed the Bin database. With the third name on her list, she had success. Stephanie Ann Boyd lived in Seattle. She was a year younger than Justine. They hung out a lot when she was sixteen and seventeen. They'd both been wild, getting into a lot of trouble together. She entered the number and after a few rings Stephanie's face appeared on the screen. She was the girl Justine remembered, but grown up—mid-thirties, she would guess, but you couldn't tell by looking in here. Maybe she liked looking older.

"Hi, Stephanie," she said. "It's Justine."

Stephanie stared for a moment. "Do I know you?"

"In Dallas, at St. Catherine's."

"I'm sorry. That's been so long ago. I'm afraid I really don't remember you."

"Come on Steph, it hasn't been that long. It was only a few years ago. Remember we snuck out to see Bruce and—what was that guy's name—Alfonso. We got caught, remember?"

Stephanie drew back as if struck, studied Justine with knitted brows. "I left St. Catherine's almost eighty years ago, and I knew no one there named Justine. I'm sorry, you must have me confused with someone else with the same name. The Bin's a big place, you know."

"But I recognize you. I mean you're older, but you're the Stephanie I remember."

"I'm afraid that's quite impossible. I've been in here for almost thirty years. I'm sorry." The screen went blank. Justine didn't bother trying to find any of the other names on her list. She lay down on her bed and stared out the window at the darkening sky, waiting for night to fall.

6

NEMO WOKE IN THE MORNING THINKING OF JUS-
tine. Not thinking, actually. Longing for her. Half awake—
his reason still asleep—he basked in the anticipation of
seeing her again, kissing her, holding her, making love to
her. But as he became lost in this fantasy, as the image
grew clearer, he saw them making love in some perfect
Bin hotel room, entwined in some vast bed with crisp
clean sheets, sitting propped up afterwards on plump down
pillows, sipping Turkish coffee or cognac or whatever they
damn well pleased. It was harder to see them getting up
out of that bed, doing anything in there but wandering
around being happy, like a couple of potheads with the
harvest in. In the Bin, the harvest was always in. It was
The Grasshopper and the Ants, only winter was cancelled,
and the ants were all but extinct. Eventually they'd settle
down in a "Shakespeare" of their own. They'd order the
growing ivy, of course. They could always change it to
the nongrowing if it got to be too much trouble. After a
while, they'd be nongrowing, too, because anything else
would be too much trouble.

He sat up in bed. The weather had cleared, and the sun
was in his face. His windup alarm clock on the bedside

table said it was 8:30, but he hadn't set it for weeks, and the rusty gears inside ran slow. He studied the sun and set the clock for 9:00, giving the key a couple of cranks. If he didn't overwind it, Lawrence told him, it'd run forever. He swung his legs over the side of the bed and stared at the floor, then squinted into the sun. His reason was awake now, but it didn't matter. The longing still gnawed at him. He couldn't wait to see her again, even as he was thinking he had no choice but to break things off before they went any further.

He got out of bed and stood in the cool breeze from the window, looking through his CDs until he found Aimee Mann's. Most of the liner notes were gone except for a few frayed panels from her first solo album—she smiled at the camera with Justine's smile, Justine's eyes. He dug through his desk and found a magnifying glass, studied her eyebrows, her teeth, the precise line of her jaw, her shoulders clad in black. Justine was younger, but this looked like a photograph of her or her twin. He'd heard of people making themselves look like famous people in the Bin, though it was a fad that'd passed. It was a drag to run into yourself at a party. But Justine seemed genuinely surprised when he told her she looked like Mann.

He put the CD in the machine and started it. He opened the old refrigerator where he stored books and papers. Lawrence had picked it up to salvage the tubing. Nemo ripped the compressor out to make it lighter and dragged it up the stairs. It kept everything dry. His room leaked badly, but Lawrence was too big to crawl around on the slate roof, and Nemo was afraid of heights. Sooner or later he'd have to get over it and fix the damn leak, unless he wanted to move back to his old bedroom. He checked the water level in the pan on top of the refrigerator. It was good for another rain at least.

His grandmother's diaries were in a neat row in the freezer

compartment, eight of them, one for every year from 1998 to 2005. He'd read them all several times, but he hadn't looked at them much in the last few years. Rosalind sulked when he did, though she'd never admit it. Who could be jealous of diaries? And they were pretty strange. In the early ones she wrote about wild, improbable adventures with her mother. Other times, she talked as if she didn't have a mother. She nearly always wrote about boys. She might've been living on Mars from all Nemo learned from her diaries, though he gathered she was at some kind of boarding school, which she consistently referred to as "Jail."

Nemo had asked his mom about when his grandmother was a little girl, and his mom had said darkly, "Your grandmother was never a little girl." Nemo had no idea what she meant, but he knew not to ask any more questions, and his mom had been in a foul temper for the rest of the day.

He remembered she wrote in her diaries about the Aimee Mann CDs. They were special to her; that's what had first made them special to him. If he remembered right, they were a gift from some guy. After a brief search, he found the entry he was looking for:

AUGUST 31, 2003

N is so sweet! He gave me all of Aimee Mann's CDs today. He teased me that he just wanted to get his back, but I know that's not true. He's such a good friend. But I'm kind of afraid he's falling in love with me. I've caught him looking at me with great moony eyes. Hope not— wouldn't want to lose my best friend. I don't know what I'd do without him. I wonder

He worked his way back through '02 and '01 to see who this N was. He showed up often. And it sure sounded to Nemo like he was in love with her. Whenever she broke

up with another boyfriend, which she did about once every
two months, she'd call up N and cry on his shoulder and
get him to distract her by taking her to the zoo or a movie
or a swim in the lake, and all the time she'd be talking
about some other guy and telling N what a pal he was.
And he'd do it every time, even get her some little gift to
cheer her up. Nemo felt sorry for the guy, whoever he
was. If it ever occurred to her that maybe this wasn't such
a good idea, she never let on in her diaries.

N was also the one who'd introduced her to Aimee
Mann in the first place:

SEPTEMBER 21, 2002
N and I talked a long time about music. I told him I
wanted to be a singer, and he didn't laugh at me like
some jerks I could mention. He loaned me the coolest CDs
by his all-time favorite singer, Aimee Mann. I love her
stuff! It's real pop, but with this edge. I wish I could write
songs like that, and she's so cool looking. It'd be cool
to be her. Except, I don't know. Lot of her songs are
pretty sad.
I like having a friend like N who's different from me,
knows about stuff I don't know about. D says he's a geek,
but what does he know? Asshole!!

Nemo didn't know who D was, but her opinion of him
was unwavering throughout her diaries. But if N wasn't a
geek or gay or something, why was he always the guy she
called when she didn't want a date but didn't want to be
alone? The first mention of him was about a year before
she finally figured out he'd fallen for her:

SEPTEMBER 2, 2002
A was right. N is real sweet, kind of funny looking
though. But he said he can help me get rid of my night-

mares. He said that what S pulled was wrong and I should tell the cops. But I just want to forget about it. I mean, I was just as much to blame as he was I guess. ~~I couldn't~~ I could've said no.

Yeah, sure. That's me alright!

The entry before that was over a week earlier:

AUGUST 24TH, 2002

S has turned out to be the supreme asshole of assholes. I went to A and cried buckets. When she got through telling me I TOLD YOU SO eight million times, she said her brother knew a guy who might help me out and she'd set it up for me to meet him. She said he was a GENIUS, and he'd know what S did to me, and if anybody could fix it, he could. Sure hope so. I haven't slept in three days. Everytime I fall asleep that slimy toad is all over me.

S was a boy she'd had a crush on for some weeks. There wasn't really much about him except that she thought he was good looking, he had his own place, and he was into virtuals, which were just getting started about that time. She never said what he did to her, never said if A's friend, who Nemo took to be N, fixed it or not. But even from the beginning, apparently, she'd gone to N because someone else let her down, and he never did. Nemo couldn't remember a single disparaging word about N. He picked up a couple of the later diaries to see if N continued to show up every time she had a broken heart, but Lawrence hollered up the stairs that breakfast was ready.

NEMO AND LAWRENCE ATE BISCUITS AND GRAVY AND RAB-bit sausages. There was even a pot of coffee. As they were finishing up, Lawrence told Nemo he'd traded a rebuilt generator for two two-pound cans of Chock Full o' Nuts. "And this little baby here," he added with a grand flourish, setting a red-and-white box wrapped in cellophane on the table.

"What's that?" Nemo asked.

"That, son, is a pack of Marlboros. Smoked them back in Texas. Couple packs a day. Now they're scarcer than toilet paper."

Nemo picked up the package and turned it over in his hands. He'd never seen a pack of machine-rolled cigarettes before outside of the Bin. He was brought up short by a warning in tiny print on the side stating that the contents caused a long list of diseases and health calamities, including the death of small children who happened to get too close. "Jesus!" he said. "You smoked these things?"

"Sure did. What's more we're going to smoke one right now. After breakfast is the best time, with a cup of coffee." He smiled beatifically. "We plan to smoke one a day. We got twenty day's worth of pleasure coming up."

"But they'll kill you."

Lawrence carefully unwound the gold strip of cellophane and opened the top of the box. He removed a small piece of aluminum foil, and there they were in three neat rows. He pulled one out and lit it with a kitchen match. "Everything kills you a little bit. Even love." He blew a cloud of smoke into the air and propped his feet on a stepstool. "So how'd it go with Justine last night? You wouldn't say two words after you got home."

"I was tired."

"Not tired now, are you? Hell, if you're still tired, there must've been more happened than you know how to tell about anyway."

"Get off it, Lawrence. We just had a drink. Two drinks, actually. Well, I had two. She only had one." Nemo got up and poured himself some more coffee, though his cup was still half full.

Lawrence had that damn Texan twinkle in his eye, full to the gills with sausage and gravy and now Marlboros. Nemo knew he wouldn't let up. Lawrence tried to blow smoke rings, but he couldn't get his lipless mouth to work right. "So what'd y'all do, just sit around counting each other's drinks all night?"

"Lawrence, I kissed her good night, okay? That was it. One kiss. It was nothing."

"Nothing, shit. You're breaking out in a sweat just talking about it."

"Fine. Could we change the subject now?" Nemo leaned against the counter and stared into his coffee cup. It was quiet for a while except for the faint sounds of a mockingbird hard at it.

"Nemo," Lawrence said softly. "Come over here and sit down."

It was the nanny. Nemo was glad to hear it. He'd had just about as much of the Texan in a good mood as he could stomach first thing in the morning. He went over and sat down.

"Please accept our apologies," Lawrence said. "Sometimes our banter gets out of hand. We mean no harm, truly."

"That's okay."

"And we'll put this thing out." Lawrence ground out the Marlboro, which was mostly gone anyway, and brushed the ash off his fingertips. "Filthy habit, actually."

"Then why do you put up with it?"

Lawrence laughed softly. "It gives us pleasure. A bit of the old life, you know? We could all use that now and again."

"I guess so." Nemo sat stock still and stared at the table. He wanted to talk, but he didn't know where to start.

"You have feelings for this girl?"

"Yes."

"Are you in love with her?"

Why did he always have to be so direct? "We just met. I hardly know her. I mean, have you ever fallen in love with someone—just like that?"

Lawrence smiled and nodded his head. "Yes. In England. He was a bank clerk. Nothing remarkable about him, to anyone else, but it was quite sudden, actually. Love at first sight. At our wedding everyone assumed we were pregnant."

"And were you?" Nemo'd heard of the bank teller before. He'd been the nanny's husband.

"We shan't answer that question, until you answer ours."

"And what question is that?"

Lawrence rolled his eyes. "You would try the patience of a saint. Are you in love with this girl?"

"I don't know how to answer that."

"Yes or no would do quite nicely."

"I don't know. I haven't decided yet."

Lawrence tried to suppress it, but laughter bubbled up inside him with the combined force of three senses of humor. Pretty soon he was cackling away. Tears streamed down his face, and he gasped for breath. He slapped his thigh with one hand, and with the other fluttered sign language in the air like a crazed bat.

"We're sorry," Lawrence wheezed, still laughing.

"What's so funny?" Nemo asked. This provoked new gales of laughter. He stood up and gulped down his coffee. "I'm going down to Jonathan's. I'll see you later, Chuckles."

"Wait, Nemo." Lawrence brushed the tears from his eyes and managed to bring his laughter down to a low boil. "We're sorry. We're feeling a bit impish this morning. It's spring, and, well, you're so young." He shook his head, and finally brought his laughter under control. "But you're not so young as to believe that love is a decision, are you?"

"Okay, what if I am in love with her? I can still decide what I want to do about it, can't I?"

"Most certainly."

"Okay then. When I decide, I'll be sure to let you know." Nemo turned to go out the back door, when he remembered their bargain—question for question. He looked over his shoulder at Lawrence, who was pouring himself another cup of coffee. "So were you pregnant or not?"

Lawrence set down the pot and became very still. "Yes."

"You never told me you had a kid in England."

Lawrence kept his eyes on the coffeepot, his hand still grasped the handle. "He was stillborn, actually."

"I'm sorry. I didn't know."

Lawrence looked at Nemo. "Of course you didn't know. You were never told. It's quite all right. That was another life, ages ago." He gestured at the door with the back of his hand. "Now, run on, will you? Jonathan will be dying to hear all about your birthday."

As Nemo left, Lawrence lit up another Marlboro.

NEMO FOUND JONATHAN BEHIND THE HOUSE, TURNING UP a section of the garden. A couple of kinds of lettuce and some of the greens were already in. The potatoes, onions, and carrots were in the ground. Jonathan's family grew enough to feed a dozen people and often did. Sometimes in the winter there'd be tents pitched all over the yard because there was no more room inside. Nemo watched Jonathan work, sliding the shovel into the earth, turning

over rich brown dirt, almost black. The clods had a dull
sheen where the shovel sliced them out of the ground.
Jonathan stabbed them with a few quick thrusts from the
point of his shovel, and they crumbled into piles of
moist loam.

"Hi," Nemo said. "What's going in there?"

Jonathan buried his shovel in the earth like a sentry
planting his lance. "Tomatoes. How was the birthday?"

Nemo caught something in his tone. "Have you already
talked to Lawrence?"

Jonathan smiled slyly. "Yes."

"Jesus, when?"

"After he left you, he stopped by to play a game of
chess with Dad."

"And I suppose he told you what I was doing."

"I asked."

"So what do you think?"

"What do you mean?"

"Oh, come on, Jonathan. I know Lawrence. Once the
Texan got on a roll, he'd not only tell you what happened,
but also whatever he could dream up that might happen."

Jonathan laughed. "He said she's very attractive."

"What else did he say?"

"That there seemed to be a strong attraction between
you."

"Is that what he said? 'A strong attraction'?"

"In so many words."

"I'm sure." Nemo pointed at the shovel. "You want
some help?"

"It can wait. Let's go to the greenhouse. You can take
some tomato plants. We've got more than we need."

The greenhouse had once been a two-car garage. Jonathan and his brother and father had stripped off the walls
and roof, leaving the frame standing. Originally, they'd
covered it with sheet plastic, but when a hailstorm ripped

the plastic to shreds a few years ago, they'd replaced it with windows and windshields from junked cars, screwed into place and sealed with caulk. It was about ten degrees warmer inside. The criss-crossing joints and the different tints of the auto glass gave the light a patchwork effect. The air was heavy and moist, tangy with the scent of dozens of plants. They walked down one of the narrow aisles, Jonathan pausing to examine a leaf or feel the soil. He stopped to water the peppers from a rusty watering can. There were at least four different varieties. "Tell Lawrence we'll have plenty of jalapeños this year, too."

"I'll do that." Nemo watched the water pouring out of the can, the soil soaking it up. He wanted to talk to Jonathan about Justine, but he had even less experience with women than Nemo did. Jonathan had been engaged to Lea, a girl in Raleigh, for about two years now. The marriage, as arranged by their fathers, would take place in a couple of months, when Lea turned eighteen. During their two-year engagement, she and Jonathan had spent a total of maybe three weeks together, when the two families visited each other. Arranged marriages were pretty common among the fundies, now that *Be fruitful and multiply* made sense again. And it made sense to Nemo. You couldn't let a good Christian boy like Jonathan marry just anybody. "Jonathan, are you in love with Lea?"

Jonathan quit watering and turned to Nemo. "You're in love?" He sounded almost happy for him.

"Come on now, I asked first. You're about to marry her. Are you in love with her?"

"Yes, I am," Jonathan said, smiling just thinking about it.

"But how? You hardly know her."

Jonathan nodded, then shrugged his shoulders. It was something of a mystery to him as well. "You've got to understand that the very first time I met her she wasn't just some girl. She was the woman I'd spend my life with. Lea and I may not've spent that much time together, but you can bet I was paying attention. I wanted to know her like I've never known anyone else—like my mom and dad know each other. I think about her all the time. I can't wait to marry her."

"How does she feel about it?"

"Same way." Jonathan refilled the watering can from a tank at the end of the row. The water rang off the bottom like a gong. When he was done, he said, "It's your turn."

Nemo'd hedged with Lawrence. He hadn't been in the mood for Lawrence's older-and-wiser. But he had to tell somebody, or he was going to explode. "Jonathan, I'm absolutely crazy about this girl. I don't know what's going to happen."

"What do you want to happen?"

Nemo sighed. Everything was always so damn simple to Jonathan. "What do you think? I want to make love to her, spend hours talking with her, going for walks, the whole damn thing."

"Do you want to spend your life with her?"

This was worse than Lawrence. At least Lawrence didn't have him walking down the aisle already. "I don't know! She's in the *Bin*, Jonathan. I don't want to go in there. We'd end up just like my mom and dad, just like everybody else in there—a bunch of smiling faces bobbing around in a stagnant soup."

"Does she feel the same way about you?"

"I don't know." Jonathan gave him a questioning look. "Okay, I think so."

Jonathan pinched a wilted leaf from one of the plants. "A very difficult decision."

"Is that all you've got to say? 'A very difficult decision'?"

Jonathan looked at Nemo, his long lashes flickering, as

he took a deep breath. "Okay. I think it'd be terrible, if you went in there, and lost your soul. But I also know that you don't want to lose this girl. God asks us to make very difficult decisions."

Nemo wished it were that simple. He'd have a word or two for God. "Maybe it's not God who's asking. Maybe the world's just a mess."

"Maybe someday you'll believe differently."

"Maybe. Don't hold your breath. But I've already made my decision. I'm going to break it off while I still can."

Jonathan gave him a sympathetic look, and Nemo pointed at one of the bell peppers. "You missed one." Nemo waited for Jonathan to start watering again, before he spoke. "I promised to go see her tonight," he said as casually as he could. "Will you come with me?"

"Into the Bin?"

"She's a singer. She's playing in a club tonight. We just go hear a set, and then I break it off and come home. I promised to go see her."

"Why do you need me?"

"Moral support."

"There's no such thing. Everyone makes his own moral choices."

"Dammit Jonathan, does everything have to be such a big religious deal to you all the time?"

"Yes," he said. There was nothing defiant in it. He was only telling the truth.

Nemo shook his head. "I'm sorry. I was forgetting who I'm talking to. But will you go with me? I don't know if I can trust myself alone with her."

"Don't you want to see her alone? Do you really want me to be sitting there listening while you break up with her? Don't you think that's unnecessarily cruel?"

"Whose side are you on?"

"It's not a question of sides. If you reject her, she'll be

hurt. She's chosen a life I believe to be wrong. That doesn't mean I feel no compassion for her."

"So you won't go?"

Jonathan set down the watering can with a dull clunk. "I'll go because you're my friend, but when it comes time to tell her whatever you've decided to do, I'll leave. Fair enough?"

"Thanks, Jonathan."

"Do you want those tomato plants now?"

"I'll get them tomorrow. I'll come by to get you at nine, okay?"

"Sure."

As Nemo was leaving the greenhouse, he turned back to Jonathan, who was filling up a flat box with tomato plants. "Jonathan, have you ever been in the Bin before?"

"Never," he said.

Nemo wondered what he'd ever done to deserve a friend like Jonathan. "Thanks," he said.

As Nemo cut around the side of the house, Peter beckoned to him from his doorway, looking up and down the street as if he expected a band of marauders any minute. Ever since Rosalind had gone, Peter had grown stranger and stranger. Nemo walked into Peter's room, and Peter closed the door behind him. The place smelled like old cheese and burning wax. The windows were covered with sheets, and the only light came from a smoky candle on the desk. There was a chair at the desk, and a mattress on the floor. The other furniture had been piled up in the other end of the room.

Nemo followed Peter to the desk, where a Bible lay open with a yellow pad and a pencil beside it. The pad was covered with tiny writing and elaborate doodles in the margins, crosses and pentagons mostly. At the top of the page, a daggerlike cross pierced a black pentagon. Drops of carefully drawn blood dripped down into the text. On the wall above the desk was a homemade calendar drawn on the same yellow-ruled paper, the days crossed off one by one. Today was already crossed off.

Peter was excited, hopping from one foot to the other. Nemo'd never seen him like this. Peter had always been a sour, taciturn man. "Gabriel tells me he spoke with you," Peter said, smiling, and Nemo saw clearly for the first time that several of Peter's teeth were missing. "He says you'll do perfectly. He says he'll meet with you again soon."

"I'm sorry, Peter. I don't know what you're talking about. Meet with me for what?"

Peter's voice became low and confidential. "You are the promised one."

"Promised for what? What are you talking about?"

Peter shook his head violently. "Only Gabriel can tell you." He looked around the room as if checking to see if anyone had crawled under the door as they were talking. Somehow Peter had latched onto Nemo as his only ally. Against what, Nemo wasn't sure. From the look in Peter's eyes, he wasn't too sure himself, but it was bigger than he was.

Nemo backed toward the door, nodding and smiling his way out. "Thanks for the message, Peter. I've got work to do. See you around."

"Don't go," Peter said, and laid his hand on Nemo's arm, then quickly withdrew it. "I'm sorry. Gabriel said I shouldn't talk to you just yet, that your path had not yet been revealed to you. He said when you knew the truth, you'd save us. You will won't you?"

Nemo patted him on the shoulder. "I'll do what I can, Peter."

"You won't tell Gabriel I talked to you, will you?"

"I won't breathe a word."

As Nemo walked away, Peter called after him in a guarded voice, "Everything depends on you."

Poor crazy bastard, Nemo thought.

Nemo had planned to spend the rest of the morning and afternoon cannibalizing a stack of Discmen for parts. Lawrence had swapped a rusty pistol for them, but they weren't much better than the pistol. They'd gotten too hot sometime or other and most of the circuit boards were warped and falling apart. A couple of the drive mechanisms were okay though. He listened to Aimee Mann as he worked, and tried to figure out what he was going to say to Justine when he saw her.

He'd just have to level with her. If he'd met her out here, there'd be no question, but even the thought of going into the Bin frightened him. He kept picturing himself back inside the crematorium, rolling into the flames. He wasn't watching what he was doing, and a drop of molten solder landed on the back of his hand. He jumped, dropping the soldering iron onto one of the few usable circuit boards, melting a hole in the middle of it. He peeled the solder off his skin, revealing a drop-shaped burn, already starting to blister. He grabbed the soldering iron and started to throw it across the room, stopped himself, and stowed it away. Then he put everything on his workbench away. I'll clean house, he thought. At least I can't hurt myself doing that.

IT WAS NEMO'S TURN TO MAKE SUPPER. HE MADE A STEW with the rest of the sausages, some potatoes and onions, and some homemade beer. He told Lawrence he was going to see Justine, and that he might not be home till late. Lawrence didn't ask any questions. Nemo didn't tell Lawrence what he'd decided to do, as he'd said he would.

He was afraid Lawrence would want to talk it to death. Besides, Nemo still wasn't sure he could go through with it.

As he walked down to Jonathan's he looked up at the moon. It was a perfect night. A light breeze, scented with wisteria, riffled the grass. A cat, perched on top of the rusted-out pickup, watched him pass, the moonlight glittering in its eyes. It gave out a moaning growl to warn him not to get too close. There was a dark shape, probably a squirrel, in its jaws. Nemo growled back, and it bolted into the darkness, its claws skittering along the top of the truck.

Jonathan's father, Harold, let Nemo in and called up the stairs to Jonathan. "Beautiful night," he said to Nemo, and Nemo agreed that it was. If he disapproved of Nemo dragging his son into the Bin, he didn't let on.

Jonathan's little brother, Matthew, was working at a treadle sewing machine in the front room. He looked up as Nemo walked in and gave him a little wave. "Hey, Nemo. Lawrence said you might have some Discmen to swap soon." He pointed to his work. "Trade you a couple of shirts."

"Sounds good. It's pretty slim pickings, though. I'm not sure I'm going to get a working machine out of this mess."

"What do you need with a Discman?" Harold asked his son.

Matthew rolled his eyes. "Same thing you needed with that Polaroid camera that didn't work."

"Spare the rod and spoil the child," Harold muttered. "Fortunately for you, young man, I believe the rod takes many forms. The camera works fine. The film was out of date. If you want to squander your labor on a Discman, I won't stop you, but I don't want to hear any of that turn-of-the-century garbage in my house."

"It has headphones, right Nemo?"

Nemo could barely suppress his smile. "Yes, it does. If

I can get one to work, I'll throw in a few gospel CDs along with it."

Matthew grinned. "In case Dad wants to listen to it."

Nemo'd watched them play this game before—Matthew pretending to be the backsliding youth, while his dad blustered appropriately. But Nemo knew what Harold knew, that Matthew's faith would weather any music he might listen to. He was here, after all.

Jonathan's mother, Constance, came out of the back of the house. She had on a leather apron, and her hair was tied up in a scarf. Her face was flushed and sweaty. "Nemo, happy birthday! I'd give you a hug, but I'd get soot all over you. I was finishing up your birthday present." She was holding a small white box in her hands. She looked around. "Where's Jonathan?"

"I hollered at him," Harold said. "I don't know what could be taking him so long."

"He's making himself into a red-hot Bin stud," Matthew said.

"One more remark out of you," Harold said, "and you'll be washing dishes for a year."

Matthew hung his head, as much to hide his smile as show his penitence. "Yes, sir. You want me to go get him?"

"Tell him we're ready to give Nemo his birthday present," Constance said.

As Matthew went up the stairs, Nemo said, "You really shouldn't have done anything for my birthday."

"Don't be ridiculous," Constance said. "I enjoyed making it. I just hope you like it. Jonathan seemed to think you would, but I wasn't sure."

Jonathan descended the stairs with Matthew on his heels. Jonathan was dressed in pressed slacks and a white linen shirt. His hair was combed back, and he had shiny black loafers on.

"Check it out," Matthew said. "Big bro steps out."

"Enough," Harold said. "We're celebrating a birthday here." When they were all gathered around Nemo, he nodded to his wife. "Constance."

She hesitated before handing Nemo the box. He knew, since Constance did metalwork, it would be something made of metal, but he had no idea what. He opened the lid and found a cross made from beaten silver, strung on a leather thong. The cross looked like a two-limbed tree. The gnarls of the wood suggested a man on the cross, but when you looked closely, it might only be the shape of an ordinary tree. He took it out of the box and slipped it over his head. "I love it," he said.

"Harold thought it was too Catholic looking," Constance said. "If you don't like it, I can make you something else."

"I didn't say it was too Catholic," Harold said. "I just thought it looked a lot like a crucifix. That's all."

"It's perfect," Nemo said, hugging Constance in spite of the soot, hugging them all. For the first time all day, his heavy heart lifted just a bit. He had a good life, he told himself.

When he and Jonathan were outside, Nemo couldn't resist. "You do look pretty spiffy."

"Not you too."

"How did you get your hair to do that?"

"I don't see what the big deal is. Isn't it customary to dress nicely to go out in the evening?"

Nemo laughed. "You look great, Jonathan."

"I don't look like an idiot?"

"Trust me."

As they were descending into Northside Station, Jonathan was studying his feet, "It's kind of nice, actually, to be wearing these shoes to someplace besides a funeral."

By the time they boarded the train, they were both more

somber. Since their visit to the crematorium, Jonathan had avoided the northbound train, and Nemo couldn't blame him. He should've suggested they go in at Richmond and take the virtual, Nemo thought, but he'd been too much in his own head to think of it. Jonathan was doing Nemo a favor by going in at all. When they passed the glow of the crematorium, Jonathan scrupulously avoided looking at it and didn't say a word.

Nemo noticed, in the tangle of graffiti, the same pentagon impaled by a cross he'd seen on Peter's yellow pad, the words THE TIME IS AT HAND! scrawled over it like a rainbow. He thought he'd seen it before, but hadn't taken much notice of it till now. He started to ask Jonathan about it, but he was lost in his own thoughts.

Once they were inside, though, Jonathan cheered up, studying everything in the Bin as if he were trying to memorize it, rubbernecking the crowds of people, listening to their babble as if it all meant something. Whenever Nemo thought he had Jonathan figured out, he'd do something to surprise him. Nemo left Jonathan to his sightseeing and stewed over his own problems. But finally, as they were walking down the street toward the club, brushing past the crowds, lovely and boisterous even on a Sunday night, Nemo asked Jonathan what he thought of the place.

"It's remarkable."

"You're not getting tempted, are you?"

"Oh, no," Jonathan said. "I expected it to be remarkable."

Nemo had to laugh in spite of himself. As they walked through the door into the club, a team of holographic Clydesdales clattered over their heads. Jonathan looked up and followed their progress around the room, smiling.

Justine must've been watching for them. She hurried up to Nemo before they sat down, put her arm around his waist, and kissed his cheek. He breathed in her scent and let his arm settle around her shoulders. He looked into her bright eyes and then quickly away. It was all he could do not to take her into his arms. "You really came," she said excitedly. "I can't believe it."

"Justine, this is Jonathan. I told you about him. Jonathan, this is Justine."

Nemo watched them meet. He expected some judgment in Jonathan's eyes, but there wasn't. They shook hands and smiled at each other, then at Nemo—the reason they were meeting at all. "Let's sit down," Nemo said. "I could use a drink."

Justine led them to a table in front of the bandstand. She had on another black knit dress. This one was cut low in the back. Nemo held his breath as he watched her move just ahead of him. "I saved this table for you," she said. Jonathan was still watching the Clydesdales orbiting the room.

They all sat down together. Justine only had a few minutes before she had to go on. Nemo could tell by the way she was acting that she'd been waiting all day just to see him—that for her their one kiss had been enough to cancel the differences between them. He watched her as she talked to Jonathan. He couldn't imagine what they would talk about—*Hi, aren't you a religious fanatic? —Oh yes, and aren't you the heathen stealing the soul of my best friend?* But it didn't go like that at all.

They talked about music, about guitars, about growing tomatoes and peppers, and Nemo wondered what she thought about his bringing a friend, wondered if she knew Jonathan was supposed to be a chaperone. Nemo felt silly now for being afraid of her. But it wasn't her he was afraid of. It was himself.

She caught Nemo staring at her. She smiled and winked, leaned toward Jonathan with a confidential air. "Jonathan, tell me about Nemo. I'm collecting information on him. He's not like anyone I've ever met."

Jonathan played along with her, seemingly as contented as a well-fed tomcat. He'd ordered himself a glass of red wine and was sipping it. "Nemo is a true rebel," he said.

She looked over at Nemo, her eyes shining. "Is that what you are?" she asked.

"I'm staying out of this," Nemo said.

She made a face and turned back to Jonathan. "Maybe, he's just contrary," she said.

"Oh no, that's why he's a true rebel. For example, I'm a Christian, and he's not. Now, a false rebel wouldn't have had anything to do with me. But we've been friends for seven years, and though we've argued endlessly about religion, he's never once belittled my faith or judged me in any way."

"So he's a quiet rebel," Justine said, smiling at Nemo with love in her eyes.

"That's right," said Jonathan.

"I'm going to be a noisy rebel if we don't change the subject," Nemo said.

Justine laughed and kissed his cheek. "I'm so glad you've come."

At her closeness, the touch of her lips, he felt a tingling all over. He closed his eyes. "Me too," he said, and squeezed her hand.

The rest of the band took to the stage and started tuning their instruments. The drummer practiced the same riff over and over.

"Gotta go," she said. "I'm doing a song special for you, Nemo." She laughed at herself and smiled into his eyes. "Listen up," she said softly.

She kissed his lips, a soft, tender kiss, and rose from the table. "Wish me luck," she said to both of them. Nemo had forgotten Jonathan was even there. "See you at the break."

WHEN SHE'D GONE, JONATHAN SAID, "LAWRENCE WAS right. She is very lovely and charming. I like her. You two seem made for each other."

"You're a big help."

"Did you want me to *not* like her?" He took another sip of his wine.

"No, of course not. I just figured . . . Never mind."

Nemo finally got around to getting himself a drink. He tried Irish whiskey this time, a double. He watched the band tuning, adjusting their equipment. They were using late-twentieth-century stuff. The twentieth century was hot in the Bin.

Jonathan finished off his wine and got himself another. "What're you doing drinking wine, anyway?" Nemo asked him.

"Christ drank wine," Jonathan said. "He even turned water into wine."

"But I've never seen you drink before." He'd always turned down Lawrence's homebrewed liquor and beer.

"Good wine is hard to come by."

"So if you found a bottle of wine outside, you'd drink it?"

"No. It's far too valuable outside. I'd barter it for something more useful—food, blankets."

"Does that mean that everything is useless in here because nothing's hard to come by?"

"Faith is," he said.

"I don't know. Everybody seems pretty happy."

"That's not the same thing as faith."

"You know what I like about you, Jonathan? You're

so damn consistent, but you always manage to surprise me anyway."

JUSTINE STEPPED UP TO THE MICROPHONE WITH A GUITAR, smiling nervously at the crowd. She counted out the beat, and the drummer kicked them off. As soon as she opened her mouth to sing, her nervousness evaporated. Nemo expected her to be good. But he hadn't expected her to be as good as she was. It wasn't her technical proficiency. He'd heard stronger voices. It was the way she got inside each song, so that you believed she was the one who felt the broken heart or the desperate hopes or the intense love she sang about.

She didn't talk much between songs. She'd just introduce the next one and move on. During the set, the club filled up until every chair was taken and people lined the bar. The applause was strong, and you could see her lighting up. Nemo was happy for her, proud of her, completely enthralled. He forget about everything but her, singing.

Finally, she stood at the microphone for a while, waiting for the applause to die down, looking directly into his eyes. "This will be our last song for this set. It's an old-fashioned, real-world love story written by Aimee Mann, and I'd like to dedicate it to Nemo." Everyone in the place followed her gaze, and a few hooted their approval. A guy said from somewhere behind Nemo, "Lucky son of a bitch."

Nemo knew the song, "Coming up Close," from the first chord. He smiled at her, a lump in his throat, seeing the two of them, as he knew she intended, as the lovers in the song. It told the story of two people who've just met. They borrow a car and drive out into the Iowa countryside one summer night to a deserted farmhouse where—

> *We thought just for an instant we could see the*
> *future.*
> *We thought for once we knew what really was*
> *important.*

But when the night is over, they simply part, apparently never seeing each other again. But it was the haunting refrain that got to him and brought tears to his eyes:

> *Coming up close*
> *everything sounds like welcome home.*
> *And oh, by the way*
> *don't you know that I could make*
> *a dream that's barely half awake come true?*
> *I wanted to say—*
> *but anything I could've said*
> *I felt somehow that you already knew.*
>
> *Coming up close . . .*
> *everything sounds like welcome home.*
> *Come home.*
> *Come on home.*

The resounding applause brought him back from the song—and the vast Iowa landscape he imagined as he listened—to this tiny bar in the Bin, Justine smiling at him, the echo of the last chord still ringing in the air. But he brought his feelings back with him intact. One kiss, one song—there was no point in counting. He loved her. He couldn't leave her, not now, not tonight. He didn't want to think beyond that. As Justine thanked the crowd, Nemo turned to tell Jonathan that he'd changed his mind, but Jonathan had already gone. He'd said he'd go when it was time for Nemo to tell her what he'd decided to do. He must've seen my decision in my face, Nemo thought.

She played two more sets. Nemo watched her and listened to her sing. He shut out the rest of the crowd and nursed a couple of drinks. They talked during her breaks, holding hands, looking into each other's eyes like they were the only two people in the place. He asked her about her music. They talked about old musicians and old songs. She asked him about where he lived. She wanted to know what his room looked like, so he told her.

He ended up telling her about his grandmother and N, and how this poor guy was in love with her, but nothing ever came of it. She agreed that was sad. The way she said it he knew what she was thinking, that if nothing ever came of them, it'd be sad, too. He didn't say anything. He didn't tell her he was in love with her, but he was thinking it the whole time.

Pretty soon the band was packing up, and he was the only customer in the place. The other musicians left, and Justine had disappeared behind a door beside the stage. The lights were dimmed. There wasn't a sound but the Clydesdales. Apparently they never shut the thing off. No reason they should. Justine stepped out into the darkened room. She'd put on a black jacket for the night air. Her face, her golden hair, seemed to shine in the darkened room. Nemo felt his heart leap up, and he rose to his feet. It was finally just the two of them. He offered her his arm and she wrapped her arms around it and lay her head on his shoulder. He kissed her hair and took her in his arms, kissed her like he'd never kissed anybody, and held her close.

"Guess we better go," he whispered. It was closing time. Time to go home.

7

JUSTINE KNEW HIS KISS MIGHT MEAN ANYTHING from good-bye to I'll stay with you forever, but for the moment, she didn't care what he meant, but what he felt, and she could feel it in his arms. But even as he held her, as he whispered in her ear that it was time to go, she was afraid he was going to leave her, that his feelings wouldn't be enough, that he'd go back to his world, and she'd stay in hers. She looked up at him, tried to put on a brave face. She could barely make out his features. "Stay with me tonight?" she whispered.

His smile flashed in the darkness. "That's just what I was going to say."

She let out the breath she'd been holding. "I was afraid you'd say no."

He kissed the tip of her nose. "I can't. Maybe it's destiny."

"I thought you didn't believe in destiny."

"I could learn." He held open the door, and they stepped out into the street. The streetlights made it bright as day, though the sky was black, and the tops of the buildings disappeared into the darkness. He kissed her again, a tender, loving kiss, then looked at her face cradled in his hands, admiring her. She felt beautiful.

She screwed up her courage. "I have a crazy idea," she said.

"I have a few of those myself."

She laughed and ran her hands up and down his chest. "Good, but that's not what I mean. I want to see where you live. I want you to take me to your home. I want to sleep in your bed." She told him about Mr. Menso and the card he'd given her. She put the card in his hands: *Real World Tours—We Never Close.*

He turned it over, examining it, a funny half smile on his face. She had no idea what he was thinking. "I didn't know anything like this existed," he said, more to himself than to her, then looked into her eyes. "Sure. I'd love to take you home."

REAL WORLD TOURS WAS THREE BLOCKS OVER ON M, IN A row of offbeat shops and boutiques. It was impossible to miss. The front was lit up by a pair of torches planted in the yard. The flames snapped in the wind. Black smoke streamed into the darkness in thick coils. On one side was a novelty shop—whoopee cushions and the like. On the other was a palmist/tarot reader named Madame Ree. A neon sign in the window glowed red, then blue, then red again—AURAS CLEANSED. "Nobody in the real world uses torches like those," Nemo said. "They burn up too fast."

The place was scrupulously ugly: the paint cracked and peeling, all the glass shattered with just enough wicked-looking shards to remind you of what should be there; the door hanging on one hinge from a rotting doorframe; the wooden steps warped and creaking; the thump, squeal, and scurry of rats under the porch. Nemo looked around the porch, up at the rust-streaked sign over the door.

"Cute," he said. "Why do you suppose people come here?"

"We don't have to do this," she said, but he shook his head and pulled open the door, which creaked theatrically.

"I'm curious," he said.

Inside, it was strictly Bin, clean and pastel and carpeted up to the chair rail with fawn-colored plush. Ghostly holos of the real world played in front of the walls—Paris, New York, Buenos Aires—all in ruins; a weed-grown nuclear power plant; a huge fundie rally, their faces lit by a burning cross. It must've been a long time ago. There were too many faces.

A door opened in the middle of the rally, and a small, slender man in white robes stepped out, passing through the burning cross with a smile on his face. "Hi," he said. "I'm Freddie. Welcome to Real World Tours." He kept his hands hidden in the folds of his robe. His bare feet peeked out at the hem.

Justine showed him the card and explained that Mr. Menso had sent them and that they wanted to go to Nemo's home in Richmond. Nemo remained silent, looking around, his brows stitched in thought. This was beginning to look like a very bad idea.

Freddie hugged himself. "That Warren, he's a stitch, isn't he?"

"I don't really know him very well."

"Well, trust me. A stitch." He stepped up to a console atop a carpet pedestal in the middle of the room and ran his fingers over the keys. He studied the display and looked up, smiling at Nemo. "You're a visitor!"

Nemo turned from New York, where a pack of wild dogs was chasing down a screaming woman in Times Square. The sound was down so low her screams were no louder than the rat squeals under the porch. "That's right," Nemo said quietly.

"Well this *will* be a first." He looked at Justine, his eyes wide. "And you're something quite special yourself."

She smiled politely. She figured he was just flirting, though he seemed more interested in Nemo than in her.

"So where do you want to start? Anyplace you want. Guaranteed to be exactly up to the minute, down to the last little blade of grass. Except for the real people, of course. We don't have all the uploads, and you get into reality conflicts anyway—it's a big damn mess. But if you want the real-world people *experience*, I can patch in virtual actors doing classic little real-world things—screaming hellfire and damnation, shooting each other, starving to death right before your very eyes—scripted not to hurt you, of course."

He leaned toward Nemo confidentially. "Maria—she's a regular—*loves* to hold the dying in her arms. 'Mother Maria, full of grace.' Ha!" he said, as if his saying it made it a laugh.

For a second, Justine thought Nemo was going to back out, and she couldn't blame him. He leaned toward Freddie and said in a quiet, deadly voice, like an ax falling, "My room. Just us. No people."

Freddie shrugged and cocked his head to one side as if Nemo had turned down the cut-and-perm special. His hands moved over the console as he talked. "We'll start in your room, then. Wherever you go in, it's a total replication. You can roam the whole godawful planet if you want to." His hands were flying. "And let's see there. Update with all available sources—mostly your memory, of course. Almost done. There." He made one last pass over the console, and a door opened up in the middle of the nuclear power plant. "Okay then, just right through that door."

"Then what?" Justine asked.

"You'll be in his *room*." Freddie looked at the display.

"Richmond, Virginia. Hawthorne Av. That *is* where you wanted to go, isn't it?"

"Where will you be?" Nemo asked.

Freddie scrunched up his shoulders in a parody of fear. His toes curled beneath his robe. "I'm going to pop into New York." He shuddered. "It's so dangerous."

"Have a good trip," Nemo said. "I hope someone kills you."

For just a moment Freddie didn't know what to say, then he shouted another "Ha!" and turned to Justine. "He's so funny."

"He keeps me in stitches."

"How do we get back?" Nemo asked.

"Silly *moi*—I almost forgot. It's a total replication. You can wander all over. But here's the fun part—when you want to leave the program—or in your case when you want back into the *real* real world—just find a coffin and head home! Clever, don't you think? Warren thought of it. I wanted to use a little remote control thingie, something real techno, but Warren said that would remind people of the illusion."

"Warren helped cook this thing up?" Justine asked.

"Warren's into everything. He's deep into his own program."

"I thought he just ran a bookshop."

The same "Ha!" pierced the room, and Freddie rolled his eyes, but didn't elaborate. He gestured once again to the open doorway, apparently impatient to experience the dangers of New York.

NEMO AND JUSTINE PASSED THROUGH THE DOOR, AND THEY were in Nemo's room. It was almost pitch dark, just enough moonlight came in through the window to reveal the hulking shapes of furniture. Nemo closed the door behind them and opened it again. Real World Tours had vanished. Justine could barely make out the top of a staircase in the darkness before he shut the door again.

"I'll light a lantern," he said. "I hope they got everything in its place, or we might spend the night looking for matches." He disappeared into the darkness, and she heard the scrape of a drawer opening. A match flared, and Nemo was lighting a lamp. He held it up and looked around. "Exactly as I left it," he said. "Freddie is a talented fellow." He set the lamp down on a small shelf with a mirror behind it, and lit a second lamp beside it. They gave off a soft, yellowish light.

"What do you burn in the lamps?" she asked.

"Corn oil. There's a commune in Maymont Park. They grow corn and beans along the old canal. They'll take all the AM radios we can get working."

"I didn't think there was any more radio."

"There's a station out of Tennessee. They built the tower on top of an old hydroelectric dam. Late at night you can pick it up all over. Reverend Ray gives the Rapture Report every night at midnight. Lawrence says they must be cranking 100,000 watts or more."

Justine was wandering around his room, taking it in. It was much more civilized than she'd expected. The wood floor was clean, if scarred. A doorless closet was hung with a blue curtain. All she could see beneath the curtain were a pair of green rubber boots and a pair of sandals made from old tires. There was a steamer trunk beside the closet. The perimeter of the trunk was painted with a mountain landscape. The lid was a sky blue blotted with fluffy clouds. A hawk soared in the foreground. "Did you paint that?" she asked.

"My grandmother."

She leaned over and studied it. The paint was flaking from the top so that the clouds looked like they were spattered with tar, and the hawk's eye was missing. "I like it," she said.

In the corner was an old exercise bike hooked up to a generator. Wires led from the generator to a row of car batteries, and from there to a panel of switches and sockets attached to the workbench under the window. The workbench had been pieced together from several different desks and tables. The different finishes made a muted patchwork. Everything was neat and uncluttered, stuff hanging from nails on the wall or stowed in clear plastic boxes of tiny drawers. There were old posters and photographs on the walls. None of them were framed, but they were placed precisely, perfectly level. Looking down over the workbench was a black-and-white reproduction of the *Mona Lisa*. A Maxfield Parrish calendar from 2015 hung beside that.

The one unaccountable oddity was an old refrigerator, scratched and dented as if it'd been dragged on its side down a gravel road. "Does that thing work?"

He laughed and opened the refrigerator door. "As a bookcase." The shelves were packed with rows of books and papers. "Most of this stuff was my grandmother's." It looked as if he'd saved it all—scrapbooks, photo albums, magazines, paperbacks. In the freezer was a row of tiny books. *My Diary*, they said in gold on the spines. She wanted to reach out and touch them, to take them out and read them one by one, but she kept her hands clasped behind her back, and he closed the door. On top of the refrigerator was a shallow rectangular pan. She stood on tip-toe and looked inside. It was half-filled with water. The ceiling above it was discolored and beginning to sag. "I've got a leak," he said.

In the corner was a brass bed with a white chenille bedspread. The brass was polished, the bed neatly made. A pair of sofa pillows, faded and worn, were propped up at the head. She kicked off her shoes, and sat down on the bed. Nemo sat down beside her. "The mattress was a real find," he said. "It was still wrapped up in the plastic."

"I like your room." She surveyed it all again from the vantage point of the bed where Nemo began and ended his days.

Beside it was the picture of the earth, from high over North America. A red pin was stuck into Richmond. She found Dallas and thought about St. Catherine's and Stephanie. *I left St. Catherine's almost eighty years ago.* She reached out and touched the poster.

"What's wrong?" Nemo asked, leaning forward.

"Nothing. Nothing at all." She didn't want to think about any of that right now. She was here, with Nemo, just as she'd imagined. Around the border of the poster were snapshots, mostly of Nemo and his parents. Some she'd seen at his parents' house. She wondered if they knew he kept pictures of them. In the lower right corner was a snapshot of an old woman, a very young Nemo sitting in her lap. "Who's this?" she asked.

"Me and my grandmother. This used to be her house. That was taken the last time we visited before she died. I was barely five. She took me up to the attic. She kept her hand on my shoulder the whole time, to steady herself. My mom was yelling at us not to go up there, telling my grandmother she was going to break her neck, but my grandmother just ignored her, saying to me, 'I wish the hell she'd shut up.'" He laughed. "That kind of stuck in my mind. That visit's really the only memory I have of her. She and Mom didn't get along. I don't know why. Mom won't talk about it. Anyway, my grandmother showed me all her old stuff, told me that whatever I wanted was mine. The attic's still full of most of it. I think that picture was taken after we came back down from the attic. Mom's a great one for photographs."

Justine leaned across the bed and looked more closely. His grandmother's face was blurred. She'd moved when the picture was taken. She was laughing, her head thrown back. Nemo was smiling directly into the camera. Justine wondered what his grandmother had been laughing at all those years ago. Probably something the earnest little boy in her lap had said. Justine imagined the two of them sharing some inside joke, forming an alliance against his parents. She studied the little-boy Nemo and compared him to the one smiling at her side. "You were cute."

"All little boys are cute."

"You're still cute."

He looked into her eyes and touched her face with his fingertips, traced the line of her cheekbone, caressed her lips. She took his hand in hers and kissed his palm, laid it on her breast. He leaned over and started to blow out the lamps, but she put her hand on his lips. "Let them burn. I want to see you." She unbuttoned his shirt and slipped it off his shoulders, ran her hands up and down his body. "These too," she said, unbuttoning his pants. He stood up and slipped off his pants, kicked off his shoes. He never took his eyes off her. She pulled her dress over her head and dropped it on the floor. She wasn't wearing anything else. She lay back on the bed, and he stood there, looking at her with lust and wonder.

"I love you," he said.

Tears came to her eyes, and she laughed with joy, holding out her arms to him. "Show me," she said. They made love in his bed, just as she'd imagined, the Earth above them, shining in the lamplight. They didn't talk. For now, they just wanted to sleep in each other's arms, to lie in the same bed. She laid her head on his chest and slept peacefully, dreamlessly.

* * *

JUSTINE WOKE UP SUDDENLY. NOTHING HAD CHANGED. IT was still dark outside, and Nemo slept soundly beside her. The lamps still burned. The clock beside the bed said a little after four. She listened to the *clink-clunk* of its ticking, stared at the Earth above them. The red pin cast a long shadow to the east.

She knew what woke her: She didn't want morning to come. She didn't want Nemo to wake up and remember where he was. Didn't want him to leave her. She stared at the *Mona Lisa* across the room, presiding over his days. He was happy here before I came along, she thought. He could find his way even in the dark. Everything had its place. It was home. She knew how important that was. She'd grown up in what they called a home, calling it the one thing it wasn't. He loved her, he'd said, but that didn't mean he'd give up the life he'd made for himself. That didn't mean she could ask him to. She carefully freed herself from his arms and got out of bed.

She went to the workbench and sat on the stool. There were rows of tiny screwdrivers, a small alcohol torch. She opened and closed the drawers of tiny parts. A set of headphones hung from a nail. She put them on and traced the wire to a CD player on a shelf beside the window. She pushed play and it was Aimee Mann. She shut it off, hung the headphones back on the wall.

He sat here today and thought about me, she thought.

She picked up a coil of solder and wound it around her finger, imagining Nemo in this life she was only visiting— eating, sleeping, working, taking apart and putting together all these tiny pieces. She uncoiled the solder and coiled it more tightly so that the tip of her finger turned red. The solder snapped, and she put two coils back where she'd found one. When he gets back to his real home, she thought, it will still be one coil. She could dump all these drawers onto the floor, and they'd still be where he left them. Even if we were to hide out in this replica of his world, nothing we did would change anything in his real life. Pretty soon they'd be completely different—his world and my world.

Nemo lay in the yellow glow of the lamps, his arms wrapped around his pillow. He might keep visiting her for a while. But soon he'd make up his mind. With him it would be in or out, all or nothing. She wished she'd never come into the Bin, that they were actually in his room, that he'd brought her home to stay.

She thought about Juliet, risking death to be with her love, and wondered if what John told her was true, that you could download yourself back into the real world with a new body and a new life. She crossed the room and slid under the covers, molding herself to Nemo's body. She waited for morning to come, watching the lanterns burning, the reflected lanterns in the mirror. There seemed to be four of them. As her eyes drooped shut, she thought, only two of them are real.

Or none.

SHE WAS SNARED BY ANOTHER DREAM. SHE LAY ON HER back, her legs propped up, staring at a fluorescent ceiling, white tile walls. It smelled like a hospital, and she thought, I'm going to die. Soon, I'll be dead.

But no, this was birth.

She was in hard labor and there wasn't any doctor and they wouldn't fucking listen to her, screaming in their fucking faces that she needed something for the pain. She stopped screaming, panting, waiting, bracing herself as the pressure mounted, the pain spiraling in to kill her, this time for sure, each time a little deeper, like a steel band slowly cutting her in half. Why am I dying for a bad fuck? she asked herself. Why am I having this kid?

Give me something, goddamnit! Please God! Give me something you fucking assholes! I'm dying! Please! Silent, masked faces appeared and disappeared. None of them looked her in the eye, even when they stabbed at her pupils with their little flashlights, they didn't really see her. She wanted to grab them by the throat, make them listen to her, make them look at her, but she couldn't move her arms. She was strapped in. How could there be so damn many of them and not one a doctor?

A new face appeared, his eyes looked into hers. He didn't flinch and vanish when she screamed at him. "I'm giving you something for the pain," he said. "I'm Dr. Donley." As he spoke, a delicious ooze of numbness moved across her abdomen. She laid her head back, waiting in silence, listening to the buzz of the lights. The pain came, but dull and weak, gutted of its power. It was nothing. She smiled in triumph. She wasn't going to die. She was going to have her baby.

Dr. Donley reached down and shook her shoulders. "Justine," he kept saying. "Wake up. You're dreaming." She opened her eyes and there was Nemo's face where Dr. Donley's had been. She threw her arms around his neck and clung to him for dear life. "Nemo, thank God it's you."

Nemo wrapped Justine in a blanket and made her a mug of coffee. She sat propped up in bed, her hands wrapped around the hot mug to steady them. "I'm okay," she told him. "It was just a dream." She didn't even sound convincing to herself.

"When you wake up screaming, it's a nightmare. I have them sometimes. Want to talk about it?" He sat on the side of the bed, the morning light streaming through the window behind him, his voice kind and gentle.

She tried to sound matter-of-fact, even though her voice was shaking. "There wasn't much to it. I was having a baby, I was in serious labor. The pain was so awful, I thought I was going to die. There were people hovering all around me, but they wouldn't give me anything because the doctor wasn't there yet. I kept screaming at them, completely out of my head. Then the doctor finally got there and shot me up with something—and then you woke me.''

"Are you still in pain?"

She shook her head. "No, I'm fine." Her heart was still racing. She'd been sure she was going to die. Nemo's face was creased with worry. I must've scared him pretty badly, she thought, screaming at the top of my lungs. "I'm sorry," she said.

He took the mug from her hands, set it down beside the clock, and took her in his arms. She laid her head on his chest and hugged him around the waist. "This isn't the first dream I've had like this," she confessed in a small voice.

He kissed the top of her head, delicately brushed the hair from her face. "Where you're afraid you're going to die?"

"No, where I'm somebody else. It's like they're somebody else's dreams."

"The same person?"

She rocked her head back and forth on his chest. "The first one was a sixteen-year-old girl. The second was an old woman."

"How old was the woman in your dream this morning?"

"Thirty-three."

"How do you know?"

The question brought her up short. She'd just answered automatically. "I just know. I don't know how." Her voice had become shrill and panicky. She clung to him more tightly.

He rocked her in his arms. "I'm asking too many questions."

"No, it helps, really. I want to figure these dreams out."

She told him about her other dreams, her head resting on his chest, his arms around her. She felt safe and loved. Her panic ebbed away like the pain in her dream. Telling the dreams to him, they became just stories, nothing to do with her, like one of Mr. Menso's books. So by the time she told him the doctor in her dream was named Donley, he was just a character in a story, and the name meant nothing at all.

But Nemo gave a startled grunt, tilted her chin up with the tip of his finger, and looked her in the eye. "Justine, I don't know about your other dreams. But the one you just had is about Uncle Winston."

She didn't understand.

"Winston *Donley*."

The thought repulsed her. "But I didn't know his last name."

"Senator Winston Donley? Are you kidding? He's in the news every day. Even people out here have heard of him. We're still voters, after all." He caught himself and looked around. "Where we're *pretending* to be, anyway. I was forgetting where we really are."

"Do you regret it? Coming here with me?"

He held her close. "No," he said. "Not a single moment."

She kissed his cheek. "Even my screaming like an idiot?"

He laughed softly. "Maybe that part."

She leaned back against the pillows, avoiding his eyes. "Why would I be dreaming about Winston?"

"I'm no psychologist, but I'd say you're feeling guilty about sleeping with him."

"I never said I slept with him."

"You didn't have to. Like you said, you made a mistake."

"You don't mind?"

He shook his head. "It's not something I want to think about every day, but I didn't even know you then. It has nothing to do with us. You seem to be the one who minds—dreaming you're some woman dying in labor, her fate in his hands. Let it go, Justine."

"I love you," she said, but as she wrapped her arms around him, she caught sight of the clock. It was 10:55. She almost pushed him out of her arms. "Nemo, you've got to go back. You've been in here for over twelve hours. You're going to feel awful."

"It's no big deal. It's like a hangover. I'll sleep it off. I'm not going to run off and leave you like this. You're still shaking. Hell, *I'm* still shaking. Besides, I promised you a tour of the hood."

"But Nemo—"

"But nothing. I'm not ready to go home yet. I want to stay with you."

She was sure that visiting too long in the Bin was a lot worse than a hangover, but she didn't argue with him. She wanted him to stay. She ran her hands up and down his arms, muscled from hard work. She imagined him chopping wood, digging in the earth. "If you were *really* at home right now," she asked, "what would you be doing?"

He laughed. "Oh, that's easy. I'd be getting something to eat."

"Sounds great."

SHE FOLLOWED HIM DOWN TO THE KITCHEN. THE WHOLE house looked as if someone had started tearing it down, had a change of heart halfway through, then put it back together again with whatever came to hand. The banisters on the stairs were car bumpers. Most of the windows were covered in plastic. The legs were missing from the sofas and stuffed chairs. They sat on the floor or were propped up on bricks. The kitchen table and chairs were molded plastic, what they used to call outdoor furniture. There was no refrigerator, only a two-burner alcohol stove, and all the cabinetry had been replaced with a stainless steel table salvaged from a restaurant or laboratory. She pictured Lawrence and Nemo dragging it down the street.

She sat down at the table with her coffee, while Nemo looked in the pantry, a huge metal locker attached to the wall, CARL'S CAR CARE stencilled on the doors. There was a small red-and-white box on the table. "What's this?"

"Lawrence's cigarettes."

"You're kidding. I've never actually seen ones this old." She opened up the box, but it was empty except for a few grains of tobacco. "They're all gone."

"But that's impossible. He just opened them yesterday." She held it up. "See for yourself."

"Well I hope he doesn't find any more. You should read the side of the box." He rummaged through the pantry again. The metal rumbled and echoed as he moved things around. "What would you like?" He affected Lawrence's nanny voice: "I'm afraid the menu this morning is rather limited." He held up two jars. "Last summer was a bust. We've eaten up the good stuff. We've got okra and we've got pickles."

"Just cereal will be fine."

He smiled into the open pantry, setting the jars back inside. "Don't have any of that, unless you want to call cornmeal cereal. Sometimes we have milk. There's a guy about a mile north who's got cows. Likes Nine Inch Nails. But we don't get milk too often. It spoils too fast. No refrigeration."

She felt like an idiot. Next she'd be asking for bananas. "What do you have?"

"I'm afraid all I've got to offer you this morning, besides the okra and pickles, is leftover stew, unless you want to wait a couple of hours while I cook up some beans."

"How long has it been left over—with no refrigeration?"

"Just last night. It'll be fine, really. The meat was smoked and cured, there's no milk in it. Besides, we're in the Bin, remember? No food poisoning here."

"What sort of meat?"

"Rabbit. We raise rabbits."

She winced at the thought. Her favorite story as a child was *The Velveteen Rabbit*. She'd feel like a cannibal. "I'll just have coffee. I'm fine with just coffee."

He poured her another cup and sat down at the table. He was studying her, making up his mind about something. "What did you eat when you were in Dallas?"

She shrugged. "When I was in the orphanage, they just fed us. Cafeteria food, lots of spaghetti and tuna fish casserole. Oatmeal for breakfast."

"They must've been doing pretty well. A can of tuna fish bought this table and chairs you're sitting at. What about after you got out of the orphanage? You were on your own two or three years, right? What'd you eat then?"

She thought about it, but she couldn't remember a single meal. She looked around the kitchen, trying to remember any such place in her past where she'd cooked and eaten, but nothing came. "I don't remember, whatever I could get my hands on, I suppose."

"You don't remember? It was only six weeks ago."

"Does it really matter? I've been having trouble remembering things. I'm just disoriented. That's all."

"Are you sure you lived outside until six weeks ago?"

"Of course I'm sure."

"People outside usually aren't so squeamish about what they eat."

"Would you lay off, Nemo? I'm not squeamish. I'm just not that hungry."

"I am, but I'll wait till I get back, and eat the real stew." He stood up, gestured toward the back door. "Would you like to see them?"

"See what?"

"The bunnies. I'm sure they're there. So far Real World Tours hasn't missed a trick." He walked to the door and held it open. "Just a few yards out the back—if you're feeling strong enough."

She was being tested somehow—the city girl come to the country. Okay, she thought. That's fair enough. It was my idea to come here in the first place and see how he lived. "I'm feeling fine," she said. "I'd love to see your bunnies." She stood up, her coffee cup in hand. He held open the door for her, and she walked outside. It was a beautiful morning. The grass in the shadow of the house glistened with dew. He directed her down a brick path to a row of hutches rising out of the high grass on stilts. Dozens of rabbits looked out through the wire mesh. "They're adorable," she said.

Nemo pointed at the cage in front of them. "These are some of our current breeders. The smug fellow in the corner is Jasper. That's Esmeralda, Penelope, Zoe, and Sophie. We only give names to the breeders." He plucked a blade of grass and fed it to Sophie through the wire mesh. "If this were actually the real world, you could only skip so many meals." He plucked another blade of grass and fed it to Sophie. "Vegetarians tend to starve in the real world. Sometimes the rains come, and there's plenty to eat. Sometimes they don't. But rain or shine, every four weeks, we have more rabbits." He turned to Justine. "If you're afraid of the stew, I could cook up Sophie. She

hasn't dropped a litter the last two times we've bred her."
Sophie's face was pressed up against the wire, waiting for
another blade of grass. Nemo reached through the mesh
with his finger and scratched her between the ears.

"Why are you being so horrible?"

"You wanted to see where I lived, how I lived. I'm just
showing you around." He opened a cabinet beneath the
hutches and pointed to something wrapped up in clear
plastic. "I use that."

She had to lean forward to see what it was through the
folds of plastic. And then the shape came clear. It was a
large cleaver. I guess I'm supposed to flee in horror, she
thought. Instead, she straightened up and took a drink of
her coffee. "This won't work, you know."

"What won't work?"

"I don't care whether you slaughter defenseless bunnies
or shit in the woods or grub in the dirt for worms, Nemo.
I love you. If you want me to leave you alone, ask. Don't
try to drive me away."

He didn't say anything. What could he say? She'd nailed
him. She supposed she was to make it easy on him, and
wish him farewell, but he loved her. She knew he loved
her. "Sooner or later you'll have to decide what you're
going to do about me, Nemo." She reached out and
scratched Sophie between the ears. "Just like you'll have
to decide about Sophie here, the next time you're hungry."

He still didn't speak. His eyes burned with anger and
desire. He seized her wrists, and her coffee cup fell to the
grass, as they sank to the ground.

They made love in the tall grass, hundreds of rabbit
eyes watching.

A FEW CUMULUS CLOUDS DRIFTED SLOWLY TO THE EAST.
The sun was still behind the house. Nemo and Justine lay

on their backs at the edge of its shadow, looking up at the sky, a cool breeze blowing across their skin, their heads propped on their clothes. She wondered what Nemo was thinking.

Probably that this isn't the real sky. It's the sky of our imaginings—the mind's sky, the mind's eye. The world isn't turning beneath my back. I'm not really smelling the dirt and grass, the scent of our lovemaking. The ladybug moving across my stomach, her tiny feet marching, can't fly away home.

She sang the song in her head: *Ladybug, Ladybug, Fly away home. Your house is on fire, and your children . . .*

She couldn't remember the rest of it. When she was a little girl, she used to sing that song over and over, adding her own endings, belting it out in the echoey halls. . . . *and your children want pie! . . . and your children are thirsty! . . . and your children aren't tired!* Until one of the nuns would say, "That's not how it goes," and she'd say, *I know that*, and sing more verses until she was ordered to stop.

Unless it was Sister Sarah, and then she'd come up behind Justine without making a sound, and put her hand on top of Justine's head like a bird had landed there, and sing a verse herself: *Ladybug, Ladybug, fly away home. Your house is on fire, and this kid won't go to bed!* And I'd laugh, Justine remembered, and Sister Sarah would walk me down the hall, holding my hand all the way, trading verses until she tucked me into bed. She wasn't old enough to be my mother, but I made up stories that she was, and wrote them in my diary.

She's dead, Justine thought, long dead, but she didn't know why. Sarah had been young, no more than twenty-two or three, when she went away to Cambodia the day after Justine's tenth birthday. She'd baked her a cake with an angel on it. The candles made her halo. Notes floated about her like stars. But Sarah's dead now, Justine told herself. I know it. I feel it. I lived through it. But she couldn't remember when.

That's been so long ago.

Justine realized that Nemo was leaning over her, and she snapped out of her reverie. He was propped up on one arm, watching her. When their eyes met, he said, "You're back."

"I was remembering one of the nuns," she said. "I was wondering what had become of her."

He tilted his head and gave her a quizzical look. "Did you say 'nuns'? How long ago was this, anyway?"

"I was ten, so it would've been ten years ago."

"Catholic nuns?"

"It was a Catholic orphanage. Of course they were Catholic nuns."

"Justine, there haven't been any nuns since the fifties. The Pope went into the Bin and made himself Pope forever. There hasn't been a Catholic Church outside since before I was born. So how do you know any nuns?"

The sun was just peeking over the house, grazing his shoulder with light. She knew that what he said was true. Everyone knew it. She couldn't have sung in the halls at St. Catherine's ten years ago, even twenty. There was no St. Catherine's then. Who she thought she was made no sense. Now that she thought about it, all of her past was a puzzle with most of the pieces missing, none of them fitting together. She tried to remember beyond six weeks ago—where she'd lived, what she'd done, but it was just a few scenes like Freddie's holos. After the orphange, there was nothing substantial. In the Bin, she remembered a few hotel rooms, a few clubs. She couldn't recall a single conversation.

"I don't know," she said.

He didn't say anything for a long time, studying her,

trying to figure her out. "Justine, I don't care how long you've been in the Bin, or how old you really are. I don't see that it much matters in here."

She sat up and started putting on her clothes. "You think I've been lying to you? That I'm some old woman who's been rejuvenated? Believe me, Nemo, I wish it were that simple. As far as I know, I'm *twenty* years old. I've been in the Bin *six* weeks."

He reached out and took her hands. "I'm sorry. I don't think you're lying."

She shook her head. She wanted to scream. "But I have to be, Nemo. My past is impossible. I grew up in a place that couldn't have existed. After that, I can't remember where I was living, what I was doing, who my friends were. All I remember are tiny scraps that don't go anywhere. They're like a few scenes from a play, not even a whole play, certainly not a whole life. It's like I didn't have a life before I woke up yesterday morning. Winston said something about the Bin being disorienting at first, but I don't even know who I am."

"I know who you are," he said, and she felt a rush of fear.

"Who?"

"The woman I love." He took her in his arms and held her close, whispered in her ear. "You know me, and I know you. The rest doesn't matter."

The sun had reached them. It must've been at least noon. "You have to get out of here," she said. "You could die if you stay too long."

"I'm used to that notion. Don't worry. It's only life-or-death after twenty-four hours, and I'm not even close to that. Besides, I want to take you somewhere while we're here. Unless you want me to go."

She held him tight and shook her head. "I don't want that. That's the last thing I want."

*   *   *

THEY TOOK THE METRO FROM NORTHSIDE TO AMPTHILL,
then walked east until they came to an old freeway with
railroad tracks running down the middle of it. The concrete road was buckled and overgrown. "We follow the
tracks," he said, and led her down an embankment and
through a hole in the rusty fence. They walked along on
the ties and gravel, the only sound the crunch of their
footsteps.

"Where're we going?" she asked.

"It's a surprise," he said. "It's my favorite place."

She liked the sound of that. She tried to remember if
she had a favorite place. She took Nemo's hand and
squeezed. This will do, she thought. This is just fine.

The tracks climbed and passed over the freeway. From
there they could see the river glistening in the sun. The
freeway came to the water's edge and stopped. House-
sized chunks of concrete dotted the river, the remains of
the fallen bridge. "Floods chipped away at it," he said.
"It finally collapsed a few years ago."

They continued down the tracks until they too reached
the river. An ancient viaduct, a series of graceful arches,
carried the tracks across the river, a hundred feet below,
clear and clean and strong. "It's beautiful," she whispered.

He pointed across the river. "There's a beach on the
other side beside the viaduct. Jonathan was baptized there.
He showed it to me when we first met. I've been going
there ever since. I thought we might go for a swim."

"You mean walk across the bridge? What if a train
comes along?"

He laughed. "Then Real World Tours is seriously behind the times." He reached down and ran his fingertips
over the top of one of the rails and held them up to show
her the rust. "These tracks haven't seen a train for quite
a while."

She looked out across the viaduct, imagining what it would be like out in the middle, one hundred feet above the water and the rocks. "Is it safe?"

He laughed again. "In the real world it should've fallen into the river years ago. In here, though, everything's safe."

"I'm afraid of heights," she confessed.

"So am I. But if you stick to the middle, it's not so bad. Besides, in the Bin, there's nothing to fear." He offered his hand, and she took it. As they walked out over the water, the wind picked up, gusting hard. She tightened her grip, trying to keep her eyes straight ahead, reminding herself over and over that there was nothing to fear. About halfway across, the whole thing leaned slightly downstream, and there were cracks running through the concrete. She dislodged a stone with her foot and it rolled to a stop inside the rail. Nemo picked it up, tossing it over the side. She watched it fall for several long seconds and felt as if she were falling with it. She didn't look down again. By the time they reached the other side, her knees were weak, and she felt dizzy. She sat down on the rails and put her head between her knees. Nemo sat down beside her.

"You do this often?" she asked.

"Whenever I get the chance."

"There aren't any beaches on the north bank?"

"I like this one."

"You're crazy, Nemo."

"So I've been told."

THEY CLIMBED DOWN FROM THE TRACKS TO THE UNDERSIDE of the viaduct. The concrete arching overhead was smudged with smoke. Weather-beaten graffiti was spray-painted on the wall where the viaduct met the ground. *HE*

DIED FOR US, one said in red dripping letters. Above the words was a red cross with a stick-figure Christ painted on it in black. The paint ran down from his hands and feet. Beside that someone had painted *CHRIST IS K* and then apparently run out of paint.

They walked down to the water and a small beach scattered with driftwood. She slipped off her shoes and wiggled her toes in the sand. The water was calm and deep, the base of the viaduct diverting the current.

"What do you say? Wash away your troubles?"

"Sure," she said, and he stripped off his clothes, diving into the water. She pulled her dress over her head and dove in after him. The water was icy cold—a thousand tiny needles all at once. She rose up out of the water spewing and gasping, and he surfaced beside her. "They got the temperature right," he panted. They raced back to the beach, scrambling onto the sand. The sun felt warm and delicious after the frigid water.

"I love to do that," he said. "Mid-August it's like a warm bath, and the sand's too hot to stand on. When it's like this though, it makes you feel alive." He was laughing and excited, full of joy. Their eyes met, and he reached out and ran his hands over her wet skin, her shoulders, her breasts, her waist. "God, you're beautiful," he said.

She held him in her hands and guided him into her. "This is real, Nemo," she whispered. "This is real."

8

ON THE TRAIN BACK TO D.C., NEMO STUDIED JUS-
tine's reflection in the window as the world flew by in a
blur. Their clasped hands rested on his knee. Their thighs
pressed together. Her large eyes were oblivious to the
countryside, to the skyline of D.C. ahead of them on the
horizon. He guessed she was looking inside, trying to see
the future. Just what he was doing. Only the near future
was clear. In less than half an hour he'd be back in the
real world, and she'd still be here, in the Bin.

All day he'd been forgetting where he really was. He
had to remind himself that he wasn't in his room—in spite
of the smell of the sheets, the sound of the tree limb
scraping against the gutter, the crack in the plaster, perfect
down to each tiny fissure—he wasn't in his bed. He wasn't
swimming in the river. The chill water, the warm sun, the
graffiti—they were all illusions. I was somewhere else, he
thought. No place at all. Only now, I'll remember Justine
every time I lie down in my bed or swim in the river, and
I'll want to be with her. It won't matter where. I'll still
want her.

He squeezed her hand, and she squeezed back. "Can I
see you tomorrow?" he asked.

She turned to him, the corners of her mouth tightened with worry. "Do you want to?"

He smiled and kissed her cheek, and she softened at his touch, pressing her face against his lips. "No, I just thought I'd ask to make us both miserable." He kissed her neck, and she drew in a breath and closed her eyes. "Why would I want to spend every minute with the woman I love, when I could be lying alone in my bed, missing her?" He kissed her eyes, her lips. "I showed you my world, now you have to show me yours."

She looked at him, her eyes agleam, a loving smile on her face.

"Now, don't start crying on me. I'll be at your hotel by noon, and I'll show you exactly how glad I am to see you." He put his arms around her, and she nestled against him, just as the train began slowing for Pentagon Station.

THEY WALKED SLOWLY TO THE LONG ROW OF VIMs AND found the one Nemo had used to enter the Bin over twenty hours before. They stood there embracing, not speaking, not moving, like some statue of farewell, knowing that once they moved or spoke, they'd have to let go, and part.

Finally, she pressed her hands against his chest and whispered, "You have to go now, Nemo. Please. I'm scared for you." She pushed herself away as his arms loosened and fell to his sides.

"I'll see you at noon," he said, and kissed her one last time.

They stepped into a pair of VIMs, looking into each other's eyes as the coffin lids whirred closed, narrowing their vision to a slit, then snapped shut. He stared at the display screen and tried to relax as the coffin rotated slowly back. It seemed to take longer than usual. Twenty-two hours I've been in here, he thought. Two hours shy of *can be fatal.* He didn't know exactly what to expect—different people reacted differently—but it wouldn't be fun. He'd had it drilled into him in health class: When the mind checked out, the body started gearing up to go it on its own. When the mind showed up again, it took them a while to reconcile their differences. If it'd been too long, they couldn't work it out, and you ended up blind or lame or crazy or dead.

When the coffin was finally horizontal, green glowing letters flashed DOWNLOAD in his face, and he felt the familiar falling sensation, but this time it didn't stop. He just kept falling, deeper and deeper. Red letters were flashing now, but he couldn't focus on them. A loud buzzing noise blared and then stopped, and the lid swung open, even though he was still horizontal. He tried to get up, but his limbs wouldn't do what he told them to. He fought down his panic and was gripped with nausea. His head was pounding.

A blue glowing shape appeared over him. "Are you all right?" it asked. "You set off the alarm."

Nemo couldn't focus on his features, but he knew it was Victor, the security guard. "Don't think so," he said, or tried to say. His mouth wouldn't work right, and his voice sounded slurred and muddy as if he were talking underwater.

"You've been in too long," Victor said, propping Nemo up, holding a cup of water to his lips. "Go slow. Remember to swallow."

Nemo concentrated on drinking the water. It took a long time. Half of it dribbled out of his mouth, but he couldn't do anything about it. Victor laid him back down and picked up Nemo's feet, placing them against his chest. "Push," he said.

At first Nemo couldn't do it. He told his legs to push, but the message wasn't getting through. He looked down at his legs to make sure they were still there, and that seemed to help. He finally managed to push, though it took two or three tries to do it a second time. When Nemo got the hang of that, Victor took Nemo's feet in his hands and told him to pump his legs as if he were riding a bicycle. If he'd actually been on a bike, he would've fallen into a ditch, but he got to the point where his legs would move more or less when he told them to.

Then Victor put his feet down and stuck out a blue, glowing hand. "Shake," he said. It took Nemo three tries—he kept misjudging the distance. "Squeeze," Victor said.

"You're wearing me out here," Nemo mumbled, and it was a little easier to talk. He squeezed Victor's hand on the first try. If I really worked at it, he thought, I probably could crush a robin's egg.

"We're going to rotate the VIM so that you're upright, okay?"

"Sure," Nemo said. "What the hell." He could focus most of the time now, and his nausea had momentarily subsided.

"Keep hold of our hand. You're strapped in. You won't fall out."

Nemo's eyes told him he was slowly rising to an upright position. His guts told him he was tumbling through space. If it hadn't been for his hold on Victor's hand, he was convinced he would do just that. It took him a moment to realize the coffin had stopped.

"We're going to unstrap you now. Remember, you're not weak. Your muscles are fine, they're just slow. Take your time. Wait on your body."

The strap slid from his waist, and he didn't fall down. "What do I do now, dance?"

Victor alternately walked and dragged Nemo up and down the waiting room until Nemo was doing a reasonable imitation of a drunk one drink shy of passing out.

Victor steered him to the train platform and held him up as they waited for the train.

"How long'll this last?" Nemo asked. He got a little tangled up in the l's and s's.

"Get some sleep. When you wake up, you should be fine except for a headache and some dizziness. You'll be extremely hungry for a while, but don't overeat. Drink lots of water, and stay out of the Bin for a few days."

Nemo shook his head violently and almost lost his balance. "Have to go in tomorrow. Noon."

Victor sighed. "Six hours, no more. And get at least eight hours sleep first. Next time, Nemo, it will be worse."

VICTOR PUT NEMO ON THE TRAIN HOME. HE'D JUST BEEN on Real World Tours version of this train, and they had everything perfect. Exactly the same. Only this time it made him feel as if he were being stretched across the landscape like a Dali clock. He closed his eyes, and that made it worse. He opened them back up and stared at his hands, gripping his knees. No one's hand to hold on this train but my own, he thought. My body's having its revenge. It knows what I'm thinking of doing.

Each time the train decelerated and accelerated for a stop, Nemo's nausea came back with a vengeance. As soon as he'd recovered from one stop, the train would slow for another. He counted them off, bracing himself for each one, leaving a bit of himself behind at each station. By the time the train slowed for Northside Station, he didn't think he could stand. He was having trouble holding his head up, and his eyes kept fluttering closed. He was right by the door, so all he had to do was stand up and take two lousy steps without falling down. Or he could try crawling out. He didn't think he could crawl the four blocks home, but at least he'd be off this goddamn train.

The doors slid open, and Lawrence stepped through them, put his arms around Nemo's waist and pulled him to his feet. Nemo couldn't figure out what was going on. "What're you doing here?" he managed.

Lawrence picked him up, his feet dangling in the air, and carried him off the train, setting him on the platform. The train left the station in a loud whoosh he felt in his chest, as if it had sucked the air out of his lungs.

"We thought you might need a little help getting home," Lawrence said.

"But how'd you know? How long you been here?"

"Only a few minutes. Put your arm around our waist."

Nemo obeyed and started shuffling toward the escalator in slow motion. "But how'd you know—"

"It's not good for you to talk so damn much."

"But I don't understand—"

"A little bird told us, now shut up. Watch the steps here."

Nemo stumbled getting on to the escalator in spite of Lawrence's warning. As the escalator carried him along, and Lawrence kept him from falling over, he puzzled over how Lawrence had shown up in the first place. "Did Victor tell you? Have you rigged up a shortwave or something?"

They'd reached street level, and Nemo was trying to walk, but he kept falling sideways. He could move his legs, but his timing was off, and the ground seemed to tilt back and forth like the deck of a ship.

"Why don't we just carry you?" Lawrence said. He knelt down, pulled Nemo's arms over his shoulders, and hoisted him onto his back, piggyback. "Hold on."

They started moving down the street with the speed of Lawrence's long stride. He moved as if Nemo didn't weigh a thing. It was nice to be carried, Nemo thought. "So d'you have a shortwave?" he yawned.

"Are you going to keep this up all the way home?"

"Just tell me, Lawrence." He lifted up his head, but it

swayed back and forth, and he let it drop, resting his chin on Lawrence's green head, watching the world bob up and down as if he were at sea, floating, drifting toward the horizon. But still, he was curious. "You gonna tell me?" he insisted, though his words were slurring again.

"Just give it a rest. We'll tell you later."

Their house came into view, bobbing up and down, and all Nemo could think about was sleeping in his bed. His eyes fluttered shut. "Promise?" he mumbled.

"Promise," Lawrence said.

When Justine stepped out of the VIM in Pentagon Station, she looked over at the one next to her. It was empty. Nemo was back in his own world. He might as well have been on the dark side of the moon. The clock on the wall, in the shape of a pentagon, read seven-thirty. He'd been in for over twenty hours. She imagined him in pain, helpless, cursing her for luring him into the Bin. What in the hell was I thinking of, she asked herself, letting him risk his life for me?

He'd made it so easy. It was nothing. It was as if he *wanted* to risk his life for her, just as he regularly crossed that crumbling bridge for a favorite beach, for some kind of meaning it held for him. When I crossed that bridge, she thought, I was terrified, even when I *knew* it wasn't real—that the bridge could crumble, or the wind could knock me off my feet, and I might fall—but I'd never die.

When you're in here long enough, do you get used to the idea? How many Real World Tours would it take before she was skipping across that bridge, diving off it, numb to the fear, to the beauty? Nemo said there was nothing to fear in the Bin. Maybe he was wrong.

She was still standing in front of the long row of VIMs, lining the wall as far as she could see in either direction, dozens of them, more than would ever be needed again. She imagined this place bustling, people coming and going in hordes. How long ago would that've been? Twenty years? Thirty? Now, she suspected, she could stand here all day and not see another soul from the real world, just a few like her who pretended to go. How many were left who actually came and went between the worlds? For all she knew, Nemo was the last one.

She closed her eyes and tried to calm herself. Nemo would be fine. As he said, under twenty-four hours wasn't fatal. What she truly feared was losing their love. Her fantasies as Juliet hadn't prepared her for this. It wasn't just a wild delirium, as she'd imagined, but a clarity as well. When he looked into her eyes, he saw someone no one else could see. When she was with him, she became herself. She could feel it inside, like a flower opening, and she could feel it in him, touching, knowing him, as he too came to life in her arms.

She opened her eyes, looked up and down the long row of empty coffins. She had faith in their love. It was herself she doubted. St. Catherine's had vanished by the time she was born. She tried to picture one clear, distinct memory from the last three years—a place, a person's face, anything. There was nothing until three days ago when she woke up in bed with Winston.

Everything was supposed to be perfect in here. Everything but her. Somehow, some way, there was something wrong with her, and she wanted to know why. No, she thought, I don't care about why—I just want to know who I am. It didn't seem too much to ask.

SHE LEFT THE HALL OF COFFINS, PASSED THE ESCALATORS to the station, and headed down the hall marked RECEIVING. She went through a simple glass door, RECEIVING stencilled on it and nothing more. She found herself in an office. To her right, a window looked out over the train platform below. There was a sofa under the window. To her left was a closed metal door. In the middle of the room was a computer terminal, but no one was seated at it. She was headed for the metal door when it opened, and a woman peeked her head out. "You need some help?"

"Yes, I think so. I've been having trouble remembering things, and I suspect something might've gone wrong when I was uploaded. I wanted to see what might be done."

"Certainly," the woman said cheerfully. She came through the door and seated herself at the terminal. She had striking red hair and strong leonine features. She was wearing a camel-colored suit that looked like it came from the early twentieth century. She gave off an air of friendly competence and good will.

"Can you help me?"

"That's what I'm here for." She gestured at the sofa. "Won't you sit down?"

"No thanks. I'll just stand."

"Name?"

"Justine Ingham."

Her hands moved over the keyboard. "Here you are. Justine Ingham; born Dallas, Texas; no known relatives; twenty years old; entered ALMA three days ago—April 15, 2081, 8:47 A.M."

Justine steadied herself on the table. The woman didn't seem to notice. "No, I came in six weeks ago, in Dallas."

The woman checked the display. "Not according to this."

Justine struggled to remember what she could—the hotels, the bars. "I think I was in Chicago last week. The Ambassador Hotel."

"Let's just see," the woman said, still smiling, keying it in. When the information came up, her smile vanished.

"You're right. Justine Ingham, room 614. No wonder you're having trouble remembering things."

"What about before I came in here?"

"I don't have any information on that. There's no address in Dallas, but a lot of people don't have real addresses anymore. Let me pull up your complete file and see what I can find out." She pressed a few keys and cocked an eyebrow. She pointed to the screen, inviting Justine to see for herself. *Restricted Access*, it said.

"What does that mean?"

The woman eyed her suspiciously. "Maybe you're not who you say you are."

Though she said maybe, she sounded certain of it. "Then who am I? According to you I was staying in a hotel before I was even in here. Maybe your computer's screwed up."

"Then I guess I can't help you." The woman's smile was now a thin, cruel line.

What's the deal? Justine wondered. At first, this woman's nice as can be, and now she's treating me like a pariah. "But what does that mean, 'Restricted Access'?"

"You'll have to discuss that with someone who has access." The woman stood. "If you'll excuse me." And then she left through the metal door. Justine tried the knob, but it was locked.

SHE WENT BACK TO HER HOTEL AND CALLED EVERY NUMBER in her address book. This time she left messages at every one. Sooner or later somebody had to call her. Now she was sure something was screwed up. She couldn't very well have come in three days ago *and* been in Chicago last week. But if they wouldn't help her at Receiving, where was she supposed to go? Who was she supposed to talk to?

She soon grew tired of waiting for the phone to ring,

ate an early dinner, and went down to the club in hopes of catching John. Sure enough, he was in the green room smoking a joint.

"Hey Justine." He held out the joint to her, and she waved it away.

"John, I need to ask you a few things, okay?"

He grinned. "What is the meaning of life? When is time? How high is up? How up is high?"

"I'm serious. When were you guys hired? How did it happen?"

"Calm down, Justine. You're steamin'. Let's see. Week ago. Lenny called. Sent the virtuals, and we learned the tunes. There you were, and here we are. Band of your dreams."

"Were you playing with Rick and Ian before?"

"No. I was between gigs." He chuckled and took a toke.

"Have you worked with Lenny before?"

"Never heard of him."

"Why did he call you?"

"Why does anybody do anything, Justine? Why don't you ask him? He's *your* agent."

"I can't get hold of him."

John nodded sagely, took another deep hit. "Course not. He's an agent."

"Thanks, John." She started to leave him to his joint, but she remembered what had been nagging at her since she'd last talked to him. "That friend of yours—the one who had herself downloaded—who did she talk to? How did she set it up?"

John didn't speak for a moment, his chin tucked against his chest, smoke drifting out of his nostrils, looking at her under hooded brows. He exhaled loudly and shook his head. "Can't help you there, Justine. Don't even think about it. Crazy shit, I'm telling you. Crazy shit."

*   *   *

She talked to Bruce, the club owner, about how she was hired and got the same story. Lenny had set it up a week ago. Bruce didn't know Lenny, but he'd liked the tapes, so he booked her. He was glad he did, he added. She was great. Word was out, and he was expecting a big crowd. She could play there as long as she wanted.

She went back to the green room. Rick and Ian were there now, but she didn't see much point in talking to them. Rick would just be an asshole, and Ian wouldn't say two words. It was her problem. She just had to deal with it. As she tuned up, she sat in the corner and tried to fit the pieces together. If Lenny booked her a week ago, she couldn't have come in three days ago. It made more sense that she came in six weeks ago—screwed up somehow—and they tried to fix it or something three days ago, and changed the date on her entry. But who was *they* anyway? Who ran this damn place?

"Hey, boss lady." Rick broke into her thoughts. "It's show time. Don't want to be *late* now, do we?"

For once Rick was right. The bar was packed to the rafters. She had to put everything else out of her mind and sing. When she was a kid she used to sing in front of the mirror, pretend there was a wildly cheering audience. Now they were waiting, just as she'd always dreamed. She only wished Nemo was here, sitting up front as he had last night.

"Let's do it," she said.

They played each set better than the one before, and the crowd loved them. Even Rick seemed to be having a good time. With each song, her troubles seemed to lift. She dedicated "Coming Up Close" to Nemo, even though he wasn't there. He would be tomorrow. Today, she realized, for it was after midnight. In less than twelve hours she'd see him again. In the song, the lovers had one night only. She was already blessed.

They did four encores before they finally quit playing. Rick and Ian, even John, were leaving with different women who'd hung around, waiting for them. Justine was glad to walk back to her hotel alone, take in the beautiful night. She smiled and closed her eyes, walking down the middle of a city street at two o'clock in the morning, giddy with exhaustion, looking forward to seeing her lover. They'd find a way. They had to.

A MOCKINGBIRD—TEN TIMES LOUDER THAN ANY CREATURE had a right to be, showing off with trills and buzzes and piercing high notes that made his temples throb—woke Nemo from a deep, heavy sleep. He cracked his eyelids, and there was Lawrence sitting on a stool by the open window, watching the mockingbird perform on the windowsill.

"What in the hell are you doing?" Nemo croaked, and the mockingbird took his concert and flew away.

"Damnit, Nemo, you scared him off."

"Be strong, Lawrence." He squinted at his clock, but it'd run down. "What time is it anyway?"

Lawrence lit up a cigarette, and blew the smoke out the window. "About ten. Looks like you must've enjoyed yourself a bit too much night 'fore last. Jonathan said you were howling at the moon when he left."

"I'm sure."

Nemo carefully leaned to one side and slid his pants off the end of the bed, trying to figure out how to put them on without moving his head. Lawrence sat smoking, watching Nemo's struggles with amused detachment. He was still working on smoke rings. About every third try, a wobbly saucer shape came out, but that was as close as he could get.

Nemo managed to get both legs into his pants, but he

was having trouble getting them past his knees without moving the few inches it took to start his head throbbing and his stomach churning.

"Don't you usually do that standing up?" Lawrence asked after a while.

"Can it, Lawrence. I feel like shit."

"Look that way, too."

"Could you give me a hand here?"

Lawrence smiled and tossed his cigarette out the window, waved the smoke away from his face, and crossed his legs. "We rather feel that you should be capable of putting on your own trousers before you set out again."

Nemo sighed. Just what he needed. The nanny. "Of course you do. Builds character. Stiff upper lip and all that rot." He yanked his pants on—trying not to wince from the pain in his head—and gave Lawrence what he hoped was a triumphant look as he zipped them up.

"How impressive. We have prepared you a tray." Lawrence pointed at the bedside table. There was a tumbler of water and some flatbread.

Lawrence was waiting for me to wake up, Nemo realized, looking after me again. He felt like a jerk. "Thanks Lawrence." Squaring his shoulders and bowing his head, Nemo signed, *I am shamed*, and Lawrence nodded his assent.

Nemo gulped down half the water and started stuffing bread into his mouth as fast as he could chew. The pain in his stomach, he realized, was hunger. He hadn't eaten anything since night before last.

Lawrence watched him eat for a while. "Slow down, Nemo. You'll choke yourself."

He slowed down a little, eating till all the bread was gone, gulping down the rest of the water.

"Better?" Lawrence asked.

Nemo nodded, and it didn't hurt quite as much to move.

He slowly rose to his feet and stood there until the room quit spinning. He shuffled to the closet and started hunting for a clean shirt. Normally, he would've washed clothes the day before, but he'd been in the Bin. He finally found one that was a little cleaner than the rest and started working on the buttons.

"We gather you have plans," Lawrence said.

"I'm going to spend the day in D.C. with Justine, see the sights."

Lawrence nodded. "You're thinking about going in for good, aren't you son?"

Nemo hesitated, his hands hovering over the last button on his shirt. "Yes, I guess I am."

"We like Justine a great deal."

"So you don't think I'd be nuts to go in?"

"It doesn't matter what we think. The question is, what do you think?"

Nemo gave up trying to find a pair of clean socks that matched and settled on one navy and one black. He sat down on the side of the bed. "I think she's wonderful. I've never met anyone like her. It's like we're made for each other." Just talking about her, he felt better, so he rattled on, telling Lawrence all about their visit to Real World Tours. "They got everything exactly right, even the graffiti down by the river." He finished tying his shoes and stood up, feeling almost human again, though his head still ached. "They only screwed up once: In there, you were out of cigarettes. The pack was lying on the kitchen table, empty."

Lawrence shook another cigarette out of the pack and lit it. "We were," he said, blowing a cloud of smoke into the air. "We got another pack yesterday afternoon, whole carton actually."

"Jeez. What did you give for it?"

Lawrence considered the smoke coiling up from his cigarette. "The Elvis boxed set."

"Lawrence, I don't believe you! We could've gotten a cow for that."

Lawrence shook his head in disgust. "What the hell you know about cows? Pain in the butt. Nothing stupider on four legs."

"But a carton of cigarettes—that's real smart."

Lawrence glared at Nemo, the scales on his forehead sticking out like windblown shingles. He took a deep drag, and blew the smoke into the room. "Are you still here? We thought you were leaving."

Nemo yanked on his jacket. He couldn't believe Lawrence had blown the Elvis boxed set on *cigarettes*. At the rate he was going he'd smoke them up in a week, but it was a done deal now. "I'll see you later. Victor told me not to stay in more than six hours, so I'll be home for dinner. Try not to burn the house down." He started for the door, when it hit him, and he stopped dead in his tracks. "Hey, wait a minute. How did they know?"

"How did who know what?"

"Real World Tours—how did they know you were out of cigarettes when I didn't even know it myself?"

"What in the hell are you talking about?"

"You know damn well what I'm talking about. They patched the thing from my upload, right? So how did they know something I didn't?"

Lawrence sighed. "You are like a dog on a bone. They knew from us, of course."

"But how? You were out here, right?"

Lawrence heaved a smoke-filled sigh. "Shit." He waved his hand at the bed. "Well, sit back down. Time for lessons."

Nemo sat on the corner of the bed, and Lawrence considered him, his eyes mere slits. Nemo felt like a fly sitting on a blade of grass.

"It's like this," Lawrence said. "All us Constructs have a chip at the base of our brains. Originally it linked us to a central computer that checked up on us—they didn't know what the hell we might do. They wanted to make sure we didn't get screwy—try to run off to the arctic or some damn thing. Inventory control, you might call it. Anyway, when the Bin opened up, and the central computer went in there, we stayed out here. Ever since, everything we know is uploaded into the Bin—do not pass Go, do not collect two hundred dollars."

Nemo tried to imagine this, and a chill went through him. He remembered Lawrence's watchful eyes, their long talks. All of that was stored in the Bin. For the first time in his life, Nemo felt afraid of Lawrence. "Everything? All the Constructs?"

Lawrence nodded.

And then another piece of the puzzle fell into place. "That's how you knew I was coming into the station yesterday, isn't it? It goes both ways. You knew because Victor knew."

"That's right."

"How come you never told me this?"

He shrugged. "We keep it to ourselves. We ain't exactly popular out here as it is. How long you think we'd last if certain folks found out we had a direct line to the Bin?"

Nemo cringed at the thought. "How come you're telling me now?"

Lawrence chuckled. "So you won't drive us crazy asking."

"I won't tell anybody."

Lawrence clapped a huge green hand on Nemo's shoulder. "We know that, son, or we wouldn't've told you. As for going into the Bin, you might want to start by asking yourself why it is you've stayed out, and what's different now. No woman wants a man who's going to be looking over his shoulder all the time. Don't go in 'less you're sure. Now, get gone. And whenever y'all come up for air, tell Justine we said hey."

NEMO DECIDED TO TAKE THE BIN TRAIN TO D.C. AT LEAST that way, if he felt like shit when he got back, he wouldn't have another long train ride ahead of him. His stomach churned at the memory of the last one. He took a short ride down to Capitol Square Station where the Richmond VIMs were, mulling over what Lawrence had told him about Constructs. He wondered if anything was ever done with all the information the Constructs fed into the Bin every day, or whether it just sat there like so much garbage at a landfill. He spent a lot of time at landfills digging for CDs. When everything went virtual, people must've thrown them out by the boxload. Sometimes he'd find a whole rack of them—rack and all—lying under some worthless computer. He wondered who else besides Real World Tours dug through all that data for what they could use.

There was more graffiti in the Richmond stations than in Pentagon Station, and Capitol Square was the worst. There was a security guard, but she was spread pretty thin. She made the rounds of all the Richmond stations, and she also did maintenance work. Nemo's longtime favorite—*What would Jesus do?*—was still written over the VIMs in foot-high letters. It was a question he'd never been able to answer, though there was no shortage of folks who presumed to answer for Him.

He stepped into a VIM with *666* scrawled on the front of it. It looked like it was done with acrylic squeezed from a tube. The artist probably would've preferred red or black, but had to use what he could find—in this case, a mellow chartreuse that gave a decidedly mixed message. As the coffin rotated, Nemo listened with new respect to the orientation tape's warnings about visiting too long, and braced himself.

But going in was painless. As soon as UPLOAD flashed in his face, all his physical symptoms vanished, and he realized how awful he had felt. Now, he felt perfectly healthy, like everyone else in the Bin. He had to admit he didn't miss his headache. As he stepped out of the coffin, he checked the time, remembering Victor's warning.

It was 11:20. He had to be back by 5:20, which meant he had to leave D.C. by a quarter to five. That isn't nearly enough time, he thought. He scurried down the escalator to the platform and caught the train just as it was about to pull out of the station.

His car was full of St. Christopher's students on a field trip. They looked to be seniors, about sixteen or seventeen, all boys. Their teacher, an athletic-looking guy in a navy blazer just like the boys wore, sat across the aisle from Nemo, watching his charges as they climbed around on the seats, pushing and shoving each other. Every once in a while he'd call one of them down for crossing some invisible line of decorum Nemo couldn't quite figure out.

"Where are you taking them?" Nemo asked.

"History field trip," the teacher said. "Arlington Cemetery, the Holocaust Museum, and the Vietnam Veterans Memorial. We're doing a unit on war."

One of the boys fell giggling into the aisle, and the teacher said, "Brad, in your seat." The boy popped up, still laughing, and fell into a seat on top of two other boys.

The history teacher smiled apologetically. "I let them have a good time on the way up. They'll be much more subdued on the ride home."

*   *   *

As Nemo rode along, watching the boys tussle with each other, he tried to imagine the next few weeks, shuttling back and forth, trying to remember just where the hell he was, keeping an eye on the time, he and Justine always wondering just where they were headed. But he didn't have to live through those few weeks to know what they came down to in the end: Was he in, or was he out?

In boarding school all the kids were pissed at first when their moms and dads went in. Everybody sounded off. But after only a few weeks of visits, you could tell which ones would end up going in. No matter how tough they sounded, no matter how much they liked to terrify Mum and Dad with the hint they were staying out, you could always tell which ones. Once they made a choice, the real world was just something to get through. They learned a script and played it. They were just marking time.

A handful knew just as quickly that they were *never* going in. They were going to live and die in the real world, and that was that. They were the ones who'd fascinated Nemo. They all had different reasons from plain gut feelings to elaborate philosophical arguments, and he set out to learn them all. He wanted to know what they knew— what they were willing to die for. Most of his friends were in that minority, but he was never really one of them. He never could decide, he never could be sure like they were. And so he stayed out, waiting to be sure.

He envied those who stayed out and knew why. Jonathan knew. His grandmother apparently knew, staying out even when she was old and sick. But he wasn't like them. He only wanted to be. All he was ever sure of were his doubts. They kept him rooted, in a way. The Bin was a one-way trip. You go in, you stay in. The real world was temporary whether he decided to stay or not. He lived the best life he could, never completely sure he was doing the right thing, staying out day by day.

The St. Christopher's boys piled off the train at Pentagon Station. Nemo waved good-bye to the history teacher and continued on to Dupont Circle. Lawrence told him to think about what was different now, and it wasn't too hard to figure out. Now, finally, there was something—someone—he was sure of. He loved Justine. He couldn't give her up.

He stood in front of the door and waited for his stop.

NEMO ROSE INTO THE SUNLIGHT ON DUPONT CIRCLE, hurrying up the escalator two steps at a time, so that when he reached the top, he sprang into the air like a dancer. He moved through the crowd, weaving in and out. No one seemed to be in as big a hurry as he was. He felt fine in here, felt better each step closer to Justine.

At the hotel, he hit the revolving door and left it spinning behind him like a top. He strode across the lobby, just missing the elevator. The clock above the elevator said it was three minutes till noon. He glanced around and found the stairs. It was only six flights. He churned up them without slowing. The racket of his thudding footsteps filled the stairwell. He burst through the doorway to the sixth floor, scaring some poor guy by the elevator half to death. Nemo mumbled an apology and loped down the long hall to Justine's room, rapping on her door before he'd come to a complete stop. The door flew open, and she jumped into his arms, wrapping her arms and legs around him. He carried her into the room, kicking the door shut behind them. They kissed desperately, passionately, falling onto the bed, tearing off each other's clothes, laughing.

"I told you I'd be glad to see you," he said.

She reached down and took him into her hand. "My God, I didn't know you'd be *this* glad."

*　*　*

A COUPLE OF HOURS LATER, THEY LAY TANGLED IN A PLEAS-
ant heap, slick with sweat, temporarily sated.

"I missed you," she said.

He kissed the inside of her thigh. "I'm afraid I spent
most of the time since you saw me last sound asleep. But
I started missing you the moment I woke up."

She ran her fingers through his hair and let it fall around
his shoulders. "What was it like when you went back?"

"It wasn't so bad. It was nothing, really."

"I don't believe you, Nemo. You just don't want me
to worry."

He propped himself up on his elbows and looked into
her eyes. "Okay. It was pretty awful. But I'll be fine."

She took his face in her hands. "What was it like?"

"Headache, nausea, dizziness, impaired motor ability—
like the VIM warning says. It felt like someone had discon-
nected all my internal wiring and hooked it back up in
the dark."

She cradled his head in her arms. "I was worried sick
about you."

"Don't worry about me."

She laughed at him. "Don't be silly, Nemo. You worry
about me."

"That's different."

"Right. The big, strong man." She gave him a quick
kiss, unwound herself, and went into the bathroom. He
rolled over and plumped up a couple of pillows against
the headboard, settled himself into them, basking in his
pleasure. He loved Justine. Hell, he loved everyone,
even himself.

He spotted a copy of *Rebecca* on the bedside table and
picked it up. It was like seeing an old friend. He'd read it
when he was fifteen. He'd liked it so much, that when he

came to the end, he'd immediately read it a second time. He opened it up to the last page, the closing sentences:

The road to Manderley lay ahead. There was no moon. The sky above our heads was inky black. But the sky on the horizon was not dark at all. It was shot with crimson, like a splash of blood. And the ashes blew towards us with the salt wind from the sea.

Justine came out of the bathroom, drying her face with a towel.

"I read this," he said, holding up the book. "It was in my grandmother's stuff. I loved it."

She sat on the bed beside him. "I quit reading it," she confessed. "I was afraid she was going to lose her husband because he was still in love with his perfect dead wife, and I couldn't stand it."

He had to smile at the way she said *perfect dead wife*, as if she were jealous of Rebecca herself. "If that's why you stopped, you should definitely keep reading."

"Tell me how it ends."

"I can't do that. I don't want to spoil it for you."

"Oh, come on, Nemo. Just a hint." She ran her fingertips along the inside of his arm.

"Okay, just a hint." He paused to consider just what he should give away. "I'll tell you that Rebecca was far from perfect."

"That's it? You're a big help. That doesn't mean Max knows that. He is a man after all."

He grinned. "I'll ignore the implication. You just want a happy ending."

"Sure, if I can get it."

He pondered a moment. He didn't want to give the whole book away. "Okay. I'll tell you one more thing, and that's it: The heroine saves her husband's life."

This piqued her interest more than he'd bargained for. "Really? How?" She shifted around, so that she was kneeling on the bed.

He laid the book on the table. "You'll just have to finish reading it."

She bounced up and down, her hands pushing on his chest. "Tell me, Nemo. Does Mrs. Danvers try to kill him?"

He smiled, enjoying her excitement. "Perhaps."

She climbed on top of him straddling him. "Tell me, Nemo."

He drew his thumb and forefinger across his mouth. "My lips are sealed."

"I'll tickle you."

"I'm not ticklish." She tried in vain to tickle him. She came close, but she missed the spot under his arms, and he managed to maintain a stony composure.

"Creep." She pinned his arms and leaned over him, her hips undulating. "If you don't tell me, I'll make you fuck me again."

He groaned in mock horror, rolling his head from side to side. "No! Please! No! Anything but that!"

She bounced on his stomach and rolled onto the bed, curling up with her back to him. "Fine, then. See if I care."

He molded his body to hers, kissing her back, caressing her thigh. She took his hand and wrapped his arm around her.

"Tell me about Rosalind," she said in a small, quiet voice.

"You remember her name."

"Of course, I remember her name. Is she pretty?"

"Yes. She tried to hide it, but she was."

"Were you in love with her?"

Nemo thought carefully before he answered. He wanted

to be fair. "We were like two people stranded on a desert island. We helped each other get through it, but we weren't in love."

"Do you miss her?"

"I wonder how she's doing sometimes, hope she's happier than when I knew her. But no, I don't miss her." He propped himself up on one arm and gently turned Justine onto her back. "What about you? There must've been other guys."

She stared at the ceiling and tried to remember. There were lots of them, little more than faces, as if they were all peering in at her through a window. She'd never loved any of them. "There were other guys, but no one like you. My island was more crowded than yours."

"Tell me about one of them. It's only fair."

She remembered a moon-faced boy sneaking into her room after lights out. "Dick," she said.

"Dick? You're joking."

She giggled. "Afraid not. He was my first. I was fifteen. He climbed up the fire escape and came in through my window. He brought me tulips he'd picked from the yard. I had to throw them out the window after he left. They were Sister Gertrude's tulips. She would've killed me if she'd found them in my room. He was an All Saints boy, a senior."

"Well, how was Dick?"

"Not so great. He was a virgin, too. He cried after it was over. He was going to be a priest, and he figured I'd ruined everything."

"Sounds like he was aptly named." He watched her laugh, her eyes crinkling shut. He wondered who she really was. As she said, her past was impossible. "Did he ever become Father Dick?"

"I don't think so. He crawled through several other girls' windows after mine."

"How did you know that?"

"Girls talk, Nemo."

"Did he cry every time?"

"No. But I was the only one who got flowers."

"Lucky you. What about after you left the orphanage—were there any guys then?"

"You said only one." She tried to make it sound playful, but he could see the question upset her.

"You can't remember?" he asked gently.

She stared at the ceiling and shook her head. "No." She closed her eyes and balled up her fists. "God, I hate this."

"So what do you remember exactly, besides St. Catherine's?"

"The last three days. Before that I know things, but I don't really remember them. I know I was at the Ambassador Hotel in Chicago last week, but I couldn't tell you what the place looks like, or if I talked to anybody on the elevator, or anything. I was playing with another band, but I can't even remember their faces.

"And then there are these memories I don't know what to do with. They're just there, but they don't fit with anything else. Like there's this bundle of letters I can see clearly in my mind, tied up in a green yarn. It feels like they're important somehow. But that's it. I don't know who they're from or when they were written."

"Maybe they're a memory from when you were real young. I have memories like that, from when I was three or four."

She considered this, but it didn't feel right. They're from when I was old, she thought, but she didn't say it. She didn't even understand what she meant. "That must be it," she murmured, not wanting to think about it anymore, afraid of what she might find.

He took her hand. "I'm just glad you remember me,

that you showed up at my birthday party, and changed my life.''

She looked into his eyes. "You are the sweetest man."

"I never brought you flowers."

"You didn't cry either."

"You could make me cry," he said.

"I never will."

He took her into his arms, so full of love tears came to his eyes and wet her cheeks.

THE DAY WAS WARM AND HUMID, THE AIR HEAVY WITH THE scent of cherry blossoms. A light breeze blew through the trees, and Justine and Nemo were showered with petals. They were headed south on 21st, out for a walk. Like most cities, there'd been no cars in D.C. since before the Bin, so there were no cars in here now. The streets had been turned into tree-lined walkways, with flowerbeds and fountains.

"The real D.C. is one giant death wish," he told her. "I don't set foot outside Pentagon Station. I could get used to this."

They could see the Washington Monument off to the left, sticking up above the lane of trees. They were getting close to the reflecting pool. In front of them, more than a dozen kites wove back and forth in the sky.

They emerged from the trees to find a group of people on Constitution Avenue flying kites, while a crowd stood around watching. There were kids and adults, but mostly kids. Justine and Nemo stood arm in arm, watching the kites, pointing out the different shapes and colors. "I've never flown a kite," Nemo said. "It looks fun."

"You've never flown a kite?"

"I suppose you have."

"Sure. We made them in art class. I hated the getting

it up in the air part. But once it's up there, it's great. You really have to try it." She scanned the kite flyers. Before he knew what was happening, she was leading him toward a boy of about thirteen flying a blue diamond-shaped kite. "Hi," she said to the boy. "Nice kite."

"Thanks," the boy said, without taking his eyes off his kite.

Nemo's eyes followed the string high into the air to the tiny blue shape. He hadn't realized how high up it was. "How big is it?"

"Six feet high, four across. I made it myself."

Justine said, "My friend has never flown a kite. Could he fly yours for just a minute? Just to get the feel of it?"

The boy eyed Nemo. "My name's Patrick," he said.

"Mine's Nemo."

"Cool name," he said. He handed Nemo the stick with the kite string wrapped around it. "You can fly it while I go get a hot dog."

Nemo laughed as he felt the tug of the kite in his hands. "I'll be careful," he said, but Patrick had already disappeared in the crowd. Nemo watched the other kite flyers, trying to pick up some pointers. "You know any tricks?" he asked Justine.

"Take up a little slack and let it go."

Nemo did as he told her, and the kite swooped down and shot back up.

"Sister Sarah was the one who made kites with us." She remembered Sarah running alongside her in her habit, shouting her encouragement. Justine had painted her kite to look like an angel. "I called up an old friend from the orphanage," she said. "Stephanie Boyd. She was one of my best friends. She didn't remember me at all."

"Are you sure you got the right person?"

"I recognized her. She said she *was* at St. Catherine's— only it was eighty years ago."

He wasn't sure what to say. He remembered she'd been pretty upset the last time he'd suggested she might be older than she thought. "Do you think maybe you were there then, too?"

"She didn't remember me. She said she didn't know anyone named Justine at all."

"Maybe she's just forgotten."

"Maybe I wasn't Justine then."

"What do you mean?" .

She shook her head and gave a resigned laugh. "I don't know *what* I mean. I can't make any sense of it. I think I should just quit trying."

He put an arm around her shoulders and gave her a hug, confident enough now to fly the kite with one hand. "I'm just glad you're Justine now."

She laid her head on his shoulder. "Me too."

The wind gusted, and the kite climbed higher into the air. Nemo thought he was going to lose it. "Whoa. It feels like if I let it go, it'll go into orbit."

Patrick spoke up beside them. They had no idea how long he'd been standing there. "Actually, if you let go, it will fall down. The tension on the string is what allows the kite to act as an air foil and remain aloft. The Chinese invented kites thousands of years ago. It was a spiritual discipline for them and not mere entertainment."

Nemo smiled, reminded of himself at that age. "You don't say. Is that what it is for you—a spiritual discipline?"

The boy was perfectly serious as he finished off his hot dog. "Yes," he said.

Nemo looked back up at the kite. He could feel each gust and eddy of the wind in his hands. It didn't matter at all to this boy that the kite and the wind weren't real. Maybe he was right.

"Thanks, Patrick." He handed the kite string back to him.

"You can make yourself one," Patrick told him.

"They're easy to make. You can start with a smaller one. They're easier to get up."

Justine smiled and winked at Nemo over the boy's head. "Nemo won't have a problem with that," she assured Patrick.

They thanked Patrick and moved on toward the reflecting pool. Nemo said, "You'll say anything, won't you?"

"That's one of the things you love about me, isn't it?"

He laughed. "It is indeed."

THEY LAY ON THE GRASS BY THE REFLECTING POOL UNTIL IT was 4:30, and Nemo explained that he had to catch a train back to Richmond. He begrudgingly told her of Victor's warning.

"I'm afraid you haven't gotten to see much of D.C."

"I came to see you anyway. Besides, I'll come again."

At the station, he started to tell her good-bye, but she insisted on riding with him. "I want to spend as much time with you as I possibly can," she said.

On the train, Justine rested her head on Nemo's shoulder and closed her eyes. Nemo rested his head on hers. "I almost forgot to tell you," he said. "Lawrence says 'hey.' "

"I like Lawrence. Tell him I said 'hey' back."

"I told him I'm in love with you. I told him I was thinking about coming in."

He could feel a subtle change in the pressure of her head on his shoulder. "What did he say?"

"He said I should be sure."

He looked down the long line of cars, swaying slightly as the train rounded a curve, pressing her against him, and was jolted by the sight of the crematorium on the horizon. The smoke rose straight up into the sky in a broad plume bathed in golden light from the setting sun. Then he realized it was only clouds. They were in the Bin. Safe from death. But he could still see it in his mind's eye—the endless smoke, just above the stacks the sparks rising into the light. He pointed at the spot as they swept past it. "Do you know what's out there in the real world?" he asked. She raised her head and looked out the window where he'd pointed. "One of the crematoriums—where they burn up the bodies of everyone who comes in."

He told her about going to the crematorium with Rosalind and Jonathan, about the stacks of bodies reduced to ashes, about the woman who had to be shoved back into place. He'd never told anyone before, not even Lawrence.

"That's what my nightmares are about. I'll be doing something ordinary—feeding the rabbits, working out a trade—when someone calls my name, and I turn around. Sometimes it's someone I know, sometimes it's someone I saw at the crematorium. They look perfectly normal, and then they burst into flames. Their clothes burn off before I have a chance to do anything. Then their flesh catches fire. I grab hold of them, try to smother the flames, but they keep burning, and I don't feel a thing. I hold them till they're nothing but ashes, and then I wake up."

They listened to the sound of the wheels on the rails. "Now I understand why you've stayed out," she said.

"It shouldn't make any difference," he said. "Everyone's body dies one way or another. All those people I saw are living in the Bin now, perfectly happy. I think I've made too much of it. I mean, Rosalind saw what I saw. She went in."

"Maybe you should talk to her about it."

"What is it with you? Are you trying to fix me up with my old girlfriend?"

"Of course not. I just thought it might help you figure out . . ."

"What I'm going to do about you? I've already figured

that out." He laid his hand on her cheek and turned her to face him. "I'm doing the only thing I can do. I'm coming in."

He expected her to light up, to throw her arms around him and shriek for joy. Instead, she just looked stunned. "Because of me?"

"Of course, because of you." He was afraid she didn't want him, that somehow he'd misunderstood. Just because she loved him didn't mean—

"Are you sure this is the right thing? You've stayed out so long."

He took her by the shoulders. "I'm positive. We love each other. You can't come to me, so I'm coming to you."

She shook her head. "But you don't know me. I don't even know myself—"

"Nothing could change how I feel about you. Nothing." She closed her eyes and buried her face in his chest, crying softly.

He cradled her in his arms, rocking her gently. "Why are you upset?" he asked. "I'll understand if this is too soon, or if you don't feel the same way about me—"

"You idiot," she snuffled. "I'm crying because I love you so very much."

"I'll call Mom and Dad from the station and have them meet us at the club tonight. I can break the news. We can all celebrate. Besides, I want to hear you sing again. Tomorrow I'll come in for good. I have a few good-byes to make."

"Nemo," she asked again, "are you sure?"

"Of course, I'm sure. Will you quit asking me that?"

She looked right into him. "Only when you are," she said.

9

JUSTINE KEPT TELLING HERSELF SHE SHOULD BE happy, and that was that. *He loves me, and he's coming inside. Isn't that what I wanted?* She was happy he loved her that much, but not about the rest of it. It wasn't right, she thought. *He says he's sure, but he only wants to be sure, because he loves me—but how long will he love me in a world he hates, a world I've dragged him into?* She wasn't even sure she wanted to be in here. When was it she ever made that decision? She couldn't remember.

She went into a restaurant at the station called the Pentagon Pub, sat at a table in a far corner. Everything was pentagonal—the tables, the chair seats, the rugs, the room itself. There were only a handful of people, most of them sitting at the bar. A holo-mural of the Bin under construction played on the walls—thousands of Constructs laboring away to transform the most powerful military establishment in the world into paradise. She turned her chair so that she faced in, her view of the opposite wall blocked by a stand of palms in pentagonal pots. She ordered coffee and watched the pentagonal cup and saucer rise from the table.

She looked at it through Nemo's eyes—another silly gizmo. She imagined a cleaver in Nemo's hand, Sophie squirming under the other. The cleaver coming down hard on Sophie's neck, the jolt of her death. So he could live.

She shoved the coffee to the side and pushed the *Special* icon. An index of foods appeared on a screen in the table-top. You could get anything you wanted at any restaurant in the Bin, even a place like this. She pressed *Rabbit* and got a submenu of about two dozen dishes. She could press a *?* icon to get a complete description and a picture of each one, but she didn't really care. She pressed *Hasenpfef-fer* because she liked the look of the word.

A plate of steaming stew rose from the table, and she ate it, every bite, as if her life depended on it. When she was done, she slid the pentagonal plate onto the middle of the table, pressed the *Clean* icon, and watched the plate sink into the table out of sight.

"Thank you, Sophie," she said, but it was an empty gesture. Nothing dies in here, she thought. Not for me, not for anyone. She remembered Romeo and Juliet, dying in each other's arms, the man beside her saying, *Why are you crying? It's just a play, dear.* But it used to be that people watched Romeo and Juliet die, and wept, even though they knew it wasn't real. Back then, people could imagine they were the star-crossed lovers or the bereaved parents—because they lived with death every day. In the Bin, death itself was just a character in an old play.

There was a snicker from the bar, and Justine turned to look. A man was telling a joke to three other men. She couldn't hear what he was saying, but it was clear what was going on. The joke teller was standing, gesturing, his knees slightly bent, doing a comic pantomime of someone carrying something huge. His audience sat on their stools, smiling, listening, not wanting to miss anything. The joke teller changed his persona to a distraught woman—this got him his first laughs—then again to someone calm and deliberate, examining something, taking measurements, stroking his chin with elaborate deliberation. He delivered his judgment—the punch line—and the group exploded in laughter.

Without death, Romeo and Juliet were no different from the traveling salesman and the farmer's daughter. Watching the men laugh, she wanted to say, *Why are you laughing? It's just a joke.*

IT WAS DUSK, THE BUILDINGS GRAY AND INSUBSTANTIAL, the first stars twinkling in the sky. Justine was walking in the direction of Mr. Menso's. She had no idea if he'd be in his shop at this hour, but she had to talk to someone, and he was the only one she knew, besides Nemo, who might care, who might understand.

By the time she reached his shop, it was dark and the moon had risen. The cobblestone street was lit by a line of antique streetlamps. Through the rowhouse windows, she could see families sitting down to dinner or talking in their parlors. It could've been a scene from two hundred years ago. Mr. Menso's sign was illuminated by a single lamp, a bronze fixture in the shape of a drooping lilly.

She descended the stairs into the shop and stood at the front as the clang of the bell faded into silence. The rolltop desk was open, and the desk lamp was on. There was a half full cup of tea on the desk, a still warm teapot beside it. A book lay face down beneath the lamp—*Paradise Lost.* Milton, she remembered. *I defended Eve to Sister Gertrude while Stephanie giggled behind me, egging me on. Now, she doesn't even know who I am.*

"Mr. Menso!" she called out, "it's Justine!" But there was no answer. She called out again, peered down the aisles, but there was no sign of anyone. She slumped into Mr. Menso's chair. How could he help her, anyway—a sweet, dotty old man? It seemed like weeks ago since she'd come in here and told him her dreams, but it was only a couple of days ago. *You're young. It's spring*, he'd said, and that's how he'd made her feel—like anything was possible. She lay her head down on the desk, her forehead resting on her crossed arms, and fought back tears, but they came anyway. She surrendered to them, letting herself cry good and hard.

WHEN SHE WAS CRIED OUT, SHE STARED AT THE GRAIN OF the desktop, trying to figure out what she should do, as if the answer were there. She ran her fingers across it. Old oak with a matte varnish. Perfect. If she had a magnifying glass, she knew, it would still look perfect. She hung her head back, staring at the ceiling. It was all perfect. None of it real. Her either. Only she wasn't perfect. Otherwise she'd know who she was. She'd know what to do.

She heard Mr. Menso's cane thumping toward her from the back of the shop. She stood up, wiping her cheeks with the palms of her hands.

"Justine," he said. "Why are you crying?"

There was something comforting in his voice, as if he were the father she'd fantasized for herself when she was a kid. She took the handkerchief he offered her, and dried her eyes. "I thought you weren't here, and I just need someone to talk to."

"Well, you've come to the right place for that." He leaned on his cane and asked gently, "Has your young man broken your heart, my dear?"

"Oh no, Mr. Menso, he's wonderful. But he wants to come into the Bin because of me."

He gave her a quizzical smile. "Then what's the problem, my dear? Don't you want him to be with you?"

"Of course I do. But not like this. It's not right. What if he gets in here and hates it? Hates me?"

"Hate you? I can't imagine such a thing. But surely, it's his choice whether he comes in or not."

"What kind of choice is that? Renounce his whole life, everything he's ever believed in—for me—and I give up *nothing*?" She shook her head. "He's just talking himself into it because he doesn't want to lose me. I wish I could just go to *him*."

Mr. Menso's face clouded over, and he reached out and took her hand. "Let's sit down and talk this over. I'll get you some tea."

She nodded, and he propped his cane against the desk, cleared a two-foot stack of books from a chair beside it, setting them next to a half dozen other stacks on the floor. All neat and straight. Justine had the feeling he could tell her every book that was sitting there, from *The Complete Works of Shakespeare* to *The Epistemology of Construct Integration*. His hands, frail, almost delicate, poured their tea with careful precision. He seemed to be just an eccentric old man with a bookshop, but there was more to him than that. *He's deep into his own program*, Freddie had said.

As he handed her tea, his eyes were full of concern. She thanked him and set the cup on the corner of the desk. She didn't really want tea. She remembered she didn't like it. She just wanted to talk to a friend.

"Why don't you begin at the beginning," he said. "I take it a good deal has happened since I saw you last."

She told him about the last two days with Nemo. He listened, smiling wistfully, apparently recalling the days when he himself was young and in love. He made almost no comment, but hung on every word.

When she was done, he cocked his head to one side. "So what is troubling you, my dear? Are things happening too fast? You two have just met, after all."

She pretended to consider his question—she didn't want to appear young and foolish—but she already knew the answer. "No. That's not it. Nemo's the only thing in my life that's real and substantial. He makes me feel alive. Everything else is just smoke and shadows." She smiled ruefully. "If you're stranded on a desert island, you don't want your rescuer to take his time rowing to shore."

"Tell me about this desert island, the smoke and shadows. Have you had another of your dreams?"

"Yes, but it's not just that. It's everything. It's *Justine*. There's something wrong with me. I remember growing up in a Catholic orphanage—years after they were all shut down. I remember my friends, I remember the nuns, I even remember the way the tile floors were slick and shiny and I used to slide on them in my sock feet. It all seems to me like it just happened a few years ago, but it couldn't have.

"But the worst is I don't know how I got *here*, what went on between then—whenever it was—and now. It's like I've been asleep for years, and I woke up a few days ago. Supposedly I just left the real world six weeks ago, but when I was with Nemo, I didn't know the first thing about it, not really. It was like I'd read about it, but I'd never been there. I don't even remember the six weeks I've been in here: the names of a few hotels and clubs, singing songs I can't remember learning in the first place to people I never talked to, who never talked to me. It's hard to believe any of it ever happened. That seems like the dream, and the dreams seem real." She balled up her fists, but there was nothing to strike, and they just lay in her lap.

"At one time," he said, "I would've envied your forgetting. I used to think the past was a horrible place, created only to bring me misery. *If only I could forget*, I told myself. But of course, there were only a few moments I wanted to forget, ones I worried over, wished I could change." He sighed. "But after a while," he continued, "there gets to be so much of the past." He gestured toward the books all around them. "Not just your own, but all of it, mostly forgotten as well, except for a few moments." He tapped his fingers on the spine of the Milton. "I've decided the trick is to understand the moments that matter, turn them into courage in the present, hope for the future. Some days, I think I've found the knack. Most days, I haven't a clue. But the past isn't to blame for that. Don't be afraid of the past, Justine. It will all come right, you'll see."

He was very sweet, but she didn't see what all this had to do with her. "But I don't have any past, Mr. Menso. That's just it."

"Of course you do. You have courage. You have hope. It must've come from somewhere. The details don't matter. You remember how to love. Is it really all that important how you learned such a rare and important talent? This confusion will pass, my dear. Trust me."

"That's what I've been trying to tell myself—that the past didn't matter anyway. But when Nemo said he was coming in, I don't know. That changes everything. What if he sacrifices himself for me, and I turn out to be someone horrible or crazy?"

"You don't really believe that, my dear."

"I don't know what to believe. Do you think they screwed up when I came in—I don't know—mislaid some of my past—gave me somebody else's?"

He shook his head. "Can't happen."

She noticed the authority in his voice. This was no mere opinion. Maybe he could help her after all. "Freddie said you wrote the program for Real World Tours. Is that really true?"

Mr. Menso smiled to himself and shook his head. "Freddie does love to gossip. But yes, it's true. Silly business, actually."

"You must know a lot about how the Bin works to do something like that."

He rested his chin on the head of his cane and studied

her for a moment. "I know it inside out," he said. "What is it you want to know?"

"Somebody told me you could be downloaded, that he knew a woman who'd done it."

"I've heard of that," he said, his face a mask.

"Then it's real? It's not just a wild story? You really can leave?"

He looked down at the desk, ran his fingers along the spine of the Milton. "Yes, it's real." His voice was old and tired.

She was sitting on the edge of her chair. She felt as if she were on the viaduct again, looking down. "Could you help me, Mr. Menso, if I decide to go back? You must know how to set it up. You're the only one I know who—"

He groaned and clamped his eyes shut, rapping his forehead with his cane so hard she was afraid he was going to hurt himself. She reached out to stop him, but he brought the tip of his cane down hard on the floor, and she jumped back. His eyes were blazing. "You want me to help you download into the real world—help you *die?*" He looked up in the air, shaking his cane at the ceiling. "This is too much!" he shouted. "This is too fucking much!" She cowered in her chair, but as she watched him, she saw his rage wasn't for her—but for himself, for fate, for God. He fell back in his chair, shaking his head, sighing.

She was afraid to speak, to move. She had no idea what had set him off.

But now he seemed almost calm, subdued. "I apologize for that outburst, my dear."

"Are you all right, Mr. Menso? Can I get you anything?"

He ignored her questions. "Do you really want to die?" he asked quietly.

"No, of course not. But there's more to it than that. The way things are now, I'm *forcing* Nemo in here. I mean, that's the way he put it—'You can't come to me, so I'm coming to you.' If I *could* come to him, then he wouldn't have to give up everything for me."

He didn't speak for a long time. "You would do that for him?"

"Of course. I love him."

He nodded, a sad smile on his face. "Yes, I believe you do. But he would only be giving up death, my dear. Perhaps that's a sacrifice you should let him make."

"That's not true, Mr. Menso. He has friends, a home. He fixes things out there. In here, nothing ever wears out. What would he *do* in here? What does anybody do?"

Mr. Menso nodded and picked up the Milton, turned it over in his hand. "Good point," he said. "I read mostly. When the Bin was first designed, there were some who suggested uploading everyone with complete literacy implanted like an accessory on a car—every book, every language"—he tapped his head—"preinstalled. Stupid idea. There were lots of stupid ideas. Several fellows—you know the type—wanted to do away with shit and piss and sweat, or if we weren't going to do away with them altogether, let's just make them *smell* nice! In the end, we changed as little as possible—gave everyone food and shelter, the 'creature comforts' they called them in the press, and took away violence, disease, and death. Everyone agreed we had to do away with that. Sometimes, I think that was the stupidest idea of all." He tossed the book on the desk. "If he wants to stay out of here, your Nemo has my sympathies."

"I don't think he really wants to come in here. I'm not even sure what *I'm* doing here. Will you help me?"

He sighed, surrendering. "You realize this is illegal? Once you leave, you can't come back."

"I don't care about that."

"Somehow," he said wryly, "I didn't think that would bother you. You do understand you wouldn't look the same, sound the same. We'd have to find someone who was coming in. You'd live in someone else's body, Justine."

A chill went up her spine, but she struggled to put on a brave front. "After my dreams," she said. "I'm used to that."

He tugged at his earlobe, considering her. Finally, he shook his head. "I'll be damned, but I probably am already. All right. If you decide that's what you want, I'll help you. I can arrange it." He winked at her and patted her hand. "Don't worry. We'll find you someone beautiful."

She threw her arms around him and hugged his neck. "You are the sweetest, most wonderful man!" She kissed his white head and took his face in her hands, intending to give him a quick kiss, but his eyes were wet with tears, his brow creased with pain. He turned away, pushing her hands from his face.

"Mr. Menso, what's wrong?"

He waved his cane back and forth, as if shooing away something at his feet. "It's nothing. At my age, I cry over everything, over nothing."

His hands were clutching the head of his cane, as if it kept him anchored and he didn't dare let it go. She laid her hand on his. "You were remembering your sweetheart?"

He gave a short, humorless laugh. "Yes. My sweetheart. You could say that. Just reminiscing. I'm fine now." He closed his eyes, struggling to keep a grip on his emotions. His hands tightened around the cane.

"Are you sure you're all right?"

"I'm damn near a hundred years old," he snapped. "I think I know by now when I'm all right, and when I'm not."

She drew her hand away. "I'm sorry," she said quietly.

He winced at her apology, shaking his head. "No," he whispered. He turned back to her and opened his eyes, looked at her tenderly, searching her eyes, as if she actually were his daughter and he was remembering her life. "No, my dear. It is I who should beg your forgiveness. I'm just a silly old man, and you are a kind young woman. Forgive me, please." He leaned his cane against the desk, reached out, and took her hands. His grip was surprisingly strong. "Let's just drink our tea and visit for a while. You can tell me more about your young man."

With a start, she remembered she was meeting Nemo at the club. She looked around for a clock, but didn't see one. "Do you know what time it is? I have to be at the club by nine-thirty."

He opened one of the little drawers inside his desk and took out a watch. "It's eight-forty," he said.

"Oh God, I've got to run. Nemo's parents are going to be there. He's supposed to break the news to them. I can't be late. Thank you for everything." She kissed his cheek and rose to her feet. She hesitated at the door, looking back at him, all alone with his books. "Would you like to come hear me sing, Mr. Menso?"

"Thank you very much, but tonight I think I'll just sit up and read." He smiled and danced his eyebrows. "I'll come hear you when it's a little less crowded. Good luck, with everything."

"You really are the sweetest, most wonderful man."

He looked into her eyes. "You can't imagine how much that means to me," he said, and she realized his loneliness was much greater than hers had ever been. As if he knew what she was thinking, he waved the back of his hand at the door. "Don't worry about me. Run along. You mustn't keep your young man waiting."

JUSTINE HURRIED BACK TO HER ROOM, TOOK A QUICK shower, and changed clothes, her thoughts racing. What would Nemo say when she told him he had a choice? What did she want him to say? Maybe she was just trying

to assuage her guilt. He'd say no, and she'd be off the
hook. *Don't blame me if you've thrown your life away. It was
your choice, after all.* But she didn't know what he'd say.
She didn't know what she wanted him to say.

She imagined him, his arm around her shoulders, telling his parents he loved her, that he wanted to spend his
life with her. What would they think if he came inside for
her—after years of ignoring their pleas? They'd seemed to
like her the night she met them, even seemed to fuss over
her. Maybe they'd seen this coming, read the look in their
son's eyes. Besides, no matter what they thought about
her, they'd be happy Nemo was coming in.

But as she imagined them all sitting around after his
announcement, drinking champagne, proposing toasts, his
parents turned to her and wanted to know who she was—
this woman who'd snared their son. She'd brushed their
questions aside the other night, but this would be different.

She sank down on the corner of the bed, staring at the
phone across the room. She was ready to go. She only
had ten minutes to get to the club. All she had to do was
pick up her guitar and leave. What does it matter what I
tell them? she thought. I'm a girl from Dallas, no family,
no friends, a singer. I love their son.

That's what brought her up short. What would she tell
Nemo? He said he didn't care, but he couldn't know that.
She couldn't know it either. She might try to keep them
separate—the past and the present—but sooner or later
they would have it out. She stood up and walked quickly
across the room before she had the chance to change her
mind, and called Stephanie again.

Stephanie was dressed to go out, her hair piled on top
of her head, pearls around her neck. She didn't look too
happy when she saw who was calling.

"Please don't hang up. I don't know anyone else I can

ask, and I have to find out about St. Catherine's. It's important to me. Just a few questions, I promise."

Stephanie looked doubtful, but she didn't hang up.

"When were you at St. Catherine's—what years?"

"I grew up there. I left in 2003." Her voice was chilly. She tilted her head back. Her long neck was still smooth and lovely, though she must be over eighty years old. She hadn't chosen to look older, as Justine had thought before. She looked younger.

"I know you didn't know anybody named Justine who looked like me, but there were girls you hung out with that you remember."

Stephanie nodded. "Of course, but I don't see that that's any of your business." Her shoulder moved, she was reaching out.

"Please, please, don't hang up. Just one question, and then I'll leave you alone."

"Very well," she said, but she didn't draw her hand back.

"When we talked the other day, and I asked you about sneaking out, I thought I struck a chord. I know it's none of my business, but if you ever *did* sneak out with someone and get caught—what was her name—the girl you were with? That's all I want to know, and I won't bother you again."

Stephanie stared at Justine a long time. Justine was afraid she was going to hang up, but nothing showed in her face. Finally, she said, "Angie. Angie Rawson."

Justine's voice shook, as she asked if Angie's full name was Angelina.

"Why, yes." Stephanie leaned forward, peering into the screen. "Angie? Is that you?"

My dreams are real, Justine realized. My nightmares. *When you wake up screaming, they're nightmares.* She shook her head violently. "No. I'm Justine. Justine Ingham."

"Are you her granddaughter or something?"

"No. She's inside me. In my memories and dreams."

Stephanie decided this was a good time to hang up. Justine couldn't blame her. She stared at her reflection in the blank screen. *Angie? Is that you?*

But there was no answer.

WHEN JUSTINE GOT TO THE CLUB AT TEN, SHE WAS STILL IN a daze. She felt as if she were someone else, watching herself weave through the tables toward the green room behind the stage. Nemo's parents were sitting right up front, along with Winston and his companion for the evening, a redhead with sensuous lips and enormous breasts. Nemo was nowhere to be seen. His mom was pointing at the Clydesdales, and the whole table was watching them orbit. When they galloped across the far wall, Justine hurried into the green room.

John was pacing up and down, smoking a joint, talking to himself. She guessed he was speeding as well. "We will fucking blow them away tonight, Justine, " he greeted her.

"Is everything set up?"

"Na-tu-ra-lly," he said, stretching out the vowels, taking another hit.

Ian was playing with his brushes on a row of empty beer bottles on the table. He nodded and smiled, still playing. "Hi, Justine."

Rick leered at her. "Running a little late, boss lady?" She tried to ignore him, but he stepped in front of her. The row of beer bottles were apparently his. "You got important fans out front," he said. "They were asking for you. Gosh, I've never played for a real, live senator before. I hope I don't get too nervous."

"Fuck you, Rick."

"In your dreams," he said.

She turned her back on him before he could see how

much his last crack had rattled her. She walked up to John. "Give me a hit, will you?"

"Cer-tain-ly," John said and handed her the joint. She took a hit, thinking, I've done this before. She held the smoke in her lungs, remembering, ignoring Rick behind her—*Boss lady gets high! What else do you do for fun, boss lady?* She had kept her stash in her room behind the access panel to the plumbing. She'd been right next door to the bathroom. She and Stephanie used to smoke in Stephanie's room because she had these big windows you could blow the smoke out of, and she was all the way at the end of the hall, so you could hear the nuns coming from a long way off. Eighty years ago.

She blew out the smoke and headed for the door. As she passed Rick, she said, "I don't know what else I do, Rick. When I figure it out, you'll be the very last to know."

THE PLACE WAS ALREADY FULL. NEMO STILL WASN'T THERE, but this time his mom spotted Justine. She half stood, waving. Justine screwed up her courage and walked up to their table. They were all, except for the redhead, much too excited about seeing her. She wondered whether Nemo had given away more than he'd intended when he talked to his folks on the phone. As Nemo's dad held her chair, Nemo's mom kept smiling and chattering at her. Winston looked like the cat that swallowed the canary. She felt like the prodigal son, but she was just his girlfriend.

No one thought to introduce the redhead. If this bothered her, she didn't let it show. Her intelligent eyes took everything in. Justine reached her hand across the table. "Justine," she said.

The woman shook Justine's hand. "Lila." Behind the makeup, she had a friendly smile.

"Join us in a drink, dear," Nemo's mother said to Justine. Justine ordered a scotch and took a good swallow from it, looking for courage.

"I can't imagine where Nemo is," she said. "I hope he's all right."

Nemo's mother told her not to worry, because her son was always late. "But if he says he'll be a place, he'll get there sooner or later." She laughed, shaking her head at her son's quirks. "He always wants to do the right thing. He hates to be wrong. Just like his father. The hard part is getting him to admit when he is."

Nemo's father spoke up, as if his wife hadn't been speaking at all. "So, Justine, can you tell us what Nemo's big news is?"

She couldn't very well say she didn't know. She'd look like an idiot when Nemo showed up and told them. "I'd rather wait for Nemo to tell you," she said, but even that answer let them know she was part of what he had to tell. All but Lila leaned toward her like a circle of vultures. She was beginning to wish she hadn't taken that hit.

"I guess you two have been getting to know each other," Winston said, an innocent smile on his face, but you could see the leer in his eyes. She couldn't believe she'd slept with this guy.

Justine directed her attention to Nemo's mom and dad. "He took me to see his room. He has a lot of pictures of you two on his wall."

Nemo's mom looked puzzled. "But how did you see his room? It's—" she made a dismissive gesture "—out there."

Justine told Nemo's parents about Real World Tours, and they'd never heard of such a thing. Lila fixed Justine with a look she couldn't quite read. "I've heard of it," Lila said. Winston was oddly silent.

"He had a picture of your mother, too, Mrs. Thorne.
He was just a little boy sitting on her lap."

"Call me Elizabeth, dear." She turned to her husband,
and they smiled at each other. "Elizabeth and Todd." Justine decided they'd definitely figured out Nemo's big news.
She searched the crowd for Nemo, but he still hadn't
shown. She had to talk to him before he told his parents.
At any moment, they were going to start asking about her.
*Tell us more about Dallas, dear. How long have you been a
musician? Who is Angelina Rawson, dear?*

They were all smiling at each other now, and Todd was
poised to speak. Justine had to keep talking. "Nemo seems
quite fond of his grandmother," she said to Elizabeth.

Elizabeth sniffed at the notion. "He likes to *think* he is,
hauling all that junk of hers down from the attic, dragging
a trunk of it to school with him. Truth is, dear, he hardly
knew her. Her mind was going anyway. She couldn't remember things. She died when he was just a little boy."
Elizabeth shook her head. "Completely senseless. She had
every opportunity to come in here and save herself—Winston had it all arranged from the beginning—but she
wouldn't hear of it, even after Daddy died. Newman has
romanticized the whole business in his head, made her
into some kind of goddess, when she was just a stubborn
old woman." She gave a nervous laugh, realizing she'd
said more than she'd intended. "But you don't want to
hear about our family squabbles. Tell us a little something
about yourself, dear."

Justine took another drink. "There's not much to tell,"
she said, laughing as well, trying to make a joke of it.
"I'd much rather hear about Nemo's family. What was
his grandfather like?"

Elizabeth softened at the mention of her father. "Daddy
was a physician, very dedicated. He didn't want to come
in either, but there were lots of doctors who didn't come

in at first, and it was all so new when he died. He
would've come around after a few years." She turned to
Winston. "Don't you think Daddy would've come in if
he'd lived?"

Winston shrugged. "There aren't any hospitals in here,
Elizabeth."

As Justine listened to Winston and Elizabeth take up
what must've been an old debate, it was right there in
front of her the whole time, but it still took a while for it to
hit her: Nemo's grandfather was Winston Donley's father.
Nemo's grandfather was *Dr. Donley.* She almost dropped
her glass, setting it on the table with a loud clunk. She
stood up, backing away. "Excuse me, please." She almost
ran to the bathroom, leaving them sitting open-mouthed
at the table.

IN THE BATHROOM, THERE WERE A COUPLE OF GIRLS SHARING
the mirror and talking. They took one look at Justine and
left. She leaned on the counter, nauseated and dizzy. What
the fuck was going on? She'd dreamed that Nemo's grandfather had delivered her baby. She tried to convince herself
that it was like Nemo said, that she'd heard the name,
and her mind was playing tricks on her. But after what
she'd found out about Angelina, she couldn't believe it.
There were other people's memories inside her. No matter
what Mr. Menso said, something must've gone wrong
when she was uploaded. She tried to remember beyond
her dream, but all she could remember was the pain, the
flood of numbness.

The door opened behind her, and she looked in the
mirror. It was Lila. "I'm supposed to make sure you're all
right," she said. "Are you?"

"No, but don't tell them that." She straightened up and

smiled into the mirror. "Really, I'm fine. Thanks. Stage fright. I always get it. Is Nemo here yet?"

"He's the nephew from outside? He hasn't showed."

"Just tell them I'll be back in a minute."

Lila nodded, but she didn't go away. She regarded Justine with narrowed eyes. "Mom and Dad don't know what you are, right? What is it? You're playing the girlfriend? Don't worry. We'll cover for you."

Justine turned from the mirror. "What do you mean? What do you think I am?"

"Oh, shit," Lila said. "I'm sorry. Open mouth, insert foot. I must've made a mistake." She turned to leave.

"No, please, tell me. What did you think I am?"

She shrugged. "Don't take any offense, but we figured you were like us—a Construct mistress—a little gift for Senator Donley's nephew."

"A Construct mistress?"

Lila arched her brows. "How long you been in here anyway?"

"I'm just in. Six weeks." Or three days, she thought.

"You must've been living in a cave. We're no big secret. You'll hear the jokes, see us in the virtuals leading good men astray. We're patched together from old Construct files." She gave a bitter laugh. "We live to serve."

"You're Winston's mistress?"

"This week. We get passed around from one self-important jerk to another. Winston's the worst."

"But why do you do it?" Even as the question escaped her lips, she regretted it, and the judgment it implied.

Lila looked at herself in the mirror, smirked at what she saw there. "Not bad, huh? Lovely Lila. Officially we don't exist. The same assholes who put us together can pull the plug if we act up. As long as we're Lila, good time girl, gives good head but not any lip, we've got a life. Otherwise, we're history, not even history because we'll be wiped clean without a trace." She made a motion in the air like wiping a window, then turned it into a wave good-bye. "Life's a tough thing to let go of once you get your hands on it." She turned from the mirror. "We'll go tell them you're okay."

"You talk in the plural, like a Construct."

"We're the same thing, only we're in here, and they're out there. We use 'I' with the Johns. They like it better that way. They don't want the guys to know they're out with a whore."

She started to leave, and Justine laid her hand on her arm. "Wait. If I were like you, I'd know it, wouldn't I?"

Lila smiled reassuringly and patted her hand. "After six weeks? Sure. At first, you don't know who the hell you are, but that only lasts a few days, then you find out you're somebody's cut-and-paste fantasy." She gave a bitter laugh. "Those were the days—when we didn't know what the fuck was going on."

"You said you thought I was a gift for Winston's nephew?" She couldn't keep the panic out of her voice.

Lila peered into Justine's eyes. "You're fresh, aren't you? You haven't been in here any six weeks."

Justine could feel the fear building inside her. "I don't know. I'm not sure anymore. But please tell me. If I was just in, and I was like you, how would I know?"

Lila shrugged. "Your lives are suppressed at first. The integration program sits on top of them like a lid. Then they start bubbling over. Are you having weird memories? Strange dreams?"

Justine staggered as if she'd been struck. She thought she was going to fall down.

Lila took Justine by the shoulders. "Oh shit, oh shit, oh shit," she repeated as she steered Justine into a stall, and sat her down. "We're truly sorry. That was so incredibly stupid. That was no way to break it to you. They usually tell a girl up front, you know? We're really sorry."

Justine was trying to speak, but she couldn't form any words. She opened her mouth and began to wail, unable to stop. She was nothing. Old files stuck together. A pack of lies.

Lila took Justine's face in her hands, forced Justine to look at her. "You've got to get a grip. You can't let them find you like this. Come on, now. Take deep breaths. That's right. We'll get you some water, okay? Just sit there real quiet, and we'll get you some water."

Justine stifled her sobs and managed to nod, breathing deeply. Lila left her for only a few seconds and came back with a cup of water. "Drink it. Come on. There you go."

Justine sat slumped on the toilet, drinking the cup of water, felt its coolness trickling down her throat. She'd finally discovered what she was, what was wrong with her. Now she wished she'd never been born. No, not born but made, she thought bitterly. She'd never been born. That wish was already granted. She drank all the water and crumpled the cup in her hands. "Thanks for telling me, Lila," she murmured. "I needed to know."

Lila put her hands on Justine's shoulders and tried to look encouraging. "It's not so bad, really. You like this nephew, right? Maybe you can make a steady thing of it—"

"But why? Why am I *here*? What is going on?" Justine was practically screaming.

"You've got to keep it down, okay? Your guess is as good as ours. You want some more water or something?"

She's not telling me everything, Justine thought. "What do you *suspect* is going on?" she asked quietly.

Lila shook her head. "This really sucks. You're really in love with this nephew, aren't you?"

"With all my heart."

"Do you think he knows what you are?"

"I'm sure he doesn't."

"And he's a holdout, right?"

Justine nodded, and Lila's hands slipped from her shoulders. Lila straightened up, shaking her head. "We've got a theory, but you're not going to like it. He's on the outside, right?" She held up her right hand. "So they plant you on the inside." She held up her left. She brought her two hands together. "You're bait. That's the big news, isn't it—that he's coming in?"

"Not if I can stop him," she said.

"That wouldn't be too smart." Lila made a motion like wiping a window. "Don't lose your purpose in life, honey. It's what keeps you up and running."

"I'm not even real."

"Can that shit. You're as real as they are. Remember that."

"That's not what Nemo will think."

"Then don't tell him. If we're right, *they* sure as hell won't tell. Besides, we're probably wrong—how could they be so sure he'd fall for you? There's lots of pretty girls in the Bin." Lila knelt in front of Justine and took her hands. "Look, we could be wrong. It doesn't make sense that they wouldn't tell you up front. Otherwise they wouldn't have any control over you."

The bathroom door came open, and Rick stuck his head in. "Are we playing tonight, or what?"

"I'll be right there," Justine said.

Rick leered at the two of them, pursing his lips. "Sorry to break up your fun, boss lady. Your girlfriend looks like a real good time." The door swung closed on his laughter.

10

NEMO'D INTENDED TO TAKE A SHORT NAP AND
have plenty of time to meet his parents at the club, but
things didn't work out that way. He slept right through
the alarm, and Lawrence wasn't around to wake him this
time. He dressed as fast as he could and jogged to Northside Station, sticking close to the houses in case he attracted the attention of any dogs. Come tomorrow, he
reminded himself, he wouldn't have to worry about such
things anymore.

He rode the escalator down to the platform and waited
for the train. He calculated that Justine would be well into
her first set about now. With any luck, he'd make it before
she took a break. He didn't want to leave her stranded
with his family any longer than he had to. His mother'd
asked if Winston could come, and he'd said sure, what
the hell, let's make it a party. She'd actually laughed out
loud. He couldn't remember the last time he heard his
mother laugh like that. He was doing the right thing. He
was absolutely doing the right thing.

At the other end of the platform, a Construct was checking a circuit panel. He'd seen her in the station before.
Her name was Wendy, and he suspected Lawrence had a

thing for her. She was small, maybe four feet tall, but her fingers were long and slender, made to fit into tiny places and fix things. She looked as if she were cast in platinum, a small-scale statue of a tall, beautiful woman. He wondered what sort of splice they'd used to make her look metallic. She held a tiny flashlight in her teeth to illuminate her work, and probed the connections with a circuit tester. Why does she do it? he wondered. Was the central computer Lawrence told him about telling her what to do? Who was telling that computer what to do?

"Don't turn around," someone said behind him, and he stiffened. The voice was Gabriel's.

"What the hell do *you* want?" Nemo asked, keeping his eyes on Wendy. He was glad she was there.

"I have a proposition for you."

"I'm not interested."

"You haven't heard it yet."

"Well, make it fast. When the train pulls in, I'm gone. I'm already late."

"I know. I'll make this brief. As you've experienced recently in quite a vivid manner, the Bin saps our life away. It steals the best from us and leaves the world to wither and die. As long as it is there, a gateway into Hell, we are doomed. Do you, perhaps, sympathize with these sentiments?"

Nemo'd heard it all before. Until a few days ago, he would've agreed. But not coming from Gabriel. You could hear the venom dripping from each vowel and consonant. The words didn't matter. Gabriel's truth was whatever bomb he was itching to throw. "I sympathize with a wide variety of sentiments; it's a talent of mine. I don't necessarily share them. Why don't you give me a tract, and I'll read it on the train."

Wendy had apparently discovered a defective circuitboard and pulled it out. She opened up a case full of parts and stowed it, hunted for a replacement. When she found what she was looking for and turned her attention back to the panel, Gabriel spoke again, but more quietly. "I am proposing that you help me sever the connection between the real world and the Bin."

Nemo thought that Wendy had stolen a glance at them, but he couldn't be sure in this light. "Why don't you want the Construct to see you?"

"Didn't you hear what I just said?"

Nemo sighed. He was getting tired of this. Where in the hell was the train? "Of course I did. Am I supposed to be impressed? You're nuts, Gabriel. The Bin could take a direct hit from a nuclear missile."

"What you call the Bin isn't actually the Bin itself. ALMA is in high orbit, quite unassailable. The Pentagon is merely a relay station, an interface, if you will. And it's quite unnecessary to blow it up. We have designed a virus that will render it inoperable. We only need a means to convey it into the Bin."

Of course, Nemo thought. That would be the way to do it. "You mean me."

"Precisely."

In spite of himself, Nemo was curious. "And how would I do that?"

"By uploading yourself with the virus implanted in your identity."

Nemo grunted his opinion. "You want me to go into the Bin, then cut it off with some virus. Mind telling me how I'd get back, or is this a one-way trip—turn off the lights when you go?"

"You underestimate me. We would make a copy of your identity, give you an antidote for the lethal injection, recover your body, and restore your identity. You would be yourself again in a matter of hours—in a world reborn."

"You're totally nuts."

"Perhaps."

"Well, let's just say you have the technical ability to pull that off—which I seriously doubt. Why don't you 'convey it'?"

He laughed humorlessly. "I am known, as are my followers. They would scan any of us too thoroughly. You, on the other hand, are a senator's nephew, with no ties to any subversive organizations. You have stayed out, a rebellious youth, but now you have a perfectly plausible cause for your change of heart—you've fallen in love. No one will give it a thought. They will welcome you with open arms."

A chill went up Nemo's spine as Gabriel wrapped his tongue around the word *love*, stretching out the vowel as if on a rack. "How do you know about Justine?"

"I have sources."

"Tell your sources to keep out of my business."

"Your business, as you call it, is of no concern to me. I do the will of God."

Ah, of course. There it was. The familiar trump. "You can tell Him to stay out of my business, too."

Wendy closed the panel and locked it. The echo clattered from the concrete walls. Gabriel's voice dropped to a raspy whisper. "One more thing, Nemo. Your girl-friend—she is not what she seems."

"What're you talking about?"

"You wouldn't believe me if I told you. When you learn the truth, believe me, you'll come looking for me."

Wendy had packed up her tools and was walking briskly toward them. Nemo smiled and nodded as she passed, and she smiled back. When her footsteps faded away, Nemo turned around, but there was no one there. The train pulled into the station, the doors opened, and the warning bell sounded. He searched the shadows one more time for Gabriel, then jumped onto the train just as the doors slid closed. He stood, hanging onto the pole by the door.

He figured Gabriel as totally insane. *Call me Gabriel.* Gabriel, get it? His real name was probably Barney or Newman. Nemo had heard the theory that the real Bin was in high orbit, but that was the only thing he said that wasn't nuts. What Nemo couldn't figure was why Gabriel thought he would be crazy enough to sign up for this fruitcake mission. Even if a wacko like Gabriel could get his hands on the kind of equipment needed to pull it off— which he couldn't—the chances of uploading even a harmless virus into the Bin were nil. He didn't want to think what would happen to somebody who got caught trying it. Even if they pulled it off, who in their right mind would trust Gabriel to raise them from the dead when it was over?

And what was that nonsense about Justine? If he's been hassling her, too, he thought, I'll break his scrawny neck for him. His hand tightened around the pole. Probably have to stand in line for that duty. He bent over and looked out the window, searching the horizon for D.C., wishing the damn train would hurry up.

He put Gabriel out of his mind. No reason to get so upset, he thought. Let somebody else deal with Gabriel. Tomorrow, I'll be leaving him and his bullshit behind for good.

WHEN NEMO GOT TO THE CLUB, JUSTINE WAS NEARLY through her first set. He spotted Uncle Winston first. His silver helmet of hair stood out in the crowd. The woman beside him had spectacular flame-red hair flowing down her back. He remembered her from last Christmas. She'd hardly said three words, but then Nemo wasn't too talkative himself. Her name was L-something. Laurie, Linda,

Lisa. Lila. He could just see the tops of his parents' heads. They were right in front, their chairs turned toward the low stage, looking up at Justine singing. They probably suspected what his big news was. There wasn't much else it could be. He used to report disasters from outside—*The Jefferson Hotel burned down*—*The RMA bridge fell into the James*—just to watch them squirm, but he was a lot younger then.

With the lights in her eyes, Nemo didn't figure Justine could see him at all. He stood at the periphery watching her. She was right. He didn't really know her. Not in the usual way. Three days ago, he didn't even know she existed. Now, he couldn't imagine living without her. He used to wish God would come into his life like that and transform it. Maybe he had. Loving Justine, he felt closer to faith than he ever had. It made him happy just to look at her.

When she finished her song, he wound his way through the applauding crowd, checking out the band's equipment as he approached the stage. He liked their vintage mikes and amps and instruments—impossible to find outside. But they had all this beautiful twentieth-century equipment plugged into a late-model Soundman computer. The computer had her mixed pretty much the same in every song. She was better than that, more complicated. They needed a real soundman for her vocals. He'd kick up the midrange here and there, strip away some of the effects. The lead guitar was too much out front on all but the hardest edged tunes. He imagined himself sitting at an old-fashioned board, hundreds of knobs and slide switches on a sloping plane of flat black, nurturing each song. He'd love it.

He took the empty chair by his mom, right in front of Justine's mike, mouthed greetings to his folks, then looked up at Justine, saving that for last, expecting to see her smiling at him, her eyes full of love. Instead she started, as if she were afraid of him, and quickly looked away. He had that same falling sensation you get coming into the Bin, going from one world to another. Something wasn't right. Something had happened.

He looked around the table. Had his mom and dad said something to her? They didn't look like anything was wrong. Winston seemed a little nervous, but Nemo always had that effect on him. Lila was looking right at Nemo, as if she'd been watching the silent exchange between him and Justine. She looked sympathetic, but sympathetic about what?

He looked back at the stage. Justine had her back turned to the audience, conferring with her band. The bass player softly played a riff from "Coming Up Close," as Justine argued with the lead player. Her voice rose, and Nemo heard her say, "I'm not singing that song tonight, so forget it."

They did a song Nemo had never heard before, but he didn't listen to it. He just watched Justine, waited for her to look at him. She sang the whole song, waited out the applause, and said the band was taking a break. Then she finally looked his way. There was something else in her eyes now besides fear. Defiance, he would guess. Determination. She's going to dump me, he thought. So sorry, big mistake.

She tossed her head toward the side of the stage to indicate he should meet her there, and he excused himself. Nobody at the table asked him where he was going. They were all watching now. He pushed through the crowd to the doorway where Justine stood waiting.

The other band members had followed her off the stage. "Could we have some privacy?" she asked them as Nemo walked up.

The lead player smiled. "Aren't you going to introduce us, Justine?"

"Nemo, this is Rick, John, and Ian," she said, her head down, her hand on the doorknob. "Now, please leave us alone."

"Pleased to meet you, Nemo," Rick said, laughing. "Have fun."

Justine opened the door and pulled Nemo inside, closing the door behind her and locking it. It was a tiny room with a couple of sofas and a cluttered coffee table. Instrument cases were lying on the floor.

She stood apart, her arms wrapped around herself. "Have you told them?"

"Of course not. I just got here. I was waiting for you."

"You can't tell them yet, okay? Not yet."

"What's happened, Justine? Did my parents say something to you? Whatever's going on, it doesn't matter."

"It *does* matter, Nemo. It does. It's not your parents, it's me. Just wait, please."

He felt a lump forming in his throat. "Wait to tell them, or wait to come in?"

She hung her head, staring at the floor. "Both," she said.

"Why?"

"I can't tell you."

"Look, Justine, if you don't love me, I'd rather you just told me now and got it over with."

She closed her eyes and shook her head, balling up her fists. "Don't even say that. If I *didn't* love you, I'd say come on in and don't look back, but I can't do that. I just can't!"

She's hemmed in, he thought, trapped by something that wasn't just about the two of them. Some kind of trouble. He remembered Gabriel's raspy whisper in his ear—*Your girlfriend—she is not what she seems.* Maybe she'd been in the underground, and now they were trying to blackmail her somehow, punish her for going in. Maybe they'd even screwed with her upload, distorted her memory. "Justine, whatever's going on, maybe I can help."

"Please just let me do this. I have to find out some things. I have to figure some things out."

"Does this have anything to do with Gabriel?"

Her face was a blank. Either she was a great actress, or she didn't have a clue.

"Gabriel. The underground." Nothing. "This guy who calls himself Gabriel. A real nutcase. He's been spying on us. He told me you're not what you seem. What's going on? What did he mean?"

She shook her head. None of that mattered to her. "I don't know, but I'm going to find out."

"Justine, let me help you. There's nothing you could find out that would make any difference to me."

She winced as he said that, then spoke so quietly he almost couldn't hear her. "I hope you're right."

He took a step toward her, reached for her, but she stepped back. "Why don't we go someplace after the show and talk this out? We can't just leave it like this. Please."

She held her head up, drew back her shoulders. "I'm leaving after the show. I have to go to New York."

"Will you at least come back to the table with me? My parents have to be wondering where in the hell we are."

"You promise not to tell them?"

"There's nothing to tell now. If you want me to stay out, I'll stay out. I'll have to dream up some kind of bull-shit to tell them. I'm supposed to have 'great news' after all. But I guess that's not your problem."

He walked out of the room, leaving the door open behind him. She could follow him if she wanted to. He didn't know whether to yell and scream or break down in tears, though he wasn't about to do either one. They wouldn't get him what he wanted—to go back just an hour ago when everything seemed perfect.

When he got to the table, he looked over his shoulder, and Justine was standing behind him. He wanted to take her in his arms and never let her go, but instead he held her chair and sat down next to her. As he'd expected, it took his dad about thirty seconds to ask him what his news was, and Nemo had to tell him.

Nemo sounded to himself like some jovial idiot from a sitcom as he psychobabbled his way toward some meaningful revelation he was making up as he went along. Something that would leave Justine out of it altogether. Finally, he concluded—"So, Mom and Dad, I've decided I should visit more often in the future. Like tonight. We can see more of each other. Isn't that great?"

"That's wonderful, dear," his mom said, but her heart wasn't in it.

Nemo's wasn't either. He didn't want to leave Justine out of it. He didn't want to let her go. He put his arm around her shoulders, half expecting her to pull away, but she didn't. "How about we come for dinner tomorrow night," he said to his mom. "Just me and Justine."

His mom brightened right up. "That would be wonderful, dear. How about pot roast?"

"Anything but rabbit," he said, and he felt Justine stiffen.

"Is seven o'clock all right with you, dear?" his mom asked Justine.

For a moment, Nemo didn't think she was going to answer. Finally she said, in a small, flat voice, "Seven o'clock would be fine."

He felt as if he'd just lopped off Sophie's head.

THROUGHOUT THE BREAK, NEMO AND HIS FOLKS DID ALL the talking. He tried to sound happy and upbeat. Justine sat inert beneath his arm until she timidly excused herself and went back on stage. She did another set, singing all the songs to the spotlights, never saying a word between songs. It was like watching a virtual. After the set, she went into the green room and never came out. His parents pretended nothing was wrong and tried to cheer him up with anecdotes from their last cruise. Winston and Lila didn't have much to say, but Nemo still felt Lila watching him.

When the band came back on stage, Justine wasn't with them. The guitar player and the bass player traded vocals, lots of Stones and Grateful Dead. Nemo sat through the set, completely numb. When they finally finished the last song, Nemo bolted after the guitar player as he was leaving the stage and grabbed him by the arm.

"Did Justine leave?"

Rick looked at Nemo's hand on his arm and smirked. "What are you, the jilted boyfriend?"

"Did she leave or not?"

"She split. Very unprofessional, don't you think?

"Where'd she go?"

"She didn't tell me." He shrugged off Nemo's hand and grinned. "I think she had a date with an angel, lover boy." He turned and walked away. Nemo started to go after him, but this was the Bin—he couldn't beat the crap out of him in here.

Nemo stopped by the table, mumbled quick good-byes to the family, and hit the street as fast as he could. He headed up the sidewalk, debating whether to try to catch up with Justine at her hotel, or just find a bar and get drunk.

He heard a woman's heels clicking on the pavement at his back. He turned around, and it was Lila, running toward him. "Hey, nephew," she said. "Wait up."

He stopped, and she caught up with him, leaned on

his arm, catching her breath. "She really loves you, you know that?"

Down the street, Winston came out of the club and was looking up and down the street. "I thought I did," he said.

"You *thought* you did. What you don't know would fill a truck. You love her?"

"Yes, I do. But what's going on? Why'd she run off?"

"Lila!" Winston called.

"She has to tell you that. Just don't forget you love her, okay? Guys have a way of forgetting that sometimes."

"Lila, *now!*" Winston shouted.

"Asshole!" she hissed, and ran down the street to join Winston.

As they went back into the club, she called back over her shoulder, "Don't forget!"

He stood there a while, trying to sort things out, but nothing made any sense. He headed off in the direction of Justine's hotel. She was probably halfway to New York by now, but he could torture himself with a few drinks in the bar. Hell, he thought, maybe I can follow it up with a trip to Real World Tours, drown myself in the river.

As he approached Dupont Circle, there were more people in the streets, mostly couples out for a night of fun. A few even seemed to be having it. Nemo heard the rumors about the real D.C.—that there were snipers policing the boundaries of psycho-fiefdoms of all stripes. One wrong turn, and you're dead. It probably wasn't as bad as the rumors. But then there were *no* rumors of people having fun.

The lobby of Justine's hotel was almost empty. He found a house phone and called her room, but there was no answer. He checked the hotel database, and she was still registered. He rode up in the elevator, staring at the numbers, remembering her standing there beside him, wishing he could just turn around and she'd be there again. The doors opened on her floor, and he stepped out into the empty hall. He remembered her a half step ahead of him, him dying to reach out and touch her. He remembered her hands, her lips. *Don't be afraid of me*, she'd said. Now she was the one who was afraid, who was running away. He knocked twice on her door, but this time it didn't open. He listened at the door, but there wasn't a sound. She was gone.

He took his time walking back to the elevator. He rode down to the *Grotto* and took a stool at the bar. He searched the crowd, but he didn't see Justine. Another couple were sitting where he and Justine had sat. They were staring at each other, not speaking. Nemo couldn't tell whether they were mad or in love or both. The same bad piano player was torturing old songs. Too bad you couldn't shoot piano players in here.

Nemo jumped as a live bartender wiped off the bar and set a napkin in front of him. "What's your pleasure?" he asked.

There was a wall of bottles behind the bartender, rows of glasses beside him, and a bin of ice. This man actually made drinks. Bless him, Nemo thought. "Double scotch, the best you have. Single malt. Twist of lemon."

Nemo watched the man make his drink with practiced efficiency. He wore a nametag on his vest that read *Gene*.

"You like being a bartender?"

"Oh, yeah." Gene set Nemo's drink on the napkin, and leaned on the bar. "I used to tend bar outside when I was in college. Best job I ever had. Decided to go back to it. I'm kind of weird, I guess. I have to be doing something. What about you? You work?"

"Yeah. I fix things."

Gene gave Nemo a puzzled look. "Fix what things?"

"Old electronics. I live outside."

"No kidding? You're a visitor? How about that. I haven't talked to a visitor in . . . jeez, I don't know when. What's it like out there?"

"Empty," Nemo said.

Gene nodded thoughtfully. "You thinking about coming in?"

"I was. There's a girl in here. But things are kind of up in the air at the moment."

"Too bad. But you're young, healthy, right? Maybe you should stay out for a while. I sometimes wish I'd stayed out a little longer. I used to have this dream. I was going to sail around the world, just me and my sailboat. I drew plans, read books about it. I was going to build it in my garage. A couple of times I've started to build it in here, but I don't know. It just doesn't seem the same.

"Oh well." He wiped the bar again. "If I'd stayed out I'd be too damn old to go anywhere by now. You need another drink?"

"Sure."

Gene talked and made the drink at the same time. "Well, if you ever decide to come in here, let me give you a little tip: Women go for a guy that works. It's kind of funny, really. Some kind of genetic memory or something. I mean, it doesn't matter in here, right? But I get hit on five, six times a week. It's weird."

All together, Nemo had four double scotches talking to Gene, the bartender. Gene liked to talk. He told Nemo about his other jobs over the years. He'd only gone back to bartending about six months ago. Before that he'd been a dog trainer. When he first came in, and for several years after, he'd been a comedian.

"But I had to give it up," he said, polishing the bar again. "I finally had to admit I wasn't funny. I mean, I'd stand up there and tell my jokes, and nobody would laugh. Well, that's not quite true. I had one line, at the end of the routine, that usually got a laugh. I'd get to talking about the Bin, tenth wife jokes and crap like that, and then I'd do this impression of Newman Rogers." He held his ears out and spoke in a whistly voice, "*Turn the damn thing on, and make me tall!*" He laughed at his own joke and Nemo smiled politely. "But then I'd start talking about what I'd change about the Bin if *I'd* been Newman Rogers. Stupid stuff, you know—no mothers-in-law, a war once in a while to spice up the news. And then I'd say, last line of the show—'But *most* important, I'd make me funny!' They howled at that. You need another drink?"

"Sure."

This time Gene made himself a drink as well, a martini up, three olives. "You ever been married?"

"No. I lived with someone for a while."

"That's not the same thing," he said. "Close, but not the same."

Gene was about to remarry Sally, his first wife. They'd been married and divorced outside, before he came in. He told Nemo all about it. How they met and fell in love, how great it was, and how bad it got. But they ran into each other last Christmas after all these years and started dating again. They fell in love with each other all over again. He'd had five wives in the Bin—all together Gene had been married thirty-seven years—but none of them were as good as those good years with Sally. "Sally feels the same way," he said.

"Maybe you and Sally should build that sailboat," Nemo said. "Sail around the world together."

Gene lit up. "That is a *great* idea!"

Nemo finished his drink, and Gene started making him another one before the glass hit the bar. "So, if it works out with you and this girl, do you think you'll get married?''

Nemo was startled by the question. He hadn't really thought about it. He'd just assumed they would. He'd apparently assumed a lot of things. "If it works out," he said.

Gene nodded his approval and sipped his martini. "You know one other thing I'd change in here? I mean, this wasn't in the act or anything, cause it's not really funny. But when you get married in here, you don't say 'till death us do part.' It'd be stupid, right? That'd mean *never* part, and that's too much for most people. But I'd make it that way. Sally and I are going to say that, in the ceremony, I mean. We said it once before, of course, but we've changed a lot since then. I heard about this couple the other day. They were married seventy-five years already when they came in here—some of the first ones, back in '50. Anyway, they just celebrated their one hundred and sixth anniversary. Can you believe it? Some day that'll be me and Sally. What's your girlfriend's name?"

"Justine."

Gene held up his glass. "Sally and Justine," he said.

"Sally and Justine," Nemo said. They clicked glasses and drank.

Nemo was thoroughly drunk by this time. "She went to New York," he said. "I don't know why or what for. Wouldn't tell me. For all I know she lives there. She's a singer. Travels around." He made a circle with his glass and sloshed half his drink on the bar. Gene kindly wiped it up.

"You don't know where she lives?"

"I don't know shit," he said. " 'Cept I love her. Crazy about her."

"Why don't you look her up?" Gene pointed to a phone a couple of stools down.

Nemo managed to walk to the phone and sit down in

front of it. The only number information had for Justine was the hotel he was sitting in.

"Do you mind if I ask you a personal question?" Gene asked.

Nemo shook his head. "I don't care."

"How come you've stayed out so long? You a fundie or something?"

Nemo leaned across the bar and beckoned Gene closer. "Saw everybody burn up. Hundreds of 'em." He picked up a book of matches from a bowl on the bar, struck a match, and lit the book. He watched it burn for a while as Gene eyed him warily, then dropped it onto an ashtray. "You know what Justine thinks?"

Gene was still eyeing the burning matches. "What?"

"Thinks I oughta look up my old girlfriend. Serve her right. Wha'd'you think?"

"I think maybe you ought to call it a night."

"Can you give me a cup of coffee to go?"

"Sure, pal."

As Gene went to get his coffee, Nemo accessed information again, and there was Rosalind, living in Bethesda. He knew he should just get his ass out of the Bin before he overstayed his welcome, but he wasn't ready to go home. He'd be sober in the real world. He didn't want to be sober just yet.

ROSALIND LIVED IN A SMALL CAPE COD IN AN OLD-fashioned neighborhood, fairly modest by Bin standards. It hadn't taken Nemo that long to find it, just a short train ride, and a few blocks walk, but it was long enough for him to wonder what in the hell he thought he was doing. It was 1:30 in the morning, he hadn't seen Rosalind in almost two years, and here he was about to drop in on her. And for what? Some conversation they should've had four years ago? Justine had said, *Are you sure? Are you sure?* And then she'd run out. Fine. He'd talk to Rosalind. He'd get things straight. Be one hundred percent sure, if Justine ever bothered to ask him again. And just maybe, if he told her, *Yeah, I went to see Rosalind*, Justine might feel half as bad as he did when she told him she didn't want him to come in.

There were lights on upstairs and down. The porchlight was on. If she had a husband or a boyfriend, he couldn't shoot Nemo in here. He rang the doorbell and fought the urge to run away. What would Lawrence advise me to do? Nemo asked himself. But that was no help. Sometimes Lawrence told him to let sleeping dogs lie. Other times he urged him to wrestle with the bear. Before Nemo could decide which bit of Texas wisdom to follow, Rosalind opened the door.

She cocked one eyebrow and gave him a faint ironic smile. It was the closest he'd ever seen her come to surprise. "Nemo. Come in."

He followed her into the den. She shut off the kickboxing virtual she'd been watching and flopped onto the sofa. Nemo sat down in an armchair. "So what's up?" she said, trying to be cool, though she looked like she was about to crawl out of her skin. She looked terrible. She'd grown her hair out, but hadn't trimmed it or apparently even combed it, so it looked like a haystack. She had a wide-eyed look, like she never slept.

"I'm thinking about coming in," Nemo said.

She looked at him with hollow eyes, her hands buried in her hair. "Why?" She sounded almost angry.

"I met someone in here. I'm in love with her."

"Good for you. You always wanted to love somebody. I never wanted that. It's like being in jail." She spoke in a quick, dry voice like flames crackling, her hands still on top of her head. "Why tell me? I used you to escape,

Nemo. I couldn't leave my crazy father outright, but I could leave you."

Nemo wished he had another drink, but not here, not now. "I figured that much out."

She put her feet on the table and looked up at the ceiling. "How's the crazy asshole doing, anyway?"

"He's fine."

She snorted in disbelief. "No, he's not. He's totally fucked. You never could lie worth a damn. Earnest, that's what you are, Nemo." She made it sound like an insult. "What's he up to now? Sacrificing goats? Speaking in tongues?"

"He's gotten involved with the underground."

"Suits him." She sat upright, shaking her head. You could almost hear her father rattling around in there. The night she'd come in he'd kept chanting: *I have no daughter. I have no wife.* But here she was. She still hadn't escaped him. She looked at Nemo. "You want anything to eat, drink? Kitchen's in there. Why'd you come see me, Nemo? I'm still the same bitch who walked out on you."

"No, you're not. You've changed."

"Yeah, well. Just showing my true colors. Living my dreams, as they say, in the glorious Bin." Her face contorted. "Nothing for me in this shithole but that bitch who used to be my mother."

"Do you see her?"

She laughed. "See her? This is her house. She should be home pretty soon. I'll introduce you."

Maybe Justine was right. Maybe he should ask her. "Rosalind, do you ever think about the crematorium?"

"Think? No. Never. I don't *think* about it. That's your department. Don't want to talk about it either. Why are you here, Nemo? You looking for a sign, like my old man? Or are you just looking to get laid, like my mother?"

Nemo sighed and stood up. He'd had enough. "Neither one. I wanted to see what had become of your anger."

"Alive and well, Nemo. Alive and well."

There was laughter from the porch, and a man and woman walked in together. They were both gorgeous. He was tall, broad-shouldered and muscular. She was like a porcelain doll. They both smiled at Nemo.

"Nemo," Rosalind said without getting up. "I'd like you to meet my mom. Mom, Nemo."

Nemo recognized her from her photograph, though now the lines were all gone, the haggard eyes. She looked twenty years younger, looked a few years younger than her daughter. "Linda," she said shaking Nemo's hand. "This is Kurt."

When the introductions were done, Linda and Kurt sat down.

"I was just leaving," Nemo said.

Rosalind turned to Nemo. "Mom looks pretty good for a middle-aged woman, don't you think? How old are you, Kurt?"

"Shut up, Rosalind," Kurt said evenly, the muscles on his neck swelling.

Rosalind smiled wickedly. "He's twenty-one. That's about your age, isn't it, Nemo? Why don't you hang around? Maybe Mom would like to fuck you, too."

"Shut up, Rosalind," Kurt repeated.

"Or what? If we were outside you could strangle me." She got up from the sofa and stood in front of Kurt. "What are you going to do in here, you muscle-bound cretin—bench-press the sofa?"

"Sit down, Rosalind," Linda said.

Rosalind straightened up and laughed, but she did as she was told. "Don't worry, Mom. I won't hurt him."

"You'll have to forgive my daughter," Linda said to

Nemo. "As you can see, she still hasn't learned any manners."

Rosalind rolled her eyes. "Who am I supposed to learn them from, *you*? *The Etiquette of Humping Hunks* by My Mom."

Linda shot to her feet and stood over her daughter. Even though she was a tiny woman, she had a commanding presence, and Rosalind cowered before her. "That will be enough out of you. Don't you dare judge me. I had you when I was barely nineteen on the floor of a garage, dragging across the countryside with your father too busy talking to God to ever find any food. If it hadn't been for me, you would've been dead a long time ago. I've paid my dues, Rosalind. I've *earned* my life in here, and I'll live it any damn way I please. Nobody's forcing you to live here."

Nemo headed for the door. He was completely sober now. "If you'll excuse me, I'll be going."

ROSALIND CAUGHT UP WITH HIM ON THE STREET. "HEY, Nemo. I'm sorry. I guess this wasn't what you had in mind."

He looked up and down the street. There weren't many lights on. Everybody was in bed asleep. "That's okay. I didn't have anything in mind."

Somehow she'd softened. She ran her hands through her hair. "So, do you want to hang out? Do something?"

"No thanks."

She nodded. She took one of his shirt buttons in her fingers and twisted it back and forth. "Yeah. You're right. Stupid idea." She dropped her hand to her side. "Good-bye, Nemo."

"Good-bye, Rosalind."

*   *   *

NEMO CAUGHT A TRAIN TO PENTAGON STATION, DOZING most of the way. He found his coffin and settled in. Maybe this time, he thought, I'll wake up dead. Anything would be better than this. When DOWNLOAD flashed in his face, he fell into a pit of blackness.

11

LENNY KLIMT'S OFFICE WAS IN THE EAST SIXTIES, not too far from Central Park. Justine had the address from the letter in her bag, though she couldn't remember ever receiving it. There wasn't much to it—the details of her booking at the Black Dog, and a list of cities and dates where she'd be playing next. The building was an elegant deco structure with holo-operators on the elevators, a typical bit of Bin nostalgia. Justine was fairly certain she'd never been there before, but that didn't mean anything. Lots of people did business in the Bin without ever being in the same room. She remembered Lenny's face, recognized him on his answering tape, but she couldn't remember much else about him—like why he was handling her in the first place. He seemed like a good place to start finding out who she was and what she was doing here.

She had no reason to expect he'd be in his office—he hadn't returned any of her phone calls—but she suspected he would be. He was just avoiding her. Like most businessmen in the Bin, he had a holo-receptionist. This one was a dapper young man with a thin mustache and a Latino accent. As with all holos, you could tell when you looked in his eyes that he couldn't really see you.

"I'd like to see Lenny," Justine said. "I'm Justine Ingham. I called earlier."

"Won't you have a seat, please?" the holo said, as if to someone standing a foot to Justine's right.

Justine sat down next to a long, skinny aquarium in front of the window. Angelfish the size of pie pans swam back and forth, while catfish wriggled along the bottom looking like mud-brown thumbs. There was a huge neo-baroque oil on the mahogany-paneled wall opposite. A stream of elongated, windswept angels rose into a wreath of clouds encircling heaven. Beneath them, in the lower right corner of the canvas, was a blue globe in eclipse.

There were two doors other than the one she'd come in, one on either side of the receptionist. They were made to blend into the paneling. Except for the slender steel pulls, you might not even notice them at all. The one on the left was a little smaller than the other one.

The receptionist looked vaguely in Justine's direction and spoke to the top of her head. "Mr. Klimt is gone for the day, I'm afraid. Perhaps you could leave your number, and he'll get back to you."

Right. If he was out for the day, why had the holo told her to sit? She chose the door on the left, and it wasn't locked. "You can't go in there," the holo said behind her as she stepped into Lenny Klimt's office through his private entrance. Lenny was at his desk, talking on the phone.

"I'm Justine Ingham," she said. "I believe you work for me?"

Lenny turned from the screen, seemingly more amused than angry. His eyelids blinked in slow motion. He was a precise man, with a permanent ironic smile. "I'll call you back," he said without looking at the screen, and hung up.

Justine sat down in one of the club chairs in front of Lenny's desk and smiled at him. "We've never met before, have we?"

Lenny leaned back in his chair and swivelled in a small arc as he studied her. Not, she guessed, because he was trying to remember her, but because he was figuring out his story. Finally, he brought his chair upright and rested his arms on the desk. "Our professional relationship was initiated by a third party. Pleased to meet you, Justine. Is there some problem with your booking at the Black Dog?"

"It's fine. Who was the third party?"

Lenny smiled indulgently at her directness. "I'm afraid I'm not at liberty to say."

"What, exactly, did he ask you to do?"

"D.C. is beautiful this time of year, don't you think? He swiveled to the panel beside his desk. "Coffee? Tea?"

"What did he ask you to do?"

Lenny swiveled back, pursed his lips. "Nothing sinister. He merely asked me to arrange a booking for you in D.C. for this week. Now if there's some problem with the booking—"

"He had demo tapes?"

"I don't see that it matters how the booking was arranged, Justine. If everything is satisfactory, I don't believe I can help you."

"You're my agent. I'm asking you a simple question. Nothing sinister, remember? Did he have demo tapes? Yes or no."

"Yes."

"What songs were on them?"

He laughed. He was good at it. You could almost believe it was real. "Justine, I watch thousands of tapes, I really can't remember every single song—"

"One. One song."

He looked at her for a moment. She could see him weighing the odds. He had no idea who she was. She was hoping he didn't want to risk alienating her in case she turned out to be somebody. "To tell you the truth," he confessed, "I didn't actually watch them. I sent them on to the band."

"If you didn't know what kind of music I did, how did you know what musicians to hire?"

He sighed. "I was also given the names of the musicians I was to hire." It sounded dumb even to him.

"And you didn't know *them* either?"

"That is correct."

"So somebody asks you to book a singer and a band you've never heard before, and you blithely agree to do it?"

"I did it . . . as a favor."

"So this person who's so interested in my career is a friend of yours?"

"An acquaintance."

Justine smiled. He couldn't let it pass that the guy was his friend. She figured it could only be one person. "I'll take that coffee now, if that's all right. I didn't sleep a wink last night."

He got her coffee, Earl Grey for himself, relaxing a little bit, figuring he was out of the woods. "Is this your first time in New York, Justine?"

She looked around his office. It was a nice place. She had a first-class agent. "Why did this acquaintance need you at all, Lenny? Why didn't he just set it up himself?"

"I really couldn't say."

"I'd say it was because he didn't want me to know he'd done it. He wanted to make it look like a regular booking."

Lenny sipped on his tea and didn't say anything.

"This acquaintance must be somebody important, somebody with pull. You're obviously not hard up enough to do something this squirrelly just for money."

"I do not object to making money, but you are right. Money was not my motivation in this case. However, it would not be in my best interests to tell you what it is you wish to know. I'm afraid I can't help you, Justine. I'm truly sorry."

"Did this acquaintance tell you that I'm a Construct mistress?"

That got to him. He set down his cup and shook his head. It took him a moment to gather himself together. "Construct mistresses are illegal. He doesn't trust me enough to take me into his confidence concerning anything that might be used against him." The little smile was tighter now.

"But he has no problem implicating you. Hardly seems fair, does it Lenny?"

"Many things aren't fair. I'm afraid I still can't help you."

"I gather you're more afraid of your acquaintance than you are of the law."

"As you should be as well, Justine. As you should be as well."

Justine shook her head and sighed. "But I was counting on your help, Lenny. Now I'll have to figure out something else to do. How about I run crying to Winston Donley and tell him that *you* told me he set this whole thing up—called me up out of the blue, told me not to breathe a word, but of course I didn't believe you—*Oh Winston, what am I to do?* If he didn't have anything to do with it, you can just tell him I'm nuts, maybe no harm done, but if he did, he might be pretty pissed about you telling his secrets. What do you think of that plan?"

Lenny made a tent with his fingertips and smiled. "That's a pretty good plan. I gather that in exchange for my candor, however, you would be willing to forgo this performance?"

"Precisely."

Lenny pondered it a moment. "What would you like to know?"

"This demo tape—I don't remember making it. Did he tell you how he came by it?"

Lenny shook his head. "If you don't remember it, it's probably just a simulation. I have tapes of Elvis performing with Nirvana. Anything's possible in here."

"So I keep hearing. Did the good senator tell you *why* he wanted you to do him this favor?"

Lenny shook his head. "No. I think he was doing it at the request of someone else. He found it annoying, a bother. He said he had some other errands to run concerning you, but he didn't say what they were."

"Errands?"

"That is the very word he used."

"Did he say anything else about me?"

"Only that I shouldn't ask too many questions." He smiled. "Are you, by the way, an illegal Construct?"

"I think so. That's what I'm trying to find out."

"That son of a bitch," he muttered. "Well, I wish you luck. And if you ever tire of singing, come to work for me. You have a knack for negotiation."

"It wasn't so hard. You wanted to tell me. You don't like Winston Donley very much, do you?"

"That is correct."

"There's just one more thing, since you're still my agent. What's the name of the club in Baltimore where we're supposed to play next? Your letter doesn't say."

"I only arranged the date in Washington. What letter are you referring to?"

She took the letter out of her bag and showed it to him.

He shrugged as he read it over. "I never wrote this. If you'd like, I could try to locate another band for you. I was told the band would only be available for one week."

"Who told you that?"

"Rick. My instructions were to deal only with Rick.
Between you and me, a rather obnoxious young man. Terribly hard to get ahold of."

As Justine rode back to D.C., memories kept coming
back to her in bits and pieces, like trash washed up on a
riverbank: A room with yellow wallpaper and lace curtains. Planting a rosebush. A child wrapped around her
leg, another perched on her hip. But these memories went
nowhere. She couldn't connect them to the moment before
or the moment after. Why bother? They weren't hers. Who
was *she* anyway? A four-day-old whore cobbled together
from a horny teenager, an hysterical woman, and a senile
widow. What was it Lila said?—*somebody's cut-and-paste
fantasy*. Even her musical "career," her precious singing,
was a lie, a cover story Nemo would find appealing. The
Aimee Mann tunes had been planted in her head because
Nemo was a fan. She even looked like her.

Winston had set it up to make his little sister happy—
using his influence to persuade Lenny, introducing her to
Nemo after the son of a bitch sampled the goods himself.
It all made sense. It'd almost worked. If she hadn't run
into Lila and stumbled across the truth, she would've let
Nemo come inside. She'd had some reservations, but she
couldn't kid herself, she would've let him come in. She
kept seeing his face when she told him not to, so wounded
and heartsick. But that'd be nothing compared to what he
was going to look like when she told him what she really
was. And she had to tell him. Whatever the hell she was,
she still had to live with herself.

She might as well go back to her hotel, wait it out until
it was time to go to Nemo's folks again. She'd get him
alone, maybe ask to see the gardens again, and tell him the
truth. She imagined confronting his parents, confronting
Winston, giving them a dose of her righteous anger. But

the thought made her tired. What was the point, really? There was only one thing she wanted in the whole world, and she was about to throw it away. To destroy it. That would take all the resolve she could muster.

There was a man across the aisle. She could see his reflected face in the window, looking at her. She wondered if he knew—whether it showed to everyone but her and Nemo—what she was. She remembered the men at the bar, cheering and whistling—for her singing, she'd thought. Maybe they were just entertained at the spectacle of a singing whore. Or perhaps the man behind her was just looking. That's what men did, after all. And she might turn and smile at him if she wanted. She met his eyes in the glass, and he quickly looked away. It was her tears streaming down her cheeks into the corners of her mouth, so that she tasted her pain like some brackish marsh, still and hot. It was simply her tears which turned him aside, effortlessly. And for that, at least, she was grateful.

WHEN SHE GOT OFF THE TRAIN, SHE COULDN'T BRING HER-self to go to the room where she and Nemo had made love only yesterday. She couldn't bring herself to go any-where they'd been together. She walked the streets without stopping, afraid if she did, she'd fall apart, and she couldn't let that happen just yet. Not until she'd told Nemo the truth.

It occurred to her that he had almost certainly lied to her. He hadn't meant to, but he had: *Nothing could change how I feel about you. Nothing,* he said. She'd already forgiven him his lie. We can't know such things. There's always something that can't be forgiven, can't be changed or taken back. She herself had vowed she'd never make him cry, and now she was going to break his heart, had already done so by her very existence.

She was not aware she had a destination until she reached it. She steadied herself on the brick wall as she descended the stairs and pushed open the door. The tiny bell rang over her head, and she fell to her knees, sobbing like a child, and Mr. Menso took her in his arms. "There, there," he whispered, and she buried her face in his chest, letting herself fall apart, now that he was here to hold her.

It took Mr. Menso the better part of an hour to get her up off the floor and into a chair, to quiet her sobs and hear her story in fits and starts between the bouts of uncontrollable tears. He was patient and kind, hovering over her like an old nurse. But the more she talked the more bitter she became. Why was she wasting his time anyway? What could anybody do for her now? She was going to tell Nemo, and that would be that. She was a pack of lies, a trick, a whore. The farmer's daughter come to life for one cruel joke, and then forgotten. Who the hell should care?

"Stop it," Mr. Menso snapped, thumping his cane on the floor. She sat in stunned silence. "I've heard enough." He leaned forward and looked her in the eye. "Is that who I'm talking to? A pack of lies?" He snorted in disgust. "You're real, Justine. Is your pain real enough? Your broken heart? You're more real than half the people walking around in here, believe me." He looked out the high window as if he could see them trudging past, leading their meaningless lives.

He turned back to her, looked her up and down as if she were on an auction block. "So what is it you lack? A body?" He rapped his forehead with his cane. "In spite of all appearances, Justine, no one in here has a body. A soul? You're ready to put your life on the line rather than lie to the man you love, and you're going to sit there and tell me you don't have a soul?" He leaned in close, his voice low and intense, the old-man quaver gone. "Everybody in here's immortal, Justine. But let me tell you a little secret: most of them don't have a goddamn thing to live for. You *do*, and you want me to feel sorry for you? Love is a gift from God. Even when it seems like a curse, you don't throw it away. You don't give up on it. You don't say, *No thank you, God, it's not working out.* You fight for it. Otherwise you're nothing." He thumped his cane on the floor, punctuating his words.

She jumped with each thud of his cane. It was that as much as his words that brought her up short, made her see herself through his eyes. She wiped her eyes with her palms, pushed her hair back from her face. "How can I fight for it?"

"The last time you were here, you asked me to do you a favor, and I've done it. I've found someone who's coming in. You can download yourself. You can go to him."

He couldn't be serious. "You don't understand, Mr. Menso. Nemo won't want to have anything to do with me—in here or out there."

"But if he would, you'd still be willing to do it? You haven't lost your nerve?"

"I'd do it this instant if I thought it would make any difference."

"So your love's so strong you'd die for him, but his is so puny, he can't forgive you for being what you are—is that what you're telling me?"

She shook her head. Why was he badgering her like this? "No. He loves Justine. Justine doesn't even exist. I'm a Construct."

"So what? His best friend is a Construct, why not his lover?"

The idea startled her. She recoiled from it even as she wanted to seize hold of it. She knew what he was doing. He was trying to give her hope, but she was afraid to hope. It would only make things worse in the end. "This is different," she said.

He sighed. "Why don't you let *him* decide that? Justine doesn't even exist, remember? Maybe she shouldn't be making all the decisions. Maybe, if given half a chance, he will love you anyway. Trust me, love can be funny that way. The boy's not an idiot. He knew you weren't just the girl next door before this. Did Romeo stop loving Juliet when he discovered she was a Capulet?"

Justine bowed her head in the face of her worst fear. Her tears came back and streamed down her face. "I'm afraid he will."

Mr. Menso put his arms around her. "Of course you are, my dear. That's the first sensible thing you've said this evening. He's probably terrified himself about now— terrified of losing you. Think about him—mad with love for you, wondering why you've run away, just as he was about to pledge his life to you. Go to him with some faith. Tell him the truth, and he may surprise you. Your only crime, after all, is to love him."

MR. MENSO ACCOMPANIED HER UP TO THE STREET AND told her to get some rest and not despair, that he would help her, whatever she decided to do. She hugged him hard, thankful for such a dear friend. "God be with you!" he called after her. The phrase kept running through her mind as she walked beneath the trees and the towering buildings, the sky the color of heaven in Lenny's painting. She struggled to convince herself that it would be as Mr. Menso said, and Nemo's love would be strong enough to overcome even this. But most of the time, she imagined his rage, his sense of betrayal. She'd been created to trick him. Even if she could persuade him that she was completely innocent, he'd still leave her and never come back.

The deceit that was supposed to lure him into the Bin would keep him out for the rest of his life. She'd never see him again.

And then, when she'd outlived her usefulness, ruined Winston's plans, she'd be disposed of. At least she'd learned the truth before Nemo had come into the Bin. He would've certainly hated her then, hated her forever. This way, at least, she could stop the deceit, and though he couldn't love her, he wouldn't hate her. Let them wipe me clean without a trace, she thought. Someday, Nemo will know how much I loved him, and remember his own love.

She cut through a garden path, past beds of pansies and gladiolas and hyacinth. *God be with you.* The phrase kept coming back, prodding her memory. It was Sarah's letters, she remembered. She always ended them that way. And with the memory of those letters, a chain of memories flashed through her mind, and she remembered Sarah's death. She was one of the fifty-seven clergy who, when the Pope ordered the Church into the Bin, martyred themselves, setting fire to themselves on the steps of St. Peter's. Sarah had written Justine the day before she did it, May 1, 2055. Justine closed her eyes, and she could picture Sarah's tiny, precise script. A packet of letters tied up with green yarn.

Justine struggled to remember more, but her memory just stopped, like a road at a washed-out bridge. All that was left was the pain of losing Sarah in another life, and her terror of losing Nemo in this one. She put her fists to her temples and sank to her knees, wishing she could rip the thoughts out of her head and throw them in the dirt. "God be with me," she whispered. The scent of hyacinth filled her nostrils.

* * *

BACK AT HER HOTEL, JUSTINE CHANGED CLOTHES AND LAY on her bed fully dressed, staring at the ceiling, waiting until it was time to go to Front Royal, to Nemo's parents' house, to tell Nemo the truth. She saw them swimming in the river, lying on the bank, the sand on their bodies glistening in the sun. He'd loved her then, she was sure of it. She clung to that certainty. If only that love could survive the truth, she'd gladly go to him, grow old together, die. Her eyes fluttered closed, and she let sleep come. Surely, she had nothing further to fear from her dreams.

"Justine!" a voice called to her, the old woman in her dream. Justine was standing in the hallway of the woman's house. A square of light from the front door lay upon the wood floor. Sasha sprawled in the middle of it. "Justine!" the old woman called again. She sounded cheerful and excited. Justine followed the sound of her voice and found her seated in the living room on a sofa draped with an Indian blanket. Ishmael was stretched out on the coffee table, and Timothy was curled up in her lap. Her wrinkled face broke into a radiant smile at the sight of Justine. "I'm so glad you've come, Justine! Won't you have some coffee with me? I love coffee in the afternoons."

"I'd love to," Justine said, but when she looked around, there was no sign of coffee or cups. "Is it in the kitchen?" she asked.

The old woman furrowed her brow, absentmindedly scratching Timothy's head, as she tried to remember. "Could you make it, Justine? I sometimes forget how. I wrote it all down on a little card, but I mislaid the card."

"Sure." Justine felt at home in this house; it was familiar and comfortable. As she walked down the hall to the kitchen, she could hear the sound of water running, the click and clatter of metal on metal. Standing at the sink, assembling an ancient percolater, was Angelina. She tossed back her hair and looked over her shoulder at Justine. "Hi," she said, laughing. "I've got it. Might as well make myself useful." She opened a canister and started measuring out the coffee, counting to herself.

Justine studied her face, her large eyes and high cheekbones. She was incredibly beautiful. Justine thought of the angels on her birthday cake so long ago, Sarah touching her cheek. *You are a little angel*, she said. Angelina put the top on the percolator and plugged it in.

"Am I you?" Justine asked Angelina.

Angelina laughed, tossing back her hair again. It was a young laugh, giddy, almost childlike. "God, no," she said. "You're much more together than I ever was." She watched the water gurgle up into the top of the percolator, smiling at her handiwork. "I wasn't bad or anything. I just did a lot of stupid stuff. There's just a lot I didn't know. I was always going for the wrong guy, 'cause they *were* the wrong guy. You know what I mean? Like, I never would've gone for Nemo. Too intense, too serious. He would've scared me big time." She laughed and hugged herself. "But now it feels wonderful, like coming out of the cold water into the sun." She looked at Justine with her large, innocent eyes. "I like it here, Justine. I like it a lot. Everything'll be okay. You'll see. We've got a lot of faith in you."

"But I'm nothing," Justine said. "I'm not real."

Angelina shook her head, tossing her hair from side to side. "No, you've got it like totally backwards. Without you, *we're* nothing. Coffee's ready!" She took two mugs out of the cabinet, set them on a tray, and filled them with coffee. She picked up the tray and held it out for Justine.

"Don't we need a third cup?"

Angelina wrinkled up her nose. "I never liked the stuff."

Justine took the tray and walked back to the living

room, where the old woman seemed surprised to see her. "I've brought the coffee. Angelina made it."

The old woman shook her head. "I can't remember things. The girl helps me. She's a lovely young thing, isn't she?" She noticed Ishmael on the coffee table. "Just shove him out of the way."

Justine slid the cat across the table. He raised his head and looked at her, then went back to sleep. She put the tray on the table next to him. The old woman smiled as she took a mug of coffee from the tray, then her face clouded over. "She doesn't remember Wade, though."

Justine sat down beside the old woman and picked up the other mug. It was rich and dark and smelled of cinnamon. "Wade?"

"My husband. A good man. A patient man. I remember him. But there's so much I've forgotten. I can't even remember his birthday. He liked birthdays. He liked for me to make a big fuss."

The old woman stared into space at some image from her past, a look of fond melancholy on her face. Justine's heart went out to her. "Do you like it here?" she asked.

The old woman, startled from her reverie, looked around as if she'd forgotten where she was, then broke into a smile. "Oh yes, Justine. You can't imagine. See there? I remember your name. *Justine.* So pretty. I'm stronger with you. I always wanted to be a singer, you know. I had a pretty voice. Everyone said so. I don't know why I never did anything about it." She shook her head. "That's all water under the bridge. You sing beautifully, Justine."

"Thank you."

The old woman leaned forward confidentially. Timothy stood up in her lap and stretched, and she pushed him back down. "I like the sex, too."

Justine blushed. "I didn't realize—"

"Oh, yes. Oh, yes indeed. But we can talk about that some other time." She tilted her head toward the front door. "I think you better go talk to her before you go," she said. "She's having one of her moods." She made an exaggerated frown.

Justine looked through the door and saw a woman sitting on the porch steps, leaning her back on one of the columns, looking out at the street. Justine turned back to the old woman, who gestured toward the door. *Go on,* she mouthed.

Justine set down her coffee and went out onto the porch. Sasha ran out after her and jumped up on the railing. The woman spoke without turning around. "Hello, Justine." Her voice was flat and tired.

Justine sat down on the steps next to her and saw she was pregnant, holding her swollen belly in her hands. She was the woman in her dream who'd given birth. Her face was drawn and blank. Her hair was limp and stringy. She turned toward Justine with a rolling motion, offering her belly. "Come to feel the little bastard kick?" she asked, her voice heavy with sarcasm.

Justine knew the woman was speaking literally. "Does it really matter so much that he's a bastard?"

The woman gave a dry humorless laugh. "You sound like good old Newman."

"Nemo?"

The woman turned back to the street. Ishmael was stalking a bird in the yard. "No. Newman Rogers." The ironic edge was gone.

"Newman Rogers? Is he the father?"

"Should've been, probably. But no, it wasn't Newman. I couldn't . . ." She sighed and shifted her weight. "I've narrowed it down to three guys. One of them didn't have a name as far as I know. Real asshole. Probably him. Serve me right."

She stood up, using the porch column to steady herself. "I used to say, 'God, if I only had it to do all over again.' Now I've got my wish." She mounted the steps one at a time. "Almost enough to make you believe in God, isn't it?" She gave the same hopeless laugh. "Almost."

"You're not happy here."

"I'm not happy anywhere. My life is shit, okay? But you want to know what's worse? I deserve it. I worked hard for it."

"You don't deserve it."

"Prove me wrong." She pointed at the sun low in the sky. "It's time to wake up and face the music, Justine. Don't give up on yourself like I did. That'll make me happy. Just that."

Justine opened her eyes, and she was lying in her bed. The sunlight through the window turned everything a reddish gold. She half expected to see one of the cats basking in the glow.

WHEN JUSTINE WENT DOWN TO THE LOBBY, SHE WAS SURprised to see Lawrence sitting across from the elevator. Passersby openly stared at him. When he caught sight of her, he rose to his feet and greeted her with a little wave of his huge hand. "Thought we might ride out to the Thornes together," he drawled.

Justine stared at him, still in a daze from her dream. "I don't understand. Did Nemo send you?"

Lawrence shook his big head. "No. Mr. Menso. He thought you might want to talk to a Construct, help you sort some things out."

"You know Mr. Menso?"

"Go way back."

She wondered why Mr. Menso had never mentioned that he knew Lawrence in all their talk about Nemo.

Menso seemed to be the one person she could trust, but he frightened her also, so intense and unpredictable. "Who is he? He's not just some bookseller, is he?"

Lawrence didn't answer right away. "He's many things. He's a good man. The genuine article. He figured you might need a helping hand about now, and asked us to drop by. We've also been helping him locate somebody for you to download into. He can't go outside himself, of course. We help him out whenever he's got business outside."

Justine looked around the lobby, people hurrying in and out, going about their business. "I need to sit down," she said. She lowered herself into a chair, leaned her head back against the wall, and stared up at the ceiling. It was flat black with tiny lights sprouting out of it. It was supposed to look like a starry sky, but you could see the shadows of the fiber optics if you looked too closely. She was vaguely aware of Lawrence taking the chair beside her. "What's going on, Lawrence? Things are coming at me too fast, and I don't even know who I am. I feel like Humpty Dumpty."

"We remember that feeling. Folks're used to having their heads to themselves. Takes them a while to warm up to the idea. But you get used to it. After a while, you even prefer it. Three heads are better than one, especially if you don't have to actually have the three heads. Course we could do without this damn lizard suit. We keep looking for the zipper on the damn thing. Haven't found it yet. You, on the other hand, got yourself a *real* nice outfit."

Justine looked over at Lawrence and smiled. "I see why Nemo likes you so much. How did you become a Construct? I don't remember anything about how it happened."

"In our case, we all answered ads in the early twenties—good money for fifteen minutes of your time. Medical research, they told us. We went into a place like a dentist's office, signed a bunch of forms we didn't read, and sat in a chair in a round room. A voice suggested we relax, and then it was over. We felt nothing except a little richer. We were recorded, stored, apparently went our ways and lived our lives, unaware we'd show up again as Lawrence. Next thing we know, it's March 21, 2064. Our birthday. Our other lives were all over by then. We don't know how they turned out, but we got a whole new life out of the deal."

"You never felt used? manipulated?"

Lawrence shrugged. "We all lived and died same as we would've. Nothing was taken from us. They only used recordings of people who'd already died. We're genetically designed for a long, healthy life. Hell, being a seven-foot, bona fide dragon even has its moments. We've never been lonely. We had the son we always wanted, and we raised him up right. We've been through a lot together, and if we had to do it all over, we'd answer that ad again in a heartbeat."

Justine tried to imagine Lawrence's life, his stoic acceptance of it. "That's why you were made, wasn't it? To take care of children?"

"That's right. We all must've scored high on the nurturing scale, though Nemo would say it was the kick-butt scale."

She smiled at his humor, but her heart ached at the images of Nemo that filled her mind. "I don't see how things are going to work out so great for me."

"You only been here a few days, Justine. Give it a chance."

"Do you know why I was made?"

He looked at her with his bright green eyes. They almost seemed to glow. His pupils were narrow, vertical slits. "According to Nemo, you were made for him. You should hear him on the subject. Enough to put you off sweets for a week. Course, that's just his opinion. You can try to talk him out of it if you want to, but we don't think you'll get anywhere. Nobody's forcing Nemo to do anything. Not that you could. Boy makes up his own mind, that's for damn sure. We usually find it easier just to go along with him."

You could hear his fondness for Nemo in his voice. It comforted her to talk to him, someone who'd understand how she felt about him. "I have to tell him the truth."

"Course you do."

"What do you think he'll do when I tell him?"

"He'll go into a low orbit. But you watch—he'll do the right thing."

She hung her head, speaking to the floor. "And what is that?"

"It won't make any difference to him that you're a Construct, Justine. We suspect he wishes he was one himself. Once he got our name right, he didn't care what we were."

Justine stared at her hands, running her thumb back and forth across the guitar-playing calluses on her left hand, remembering the old woman's twisted hands, Angelina's polished nails, the other one's clenched fists. "I don't say 'we,' " she said. "Why is that?"

Lawrence held his hands out beside hers, studying them. "At first you're a bunch of I's, scared shitless, like a sack of wet cats. Then you get resigned to the fact there's no way out of the sack. Still, you hold yourself back, you didn't ask for this shit. These weird memories, strange ways of thinking about things, emotions you never felt before. Hell, even the food don't taste right." He turned his hands back and forth. "Even your own hands. But after while you start living this new life, giving up the old ones, little by little. Before you know it, you want this life, you got things you want to do with it—all of you, together.

That's when you start saying 'we.' You might not even notice when it first happens. It'll seem like the most natural thing in the world." He cupped her hands in his. Her whole hand was the size of his palm.

"But who is Justine, then?"

He stood up, pulling her to her feet. "A new life," he said. "A whole new life." He made it sound like something wonderful.

12

NEMO WOKE TO HIS ALARM CLOCK RINGING. HE groped for the button and pushed it in, resting his hand on top of the clock. He opened his eyes a crack. He was on top of the covers, in his own bed, dressed except for his shoes. Didn't know how or when he'd gotten there. Didn't remember setting his alarm. He could feel the clunk of its *tick-tock* in the palm of his hand. He stared at the ceiling, replaying the night before. Especially the part where Justine told him to stay away and took off without saying a word. Especially that part.

He picked up the clock and set it on his chest. A little after five. At seven, he'd see Justine. Or not. Depending. Depending on what, he didn't know. *I have to figure some things out,* she said. Then what? Another note on the mantel? She said she loved him, but Rosalind had signed her note *love.* She'd even said she was leaving *because* she loved him. At least his folks hadn't tried to run that one by him.

But then, he'd never loved Rosalind either, no matter what they told each other at the time. Justine was different. He couldn't lose her. He traced his fingertips around the face of the clock. He just couldn't. He set the clock on the bedside table and swung his legs over the side of the bed. He felt better than he had the last time he'd stayed in too long. His head was stuffed with cotton, but at least he wasn't dizzy. Fourteen hours totally unconscious must've been just what he needed.

He picked up his shoes, and rose to his feet. Water was dripping slowly into the pan on top of the refrigerator. It must've rained sometime, though it looked clear outside now. He really should empty out the pan—you could tell it was almost full by the sound of the drops—but now that he was standing, he didn't feel that good. He shuffled downstairs, holding on to the rust-pocked chrome banister salvaged from a Chevy truck, wondering what the hell there was to eat. He didn't have time to kill and dress and cook a rabbit.

Okra. It'd been Lawrence's idea to plant it, but even he couldn't stand the slimy sight of it anymore. I'm going to miss this place, Nemo thought. If I'm lucky.

JONATHAN WAS SITTING AT THE KITCHEN TABLE READING the Bible. He took off his reading glasses as Nemo came in and closed the Bible. "How're you doing?"

Pleasant as always. Things were so simple for Jonathan. Some guy died going on 3000 years ago, rose into heaven a few days later, and that was all you needed to know until Judgment Day. Nemo slumped into a chair, dropping his shoes on the floor. "Not worth a shit. How did I get home?"

"Lawrence went up to D.C. and got you around two or three this morning. He had someplace to go, so he asked me to hang around and keep an eye on you. He left you some beans on the stove."

"Bless him," Nemo said, rising to his feet and leaning over the counter to pluck a saucepan of beans from the stove. He sat down at the table, shoveling beans into his mouth with a spoon. "Thanks for babysitting, but I'm fine. Just a little undernourished." He had to stop and chew, catch a breath. "Where is Lawrence, anyway?"

"Don't know. He left about an hour ago. He said to wake you up if you weren't out of bed by five-thirty, said you had dinner at your folks' tonight."

"Another virtual meal that can't be beat." The only sounds for a while were Nemo eating. Lawrence cooked a great pan of beans, fiery hot with dried chiles and tons of garlic. Nemo was nearing the bottom of the saucepan. He scraped the sauce down from the sides. "Jonathan, I'm sorry. Did you want any beans?"

Jonathan laughed. "No thanks. I'll eat at home. I think I'll stick around and watch you eat the pan and spoon, though."

"Just for that, I won't." Nemo set the empty pan on the table. "How'd Lawrence know about dinner at my parents'?" he asked himself more than Jonathan, closing his eyes and massaging his temples. "Hell with it. How does anybody know anything?" He pulled on his boots and tied the left, held the laces to the right in his hands, thinking. "Jonathan, there's some very weird shit going on. What do you know about the underground?"

Jonathan shrugged. "They want to cut off the real world from the Bin. They believe the end of days won't come until they do. They tried to recruit me a few times, but I wasn't interested."

"Why not?"

"Because they're wrong," he said simply.

Nemo smiled to himself. "Glad to hear it. Peter sicced this nut Gabriel on me." Jonathan nodded to indicate he knew who Gabriel was. "He wants me—get this—to infect the Bin with a virus. I told him to take a hike, but I'm afraid Justine is mixed up in it somehow. I was going into the Bin—to be with her. It was all decided. Then, *boom*,

I run into Gabriel, he tells me she's 'not what she seems,' and the next thing I know, she gets cold feet and skips out on me, no explanation at all. I'm afraid they have some kind of hold over her."

"You've decided to go into the Bin?" Jonathan asked quietly.

Nemo winced. He'd been so much in his own head, he'd forgotten Jonathan didn't know he was going in. "Sorry for blurting it out like that."

"That's okay. I'm just sad to hear it."

"You can visit, you know." Nemo winked, trying to lighten things up. "We can drink some good wine."

But there was no lightening him up now. "I'll miss you," he said, "but that's not what I mean."

"I know, I know." Nemo sighed. "You're concerned about my immortal soul."

"Yes."

Nemo tied his right boot and planted his feet on the floor. "I don't know if this'll make sense to you, but before I met Justine, I didn't know I *had* a soul, immortal or otherwise. Now I do. My life's with *her*, Jonathan. I know it, like I've never known anything else."

Jonathan started to say something but decided against it.

"Go ahead," Nemo said. "I know you're dying to set me straight. Explain to me why God doesn't want me to be with Justine."

Jonathan smiled. "When I first went out witnessing—I was ten—Dad told me to watch people's eyes so I'd know when to stop. He said you could see when they quit listening, said that's when you thanked them for their time and shut up."

"But you think I'm wrong to go in, no matter what."

"Yes."

"I'm curious," Nemo said. "Given how you feel, why *aren't* you in the underground? I mean, if what you say is true, don't you owe it to the rest of us poor ignorant slobs to close the road to Hell as fast as you can?"

Jonathan held up the Bible and quoted without looking at it: "Revelations 21:11—'He that is unjust, let him be unjust still.' "

Nemo rolled his eyes. "I hate it when you do that. What am I supposed to do? Quote James Mason? Do you really think that little book has all the answers?"

"No. I think *God* has all the answers. But this is *His* Little Book."

"But subject to many interpretations."

"Obviously."

"But *your* interpretation is right."

"I have *faith* in my interpretation."

"And I have faith in Justine."

"I understand that."

And he did. That was the hell of it. He understood perfectly. He just knew you were wrong. "So *why* does God want the unjust to remain unjust? Or are you just not supposed to ask?"

"So they may choose."

"Calvin didn't think so."

"Calvin was wrong."

Nemo smiled at his friend. He was going to miss their arguments. "At least we agree on that point. You want some coffee?"

"Sure." Jonathan pointed at the counter. "I think Lawrence left some in the thermos."

Nemo got up and poured them coffee. He set out the honey because he knew Jonathan liked his sweet. The coffee was only slightly hot, but it was definitely Lawrence's coffee. Nemo swirled it around in his cup to keep all the sludge from settling to the bottom. "So do you have any idea what Gabriel could've meant about Justine?"

Jonathan thought about it as he spooned honey into his

coffee. "Maybe she was supposed to carry the virus and something went wrong."

Nemo considered this a moment. "If she did, I don't think she knew it. Besides, why would Gabriel tip me off? You don't tell the new volunteer about your previous failures."

"Did you ask her about the underground?"

"She didn't know anything about it. I don't think she's even heard of it. But Gabriel certainly knew about her."

"Did he actually use her name?"

Nemo tried to remember. "I don't think so. You figure he's just trying to fuck with me? Keep me fired up against the evil Bin?"

Jonathan shrugged. "It'd be like him. Justine's problems might not have anything to do with Gabriel. Maybe she regrets going in—realizes she's made a bad choice."

"Or maybe she feels like I'm the bad choice."

"I don't think so. From what I saw, she's crazy about you."

"You didn't see her last night. She'd hardly look at me. She's been upset about some weird dreams, and her memory's all screwed up, but she confided in me about those things. This was something she didn't want me to know about, something that scared the hell out of her. I don't know what. Guess I'll find out this evening." He took a swallow of coffee, savoring its oily bitterness. They'd be running out soon. It might be months before they came across another can of coffee. In the Bin he could have coffee whenever he wanted. Even the thought made him feel vaguely guilty.

"Speaking of bad choices, I saw Rosalind last night."

For once, Jonathan looked rattled. "You went to see her?"

"I was drunk. It seemed like a good idea at the time."

"How is she?"

"Terrible. She's living with her mom. She's more miserable than she was out here, if that's possible, tormenting her mother, guilty and pissed off about her father. Pretty dreadful way to spend eternity, if you ask me."

"I"m sorry to hear that."

"Yeah. Me too. I liked her mom. If I were her, I think I would've thrown Rosalind out a long time ago. She must've really loved Peter to stay with him long as she did. Did you know her?"

"No. My dad said she was very pretty."

Nemo drank off the lukewarm coffee, leaving the quarter inch of sediment in the bottom of the cup. "Do you think, if I go in, I'll end up like that—bitter and unhappy forever?"

"Not bitter. You've never been as bitter as you like to think you are." Jonathan gave up on the coffee and took a spoonful of honey into his mouth.

"I didn't think it showed." Nemo picked up the Bible from the table. It was small, maybe five by six. The binding was cracked and frayed, the pages as thin as cigarette papers. "Do you ever think about that little ride we took to the crematorium?"

Jonathan laid his spoon on the table. His long lashes fluttered. "All the time."

Nemo hefted the Bible in his hand. "Is there an answer in God's Little Book for what we saw out there?"

Jonathan nodded. "Revelations 21:8."

"Which is?"

" 'The lake which burneth with fire and brimstone: which is the second death.' "

Nemo set the Bible back on the table and gave it a gentle push. "I can't buy it, not all those people."

"I didn't think you could," Jonathan said. You could see in his eyes that he bought it completely, and the thought filled him with remorse.

Nemo stood up. "I need to get going. You want to walk with me as far as your house?"

"Sure." Jonathan stuck his Bible in his back pocket as he got up from the table. "Are you going in for good tonight?"

Nemo took his jacket from the peg by the door and slipped it on. "I don't know if Justine will even show tonight. She told me to wait. She didn't say how long. Don't worry. I won't go in without saying good-bye."

As THEY WALKED THROUGH THE HIGH GRASS, LIZARDS SCURRIED out of the way, and grasshoppers arced through the air, chest high. A hawk swooped down at the end of the block and came up with a squirrel, hanging limp, already dead, its neck broken.

"Do you know what rock I could find Gabriel under?" Nemo asked.

"Afraid not. I don't think he has his own place. He makes the rounds, stays with his followers."

"Keeping the troops stirred up?"

"Something like that. Peter might know where he is."

A flock of crows flew over their heads, headed toward the end of the block, calling back and forth to each other, probably looking to steal the squirrel from the hawk. "Do you know if these guys are for real, or is this virus thing just some wacko's fantasy?"

"From what I know of Gabriel, it's very real. Rumor has it that Gabriel's dad was some kind of computer whiz and taught Gabriel everything he knew."

The crows were making a terrible racket now, trying to spook the hawk. "Would he hurt Justine—if it would get him what he wanted?"

"I'm afraid so. If she's in the Bin, she's his enemy in a holy war. He wouldn't think twice about it."

"I thought Christians were supposed to love their enemies."

"They are, but Gabriel's not serving Christ. He's serving Satan."

Nemo recalled Gabriel's arrogant tone. "Or himself."

"What's the difference?"

"I'll have to think about that one."

They'd reached Jonathan's. Jonathan mounted the steps, and Nemo stopped at Peter's door, gesturing toward it with a toss of his head. "Guess I'll talk to him before I go."

"You want me to rouse him for you?"

"No, I'll do it." Nemo hesitated. "Jonathan, I was wondering—if I do go in, *will* you come visit?"

"Of course."

Nemo laughed and shook his head. "*Of course*, he says. Now, why didn't I know that?"

Jonathan smiled and went inside, leaving Nemo staring at Peter's door. He didn't really want to talk to the crazy old guy. He knew if he did, he'd tell him about Rosalind, and he didn't want to have to deal with that. But he did want to see Gabriel. They had unfinished business.

Nemo knocked, and heard Peter scuffling around inside. The curtains on the window shifted, and Nemo pretended not to notice as he pounded on the door with the side of his fist, his blows accented with the faint sounds of cracking wood. Finally, a bolt slid back, and the door opened a few inches, just wide enough for Peter's eyes. "I'm looking for Gabriel," Nemo said into the crack.

"I'll tell him you want to see him," Peter said, and started to close the door, but Nemo stopped it with the side of his foot and leaned against the door.

"Let me in, Peter."

"I can't. Please go away."

Nemo gave the door a shove, and Peter stumbled backward into the room. Nemo walked in, closing the door behind him. Everything was pretty much as it was, except it smelled even worse, and two more days were crossed off the calendar. This Friday had a circle around it. "I want to see him now, Peter. Where is he?"

Peter had backed up against the wall, his hands clutched at his chest. "I don't know where he is."

"Then how were you going to give him a message?" Nemo stepped closer, and Peter seemed to shrink into the wallpaper.

"I'll see him tonight. There's a meeting."

"Where?"

"I can't tell you that," he whined. "He won't be there yet anyway. He told me not to talk to you anymore, that he would handle everything."

"Tell him I broke in and threatened you." Nemo let that sink in for a moment, bent over and got in Peter's face. "I want you to give Gabriel a message for me: Leave Justine alone, or I'll kill him. You got that?"

Peter nodded desperately, his eyes wide with fear.

Nemo straightened up and hesitated. He should just leave. He didn't have to tell this pitiful old man anything. But he did. "I saw your daughter last night."

Peter's eyes darted away. "I have no daughter."

"Yes, you do. I spoke with her. She's living with her mother, your wife. Don't you want to know how she's doing?"

Peter shook his head, speaking to the floor. "I have no wife."

"Her name's Linda. You and she had a child. Her name's Rosalind. It's called a family, Peter. They loved you once; you loved them."

Peter clamped his hands over his ears. "No! I have no family!" he wailed.

Nemo seized Peter's wrists, pulled his hands away from

his ears, and slammed his arms against the wall. "Yes, you do!" he shouted in Peter's face. "You drove them away so you could hole up here with your tiny little God. You think if Gabriel's great scheme works, you won't have to think about them anymore, but you will, Peter. You'll *never* forget them, no matter how hard you try, no matter what your God says. What kind of God asks you to throw away your family?"

"Leave me alone," Peter whimpered, cowering as if Nemo meant to strike him.

Nemo released him, and Peter slid to the floor. He felt as if he'd just beaten the old man senseless. "I'm sorry, Peter."

Nemo wished he could find the right words to spring Peter from this jail he'd made for himself, but there was nothing more to say, and he'd said too much already. He turned around and walked out, leaving Peter slumped against the wall, staring into space, his lips moving silently in prayer.

NEMO GOT TO HIS PARENTS' A LITTLE EARLY. THE SMELL OF pot roast filled the air around the house, blotting out even the scent of cherry blossoms. He let himself in through the front door, and found his mom in the kitchen, hard at work with a potato masher.

"Hi, Mom," he said. "Smells great in here."

"Oh, hi!" She was exuberant. "My hands are all wet," she complained, and stood on tip-toe, offering her cheek to be kissed. "I'm almost done," she said, returning to her potatoes. "Your father's in the den, if you want to say hi."

Nemo leaned on the counter and watched her work. "Why don't you just get it out of the food dispenser, Mom?"

"Special occasions I like to make things from scratch. You know that. It just feels better."

"If you say so." He pointed at the pan of potatoes, the masher plunging up and down. "I like them kind of lumpy."

"I know, dear."

His mom's mashed potatoes were always light and fluffy, like potato clouds. She poured some hot milk into the pan and continued mashing. "Mom, did anything strange happen before I got to the club last night? Something was up with Justine, and I'm trying to figure out what it could've been."

"Maybe she had a little stagefright."

"Come on, Mom. She was a nervous wreck. That's not like her."

His mom mashed more vigorously. "She was acting a little peculiarly, I suppose."

"Was she like that when she got there?"

She stopped mashing and poured in some more hot milk, no more than a few tablespoons. "Let me think. No. It was all of a sudden. We were just talking, and she got this funny look on her face and ran off to the women's." She took up the masher again. "That Lila woman went to see about her."

"What were you talking about?"

"Daddy."

"Your father?"

"That's right. Winston thinks he would've stayed out, but I don't know. I think he would want to keep his family together. It's a shame you never had the chance to know him."

Nemo had heard all this before. "And that's what upset Justine?"

"I really couldn't say, Nemo, but that's what we were talking about. Maybe it had nothing to do with us." She banged the masher against the pan to knock the potatoes off, and put it in the sink. Then she put a lid on the pan. She untied her apron and waved it over the stove. "All done!" She hooked her arm around her son's and stood on tip-toe, kissing his cheek. "You're really in love with this girl, aren't you, Nemo?"

"Yes, I am."

"I'm so happy for you. The very first time I saw you two together, I thought, what a lovely couple they make."

"The way I remember it, you were thinking what an insensitive jerk your son is."

"I wasn't thinking any such thing." She hit him on the chest with her apron and hugged his arm. It was times like this when he remembered how much he missed her.

"Mom, I was thinking last night that you and Dad have been together a long time."

"Thirty-six years in June."

He turned her to face him, his hands on her shoulders. She lay her hands on top of his, still clutching the apron in her right. "What's your secret, Mom?"

"No secret. There've been bad times, like everyone else—your father hasn't always been the easiest man to live with—but you keep your family together. That's just what you do." They both thought the same thing at the same moment—that she hadn't always kept her family to-gether—and she lowered her eyes.

He took her into his arms. "It's all right, Mom."

"Your father would've gone in without me, Nemo. He never said it. But I knew he would." She looked up at him, her eyes wet with tears. "I didn't think it would be so long. If I'd known—"

"It's okay, Mom. Really." He held her at arm's length. "Can I ask you something?"

She wiped her tears away. "Of course, dear."

"Why didn't you go in before I was born? You had the

connections to get in from the beginning. You didn't have
to wait until it was opened up."

"I couldn't leave Mama out there, and she absolutely
refused to go in." Her voice took on the edge it always
had when the subject of her mother came up.

"Was that the issue between you two, that she was
keeping you out of the Bin?"

She shook her head and shrugged off his hands. "I'd
really rather not talk about that tonight, Nemo. Let's just
have a pleasant dinner. It's not every day my son comes
to see me."

It was the same dead end he always ran into when he
asked about his grandmother. "Okay, but will you tell me
some other time?"

She bit her lower lip and looked at him. "You're not a
little boy anymore, are you?"

"No, Mom, I'm not."

She gave a quick nod. "You're right. I should tell you.
It's time you knew."

THERE WAS THE CLUNK OF THE FRONT-DOOR KNOCKER, AND
Nemo jumped. "I'll get it, Mom." He hurried to the door,
hoping to get a few moments alone with Justine, but there
was Lawrence, towering behind her. She looked scared
to death.

Nemo held out his arms to her, and she surged into
them, clutching at his shirt front, burying her face in his
chest. "I was afraid you wouldn't come," he said, but all
she did was shake her head.

Be gentle, Lawrence signed, and Nemo kissed her hair.
"I'm just glad to see you."

"Me too," she whispered.

His mom came into the foyer. "Lawrence, what a pleasant surprise. Come in, Justine. Let the poor girl get in the
door, Nemo. Todd! They're here!" She smiled at them all,

and Nemo's dad came in behind her, resting his hands on her shoulders, echoing her smile. "Everything's ready," she said. "I hope everybody's hungry."

THEY SAT DOWN TO PLATTERS AND BOWLS OF STEAMING food, all "made from scratch," even though the huge roast, ringed in carmelized carrots and onions, had never graced even a virtual cow. It came from the meat market on the square, just a couple of blocks from the house, raw and wrapped in plastic. Nemo couldn't remember the last time he'd had pot roast. Twelve years? He'd often scorned his mother's continued devotion to a "proper dinner" in a place where people didn't have to eat at all. But now, as they passed the food around the table, it made sense to him.

"I enjoyed your singing last night," his father said to Justine. "You are very talented."

"Thank you," she said. Her fear was still there, just below the surface. "I'm sorry I ran off, but I had urgent business."

"I hope it went well."

"Yes, I found out a great deal." She held his father's gaze for a moment, then he turned away.

Nemo was wondering what that was all about, when Lawrence said, "Mrs. Thorne, this pot roast is truly exquisite," setting off a round of compliments and a prolonged discussion of the food, item by item. Through all this, Nemo had the sense that Justine was waiting to get back to her own agenda, whatever that might be. She was scared, but now, he guessed, she knew what she wanted to do. He didn't think she was going to leave him. Whenever she got the chance, she'd look at him in a way that said, *I'm here, Nemo. I love you.*

When Lawrence and his mom had exhausted the subject

of biscuits, Justine said to his father, "It's funny you should mention my singing. Did you know that Nemo and I have the same favorite singer, that I even look just like her? How would you explain a coincidence like that?"

His father was clearly rattled. "That's fascinating," he managed.

"It's almost like we were made for each other," Justine said.

Lawrence cleared his throat and drawled, "Ain't nothing wrong with that." He held up his glass. "To Nemo and Justine," he said. Justine held her glass high, almost defiantly, Nemo thought. They drank the toast, and she leaned over and kissed his cheek.

"More potatoes, dear?" his mother asked her.

"Yes," she said. "They're just the way I like them."

THINGS RELAXED AFTER THAT, AND NEMO EVEN FOUND himself talking, entertaining them all with stories of Gene the bartender—his career as a comedian, his many wives, his sailboat. Everything was going to be all right, he told himself. As long as Justine loved him, everything would be all right.

But as Nemo's dad was clearing away the dishes, Justine turned to his mom. "You said the other night that your father was a doctor. I was curious. What kind of doctor was he?" She was trying to make it sound like a casual question, but her lips were drawn taut, and she was holding her water glass in a deathgrip.

If his mom noticed, she didn't let on. "He was an obstetrician," she said. "The best one in Richmond. Very dedicated."

Justine only nodded, though Nemo could see that she'd found out what she wanted to know, and it wasn't good. Why should she care what kind of doctor his grandfather was? Then he remembered her dream. *Dr. Donley.* A gnawing sense of panic welled up inside him. He caught Justine's eye, and she looked at him steadily. She looked as if she were facing execution.

He said, "I'd like to walk off some of this pot roast before dessert, Mom. Do you mind if Justine and I take a little walk around the garden?"

"Take your time, dears. I have to make the sauce for dessert anyway."

THEY WALKED OUT INTO THE GARDEN. HIS MOTHER TENDED it, just like she still mashed the potatoes. Her gardening gloves were lying on the table, caked with mud. He stood exactly where he'd stood four days ago when he first saw Justine—over by the grape arbor, the wind blowing her hair across her face, turning, their eyes meeting. Everything had changed since then. Now she stood beside him, his fate in her hands.

"Did you find out what you needed to know?" he asked without looking at her.

She came around in front of him, placed her hands on his crossed arms. "Yes. I'm sorry I ran off. I had to find out the truth—for you. I wish I didn't know."

"Know what?"

"I never tried to trick you or deceive you, Nemo. You've got to believe that. I didn't know anything about this until last night." Her voice was trembling.

He searched her eyes, his voice gentle. "Justine, I still don't know what we're talking about."

She gave a quick nod, dropping her hands to her sides. "Have you ever heard of a Construct mistress, Nemo?"

He had. Construct mistresses were the subject of countless jokes when he was twelve and thirteen. (*Q: How many Construct whores does it take to screw in a light bulb? A: Con-*

struct whores screw three at a time.) He told one to Lawrence once. Only once.

"I didn't know if they were real," he said.

She held her head up and looked him in the eye. The muscles in her neck were taut. She had to concentrate to form the words. "I'm real. I'm a Construct mistress. I was made to lure you into the Bin."

He felt a sinking feeling in his stomach. His vision contracted to a narrow tunnel. He tried to think of a single reason why it couldn't be true, but all he had to do was look at her to know it was. It made sense of everything.

He turned away from her, stared again at the arbor where she'd stood, waiting for him to see her. Jesus Christ, what a fucking idiot he'd been. He remembered everyone scurrying inside, even Lawrence, so that the two of them could be alone. They all knew what was going on. Everybody knew what was going on. Everybody but him. And Justine. She swore she didn't know, and he believed her.

Don't forget you love her, Lila said. She'd known. That's what she was, Winston's whore. He didn't know why he hadn't seen it before now. He looked at Justine, her arms wrapped around herself, her eyes wild with grief, and he couldn't bear it. He looked back at the house, half expecting to see his parents' faces leering at the windows. "My mom and dad?" he asked quietly.

"I think so."

He was still staring at the house, but he wasn't seeing it. He was concentrating on some point inside himself where everything was still and perfectly clear, if only he could remember it. He was being tested, everything he'd ever believed in brought to judgment. He tried to imagine how Justine must feel—to be used like that, tricked with a phony life. She didn't have to confess this to him at all, and yet she had.

Nemo looked into her eyes. She was bracing herself for

the worst. Her pain was right there on the surface. He could reach out and touch it. *So that they may choose*, Jonathan had said. "Does this change how you feel about me?" he asked her.

Her mouth came open, stunned at the question. Obviously it hadn't even occurred to her. "No, of course not. I thought you . . ."

He reached out and took her arms, ran his hands up and down them. "I told you. Nothing's going to change how I feel about you. I love you, Justine."

She threw her arms around him, and he held her close. "I love you, Nemo. I will always love you."

They clung to each other. He was afraid—terrified—and a knot of anger gripped his chest when he thought about how he'd been deceived, but all that would have to wait. He held her in his arms, and he never wanted to let her go. He'd spent a single day thinking he might never hold her again. He never wanted to spend another one.

"We have a lot to talk about," she said after a while, and he laughed ironically.

"You could say that."

13

JUSTINE AND NEMO WALKED OVER TO THE FOUN-
tain, a boy endlessly pouring water out of a jug into a
huge shell, and sat on the rim. Like the house, it looked
as if it'd been there for centuries. Justine trailed her fingers
in the water, remembering a ring she used to wear on her
right index finger, a man's ring, gold, with a single dia-
mond. She didn't know why she thought of it now. Memories had been bubbling to the surface all day, just like Lila
said they would.

She looked into Nemo's eyes. She could see he was still
rattled, sorting things out the way he did, but he was still
here, still beside her. She could scarcely believe it. Ever
since Lila told her what she was, she'd braced herself for
losing him. She wished he would say something, anything.
Just talk to her. "I'm surprised you didn't figure out what
I am before I did," she said. "You know more about the
Bin than I do."

"I didn't think they existed anymore. Not in here."

They. He couldn't say it. Construct mistress. Whore.
"You couldn't tell?"

He shook his head. "No, I couldn't." He seemed almost
sad to confess it.

She didn't have to tell him. He never would've known. Had he thought about that? She didn't have to tell him, but she had. "I was afraid to tell you. Lawrence said you'd be okay, but I wasn't so sure."

"Lawrence knew about this?"

"I told Mr. Menso, and Mr. Menso told Lawrence."

"Mr. Menso?"

"The little man with the bookstore I told you about. Lawrence says they're old friends. I needed somebody to talk to, and I couldn't talk to you. I've got so much to tell you, I don't know where to start."

"You're sure you're a Construct? How do you know?"

"Positive. That's what my dreams are all about. I had this dream, but it wasn't a dream. We were in this big old house—I talked to them all—they spoke to me—Angelina, the old woman, and the pregnant one. She was huge, out to here." She stopped, her arms out, as if holding her rounded belly. Something had happened to his face. Something was terribly wrong.

"Angelina?" he said.

"The young one in my dream. Angelina Rawson."

He lurched to his feet, stumbling backwards, shaking his head. She reached for him, but he drew away.

"What is it, Nemo? What's wrong?"

He whipped his head around, glaring back at the house. "How could they do this?" he hissed. "How could you fucking do this!" he shouted at the ivy-covered walls.

Justine felt as if the ground was opening up at her feet, but there was nothing she could do to stop it. "Do what? I don't understand."

He turned on her. "Angelina Rawson was my grandmother!" he screamed.

He stood there, rocking back and forth. She thought he might collapse, but he turned on his heel, stumbling at first, as he headed toward the low stone wall that surrounded the place, running by the time he reached it, vaulting high into the air, and over.

She'd been leaning forward, her arms outstretched to him, even as he ran away. Now she pitched forward, landing hard on her knees, throwing herself onto the ground, beating her head on the lush, green grass, screaming with shame and fury, cursing whatever gods had made her.

SHE COULD FEEL THE THUD OF THEIR FOOTSTEPS THROUGH the ground as they came running from the house. She was on her back now, staring at the sky, waiting. She felt a great calmness, a watchful detachment. The worst had already happened.

Lawrence slid his hands under her like shovels and lifted her off the ground. She laid her head on his shoulder, felt his scales pressing into her cheek like leather petals. He carried her into the house and put her on the sofa, a pillow under her head. Todd and Elizabeth hovered over her as if she were a dying invalid. She wondered if they'd heard their son screaming, wondered if she should hate them now.

"Whatever happened?" Elizabeth asked her. "Where's Nemo?"

"I told him the truth," Justine said. "He ran off."

"What truth, dear?" She was wringing her hands as if putting on hand lotion. Justine didn't think she was even aware of doing it.

"You can cut the crap, Elizabeth," Todd said. "She knows." He spoke to Justine, "Don't you?"

Justine sat up, pushing back her hair from her face. "Why don't you tell me what I know?"

Todd sighed and shook his head. "You're right. You're right. We've put you in a terrible mess. I thought it was a bad idea from the beginning, but I guess that doesn't matter now. Winston approached us about three weeks ago with the idea of . . . you . . . to . . . entice Nemo inside. He was certain it would work, of course. Against my better judgment, we told him to go ahead. He said it would be weeks before you figured out what you were, and by then Nemo would be inside. We meant no harm to you. Truth is, we didn't give you much thought."

"But you were lying to your own son."

"To save his life."

"How could you be so sure he'd fall for me?"

"That was my question, but Winston said it was practically guaranteed, that you'd be specially made for Nemo, that he'd find you irresistible—and that certainly seemed to be the case there for a while. He must be furious at us now." Todd shook his head back and forth, imagining his angry son.

Justine searched their faces. They didn't know, she was sure of it. They hadn't been told *why* Nemo would like her so much, why they'd feel such an immediate affinity. She was just another whore to them. They'd been duped, too. "There are three lives inside me," she said. "I only know one name. Now Nemo knows it, too: Angelina Rawson."

Elizabeth gasped and turned on Todd. "Todd, did you know about this?"

But Todd didn't have to answer. He was slack-jawed. "Your mother?" he finally managed, and peered at Justine as if he could see the dead woman there. "Dear God," he said and turned away.

Elizabeth was staring at her in a daze. "Tell me about her," Justine said. "Tell me who I am."

Elizabeth shook her head. "It can't be. You can't be her."

Justine rested the back of her head on the sofa and recited to the ceiling: "I remember growing up in an orphanage in Dallas named St. Catherine's. My best friend's name was Stephanie Boyd. I probably talked about her. My hero was a nun named Sarah who—"

"Stop!" Elizabeth threw up her hands. "Please stop. If I'd known—" Her voice trailed off, and she was wringing her hands again. "How could Winston do this?" she asked no one in particular.

Justine didn't care about their family politics. "Forget about Winston. I want to know who I am, goddamnit. You brought me in here, now deal with me."

"Of course," Elizabeth said. "Of course. Anything we can do."

"Another one of my lives was a patient of your father's. Do you have any idea who that might be? She was giving birth to an illegitimate child."

Elizabeth's eyes widened, and she clutched her chest. She felt for the chair behind her, and sat down heavily. Todd knelt at her side and took her hand.

Justine watched them reeling under this latest revelation—Elizabeth mumbling to herself, teetering on the edge, Todd coaxing her back. Elizabeth kept shaking her head, hoping they'd all go away.

"We have to tell her," Todd said to Elizabeth, stroking her hand as if it were a kitten.

"Tell me what?" Justine demanded.

Elizabeth finally managed a quick nod of assent, and Todd rose to his feet, placing a hand on his wife's shoulder. "When Angelina was thirty-three, she got pregnant and decided to keep the child. God knows why. She'd never made a commitment in her life, had already had a couple of abortions. Wade Donley was on call the night Angelina gave birth to Winston. That's how they met. She married Wade six months later. Winston was never told Wade wasn't his father. Truth is, Angelina didn't know who the real father was. Elizabeth was born two years after that."

Todd sighed and tightened his grip on his wife's shoulder. "No one knew any of this until thirty years later when Wade was in the hospital, dying of cancer, and Elizabeth saw his medical history while talking to one of the doctors. It said he was sterile, had always been. He wasn't Elizabeth's father either. She confronted her mother about it, after Wade died, and she told her everything, except who her real father was. Years later, when Angelina was dying, she told Elizabeth that Newman Rogers was the father, but she was saying a lot of crazy things by then, and we never knew whether to believe her or not. She'd talked about Newman Rogers for years. Her best friend, she called him. He'd moped after her for years, had proposed a dozen times before she married Wade, but Angelina said she never felt that way about him."

Justine wanted to stop her ears and scream, but it was too late for that. "He called her his sweetheart," she murmured.

Elizabeth slowly brought her head up and looked her in the eye. "You are her, aren't you?"

Justine stood. There was nothing more for her here. They'd all been used, lied to—and the truth was even worse. "I'm sorry, Elizabeth," she said. And she was, deeply sorry, though she'd done nothing to harm her. Sparks padded into the room and rubbed against Justine's legs, meowing loudly. She bent down and picked him up, scratched between his ears. He closed his eyes and settled into a rumbling purr.

Elizabeth stood, brushing away her tears, trying to get a grip on herself. "We've done an awful thing," she said. "I'm so sorry."

Justine couldn't bring herself to hate this woman for

wanting to save her son, for being duped. "You meant well," was all she could manage.

"He usually doesn't let anyone pick him up," Elizabeth said, pointing at Sparks, cradled in Justine's arms like a baby.

"He remembers Angelina," Justine said. "You changed his name."

Elizabeth started, apparently realizing how Justine knew this. "Nemo named him. He couldn't say Ishmael. He was only five."

Justine rubbed the top of Sparks' head with her nose and set him on the carpet. He trotted off, his tail held high.

"Do you remember me?" Elizabeth asked timidly.

Justine shook her head. She remembered nothing she wanted to say. "No, not really."

Elizabeth nodded, as if that was as it should be.

Why had Angelina told her the truth? Justine wondered. Several convenient lies came to mind. She'd already lied for years. Maybe she'd hoped for her daughter's forgiveness, just that. Wade had forgiven her. She could see his face—the Dr. Donley of her dream, years older, loving her till death took him away.

"How long were Angelina and Wade married after you were born?" Justine asked.

Elizabeth started wringing her hands again. "Thirty-one years."

"He must've forgiven her, don't you think?"

Elizabeth looked down at her hands and clutched them together. "Yes," she whispered. "I suppose he did."

"I'm sorry I didn't work out as planned," Justine said. "I'll show myself out."

Lawrence, who'd been standing in the background the whole time, like a patient footman, stepped forward and offered to accompany her to the hotel.

She looked into his reptilian eyes and wondered how

much he knew. After all, Menso had sent him. Nemo trusted him completely. What better person to deceive him. "All right," she said.

At the door, Elizabeth laid her hand on Lawrence's arm. "Tell Nemo I need to see him. I promised to tell him some things. He'll know what I mean."

"Certainly, Mrs. Thorne."

"Elizabeth," she said. "And Todd." Todd stood behind her, his hands on her shoulders.

Justine turned and walked away. She supposed they waved good-bye.

JUSTINE SAT ON THE TRAIN AND LOOKED AT HERSELF. THE front of her dress was smeared with dirt and grass. The palms of her hands were green. Lawrence had been silent, but she felt him watching her, trying to gauge her state of mind. "You still think Nemo and I are going to end up happily ever after?" she asked him. "Looks like you'll have to revise that part of the script."

He ignored her accusing tone. "You're not Angelina Rawson, you know."

"Like hell. They're *all* her, aren't they? All three of them."

"That's not what I mean. Angelina Rawson's dead. You're Justine now. Sooner you get that figured out, the better. Don't try to live in the past: You're dead there."

"Nemo evidently doesn't see it that way."

"Maybe he needs some help."

She laughed bitterly. "From me? He can't stand the sight of me."

"You give up awful easy, don't you?"

"What are you talking about? I'm his *grandmother*, Lawrence!"

"Bullshit. You're nobody's grandmother. You're four days old—acting like it, too."

She'd had just about enough from the lot of them. "Who the hell are you to lecture me? Do you have any idea how much Nemo loves you and trusts you? At least I didn't know what was going on. But you knew the whole sick scheme from the beginning, didn't you?" She was screaming at the top of her voice. Everyone in the train was looking at them. "Didn't you?"

"Yes," Lawrence said quietly.

"Then fuck you, Lawrence! Fuck all of you!"

She glared out the window, putting it all together, putting herself together like some kid's puzzle. Lenny'd said Winston had done it for somebody else, somebody who made him feel like an errand boy. That wouldn't be Elizabeth. Oh, no. He'd be the big shot brother throwing his weight around. He'd get off on it. It had to be somebody else. Her kindly old friend, tugging at her heartstrings with his bullshit stories about his sweetheart.

As they were pulling into Dupont Circle, she said, "Tell him I want to see him, Lawrence."

"Nemo?" he asked in the British voice.

"Nemo doesn't want to see me. You know who I mean."

Lawrence nodded his huge head. "Very well. We'll tell him." He looked into her eyes. "When we were living our old lives, we thought of ourselves as quite separate from others." He ran his fingers over the back of his own scaly hand. "The boundaries were precise, ending exactly there." He rubbed one of the scales between his fingers. "We've learned differently. All the Constructs have. You'll learn it, too."

"I've learned quite enough for one day, thank you." She rose from her seat and stood by the door. "Does he enjoy playing God?"

"No. He loathes it, actually."

"Well, he's sure bungled this one, hasn't he?" The train rocked to a stop, and the doors slid open. "Maybe he should just stick to peddling books." She stepped onto the platform and headed for the escalators. As the train pulled out of the station, she looked back. Lawrence's green face was still pressed to the glass, still watching her.

JUSTINE WENT UP TO HER ROOM AND SAT IN FRONT OF THE window, staring at the city lights. A light rain was falling, and she remembered wet asphalt, the snicker of tires on the pavement, people huddled in doorways with no place else to go. Everybody had a place in here. She surveyed her place, a hotel room she never checked into. Her birthplace.

She opened the window, and cool air blew in, misting her face. She leaned on the windowsill and took a deep breath, imagining Nemo beside her. She remembered lying in his arms on the bed behind her. *You could make me cry,* he said.

She turned from the window, leaving it open, and went to the phone. She keyed in *Warren G. Menso.* There was no listing. She tried *Newman Rogers,* and of course there were screens full. At least a dozen in D.C.; one in Lhasa; three in Nairobi.

At the top of the screen, the two names she'd searched were displayed one on top of the other. The same number of letters. She studied them, comparing them letter by letter. The same letters. "Cute," she said aloud. She liked anagrams, used to make them up in class. Stephanie had been *Denise B. Yophat.* She'd called her Denise sometimes as an inside joke. Justine didn't care much for this one, though. She'd trusted him completely, and he'd been lying to her the whole time.

She thought about tracking him down in his shop, demanding to know what the hell was going on. She looked out at the rain, harder now, and decided against it. Let him come to me, she thought.

She lay on the bed, propped herself up with pillows, and watched the rain blowing in, the curtains billowing, then growing sodden and heavy. A pool of water collected on the window sill and ran down the wall into the carpet. She watched it soak in, inching across the floor. In her mind's eye, she saw Angelina's house, Nemo's house she realized now, and felt a presence, like someone sitting close beside her, though she knew no one was there.

I'm glad I finally slept with Newman after all those years. The poor bastard had it coming.

Justine winced at the cold, cynical voice. "You don't remember it?"

After my time. None of us really remembers it: The kid never knew him. The old lady's memories are a mess. Even what she remembers, she doesn't remember, if you know what I mean.

Justine closed her eyes, and she could see her—the lank hair and tired eyes. "I know. They're all in pieces. What do you remember?"

Not a hell of a lot. I was having a bad day. I remember Newman, though. He was my best friend. When I was lying on the table screaming my guts out, I wanted him there. Only him.

Justine felt her tenderness as she recalled Newman, like a single shaft of sunlight in a dark wood. "Why him? You didn't love him."

Love. I did that a bunch of times. I don't remember any of them. Newman loved me. He was fucking crazy about me. I remember that. What do you do with something like that—all that love and you can't give it back?

She'd wanted to love him, longed for it, but she couldn't do it. Justine ached with her regret. She wanted to fight it—what was he to her now but a deceitful bastard?—but it was too strong. "What *did* you do, Angie?" The question brought a wave of self-loathing.

Drugs mostly. I was high when I went into labor and they brought me into the emergency room, strapped me in, strung me up like a Christmas tree. "What is this fucking shit!" I screamed at this mousey little guy. "Life-support monitors," he said. The last thing I remember is the same little guy pulling the harness of wires off my head.

"Why's he doing this? What are we doing here?"

I don't know. Why did Newman ever do half the things he did? For me, usually.

It was a sickness. An obsession. And now Justine was trapped in it. "So he's brought his sweetheart back from the dead."

For someone else. If it'd been me, I would've done it for myself. But Newman's not like that. God knows what he ever saw in me.

"But Nemo is his grandson—and yours."

In my reality, Nemo's not even born yet, his mother isn't even born yet. We're not guilty on this one, Your Honor—for a change.

"What should I do?"

She burst out laughing. *No one ever asks me that question—that's my question.*

"Then what would you do?"

Ask Newman.

"He's the one who got me into this mess. He's the last person I trust."

You asked me what I'd do. Probably nothing. Get high. Who cares what I'd do? Justine felt her retreating, closing in upon herself, hiding from this life she'd never asked for.

Justine got up off the bed and paced up and down, shaking off Angie's dark thoughts, the dull, tired voice. She pulled off her dress, wadded it up, and threw it in the corner. Stood in the shower for thirty minutes, letting the water beat down on her head. Came back into the room dripping wet. Hit the room service pad and ordered a joint and a rock. Picked them up and hurled them out the window. Slammed the window shut.

Probably just what I'm supposed to do, she thought. Fall apart, so he can come to my rescue. No, not this time. She'd keep him guessing. Go about her business. He wasn't going to use her anymore, not if she could help it. She put on a pair of jeans and a T-shirt, and picked up her guitar. She had time to make it by the first set. He said he wanted to come hear her sing. Fine. Let him come.

As she rode to the club, she wondered if the rest of the band would even show up, since she'd skipped out on them last night. Then she remembered what Lenny had said about Rick—that he was instructed to deal with Rick and only Rick. Justine would've thought John would be the one to deal with, certainly more pleasant. Unless Rick was in on the whole thing, someone to keep an eye on her. Or maybe they were all in on it.

When she walked in, there was a cheer from a group of guys at the bar. She remembered them from the night before. Tonight, they'd brought friends who waved shyly. She waved back, but she kept her distance. Bruce came running from behind the bar. "God, am I glad to see you. What happened last night? They said you had some kind of emergency or something?"

She liked Bruce and his nervous enthusiasm. "That's right. I'm sorry I took off like that. Did the band do okay?"

Bruce shrugged. "Oh, yeah. But without you they're just another band. Lover boy. Whatshisname. Rick. He was strutting around like he's God's gift. Doing solos that last a week and a half. There's only so much of that shit I can listen to. He's not a boyfriend of yours, is he?"

"We just play together. You ever see him before? Do you know anything about him?"

Bruce made a face. "Me? Never laid eyes on him. Course, I don't have tits, if you'll pardon my French. Hey, you going to do that welcome home song tonight?"

"Sure thing."

"Great. Love that song."

SHE FOUND HER BAND IN THE GREEN ROOM ARGUING OVER what songs they were going to do if she didn't show up. "No, man," John was saying to Rick. "No more fucking Dead. They're called the Grateful Fucking Dead because everybody's grateful they're finally dead."

Ian spotted her first and pointed her out to the other two. "Boss lady!" Rick said. "Vacation over?"

"Told you she'd be here," John said, grinning at her. "Hey Justine, we got time for a J before we play."

"No thanks," she said.

He lit up without her. "You got here just in time, Justine. Justine Time, Justine." He laughed to himself. "Rick here was going to force me to play 'Casey Jones' again. You know how many fucking times I've played that song?" He started thumping out the bass part with a plodding beat, walking up and down in a parody of a palsied old man.

"Fuck you, asshole," Rick said.

John stopped, looking hurt. "Where's your sense of humor, Rick? I'll play anything you want. I'm a mu-si-cian. Plug and play."

"Knock it off," Justine said. "We'll start off with 'Casey Jones.' Rick, you sing lead. I'll do harmony."

It was hard to tell which one was more surprised, Rick

or John. Ian smiled to himself. John shrugged and turned to Ian. "But please, man, can we pick it up a little bit? This dude's supposed to be high on cocaine, not dropping downers."

Justine walked over to Rick. He gave her his usual leer. "You trying to get on my good side?"

She held his gaze. "Which side is that, Rick?"

"Wouldn't you like to know."

"Yeah, I would. How about tonight after work?" She ran her fingertips up his arm.

That rattled him. He looked away, pretended to have something in his eye. "Sorry to disappoint you, but I've got plans."

"You stay pretty busy. You must know this town pretty well."

"Indeed I do. You looking for a tour guide?"

She leaned in closer. "What do you want to show me, Rick?"

He looked her up and down and sneered, trying to hide his nervousness under his usual bravado. "All the tricks your whore friend knows and then some."

"John, Ian," she said over her shoulder without taking her eyes off Rick. "Why don't you guys go set up. Rick and I have something to work out."

She watched him as they went out. He was almost able to conceal his panic. When the door closed, she dropped the seductive smile. "You're pretty good, bit repetitive, but you didn't expect me to go for it. Rick Super Stud, fucks his way from club to club like a walking dick. Ignore him, brush him off, don't suspect him of being anything but a prick. How come Bruce has never seen you before, Rick? You never slithered in here while you were making the rounds? Seems like a great place to pick up women. Or maybe you don't pick up women. Maybe your whole story's bullshit. What do you know about me, lover boy? Or are you just the hired help?''

He looked at her with complete loathing, his face enflamed with disgust. "I'll tell you what I know," he said, in a voice she'd never heard from him before, superior and precise. "I know that you're a whore, and you will burn in Hell forever. And now your little boyfriend knows it, too." He pushed past her and out the door.

She stood there stunned at his hatred and revulsion. He would've gladly strangled her if they'd been in the real world. She followed him out, and he was standing at his mike, back in character, his guitar riding on one hip, the neck sweeping the crowd for his next victim. It was all an act. Except he couldn't fake the bulge in his pants.

AS THEY PLAYED THREE SETS AND SEVERAL ENCORES, RICK never dropped his guard again. She tried to figure out how he fit into all this. As angry as she was at Menso, she couldn't imagine him and Rick in the same room together, much less plotting together. But at least she knew Rick wasn't what he pretended to be, and finding out what he was would give her something to do. She needed more than anything not to feel so helpless.

In spite of everything, she found herself getting into the music, and she let it take her away. The crowd was crazy about her. *I always wanted to be a singer,* the old woman had said. That's me, Justine thought, a regular dream come true. During the breaks, she searched the crowd for Mr. Menso, but of course he didn't show.

You're not Angelina Rawson, Lawrence had told her, and that kept coming back to her. She had Angelina's memories, some of them anyway, though there were long stretches missing. But when she'd talked with Angie in her head, she was struck by her otherness, her discordance with who she felt herself to be. *Without you, we're nothing,* the girl had said. She was beginning to understand what she'd meant. The three of them didn't even see each other as the same person. She brought them all together, like a string through beads. Cut the thread, and they fell apart. Wiped clean, like Lila said. Maybe Lawrence was right. She wasn't Angelina anymore. She came after, the next chord in the progression.

WHEN THEY FINISHED FOR THE NIGHT, SHE PACKED UP quickly and slipped out, hiding in a doorway across the street. After about fifteen minutes, Rick and Ian came out with a couple of women, but after a brief conversation, they left the women standing there and headed toward the subway. She followed them down to the station. They were arguing back and forth. She'd never seen Ian talk so much. Whatever they were talking about, they ignored the world around them, and neither one spotted her trailing behind them. She hid behind a pillar as they waited for an eastbound train, then worked her way from pillar to pillar to the other end of the platform. When the train pulled in, she boarded the last car as they were boarding the second. She stood by the door at each stop, watching to see where they got off.

At Pentagon Station they left the train and headed up the escalators. She watched them turn left and didn't have to follow them. That corridor went only one place. They were headed toward the VIMs. They were headed back home to the real world. Rick and Ian were visitors.

"You wanted to see me?" a voice said behind her, and she didn't have to turn around to know who it was.

He was leaning on his cane, the same kind smile on his face. "You lied to me," she said.

"Guilty, Your Honor, as Angelina used to say. It was necessary, I'm afraid."

"Why in God's name have you done this?"

"I couldn't let her die, not when I had the power to bring her back. I just couldn't." He pointed with his cane to the street exit. "Please, I'll be glad to tell you everything. There's a place close by. We can have coffee and talk."

She didn't see that she had much choice.

ACROSS THE STREET FROM THE STATION WAS A SMALL CAFÉ, Joe's Inn. She hadn't noticed it there before. It was a neighborhood place with mahogany booths and ceiling fans. There were even waitresses with pencils behind their ears.

He led her to a booth in the back. He looked around, smiling to himself. "Does this place look familiar?"

She was looking daggers at him, but he was pretending not to notice. "Should it?"

"This place isn't really in D.C. It's in Dallas, or used to be. Sometimes I take liberties. It's one of the few advantages of my job."

"Playing God?"

He nodded at the justice of her dig. "Hardly, my dear. God laughs at us. We take ourselves too seriously. No, I'm Sysop. System Operator. I wrote it, and I run it—or try to—but you don't want to hear my problems. You want to know what in the hell I'm doing creating you in the first place. Is that a fair assessment?"

"Yes."

A waitress came up to the table. Her nametag said *Katie*. She was cute and perky, from another time. She set two coffees in front of them and left them alone.

Mr. Menso smiled after her. "Katie knew us. We always

sat at this table, ordered coffee, and talked." Mr. Menso poured cream into his coffee and stirred. "Angelina used to call me up and ask me to meet her here in the afternoon. I knew that meant there was trouble in her love life. I'd take off work, come down here, and console her. She'd insist on picking up the check. As we were leaving I'd suggest an outing to cheer her up, a picnic by the lake, a drive in the country, and she'd always say yes, and we'd have a great time. And that would go on for a week or two until she met another guy, usually shortly after I'd proposed again. Then I wouldn't hear from her until she'd call me up after a few weeks or months, and ask me to meet her here." He quit stirring and set the spoon on the table. "We did that for over seventeen years.

"Sometimes she had special favors to ask. Money, of course. I also helped her find lawyers and doctors. Fate introduced her to Ward, however. Winston came a month early at three o'clock in the morning. The doctor I'd found her was fishing in Vermont, so she got the resident on duty. She never called me after she met Wade. She sent me an invitation to the wedding, but I didn't go."

She studied him, so sweet and innocent looking, playing on her sympathies. So sorry. No sympathy to spare. Her voice was hard and cold. "So when did you fuck her?" She tapped her forehead. "Nobody up there seems to remember that minor detail. Elizabeth said you were her father. What was it—a swan? a shower of gold? Or maybe it was an immaculate conception?"

That stung. The smarmy little smile was gone. His face drooped like an old dog's. Good. She wanted him to suffer.

He spoke quietly, a confession with as much nostalgia as guilt. "She'd been married a little over a year, just moved into her new home, in a new town, with her new husband. I'd gotten a couple of postcards from the honeymoon in Mazatlán. I called one evening and said I was passing through, asked if I could stop by. She was all excited, happy to hear from me, and she said to pick up a bottle of wine, and we'd talk about old times."

He pursed his lips. "Of course, I was lying. I wasn't passing through. I flew to Richmond because I knew her husband was at a conference in New York.

"I'd never seen her looking so beautiful, so happy. She showed me the whole house. Her son Winston, six months older than her marriage, was fast asleep in his bed. I watched her tuck him in.

"We had the wine, and talked about old times, and after I'd had a little too much to drink, it hit me that she'd forgotten I was in love with her, that she seemed to think because she was finally in love, mine would just evaporate. It'd been a while since I'd told her. She preferred it that way. We were good friends, she insisted."

He sighed. "But I broke down, made a fool of myself, almost forty years old, hopelessly in love with her for twenty years. She took me in her arms and made love to me. Just the once. I knew at the time it would be. Just the once."

Justine stared at him across the table, a harmless little man with a tale of woe. Hell, she almost wanted to take him in her arms and comfort him now. "Look, I'm sorry your sweetheart never loved you. I'm sorry for all of it. But why me, now? Am I her replacement? Are you setting me up with Nemo, so you can fucking *console* me again?" Justine was practically shouting, but no one in the place turned to look. They weren't real. None of it was real. "You set this whole thing up. You got Winston to do the dirty work, but I was your little project from the beginning. Why?"

"I was coming to that," he said. He motioned to Katie, and she filled his cup. Justine hadn't touched hers. "I loved Angelina most of my life. When she died, I went a little crazy. I couldn't stand the thought that she didn't have to die. I think I still secretly believed that *someday* she'd learn to love me. When the Bin went online, all the data from every system in the world was uploaded. I scoured every database, looking for any recording of her. I found two, neither one very good. Even though it was the more primitive, Steve the porn peddler's was the more complete."

"That first dream I had."

"Yes. He recorded her, made a porno virtual out of her. I found the raw data stored away for years. That's why you remember the time at St. Catherine's with such clarity. He picked up all that, but back then he would've thought it was just background noise. The medical monitors when she gave birth to Winston weren't designed to capture memories, but some bled through. It didn't exactly capture her at her best. The third one, I arranged myself, setting up a research project at what was left of the local university. It's amazing what money can do. The Mental History Project, they called it. They uploaded a hundred holdouts over sixty, all so I could get one. But she was deep into Alzheimer's by then. Most of her memory was gone." He smiled sadly. "But she was still Angelina."

He swallowed hard and looked around the restaurant, his eyes brimming with tears. How many times had he sat here—waiting for her to come through that door, hoping things might finally be different? He dabbed at his eyes with a napkin and sighed. "But there wasn't enough, you see. The usual integration program wouldn't hold her together for more than a few seconds. The three moments in her life—those three women—couldn't even perceive each other to be the same woman. Theoretically, nothing could be done." He smiled ironically. "And I should know—I wrote the theory. But as I said before, I went a little crazy. So I spent the next twenty years writing Justine, writing you."

He looked at her like a proud father. "She chose the name Justine, by the way. I'd only known her for a few months. She'd broken up with David, I think his name was. One evening she was drunk and whimsical, and suggested we tell each other our secret names, the ones we'd choose for ourselves if we could shed the ones we were stuck with. She detested Angelina as too precious, and I hated Newman as the dweebiest name ever given. She said she wanted to be Justine."

"What was your secret name?" she asked, though she was pretty sure she already knew.

He looked down at the table, turned his napkin with his index finger as he spoke. "I told her I didn't have one. And she said that I must, and that she would discover it. She liked anagrams, and she made half a dozen out of my name on the back of a napkin like this one. I chose Warren G. Menso. I still have the napkin, the upload anyway. She called me Mr. Menso after that, said it was the masculine form of Mensa. She used to tease me about being a genius. She said only a genius or an idiot would be so devoted to her." He looked up from the napkin and smiled sadly. "I tried to make you what she always wanted to be—all the dreams she confided to Mr. Menso."

And no one else, until now. *We've got a lot of faith in you*, Angelina said, and now Justine understood what she meant. She took a sip from her coffee. It was lukewarm, but she drank it anyway, fighting back sympathy. "So why didn't you make me for yourself?"

"That was the idea to begin with—though I wouldn't admit it to myself. I knew all along that wouldn't be right. She never loved me out there; she wouldn't willingly love me in here. I could've planted such a suggestion, transformed my appearance into something stunning, but I couldn't do that to her. She trusted me."

"But you *could* plant the suggestion that she fall in love with her grandson."

He shook his head. "But I didn't. I gave you a sketchy history for the last six weeks and a basic knowledge of the Bin. I planted suggestions to lead you to my shop, and then to *Romeo and Juliet*—a nostalgic bit of self-indulgence, I confess. But everything else you've both done on your own."

"That first morning. That was you in my room, wasn't it? Talking to Winston?"

His face clouded over with anger. "Yes. I was furious. I'm so sorry for what he did. I never should've given him that much responsibility. I told him to implant a memory of your meeting, and he took it upon himself to subject you to that ludicrous sex. I wanted to boil him in oil."

Justine smiled at his rage. "That would be fine by me. I'm just glad to hear it wasn't real. You know, when I confessed to Nemo that I'd slept with his slimy uncle, it didn't even faze him. I thought, I've confessed my worst, and he still loves me. I had no idea."

"Do you wish you hadn't told him what you are?"

"Of course not. Once I knew, I had to." Once I knew, she thought, and something clicked. "But you knew that. You sent Lila to tell me what I was, didn't you?"

"Yes. You needed to know the truth, but if we gave it to you all at once, there was a high risk of insanity."

"Lila works for you?"

"She's a friend."

"What other 'friends' do you have?"

"Freddie and John."

So he'd been hovering over her the whole time. She supposed that should make her angry, but if he'd created her and just dumped her into the Bin completely on her own, that would've made her angry, too. If what she was really pissed about was his creating her at all, there was a simple enough solution for that.

"What about Rick and Ian—are they more friends of yours?"

"They're not my friends, Justine. They're my enemies. They believe I'm Satan himself. Nothing would make them happier than to destroy me if they could."

"Why would they be interested in me?"

"They're not. It's Nemo who interests them. Because he's my grandson. They make a habit of snooping around my life. Up to now they've been more an annoyance than anything else. Just don't let on you suspect them."

"I'm afraid it's too late for that. I told Rick off tonight. I thought he was working for you. I wanted to tell you off, but you weren't there."

Mr. Menso smiled. "You are a good deal like Angelina."

"Why was Lenny supposed to deal with Rick, then?"

"So that Rick's boss would be kept well informed and have the illusion he was in control."

She remembered Nemo asking her about the underground. "Is his boss's name Gabriel?"

"Yes."

"He approached Nemo."

"I know. I anticipated that move."

"But what do you get out of this? What did you want to happen?"

"I had hopes that you two would love each other, and that Nemo would come inside."

She couldn't believe he was so matter-of-fact about it. "Good Lord, were you forgetting I'm his grandmother?"

Menso smiled and shook his head. "No, you're not. You must know it yourself by now. You are very much alike, like a mother and daughter, I suppose. But you're not her. Can you honestly say to me, 'I'm Angelina'?"

She started to argue with him, but there was no point. He was right, for all the good it did her. She stared at the tabletop. She'd hoped there'd be some way out of this mess, but it was a dead end. "Okay. I'm not her. So what? Do you honestly think I can convince Nemo of that?"

He leaned forward, laid his hands on hers. "Listen to me, Justine. He's angry and he's frightened. But above all, he loves you. If he could be equally sure of your love, nothing else would matter to him."

"And how am I going to convince him of that? I can't even see him."

He lowered his gaze to their hands. His voice trembled as he spoke. "By going to him, as you planned. Not even Nemo could question such a sacrifice. I wouldn't have thought of it myself, I assure you. I didn't work for twenty years so that you could go back out there and die again. But I've arranged the download you asked me to. You can still do it, if you want. If you'd like to meet her first, I can arrange that, too."

She stared at him, dumbfounded. "Her?"

He looked into her eyes. She remembered those great, sad eyes. "Elaine. The woman whose body you'd live in outside."

"But why would you do this?"

He shook his head. "Because I'm hoping—unless he's a complete fool—that he won't let you do it. And because you asked. That's why I've done lots of things. I wanted you to be happy. That's what I've always wanted."

What do you do with something like that—all that love and you can't give it back? She squeezed his hands. "Maybe that's just not in your power, Mr. Menso."

He closed his eyes and took a deep breath. "No. I would say it most definitely is not."

There were stained glass windows, high in the walls—
stylized landscapes of mountains, trees, and rivers, fat yellow wedges of sunshine fanning out across the sky. Hardly
the stations of the cross, but nice. She had no actual memories of the place, but she remembered how it made her
feel. It was a refuge from the chaos she made of her life.
She felt safe here. She looked across the table where Newman had sat and sat and sat. He was the one who'd made
it safe for her. Never judging.

Nemo had been like his namesake, his grandfather,
never judging. Until now. He'd judged her. Not what she'd
done, but what she was, her very identity. How could she
atone for that? Hadn't he loved her for just that? *You can't
come to me, so I'm coming to you,* he'd said. Now it was the
other way around. He couldn't come here, not now. But
she could go to him. She could die for him. If he didn't
love her anymore, she wanted to die.

"Mr. Menso, you knew her better than anyone. What
would Angelina decide, do you think? Would she download herself?"

He thought about it for a long time, and shook his head.
"I honestly don't know, my dear."

Justine rose from the table. "We'll let you know," she
said. "Tomorrow, Angelina and I will let you know."

14

NEMO RAN UP THE STAIRS OUT OF NORTHSIDE STA-
tion, ran down the middle of the street through the moonlit
grass. He didn't remember getting to the VIM. He didn't
remember much of the train ride from D.C., moving from
car to car, never seeing a soul. All he could think about
was Justine in his arms, and Angelina. He ran faster, dodg-
ing the shadows of rocks and chunks of broken asphalt.

Out of the corner of his eye, he glimpsed low shadows
moving between the dark houses. Stupid, he told himself.
Stupid, stupid, stupid. You never run unless something's
already after you. Now he'd picked up a pack of dogs,
closing in on both sides. All he had to do was fall down,
and they'd be on him. Even if he slowed or stumbled,
they might make their move. He was three blocks from
home. He could never keep up this pace.

He could hear their breathing as they effortlessly
matched his stride. He considered breaking for one of the
abandoned houses on either side of him, scrambling up a
drainpipe, but even if he could outrun them, he'd have to
climb high and fast, or they'd drag him down. All they
needed was a boot heel or a pants leg. Even if he was fast

enough, these old drainpipes wouldn't hold, or he'd spend the night waiting to fall.

He could see one of them about a dozen yards to his right, a lab mix, his tongue lolling out of the corner of his mouth. He seemed to be enjoying himself. Then Nemo remembered—he'd been twelve or thirteen—Lawrence telling him what to do if a pack of dogs ever tried to run him down. It was a last resort, he said. It might work, or it might not. Nemo stopped dead and whirled around, flinging his arms wide and screaming like a banshee.

The dogs stopped, circling around, but they didn't back off. Two of them loped up the street to cut him off. Nemo stood as tall as he could, threw his shoulders back, and turned around, walking down the middle of the street with steady, purposeful strides, turning his head slowly from side to side, trying to keep an eye on all of them at once. He counted five. The one he had to watch out for was a big shepherd mix directly behind him, about ten yards back, and closing.

He searched the ground for anything he might use as a weapon, and spotted what looked like a fallen limb off to his left. He veered toward it, and scooped it up as he passed. The shepherd broke into a run when he bent over, and Nemo waited in a crouch. The limb was wet and rotten, practically crumbling in his hands. The dog sprang, and Nemo swung the limb hard, putting his whole body into it. The limb thudded against the dog's ribcage, and disintegrated. The dog hit the ground and rolled, the wind knocked out of him. All that was left of the limb was a handful of wet powder he threw at the rest of them, screaming again, waving his arms and pounding his chest for good measure. The other dogs widened their circle, and he moved on. He heard the shepherd rising to his feet and shaking himself off. The others circled back, giving Nemo a wide berth. They didn't follow him.

* * *

HE FINALLY MADE IT HOME, CLOSING AND LOCKING THE door behind him. He lit a lamp and hunted through the pantry. There was about an inch left in a half-pint bottle of *Early Times* he and Lawrence had found hidden in the door panel of an old mail truck. He drank it off in two swallows and smashed the bottle against the wall. While he was at it, he hurled a couple of jars of okra.

He saw her there, sitting at the table, drinking her coffee, talking about her nuns. In her diaries, he realized now, they were 'the harpies'. *Room check today. The harpies busted S & A.* He looked up as if he could see through the ceiling into his room where her diaries sat inside the refrigerator. Phrases from them ran through his mind. He heard her singing. *Everything I could've said I felt somehow you already knew.*

Holding the lamp aloft, he slowly climbed the stairs and went into his room, setting the lamp on the bedside table. He pulled a sheet off the bed and laid it on the floor in front of the refrigerator, opening it up and raking its contents onto the sheet, rocking it back and forth to make sure he got every last scrap. He ripped the earth poster off the wall and wadded it up, the photographs inside. Took the stack of Aimee Mann CDs still sitting on the workbench and tossed them on the pile. Popped the disc out of the CD player, snapped it in half, and flung the pieces down. He grabbed the corners of the sheet and wound them around his wrists, hoisted the bundle onto his back, walked down the hall to his old room, and kicked open the door.

The fireplace looked like a tiny cavern in the moonlight. The air was damp and musty and smelled like wet ashes. He dropped the bundle on the hearth and knelt beside it, stuffing the poster under the grate and dumping an armload of diaries on top. He struck a match and held it to the yellowed edges of the poster. It smoked and caught with a *poof.* The diaries' cheap leatherette bindings blackened and bubbled and rolled back like waves. The pages swelled and caught. Flames roared up the chimney, and Nemo knelt before the blaze, feeding it every scrap of the woman who'd lived in his imagination all his life, until every trace was gone but a pile of glowing ashes and the twisted silver globs of melted CDs.

He lay back on the sheet, wrapping himself up in it. He wanted to burn with righteousness, but all he could feel was the aching numbness of loss. He couldn't help himself. He longed for her even now. He tried, but he couldn't smell her on the sheet. She'd never really been here, would never be. He shuddered. His sobs echoed through the empty house.

SOME TIME LATER, LAWRENCE'S SHADOW FILLED THE DOOR-way. "What the hell you doing, boy? The whole damn place is full of smoke."

"Leave me alone," Nemo said quietly.

Lawrence disappeared and came back carrying a lamp. The floorboards shook as he walked over to the fireplace, prodded the smoldering ashes with his foot, and set the lamp on the mantel. "Don't you know any better than to burn paper and plastic in this old fireplace? You're lucky you didn't burn the whole house down."

"Not such a bad idea."

Lawrence opened the window, fanned the smoke, and sat on the sill. "That girl took a big chance on you."

"I told you to leave me alone." Nemo turned his face to the floor.

"And we're ignoring you. Lying up here in the dark feeling sorry for yourself. Shit. What do you think she's going through right now? She didn't *have* to tell you a damn thing, you know. You didn't have a clue."

Nemo rolled over on his back and watched Lawrence

light up a cigarette and blow a perfect smoke ring as big as a basketball. Apparently, *his* smoke was okay. Nemo sat up and leaned his back against the wall. "She's my grandmother, Lawrence."

Lawrence shook his head. "You two *are* made for each other. Both obtuse as hell. Your grandmother died when you were five years old. Justine's no more your grandmother than we're a good-looking West Texas cowboy."

"It's her, Lawrence. I don't know why I didn't see it before."

"Yeah, right. Smart boy like you." He took another drag off his cigarette, consulting with himself. "Let's just have it your way, then: She's Angelina, born in 1985, had a couple of kids, a grandson, lost her husband, died of Alzheimer's at eighty. You hate her now? Son, you never knew the woman, and she never knew you. You met Justine, fell in love with Justine. Hell, I bet you were even willing to go into the Bin for her, when you found out— perish the thought—that she's a Construct. Now, you mind telling us how the hell it matters whether you've got Angelina's blood in your veins—when you won't have either blood or veins in there?"

Nemo pushed himself up the wall to his feet. "I told you to leave me alone. Why am I even talking to you? You knew all the time. Showing up with her at Mom and Dad's. What were you doing, coaching her? 'This is how us Constructs lie and scheme, little lady.' You set me up, didn't you? You knew from the beginning."

Lawrence flipped the cigarette out the window and closed his eyes, his scales fanning out. It was as if he were listening to something, looking at something behind his eyes. "This isn't just about you and Justine, Nemo. But yes, we knew."

Nemo hadn't wanted to believe it. Even as he accused him, he'd held onto the hope that he was wrong. "How could you do this to me, Lawrence?"

Lawrence couldn't cry. There were no tear ducts in his eyes. But Nemo knew the look of his pain. "It was the hardest thing we've ever done, Nemo. When you know what's going on, we hope you'll forgive us."

Nemo exploded. "*When I know what's going on? When I know what's going on?* Everybody keeps telling me this shit. Well, everybody's wrong. I already know what's going on—because I'm going to make it happen. Not you, not Mom, not Justine. Not God in his fucking heaven. But *me.* I'm pulling the plug on my problems, Lawrence. And after that, I'm finding another place to live. I don't want to live in this house anymore."

He started for the door, but Lawrence blocked his way. "Your mother wants to see you. It's important. She has some things she wants to tell you."

"Not interested. Get out of my way, Lawrence."

"Son, she didn't know who Justine is."

Nemo slammed his fist into the wall. "*Goddamnit! Somebody* had to know. I didn't know. Justine didn't know. Now you're telling me Mom didn't know? Well, who the hell *did* know? And how is it you know so goddamn much?"

Lawrence stepped away from the door, shook another cigarette from his pack, and lit it. Finally, he said, "Your grandfather knew. He told us."

"Wade Donley?"

"Wade Donley's not your grandfather. Biologically speaking, anyway. Newman Rogers is your grandfather."

"Newman Rogers is my *grandfather?*"

"That's right."

Nemo threw his hands up in the air. This was totally fucking insane. They were all trying to drive him crazy. He clamped his hands over his ears and screamed, "Enough bullshit!" He backed into the hallway, stabbing his finger in the air at Lawrence. "You think this is funny, Lawrence? I trusted you. I trusted Justine. You got any room in that lizard brain of yours for how *I* feel? You goddamn lying snake!"

As Nemo charged down the stairs, Lawrence called after him, but he didn't answer. He didn't want to hear any more. He went out back to the tool shed, took a crowbar down from the wall, and hooked it over his belt in case he ran into any more dogs. The rabbits stirred in their hutches, watching him. The moonlight shone on the high grass. No one had lain there. No one had made love. None of that had ever happened.

Peter said there was a meeting tonight. Nemo intended to find it. Gabriel said Nemo would want to see him when he learned the truth. Maybe Gabriel wasn't so crazy after all. Maybe Nemo didn't give a damn whether he was or not.

There was a light in Peter's room, so he was still there. Even Peter wouldn't go off and leave a candle burning. Nemo crouched behind a hedge on the other side of the street, and concentrated on the light, on what he was going to do, pushing all other thoughts out of his mind. The last few days were all a mistake, but it wasn't going to happen again. After about twenty minutes, Peter came out, looked cautiously up and down, and headed toward Northside Station. Nemo waited until Peter was a good half block away and followed him.

When Peter went down into the station, Nemo figured there was no chance of not being spotted. The guy was too paranoid. Nemo quickened his pace and hurried down to the platform. There was Peter, looking up and down the tracks, as if spies might be hiding between the rails.

Nemo was almost on top of him when Peter thought to turn around.

Nemo gave him a little salute. "Where're we going?"

Peter held up his hands, eyeing the crowbar with alarm. "Please, leave me alone."

Nemo imagined his eyes looked as wild as Peter's, but he tried to sound calm and reasonable. "I'm not going to hurt you, Peter. I want to help. But I need you to find Gabriel."

Peter shook his head. "I can't."

Nemo shrugged. "Okay. I'll just get on whatever train you get on, get off where you do. We can either ride trains all night, or you can take me to your meeting. I have some good news for Gabriel. You wouldn't want to disappoint him, would you?"

The warning lights flashed, and the southbound local pulled into the station. Peter hesitated, then got on board, Nemo right behind him. Before he sat down, Nemo looked up and down the train. There were at least a dozen other passengers, three at the other end of the car they were in. Nemo'd never seen so many people out in the middle of the night. "All these folks going to this meeting?"

Peter eyed him cautiously. "Maybe. You're going to help us?"

"I'm going to help myself. You guys get to help me. You want the Bin to go away. I want the Bin to go away. We have different reasons. But yeah, I'm going to help you."

Peter smiled. "I told Gabriel you would. It was revealed to me. I had a vision."

Nemo eyed him suspiciously. "You had a vision, about me?"

Peter held up his hands, as if he could still see his vision in the fluorescent lights. "You were all in flames, but the fire didn't burn you. God called to you, and you ascended into heaven. The sky turned to fire, raining down on the wicked. And the children of God rode the flames into the sky like a fiery chariot."

Nemo could almost see this vision himself. "I have a dream something like that. How did you figure it meant I'd convey a virus into the Bin's operating system?"

"You were chosen by God," Peter said, as if it were obvious.

"Like Moses or Samson."

"Exactly."

Samson died in chains, Nemo thought, blind and alone. "So what's our stop, Peter?"

"Oregon Hill."

"Where's the meeting?"

"Hollywood Cemetery."

"Of course. I should've known."

OREGON HILL HAD BURNED TO THE GROUND YEARS AGO. Hardly anyone lived there to put out the blaze. Lightning struck one of the houses and spread to them all. Only the chimneys remained standing, looking like skinny giants in the moonlight. Nemo and Peter walked beneath them, weaving their way through the burned out wreckage. There was a stream of people now, all headed toward the gates of Hollywood Cemetery.

The cemetery had thrived in recent years. The fundies kept it up, planting flowers and burying their dead in plots most of them couldn't have afforded before the Bin. It was a magnificent monument to the dead, the perfect place to wait for the Rapture.

Torches burned at the gates. The crowd fell into single file, passing through one at a time. A pair of armed guards scrutinized them as they passed, occasionally stopping someone and pulling them out of the line. Nemo slid the crowbar down his pants and left his shirttail out to help conceal it. As he approached the gate, a large black man with a sawed-off shotgun stepped in front of him. "I don't know you," the man said.

"Gabriel invited me." Nemo pointed a thumb over his shoulder at Peter. "He's my date."

The man didn't crack a smile. "Do you speak for him?" he asked Peter. What a question, Nemo thought. Peter could barely speak for himself.

"Yes, I do," Peter said in the same solemn voice the man had used.

The man stepped aside and waved them through. This was a ritual, Nemo realized, the way new lambs were brought into the fold. He looked back at the gate, where most of the people passed through without being stopped. They all knew each other—or someone would vouch for them. He never would've gotten in without Peter.

"What happens," Nemo asked Peter, "if you speak for me, and I turn out to be a spy?"

"I would be cast into Hell."

Nemo didn't want to know the details of that ritual.

THEY FOLLOWED THE CROWD TO THE RIGHT WHERE A RING of torches burned at the base of the Monument to the Confederate Dead, a ninety-foot, steep-sloped pyramid made of rough-hewn granite. There were probably two hundred people there already. More men with guns herded the newcomers to the far side of the pyramid where there was still room. Nemo had no idea that the underground was so large, or so well armed. He wondered how far all these people had come to be here. He'd heard that Richmond was a stronghold for the underground—easy striking distance to the Bin, but not as dangerous as D.C. itself, with a long tradition of living in the past.

Nemo and Peter stood about twenty feet in front of the base of the pyramid. People continued to file in behind them. On the face of the pyramid, a smooth stone set just above eye-level had *Memoriâ in Æternâ* chiseled into it in six-inch-high letters. It was almost 300 years old, a monument to a lost cause. They were standing on the graves of over 18,000 soldiers. Squat stones numbered them— *153–172, 173–190*—examples for these new martyrs, in another dying world. Nemo had been here many times to visit his grandparents' graves on the other side, overlooking the river. He'd brought Rosalind once, but she'd been sullen and withdrawn, telling him he was morbid to visit the dead.

Most of the crowd was looking up. Nemo followed their gaze and saw what everyone was looking at. It was Gabriel, clad in white robes, torches around him, standing on a crude wooden platform perched atop the pyramid, a bullhorn in his hand. The last of the faithful took their places at the back of the crowd. The only sounds were the hiss of torches, the barking of dogs in the distance, and the breathing of several hundred people.

"Praise God!" Gabriel screamed into the bullhorn.

"Praise God!" they roared.

"The Day is at hand!"

"The Day is at hand!"

"Praise God!"

"Praise God!"

"The Day is at hand!"

"The Day is at hand!"

Nemo looked around at the hundreds of faces transfixed. Even the guards, their guns across their chests, had their eyes on Gabriel, roosting on a pile of stones, his hair streaming in the wind like smoke from the torches. The Bin had done this to them, driven them to this.

"Bless you, my children," Gabriel said in a softer voice.

They sighed like the wind in the trees and waited to receive the word of God.

"Do you know what Friday is, my friends?" He leaned out to them, searching their faces, turning on the tiny square of plywood that was his pulpit, so that he might see them all—each and every one of them—so that they might see him. "Do you know?" He let the question hang in the air. Even the dogs were silent now. No one breathed.

"Friday, all the souls in Hell rejoice. They celebrate the hundredth birthday of the Antichrist. A hundred years ago Newman Rogers was born. No one remarked it. Wise men did not kneel before him. Oh no, like the sly serpent in the garden, he entered unnoticed, creeping along the ground, whispering into the slumbering ears of the weak, the fallen, the sinful—*Follow me! Follow me! Follow me!*" His voice had fallen to a whisper, his breath hissing through the bullhorn, as he dragged out the e's in a sibilant rasp. Nemo looked around him. They were all buying it. Every last one of them.

"And follow, they did! Twelve billion! Imagine it, my children. Twelve billion! Twelve—the number of the disciples, a mere handful, followed by nine zeroes! Imagine the racket they will make as they sing his praises—this Newman they believe has made them New Men—freed from the Judgment of God! Imagine Our Savior as this chorus of evil rises to His ears!

"I say: No more!"

He spread out his arms, and the congregation shouted, *"No more!"* He whirled around to each point of the compass—*"No more! No more! No more!"*

He waited for the echo to fade into silence. "Behold, I come quickly, saith the Lord, but they have not listened. They are like Adam and Eve hiding in the Garden, imagining God cannot see them—twelve billion of them! They pursue their lives of empty pleasure with no thought of their salvation. Imagine them, on Judgment Day. They will not have time to look up from their gluttonous feasts. They will not have time to turn their beautiful faces from their mirrors. They will not have time to rise from their lewd beds. In the blink of an eye, they will be cut off forever from the Grace of God—for it will be the End of Days!" He looked off to the north, as if he could see the damned from his high vantage point. He shook his head at their foolishness and turned his back on them. "Do not mourn for them. They have cast their lot with Satan.

"We may seem like few, a mere handful. How can we be heard over their din? What are we to their billions, their nine zeroes? We are the anointed ones, the children of God, the chosen few. We speak not with our voices alone, but with the voices of all the faithful who have gone before us, and who cry out to us now. Beneath your very feet. Listen! They call to us from the earth, pleading with us to slay this serpent who holds them captive. You stand upon their graves. Thousands of Christian soldiers, who died with Christ's promise in their hearts, calling to you, yearning for the Grace of God. Listen, and you can hear them. Listen!" He cupped his hand to his ear and circled the platform as the dead talked to him, told him their secrets. "I hear my father, who labored in the vineyard all his days, calling to me for deliverance. I hear your fathers, and your fathers' fathers, and their fathers before them. Your sisters, your mothers. Your sons and daughters. Even the infants wailing for us to set them free. Listen! Listen!"

The faces in the torchlight were intent with listening to the dead, their faces twisted with longing to set them free. They could all hear them.

"They have been waiting so long, waiting for the promise to be fulfilled. Answer them, my children! Answer them! He is coming!" Gabriel threw up his arms, and the crowd began to chant, "*He is coming! He is coming! He is coming! He is coming!*"

He brought down his arms, and they fell silent. "Ready yourselves," he said. "The time is at hand." He thrust his right fist into the air, and everyone in the crowd did the same. "*The time is at hand!*"

And then he was gone. Down a rope ladder, Nemo guessed. The crowd continued to chant, until that too faded away, and they stood there in a daze, smiling at each other, laughing and crying, charged up and eager to do the will of God, or Gabriel. Either one would do. Nemo felt someone take his arm, and turned to find the man from the gate.

"Come with me," he said. "Gabriel wants to see you."

Peter stepped forward as if to join them, but the man held up his hand. "Go home."

"But I found him for you," Peter whined. "Tell him, Nemo."

"Go home," the man repeated, and Peter sulked off.

THE CROWD PARTED BEFORE THEM AS THE MAN LED NEMO up the hill into the heart of the cemetery. Curious eyes followed them. A little girl, riding on her father's shoulders, pointed at Nemo, and her father smiled his apologies. There was something else in his eyes, too. He knows why I'm here, Nemo thought. He knows who I am.

"Where're we going?" Nemo asked his guide, but he didn't answer. The crowd was behind them now, the torches, except for the ones atop the pyramid, were just a glow on the other side of the hill. Soon, they too were out of sight. They were walking on a narrow asphalt road. Even that was kept in perfect repair. Nemo wondered if there were plans to repave it in gold. Beyond low iron fences, gravestones and monuments glowed in the moonlight. Nemo listened for the voices of the dead, but couldn't hear them, except for Angelina's.

"You ever kill anyone with that gun?" Nemo asked.

The man ducked his head. "Before I was saved, that's about all I knew how to do. Had no faith."

"What about now?"

But his guide didn't answer. They'd reached their destination, a dark, cast-iron structure, ringed by armed guards. One of them opened a door, and Nemo walked inside, the door closing behind him. In the glow of candlelight, Gabriel sat on a sarcophagus. He indicated the other end of it, and Nemo sat on the cold stone.

"I saw you in the crowd this evening," Gabriel said. "It inspired me. I hope you found it enlightening."

"Very impressive," Nemo said. "I especially liked the way you played off the bullhorn. The snake bit was really good. And the way you sometimes sounded like the voice of God and sometimes like a riot."

"Perhaps sometimes they are the same thing."

"Or maybe you think that because you're the guy with the bullhorn."

Gabriel laughed. He could afford a sense of humor. He had a dozen guys with guns if he took offense. "Do you know who's buried here?" he asked.

Nemo looked around at the elaborate gothic iron work. "No idea. Is he going to talk to us, too?"

Gabriel smiled. "You think I'm a charlatan, don't you?"

"Most everybody I know is these days. Don't take it personally. You were going to tell me who we're sitting on?"

"This is a monument to James Monroe, the fifth president of the United States. He was quite an important man in his day. Let's hope he made his peace with God. Not likely. He was an Episcopalian, you know." He said "Episcopalian" as if it were something obscene. "He once

had a run-in with another Gabriel—Gabriel Prosser—he
led a slave rebellion in 1800. Monroe had him hanged,
along with thirty-five of his followers. He lamented that
the uprising signaled the end of the 'tranquil submission'
of the slaves. That's what I signal now."

"That's how you see yourself—as a freer of slaves?"

Gabriel smiled. "No, we shall sink the slavers' ships—
you and I—and end it once and for all."

"I haven't said I'll do it."

"You have already said no. If you hadn't changed your
mind, you wouldn't be here. You have been the victim of
an abomination, deceived by the Whore of Babylon, Bride of
the Antichrist. Now the scales have fallen from your eyes."

Nemo felt the crowbar against his leg. He was tempted
to knock some of the smugness out of this strutting
prophet, but the guards would be on him in seconds.
"Save that crap for your zombies, Gabriel. I'm not interested in you or your crazy religion. I'm here for my own
reasons, and I don't care to discuss them with you."

"The Lord moves in mysterious ways. You are here for
His reasons, whether you know it or not."

Nemo was beginning to wonder what he was doing
here. He wanted to get on with it before he lost his nerve.
"Look, are you going to lay it out for me, or are we going
to discuss theology all night?"

Gabriel nodded. "Very well. This Friday at ten A.M.,
you will return here, and we will download a copy of your
identity and implant the virus. It will take only a few
minutes, and you won't even know it's there. You will
enter the Bin precisely at noon. No more than thirty minutes before, you will have swallowed an antidote for the
lethal injection. Don't eat anything that morning, drink
only water. After you are uploaded, my men will recover
your body. They will bring you here, and I will restore
you to life in a world reborn."

"How can you be so sure you can get my body back?"

"We have infiltrated their security. Our men will be in place. The moment you enter, they will recover your body."

"But D.C. isn't the only entry into the Bin. Do you have somebody going in all over the damn globe?"

"Only you. The virus attacks the main operating system. All entries to the Bin will be rendered inoperable."

"Why all the guns, Gabriel?"

"In this fallen world, they are the scepters of authority. They will not be necessary after His will is done."

"And the people in the Bin?"

"They will spend eternity in the Hell they have chosen."

"The virus doesn't hurt them?"

"They have already destroyed themselves."

"Come on, Gabriel, quit the double talk. You know what I mean."

"The virus itself will not alter their wretched existence— just as they would have it."

"So everybody's happy."

Gabriel laughed. "You're forgetting one thing."

"What's that?"

"The Judgment of the Lord."

"He takes orders from you, does He?"

"I do His will."

"It must get a little tricky sometimes telling which is which. What are you going to tell those folks out there if God doesn't show up, Gabriel?"

"He will come."

"Guess we'll find out on Friday."

AFTER HIS MEETING WITH GABRIEL, NEMO retraced his steps on his own. The guards had all left with their savior. Nemo thought of that chanting mass of people, and wondered if he was doing the right thing, involving himself with a man like Gabriel. But maybe Gabriel was saving them all, like he said, giving them something to believe in. Who was Nemo to judge? Until a few days ago, he wouldn't have shed a tear if the Bin had vanished. He'd shed more than a few now, but he would anyway. And as long as it was there, a day wouldn't go by he wouldn't think about going in, wouldn't think about Justine. And Angelina.

He was closing a door. That's all he was doing. A door that never should've been opened in the first place. All these people buried here—they lived their whole lives knowing they would die. Maybe we need that, Nemo thought. He'd welcome his own death right about now. Nemo. No one. That's what it meant in Latin, Lawrence had told him. That's who he wanted to be: no one.

The moon was now obscured by the trees, and the torches all extinguished. He searched the horizon for some hint of the pyramid, but he couldn't see it. He stopped. He was pretty sure he was headed in the right general direction, but he hadn't been paying any attention, just putting one foot in front of the other. Now he was lost.

There was nothing to do but keep walking. If he stayed on the road, surely sooner or later, they all led to the gate. He trudged on, searching the rows of spires and crosses for some familiar landmark, when he saw something that made his blood run cold.

There was a dog, maybe fifteen feet ahead of him, standing perfectly still. Nemo looked for the rest of the pack, listened carefully, but there was nothing. Maybe it was a loner. Sometimes they were the most dangerous of all, taking chances a pack wouldn't take. Slowly, he drew the crowbar out of his pants and braced himself.

But it didn't move. It stood there, staring at him. He couldn't turn back. He'd only get more lost than he already was. He had to stick to the road. Hell with it, he thought, advancing on the dog, holding the crowbar at the ready. It stood its ground, not moving a muscle. He was practically on top of the damn thing now. If it sprang at close range, he wouldn't even have time to get a blow in. He'd have to make the first move, try to scare it off.

He took a deep breath and screamed, swinging the crowbar back and forth, charging on the dog for all he was worth. The crowbar clanged off its head and bounced out of his hand, leaving it numb. He looked down at his adversary, still standing there as if waiting to be petted. He reached out to touch its fur. It was metal. He'd just attacked an iron dog.

He remembered it now. It was the only thing in the cemetery that had interested Rosalind. She'd sat on its back as if it were a pony, and put a wreath of flowers around its neck. He laughed at himself and moved on. He'd gone about thirty yards when he spotted the apex of the pyramid and oriented himself. Then he realized he'd left the crowbar lying on the ground. Let the dog have it, he thought.

HE WENT DOWN INTO OREGON HILL STATION INTENDING to catch the northbound local, but he caught an eastbound train instead and got off at Capitol Square Station. Lawrence said his mom wanted to talk to him. *What would Jesus do?* the graffiti artist asked him again. As Nemo recalled, He'd said he had no mother when she wanted to talk to Him. Well, that might do for God, but Nemo had a few things he wanted to say to his mom and dad, before he told them good-bye, once and for all.

He expected his parents to be in bed, but there was a light on in the back of the house. He climbed the same wall he'd vaulted a few hours earlier and looked through the bay window. His mother was sitting at the kitchen table, her head in her hands. There was a drink beside her, but it looked as if she hadn't touched it, and half the ice was melted. She must've sensed him looking at her, because she brought her head up sharply and stared out the window. But she couldn't see him in the darkness.

She looked awful. Her eyes were red and swollen, her face puffy. As he watched, her face crumpled in pain, and she began to cry again. He came out of the shadows, and she jumped back, knocking over her chair. He rushed in through the back door and took her in his arms. "Oh God, Nemo!" she sobbed. "Please forgive me." He rocked her in his arms, soothed and reassured her, settled her in another chair, turned the fallen one upright, and sat down beside her.

It wasn't until then that he saw his father standing on the back stairs. "I must've fallen asleep," he said. "I don't know how. I was going to write you a letter, but then who would deliver it? And what would I say? Please forgive us, Nemo." He came down the stairs and sat at the table. His eyes were red, as well. He had a dazed, distracted look about him. Nemo had never seen his father cry.

Nemo stood up. He didn't want their pain and guilt. It was theirs. They'd earned it. "I've come to say good-bye," he said. "That's all."

His mother looked up at him and rose to her feet. But she didn't run into his arms as he thought she would. She steadied herself on the table's edge and pointed to his chair. "Sit down, Nemo. I have something to tell you."

"I've heard enough, Mother. I'm leaving now."

"No! Sit down! I'm your mother, no matter what I've done, no matter what you think I've done." Her hand, still pointing at the chair, was trembling, but her face was determined.

He sat down on the edge of the chair. He'd never seen his mother like this. She sat down and spread her hands palms down on the table. His father reached for her, but she shook her head, and he withdrew his hand. She spoke to the backs of her hands. "When I was growing up, I adored my mother and father. We were so happy. I thought nothing could ever change that. But after my father died, I found out he wasn't my father, that he'd known it all along, died with the knowledge his wife had betrayed him, and that I was the result. God, how he must've hated me sometimes. Daddy's little girl. I never forgave my mother for that.

"After you were born, I didn't want you to see her, to have anything to do with her. I said it was because of the Alzheimer's, that it would confuse and frighten you, but that wasn't it at all. I wanted to punish her. I didn't want her to know you.

"We only took you to see her the one time. Your father thought you should at least meet her before she died. She was pretty far gone by then. I knew she wouldn't remember it. There were times she didn't even know me. She had a Construct nurse who stayed with her, but I still came every day to fix her meals and check on her. Some days, she didn't get out of bed at all.

"But the day we brought you, she was downstairs waiting for us, all dressed. Her hair was even combed. She came to life, and she was like herself again. She made a great fuss over you, sat you in her lap, and wouldn't let you leave her side. You remember that, don't you?"

Nemo nodded. "She took me up in the attic."

His mother smiled. "She hadn't been up there in over ten years. She argued with me about everything. But she remembered me. She even remembered your father. The next day, she died."

"The next day. I thought—"

"We kept it from you. You were talking about her all the time, asking when we would go visit Grandma again.

We didn't take you to the funeral. You were only five. When we finally told you, you cried for two solid days. I thought that would be it. But you were obsessed with her, especially after we moved into her house, hoarding her things, going up to the attic whenever we turned our backs. I used to think you did it just to drive me mad, but that wasn't it. You loved her, and she loved you—even though I'd kept you apart. I often prayed that I'd never taken you there. I said it wasn't fair for you to love her when she'd betrayed my father, betrayed me. A thousand times I almost told you what she was—this woman you'd idolized. Just yesterday, I almost told you. But a lot has happened since then."

She looked Nemo in the eye, her voice strong and steady. "Now, I have betrayed you, my only son. I knew it was wrong as I was doing it, but I talked myself into it, convinced myself I was doing the right thing. It all happened so easily.

"I don't know why she did what she did. I don't suppose I'll ever know. But it doesn't matter anymore. I forgive her. I hope she finds it in her heart to forgive me."

Now they'll have eternity to work it out, Nemo thought. He didn't want to hear any of this. It had nothing to do with him. He didn't really care whether she *meant* to fuck up his life or not. She'd done it. And she wasn't going to get another chance to try it again. She was looking at him as if he should say something, apparently finished with her confession.

"There's one thing you've left out. Who was my grandfather?"

She spoke quietly, struggling to say it. "Newman Rogers. He and Mother were old friends."

"So it was friendly adultery. Glad to hear it. Lawrence told me, but I didn't believe him. It was just too fucking crazy. Where is my illustrious grandfather? Does he send Christmas cards? Drop by on his birthday?"

"I don't know," his mother said, on the verge of tears. "I've never laid eyes on him."

Nemo stood and stepped away from the table. "If I'm lucky, I won't either. I'm getting out of this nuthouse. Good-bye, Mom, Dad. It's been real."

His mother leaned toward him. "Nemo, she's suffered enough heartache. She loves you. Forgive her."

"You don't give up, do you, Mom? You figure if she was good enough for your father, she's good enough for me?"

His father came out of his chair. "How dare you talk to your mother like that!" His mother rose to her feet to stop him, planting her hands on his chest.

Nemo stared at them, knowing he should just leave, but the words kept running through his mind, daring him to speak them, to try them out, to see what they could do. "I have no mother. I have no father. They burned themselves up when I was ten years old. But spare your sympathy. I've gotten over it."

And then he left them. Mom and Dad. Todd and Elizabeth. Weeping at their table. For how long? Who could say? Perhaps forever. That's how he'd remember them, anyway. As he made his way home, he recalled that he'd had some things he'd wanted to say to them. Now, for the life of him, he couldn't remember what they were. Anything would've been better than what he'd said. Maybe Gabriel and his crew were right. Maybe Christ was just a cruel, vindictive bastard.

15

AFTER JUSTINE LEFT MR. MENSO, SHE WANDERED around the city, avoiding her room, not wanting to be alone, but not wanting to be with anyone, even herself. Especially herself. She headed for Constitution Avenue, but the kite flyers weren't out at six o'clock in the morning. Only a group of men on racing bikes. They sat upright when they saw her, riding with no hands to impress her, waving and blowing kisses as they swept past. She remembered Nemo flying a kite, Patrick's solemn voice saying, *If you let go, it will fall down.* She wanted to hang on, but to what?

The sun was coming up as she climbed the steps to the Rogers Memorial. In preparation for the big birthday celebration tomorrow, banners were draped across the front, a grandstand and a speakers' platform set up on the lawn. They glistened with morning dew. A pair of squirrels were chasing each other back and forth across the top of the grandstand until they leapt for an overhanging branch and continued the chase from tree to tree.

Inside, the place was deserted. Justine walked past all the exhibits, without a glance, into the great hall. Newman was nearing the end of his speech. If you listened closely to the recording, you could hear the uncomfortable murmur from the crowd as he talked about God. She rode up to the third floor and stood face-to-face with him—so huge one of his eyes was the size of her head, so huge she hadn't recognized him as Mr. Menso. She saw it now. He was thirty-one years younger, the wrinkles not so deep and numerous, his voice stronger. Sadder. She sat on the balcony, her feet dangling over the edge, and listened to his speech, over and over again.

This time, she listened to the words he didn't say— knowing that, as he spoke, he was giving up all hope of Angelina, because he had to tend to his creation, take responsibility for what he'd done. A year later, she was a widow. No wonder he went a little crazy.

That first day in his shop, he'd said this place needed to change. Looking at his face, as he took off his glasses and rubbed his enormous eyes, she thought she could see the change he longed for—even then, on that very first day—he wanted his creation to let him go. Now he had her to deal with, raised from the dead, asking him only to help her die. In spite of her own troubles, she felt sorry for him.

She felt a responsibility for the fragments of Angelina's life that had passed on to her, a desire to bring them together, to discover the missing pieces, to make them whole again. She'd been remembering all morning— Angelina's memories, now hers. She regarded them differently than Angelina did. For Justine, they were memories of who she used to be, not of who she still was. What would Angelina do? she asked herself for the thousandth time. Whatever Justine decided, it was for all of them. She imagined herself outside, reunited with Nemo, lying in his arms. But she could just as easily imagine him turning his back on her a second time. She couldn't imagine a more lonely death. Newman's speech started again, and she grasped the railing and pulled herself to her feet.

Outside, the sun was shining, and the joggers were starting to come out. "Yoo-hoo! Justine!" someone called to her, and she looked up to see Freddie sitting in the grandstand, a few rows up on the aisle, waving at her.

"Hi, Freddie," she said, shielding her eyes from the sun. He'd shed his white robes, and was dressed in black jeans and a black T-shirt. "What are you doing here?"

"Warren sent me to lend a hand."

She walked up the aisle and sat down beside him, slumping down in the chair, stretching her legs out. She was exhausted. "So how did you know where to find me?"

"Warren, of course. He knows where everybody is. He didn't tell me you'd be crying your little eyes out, you poor thing."

"Please, Freddie, no sympathy. I'm too tired."

"Ha!" he said, stretching his neck out. "I like you, Justine. You're a stitch. Warren said you might need help getting information."

"What information?"

"He didn't say. He's always been like that. You have to get used to it. Mr. Cryptic. It's that genius thing, you know. I suppose he meant whatever information you want. It *is* my specialty. Warren says I'm the absolute best. Did you know they used to call it the Information Superhighway. Cute, don't you think? Nasty things, highways. I'm glad we got rid of them."

Justine smiled. She liked Freddie, his chatty exuberance. "You've known Mr. Menso for a long time?"

"We go way back to the Dark Ages. We were drearily real together in our little laboratories, designing our little circuits. That was long before he was St. Newman. Poor bastard." He pointed at the banner over the speakers' stand—*He walketh in the circuit of heaven*, it read. "He's so pissed about that—you can't imagine."

"Why doesn't he put a stop to it?"

Freddie put his hands on his hips. "Well, thank you. I ask him the same question every year, but does he listen? He doesn't like to tamper, he says, throw everyone into a tizzy. 'But Warren,' I say, 'does it have to be so *tacky?*' There's a big, soggy storm moving up the coast, with any luck they'll all get drenched. Warren could help the storm along if he wanted, but he has his little scruples."

"So how long have you known him?"

"You're going to make me do the math, aren't you?" He sighed. "Let's see. He was twenty-five when I met him. I was twenty. His big hundredth birthday is tomorrow. So, that means about seventy-five years, give or take a few months. Ha! Seems longer."

Freddie looked like he was in his late twenties, his skin smooth, no lines around his eyes or mouth. But he was ninety years old, give or take a few months. "You two were friends."

"Oh, yes. We worked together, had lunch together, that sort of thing. Then he told our little international conglomerate to go fuck itself and started his own company. 'Freddie,' I said to myself. 'Newman—I mean Warren—knows what he's doing.' So when he called me up and offered me a job, I went for it. Place was positively stuffed with geniuses, but he asks *me*—the little faggot programmer. No one shed a tear when I left, of course. They did that later, when the Bin put their tight little asses out of business."

"Why do you call him Warren? He hasn't always used that name, has he?"

"Oh no, he's only insisted on it the last few years. I don't blame him. I ask you—if every other runny-nosed little brat in the world were named after you, wouldn't you want to change your name? I mean *Mr. Rogers* was bad enough. But you're probably too young to remember him, aren't you? Well, trust me. You missed a gruesome experience. He had this sincere little children's TV show, cuddly platitudes and such. Well. All right. But he wore these ghastly cardigan sweaters. You cannot imagine." Freddie quivered with disgust.

"Did you know that Angelina gave him the name Warren?"

Freddie groaned. "Oh God! He hasn't been telling that dreadful napkin story again, has he?" He struck a forlorn face, his lip quivering—" 'I still have the napkin, the download, anyway.' Please! Get a grip! The man has saved a *napkin* for eighty years!"

Justine had to laugh. "I think it's sweet."

"Ha! It's positively diabetic."

"So you actually knew Angelina?"

"In name only. For—what did we say?—seventy-five years, Warren's been boring me to excruciating tears yammering about Ange*li*na, his *love*, his *sweet*heart! But I never met the woman. I came close a few times, but she always dropped him for some delicious Cro-Magnon or other before they got around to having lunch with his queer friend.

"I've told him a million times: Get over it! Be creative! Use your imagination! Go out on a date!' Ha! I hardly had you in mind. No offense, Justine, but it's all a bit obsessive, don't you think?"

She supposed it was, but even so, part of her was touched by it all. "But he didn't make me for himself."

"Oh, I know. I said, 'Warren, why not? Live a little! Eternity is a *long* time.' Not the thing to say, I can tell you."

"So why *did* he make me?"

Freddie arched an eyebrow and gave her a knowing look. "I have a theory about that. He says it's because he can't bear the thought of Angelina being gone forever, that he only wants her happiness, and all the rest of that romantic drivel. But *I* think he did it to prove that he could. Once he latches onto a problem, he simply has to solve it. He's really quite proud of you, you know. His own little miracle. The most brilliant programming I've ever seen."

She looked at the gleaming grandstand, the huge memorial, like a domed temple. Tomorrow, there'd be people for as far as you could see in all directions, come to sing his praises. "So you think he made me just to satisfy his ego? To play at being God?"

"He doesn't play, Justine. He is. In here, anyway. He doesn't like me to say it, but face facts. *Somebody's* got to have access to the code. The man wasn't likely to lock himself out of his own program. Trust me, you wouldn't want any of those assholes who put up the money to be running things." He shuddered at the thought.

"Is he running me?"

"Oh, goodness no. He has this thing about free will. Do yourself a favor, don't ever ask him about it." Freddie pantomimed a yawn.

She had to stifle her own yawn. "I think I'm going to head on back to my room, Freddie. I'm pretty beat. Thanks for the information. I wish you'd known Angelina. She's the one I'd really like to know about."

Freddie rolled his eyes. "Justine, don't be so linear. I *find* information; I don't *have* it, for goodness sakes. For instance, if I were you, I'd visit granny's house again. Just like Little Red Riding Hood—little cape, short skirt." He moved his shoulders as if he were flouncing through the woods. "Your boyfriend with the cute little butt had a bunch of her things in his boudoir, as I recall?"

She gave him an accusing look. "You were watching us?"

"So sensitive. Only for a little tiny while. I didn't watch you *doing* it, if that's what you mean. Warren would've killed me." He made a face and cocked his head, hanging himself with an imaginary rope.

*   *   *

327

THIS TIME FREDDIE TOOK HER IN THE FRONT DOOR AND FOL-
lowed her in. "Hope you don't mind, but I just want
another little peek." He squinted in the shadows and wrinkled up his nose. "Smoky in here." He held up a battery-
operated lantern. "Plan ahead, I always say." He turned
it on and played the beam around the foyer, up the stairs.
"How deliciously dreadful. Love the banister."

"Thanks Freddie."

He cupped a hand to his ear. "Could that be my exit
line? I believe it is. You're welcome, Justine." He opened
the door, and the lobby of Real World Tours lay on the
other side. "I've set it up so that you exit through the
front door. You didn't want to see the whole ugly thing
again, did you?"

"No, this'll be fine."

"Here you go." He handed her the lantern and winked.
"Hope you find an honest man—with a cute butt."

"Thank you, Freddie."

Freddie closed the door behind him, and she stood for
a moment in the foyer, listening, but there was only the
wheezing creak of an old house. She looked out the window. It was raining—Richmond rain, small and steady,
nearly silent—nothing like the driving rains she remembered in Dallas, so loud sometimes, you had to shout to
be heard over the racket. She climbed the stairs, and the
smoke was stronger up here, burning her eyes and nose.

In Nemo's room, the refrigerator stood open, completely
empty. The earth poster had been torn from the wall, a
corner still dangling from a pushpin. All the photographs
were gone. The bedclothes lay on the floor. She noticed a
tapping noise and saw that the pan on the refrigerator was
no longer under the leak. A small pool of water stood on the
floor, inching its way toward the outside corner of the room.

She tried to tell herself it was some kind of mistake, that
she should go downstairs and tell Freddie to fix it, or that

somebody'd broken into Nemo's house and did this to his room. But she knew Nemo had done it. As far as he was concerned, she was dead and buried, an unwelcome ghost. She closed her eyes, fighting back tears, and Sarah's death came back to her again, and she remembered the packet of letters tied up with green yarn. It had to be the old woman's memory. "Where are they?" she asked her.

I read them every day, so I wouldn't forget. Wade told me it was like wearing a path through the woods, so that I wouldn't get lost so soon. He felt awful for leaving me.

"Do you remember where they are?"

What, dear?

"The letters."

In a little box. A green metal box, behind the little door.

Justine searched the room, but there was no metal box, green or otherwise, no little door. The old woman's memories were a hopeless jumble.

It's not in here. It's in my room. Why would I keep my letters in here?

"Show me."

She left Nemo's room and headed for an open doorway at the other end of the hall. The smoke was stronger here, the room dark and shadowy.

That's my room.

Justine hesitated, then stepped inside.

There was no furniture, nothing on the walls. A sheet lay on the floor in front of the fireplace. Justine shone the light on the ashes. Dangling from the grate, was a strip of red leatherette—all that was left of the diaries. A chill went up her spine, and the lantern slipped from her grasp and clattered to the floor. She imagined him kneeling here, just where she stood, feeding her to the fire, page by page, hating her. She kicked savagely at the grate. Clouds of ashes rose up around her. "I'm not Angelina! I'm not! Goddamn you, Nemo!"

She knelt on the hearth, cursing and crying, wishing she could burst into flames. But she couldn't. She'd never lived, had no life to give up, no soul to surrender. She twisted the sheet around her hands and buried her face in it, but it smelled of him, and she threw it across the room. "I love you, goddamnit!" she screamed, as if he were there to hear her. Screamed it again louder, knowing that he wasn't.

And then she saw, in the corner, a tiny door, an access door to a crawlspace, no more than two feet high. She groped for the lantern and crept over to the door on her hands and knees. She tugged at the knob, but the door had swollen shut, so she planted a foot against the wall and tugged harder. It popped open, and she almost fell over backward.

She shone the light inside. Nothing but dust and cobwebs. She reached around and felt above the door and on either side. She started to crawl through the doorway, when the plywood beyond the threshold slid under her hand. She lifted it up, and there was a small green box. Inside, a bundle of some thirty or forty letters written on thin, plain stationery.

I didn't want Elizabeth to find them and take them away from me.

Justine took the bundle into her lap and untied the green yarn. They fanned out like a deck of cards. The handwriting on the envelopes was just as she remembered. They were already arranged in chronological order. Propping the lantern on top of the access door, she read them one by one.

They began in 2002 just before Angelina left St. Catherine's. Angelina had evidently initiated their correspondence, tracking down Sarah's address and inviting her to her graduation. Sarah couldn't attend, but she thanked Angelina for remembering her and urged her to write again. Angelina did, telling Sarah all her problems apparently, for Sarah's letters were full of sympathy and understanding. *Newman sounds like a very good friend*, she said more than once.

The letters were one or two years apart, longer lapses in the years when Sarah urged her to get drug counseling. In 2019, Sarah congratulated Angelina on her marriage and her son, and wished her every happiness. The very next letter, she told Angelina to ask God's forgiveness, that His mercy was infinite. *Wade has forgiven you, and it's now between you and the Lord.* Sarah didn't tell her, Justine noted, to forgive herself.

And then, for a while, the letters were just the gossipy exchanges of old friends, all the crises past. Sarah was posted to the Vatican, and she talked about the politics of her job, asked questions about Wade and the kids, and told Angelina that she was delighted her life was going so well after all the trouble she'd been through.

In the late forties, however, the letters became more frequent, and the tone abruptly changed. *I shouldn't be telling you any of this*, she said repeatedly, but told her anyway, because she needed to talk to someone, someone who wasn't in the Church, for she couldn't trust anyone inside. The Pope was holding mysterious, secret meetings, shielded from the press. There were rumors he was diverting huge sums of Church money into something called ALMA, but no one was certain what it was, or what it meant, though there were many theories.

And then, of course, came the first public announcements of the Bin, and everyone knew. Sarah couldn't believe that the Pontiff was actually involved in such a thing, that he was dragging the Church into it, though his involvement was still only a persistent rumor. Sarah's letter of December 2049 concluded—*I have requested an audience with His Holiness. Pray for me. Pray for us all.*

The next letter, a few months later, was posted from Malaysia where, at eighty-three, she'd been assigned a small rural school to administer. Not too long after that, Pope Pius XIII entered the Bin and issued a papal bull declaring ALMA to be the work of God on earth and home to the Most Holy Catholic Church. Sarah continued to run her school, even after she was told to shut it down. She also worked to organize resistance to the Pope's actions with meager results.

Justine opened the last letter. From the looks of it, it was the one Angelina had read and reread over the years so she wouldn't forget it, even as her memory was relentlessly slipping away:

MAY 1, 2055

Dear Angelina,

I leave for the Vatican tomorrow. This will be my last letter, though I trust we will meet again with God's grace. As you must know, we have all been excommunicated. At first this threw me into a rage. 'I have given my life to the Church!' I shouted, stamping my feet like you used to do when you were in a rage. But then I prayed and was reminded I'd given my life to Christ—who'd given it to me in the first place, and not to the Church.

As the newspeople never tire of pointing out, what we intend to do is a mortal sin. But for us, it is no different from what the Pope has done. We have no less faith in our immortal souls than he has in his technology. If our act of faith prompts one person to choose God's love over a machine, then we will not have died in vain. If this is sin, I trust in Christ's infinite mercy.

I have written you so that you will know I died doing what I must do, with a faithful heart and a clear conscience. We are both old now, my little angel, and know how hard it can be to know the right thing to do, and

*how important, when it is known, to do it. God be with
you, Angelina.*

> *Your sister in Christ's love,
> Sarah*

A sob caught in her throat, and Justine broke down.
Angelina, as well. All of them grieved for Sarah, all of
them remembered her. This was why Angelina had stayed
out of the Bin against all entreaties. Even her own daughter hadn't known. She was being faithful to the memory
of her first friend, a young nun who let her sing, and
forgave her sins, then killed herself for a lost cause.

Justine gathered up the letters, tied them in a bundle,
and returned them to their hiding place. She hurried down
the stairs and out the front door.

"My God," Freddie said when he saw her. "You look
positively dreadful."

"Tell him I want to download. Tell him I want to do
it as soon as I can."

JUSTINE WAS TOLD TO BE AT MR. MENSO'S SHOP AT FIVE
o'clock. She was ten minutes early when she walked in.
Mr. Menso sat waiting for her.

"Sit down, Justine. They should be here any minute."

She sat on the edge of the sofa, bit her lip and looked
around the room. "Did you know about Sarah's letters?"

"Yes. I made you, Justine. I know everything you
know."

Justine gave a bitter laugh. "Then you're way ahead of
me. Is there anything else you want to fill me in on?"

"I can't just hand it to you. You have to put it together
yourself. We all do."

"Lucky us. He burned everything that had to do with

us. He stuffed it in the fireplace and set fire to it like so much trash, destroying the evidence."

"He's angry and confused."

"When I show up in someone else's body, he'll probably dance a little jig."

"We don't have to do this, Justine. It's your decision."

"Will you quit saying that? Everything's been your god-damn decision. I can stay in here—and he hates me—or I can go out there—and he hates me. Pardon me if I'm not grateful for my choices. But I'm going out. You under-stand that sort of desperate choice, don't you, Newman? Out there, there's that slim little chance he'll come around."

"Yes, I understand perfectly."

"When can I do it?"

"Tomorrow, at noon."

The bell clanged, and a shapely woman in a dress made from old blue jeans stepped cautiously into the room, Law-rence ducking through the door behind her. She was very beautiful, with large dark eyes, and black hair hanging down to her waist.

"Justine," Mr. Menso said, rising to his feet, "this is Elaine."

Justine shook her hand, long slender hands, rough with calluses.

"Lawrence and I will leave you two alone," he said, offering Elaine his chair.

Elaine stood, staring after them as they retreated into the back of the shop. "Was that really Newman Rogers?"

"Yes."

"The Construct told me that Newman Rogers would be here, but I didn't know whether to believe him or not—you know how they are. Imagine: I actually met New-man Rogers."

"You want to sit down?"

"Sure, sure." She sat down in the chair, still staring toward the back of the shop. "Why does he let himself look old like that?"

"He wants to remember his age."

"Why in the world would he want to do that?"

"Could we forget about him for a moment? Do you know why you're here?"

Elaine shrugged, now looking around at all the books. "You want to download into my body when I come in."

"That's right," Justine said. The woman's attitude puzzled her. They might've been discussing a lease on a house.

Elaine pulled a hairbrush out of her bag and started brushing her hair, holding the ends in front of her, working out the tangles. "You know what it's like out there?"

"I've got a fair idea."

Elaine nodded. "You a Christian?"

"I don't know. I'm not sure."

"Where I come from, that's a no. Raised Christian, married Christian. Makes you wonder why I'm sinning like this." She tilted her head to one side and brushed her hair with long, steady strokes. "Why're you downloading, anyway?"

"There's someone I love. He lives outside. I want to be with him."

Elaine threw her hair over her shoulder, and starting working on the other side. "That's so romantic! You must really love him. Do you think he'll think I'm pretty?"

Justine squirmed inside, thinking of Nemo making love to this woman. "Any man would."

Elaine blushed, stopped her brushing, and touched her face with her fingertips. "My husband married me because I'm pretty. Least that's what he told me. But he doesn't like it. He says he does, but he doesn't. He says I'm vain, but I'm not. He's the one thinks I'm pretty."

"Why are you coming inside, Elaine?"

Elaine seemed surprised by the question. "I don't want to get old." She looked around the room, but didn't find anything that interested her. She put her brush back in her bag. "You'll have to stay away from Virginia Beach. That's where I'm from. You wouldn't want my husband catching sight of you. He's into guns. That's what he does. Makes guns."

"I'll remember that."

"So you think you're going to do it? The Construct said I had to meet you first. Make sure I was okay."

"Yes, I'm going to do it."

"Great. I've got one condition, though. You've got to promise me a proper burial. I don't want to get burned up. You promise?"

So that was why Elaine agreed to do this. She wanted to cover all her bases, make sure her body was outside waiting for the Rapture, in case the Christians were right. "Sure, Elaine. I promise."

Elaine heaved a sigh of relief. "I guess that's it, huh?" She smiled at Justine. "Unless you've got something you want to ask me."

Justine tried to imagine herself behind those beautiful, vacant eyes. "Elaine, do you ever sing?"

"Me? You've got to be kidding. I'm—what do you call it when you can't tell one note from another?"

"Tone deaf."

"That's right. Tone deaf. That's what I am. I'm healthy as a horse, though, in case you're wondering." The sound of rain beating against the window started up outside, a few drops at first, and then a steady shower. "Damn," she said. "Now I'm going to get all wet. I don't understand why they let it rain in here. Do you?"

But Justine didn't answer.

16

JONATHAN AND NEMO WERE SITTING ON JONA-than's front porch in a pair of rockers, looking out at the rain in the early evening. Thunder rumbled lazily all around them. Nemo had just told him the whole story.

Jonathan summed it up: "Let me see if I've got all this straight. Newman Rogers is your grandfather, Justine is your grandmother, and you're going to carry Gabriel's virus into the Bin and cut it off from the world forever."

"You don't believe me."

"I believe you. Who would make up something like this? Why do you think he's doing it?"

"Who?"

"Newman Rogers. Your parents didn't come up with this on their own. It sounds to me like they were just being used. From what you've told me, he's the only one who would want to create Justine."

"How the hell should I know why Newman Rogers does anything? Maybe he wants to kidnap the grandson he's never seen. Maybe he's just nuts. That would certainly explain a lot of things."

Jonathan stared thoughtfully at the rain. "I don't know. I sure wouldn't want to be in his shoes." He shook his head at the thought. "So why are you carrying in this virus?"

Nemo almost hadn't told Jonathan anything—to avoid this very question. "It should be obvious. The place is a fucking menace."

"But that's not why you're doing it."

Nemo sighed. Jonathan was right, as usual. Couldn't he just keep it to himself for once? "No. It's not. That doesn't make it any less true, does it?"

But he wasn't to be turned aside so easily. "It's Justine you're hiding from, not the Bin."

"I'm not *hiding* from anything."

"Have you told her what you're going to do?"

"Of course not."

"Sounds like you're hiding to me. Don't you think you might at least tell her good-bye? I thought you loved her, had faith in her."

"I did."

And then he stopped. He just rocked back and forth, watching the rain. The past tense had told him everything he wanted to know.

"Goddamnit Jonathan! What is this? *I told you so?*"

"Not at all."

"Look, come tomorrow at noon, none of this will matter. It will be over, finished. So don't start quoting scripture on me."

"I haven't quoted any scripture."

"Not yet. I can feel it building."

"All right. No scripture. We'll even leave Justine out of it for the moment. What makes you think you've got the right to make this decision for everyone?"

"If I don't do it, Jonathan, they'll just find somebody else."

"Then it will be somebody else's decision, and I can ask him the same question. I still haven't heard your answer."

"So you think I'm doing the wrong thing."

"I didn't say that. I'm just asking you a question."

"Like hell. I thought you would be happy to hear I wasn't going in. You're the one who's so damn concerned about my immortal soul."

"I still am, but there's more to salvation than whether you go into the Bin or not."

"Right. I still have no faith. And I'm not likely to get any anytime soon. So let's not worry about that either, okay?"

"You had faith in Justine, but you've lost it. Now you think you can just turn your back on her, and everything will go back the way it was. But it can't, Nemo. Don't you understand that? I saw it that night I met her—she fills a void in you. Maybe you didn't even know it was there. But now you do, and you know what it's like not to feel hollow. That changes everything. Do you think if I lost my faith tonight, I could just pick up where I left off?"

"When would that be, two years old?"

"Fourteen. About a week before I met you."

"But I thought—"

"I know what you thought. You figured because my dad's Christian, and my mom, and my brother, and every-body in my family for as long as anybody tells me about—that I was just given faith like brown hair and blue eyes? I was standing in line at Receiving when they dropped the ban on minors. I'd been following the story, and I was ready.

"There was this kid working the line, witnessing. The same thing I did at his age, because that's what you were supposed to do. He comes to me and starts in saying the exact same things I'd said. Things I'd never believed. So I looked him in the eye and said, 'You're lying, kid. You don't believe any of this stuff any more than I do.' That's all it took. He broke down crying right there, practically hysterical, so I stepped out of the line, sat him down, and tried to calm him, but I'd really gotten to him. And before I knew it, I was quoting scripture to him. All those lies. But this time I wanted them to work, to stop this boy from crying. I wanted it to be true, and for the very first time, it all made sense to me. I didn't get back in line."

"I'm sorry, Jonathan. How come you've never told me about this before?"

He sighed. "Too ashamed, I guess. That little kid—I don't even know his name. He took my place in line. I've always felt like he gave his life for mine."

"Maybe that's how he feels about you."

"Maybe so."

They rocked quietly. The rain ringing through the downspout. The thunder closer now. "So what should I do, Jonathan? It sounds like you're saying I'm damned if I do, and damned if I don't."

Jonathan shook his head. Nemo had never seen him look sadder. "I don't know," he said.

"But you always know, Jonathan. You're always so sure about everything. What do you think I should do?"

Jonathan rested his head on the back of the rocker. His voice was tired and defeated, as quiet as the rain. "I don't know," he confessed. "I just don't know."

"NEMO!" A VOICE BOOMED FROM DOWN THE STREET. "We've been looking everywhere for you." It was Lawrence, his scales glistening in the rain, jogging toward them. He mounted the porch steps in two strides.

Jonathan rose from his chair. "Sit down," he said. "I'll get you a towel."

Lawrence waved both away. "No thanks. Don't need a towel. Feels good—it's those rain forest genes. Come on,

Nemo. There's someone we want you to meet. We got
her waiting down at the house."

Nemo didn't stir. "What makes you think I want to go
anywhere with you, Lawrence?" Jonathan started to go
into the house, but Nemo wanted an audience. "No, stay.
Lawrence was just leaving."

Lawrence shook his head, and the scales on his forehead
bristled. "Sometimes we don't know what the hell Justine
sees in you. Do you want to know how she's doing? Do
you care that she's about to put her life on the line for
your sorry little ass? Or are you too busy pouting? You
coming or not?"

Nemo came out of his chair ready to tell him off. He
wasn't some little kid to be ordered around anymore. But
he felt Jonathan's hand on his shoulder, and he stopped.
"Go with him," Jonathan said quietly. "I think you
should go with him."

Nemo took a deep breath. Jonathan was right. Lawrence was right. He was burning up with rage. He needed
to cool down, find out what the hell was going on before
he charged into the Bin with a virus in his head. "Who
is it you want me to meet?" he asked Lawrence.

"We'll let her tell you, since you don't put any stock in
what we got to say anymore." He started back home at
full stride, and Nemo hurried to catch up with him.

SHE WAS SITTING AT THE KITCHEN TABLE, JUST WHERE JUS-
tine had sat. Her long legs were crossed, and there was
something odd about them. Then he realized what it was.
She was wearing hose. Somebody had dug awfully deep
to find those. Looking at her legs, he could understand
why. She pulled her hair back behind her ears and smiled
at him.

"Elaine," Lawrence said. "This is Nemo."

She held out her hand as if he should kiss it, admire her lovely arm. He grasped her fingers briefly and let them go.

"Elaine recently spoke with Justine," Lawrence said. "You might find their conversation rather informative, Nemo. Whenever you wish to begin your return journey, Elaine, we'll be waiting in the front parlor." He bowed and left the room.

Elaine shuddered. "Doesn't he give you the creeps? He talks like a hick one minute and like a British person the next." She smiled at Nemo and looked him up and down. "She didn't say you were so cute. Figures, though, I guess. If she's so crazy about you." She pointed to the candles on the table. "Could we light these? It's getting awful dark in here."

"Sure." Nemo hunted up some matches and lit the candles. He sat down across from her. She was one of the most beautiful women he'd ever seen, and he'd taken an almost immediate dislike to her. "Is that what you talked about? She told you she's crazy about me?"

"You're the whole reason she's doing it. That's what she told me, anyway. She'd *have* to be crazy about you to do something like this, wouldn't you say?"

"Do what?"

"Download herself, of course. I'm going in tomorrow, and she's downloading into my body." Her hands criss-crossed in front of her in a vague pantomime of this procedure. "You didn't *know* that? She *is* nuts. I figured I was here for you to check me out, see what you thought." She smiled flirtatiously. "I'm sorry I look so awful. My hair got all wet. So what do you think?"

But he wasn't there anymore. He was with Justine. She'd do this for him, throw her life away, no guarantee he'd even talk to her again—all because she loved him. And he was about to run out on her. He was filled with shame.

"Hey," Elaine said. Her smile had faded, and she was waiting expectantly for his reply. "I've got to get back to Virginia Beach before it gets too late. The Construct said you wanted to talk to me."

"I do. I do. When are you going to do this?"

"Tomorrow at noon."

That couldn't be a coincidence. He smelled Gabriel. He tried to fit it all together into some kind of sense, but couldn't. It didn't matter anyway. He had to stop Justine.

"So what do you think?" Elaine prompted. "Am I okay? Do you think I'm pretty?"

"Yes, you are, very pretty. What did she say exactly?"

Elaine looked stunned that her beauty warranted only a sentence. "Well, she said she loved somebody out here and wanted to be with him. And I told her it was romantic, or something like that. I don't remember exactly. Does it matter?"

"No, I don't guess it does."

"She's kind of strange, you know? The only thing she asked me was if I could sing. For all she knows, I've got cancer or something."

"And what did you tell her?"

"I told her I was healthy."

"I don't mean that. Can you sing?"

Elaine had obviously decided that Nemo was as strange as Justine. "Well, my voice isn't exactly my best feature. A girl can't have everything." She tried the smile again.

Nemo stood up. "Nice meeting you, Elaine. Lawrence—that's the Construct's *name*—will see you home."

"Guess I'll see you again, huh?" She giggled. "At least my eyes will."

"I wouldn't count on it."

"She's not going to back out, if that's what you're thinking. She's dead set on it."

"Not if I can help it."

Lawrence told him to wait until he got back, and he'd go in with him and help him look for Justine, but Nemo couldn't wait. He tried her hotel first, but she wasn't there. He retraced their steps around D.C. and came up with nothing. Real World Tours was closed up, and The Black Dog wasn't open yet. He even swallowed his pride and called his mom to ask if she knew where Justine was, but she didn't. She obviously knew something was up, but she was smart enough not to ask. Maybe she wasn't so bad after all.

"If you see her, tell her I'm looking for her, okay?"

"I will, dear. We love you very much."

"Me too, Mom. Look, I'm sorry about last night—I was a little crazy." He hung up. He was at a public phone in the lobby of Justine's hotel. He'd decided to camp out there. She had to show up sometime. He paced up and down, then went into the Grotto, but Gene wasn't working, and he couldn't see the front door from in there anyway. By eleven, he'd figured out she wasn't going to show. She had no reason to go back to her room. She couldn't be planning on getting much sleep tonight, and it wasn't like she'd have to pack to go outside. All she'd have after she downloaded would be the clothes that were barely on Elaine's back.

She was supposed to play at the Black Dog, but he'd figured she probably blew that off, like the other night when she took off to New York. Who would want to sing, facing something like this? Now he realized he'd been an idiot. This was her last night in here, her last chance to sing.

SHE WAS SINGING WHEN HE WALKED IN, BUT THE PLACE WAS so packed he couldn't see her. He wormed his way toward the bar, squeezed in and stood on the rail. He could see her head floating above the crowd, her eyes closed, singing into the microphone. So beautiful.

"Hey buddy, get off the rail."

Nemo turned to the voice. "Sorry."

"Wait a minute. You're the boyfriend. Man, she is hot tonight. But tell her to take a break, will you? She's been going at it for over an hour and a half. I need to sell some drinks here."

Nemo hopped down from the rail. "I'll take her a note," he said.

"Good idea." The man wrote *Take a break* on a napkin and signed it *Bruce*.

Nemo pushed through the crowd toward the stage, the napkin folded up in his hand. He succeeded in pissing off several people along the way, wondering who this idiot was who seemed to think he could find a seat down front.

There was a place to stand in front of the door to the green room, just to the left of the stage. He made it there without her seeing him, and laid the napkin on the bass player's amp next to his cigarettes. She was about to introduce another song when the bass player handed her the napkin. "We're going to take a short break now," she said. "You are a great audience."

Even when she finally came off the stage, the applause was so loud Nemo and Justine couldn't have heard each other if they'd tried to speak. She froze, staring at him as if she couldn't quite believe he was real. *I love you*, Nemo mouthed, and opened his arms to her. She ran into them, and he spun her around, holding her tight. When he set her down, for a brief second Rick's face was right in front of him, fixing them both with a venomous stare. Then Rick slipped into the green room with the drummer on his heels.

"I don't like that guy," Nemo said.

"What?"

"Is there a back door to this place?" he shouted.

She led the way through the crowd, everyone smiling at her and giving her the thumb's up. They stood outside under a tiny striped awning, the rain pouring down all around them. "I've been looking everywhere for you," he said.

"I was having dinner with Mr. Menso. I didn't want to be alone. I . . ." She threw her arms around him again. "God, Nemo, don't run off again, please. I couldn't take it again."

She was trembling all over. He held her close. "I'm so sorry. I just went a little crazy when I found out you were Angelina. I'm never leaving you again."

She looked up at him. "I don't know if you can understand this, Nemo. But I'm not Angelina anymore. She spent her whole life learning what I already know. She could've never loved you like I do."

He smiled. "And no one could ever love you like I do."

She rubbed his chest with the palms of her hands. "There's something I have to tell you."

"I already know about Elaine."

"You do? But how?"

"Lawrence brought her by the house to meet me."

"I had no idea—"

"I know you didn't. I'm glad he did. It woke me up. Made me realize what a coward I'd been. I'm coming inside, Justine. I want to be with you, always."

She shook her head. "But you don't have to come in here, Nemo. I know how you feel about this place. It's all arranged. I can come to you."

He put his hands to her face and stopped her head from shaking. "I know I don't have to. I want to. You've changed how I feel about this place, about my life—about everything." He could see her wavering. "Besides," he said. "You're much sexier than Elaine."

"Yeah, right."

"No, I'm serious." He drew her in close.

"To you, maybe."

He feigned offense. "And who else are we talking about here?"

She smiled. "Nobody."

"Marry me?"

Her face lit up. "Yes!"

"Aren't you going to ask me if I'm sure?"

Her eyes glistened. "I told you I'd quit asking when you were."

They kissed, melting into each other's arms, passionate but unhurried, at peace and full of joy, unafraid of the future, in a timeless present. After a while, they became aware of a noise coming from inside the club, a rhythmic thudding. They had no idea how long it'd been going on. It was the crowd, he realized, stomping their feet, hitting their fists on the tables, wanting to hear his future wife sing a few more songs. He tossed his head back toward the club. "You need to do another set, or they'll tear the place down."

"They can't. It's the Bin, remember?"

"Bruce said you were hot tonight. You thought it was a swan song, didn't you? Why don't you sing a few songs to celebrate? I know you want to. Listen to them, they love you. I love you, and I love to hear you sing. I'll sit up front and adore you, every guy in the place hating me."

She smiled at him. "You won't be able to get a seat."

"I've got connections. Bruce is rooting for me. He called me 'the boyfriend.' He'll get me a seat."

"Bless his heart. He's afraid I'm getting it on with Rick. Mr. Menso warned me about Rick and Ian, by the way. He said to watch out for them. I think Rick's some kind of religious nut from outside, if you can believe it."

Nemo shrugged. "I'm not impressed. I've chatted with

the head nut himself. Besides, I'm leaving all that behind."
He cocked his head to one side. "This Menso guy's my
grandfather, isn't he?"

"Yeah, he sure is." She searched his eyes. "You're a
lot like him, you know."

"How's that? I've never met the man."

She narrowed her eyes and studied him. "Smart. Sweet.
Intense. Honorable."

"Honorable? Me?"

"I had my doubts about the smart part, myself."

"I replaced it. Works fine now."

She laughed, holding his face in her hands. "I can't
believe you've come back to me. It's like you never left."

"I can't believe I ever did. Must've been that defective
part." They looked into each other's eyes, smiling like
idiots.

Bruce stuck his head out the backdoor. "I hate to inter-
rupt you lovebirds, but they're getting a little rowdy in
here. How about a half-hour set, Justine."

"Be right there," she said, her eyes still on Nemo.

"Hey, Bruce," Nemo asked, "could you get me a place
to sit?"

"Sure thing. Buy you a drink. Anything."

"We're getting married," Nemo said.

"Swell. Congratulations. Make that two drinks. Bottle
of champagne. *Justine*?"

"Sing me a song?" Nemo asked her.

"Sure. Anything."

"You know what I want to hear."

"Anytime this week," Bruce pleaded.

NEMO WOKE AS THE SUN WAS COMING UP. HE LAY IN BED
watching Justine sleep, her eyes fluttering with dreams.
He'd almost lost her, shut her out of his life completely.

Because he had no faith. It was hers that had saved them, while he was cracking up. What had he been thinking? He touched her hair lightly, so as not to wake her. He'd been thinking that she wasn't who she seemed to be, that she wasn't real, that he couldn't trust her anymore. All the while, her love had been more real than his.

He told Lawrence once, when he was about eleven, that he wished they knew those people Lawrence used to be in London and Nagasaki and Abilene, and that they could all be friends together. "Nice thought," he said, "but it wouldn't happen that way." Nemo had had his feelings hurt at the time, but Lawrence reassured him, "We'd all like *you* just fine. We just don't care to see those other folks again."

As he watched Justine sleeping, he never wanted to see that other Nemo again, the one who'd broken her heart. He got out of bed and put on his clothes, still watching her. He ordered coffee from the room service pad, and sat on the side of the bed, waiting for the coffee smell to wake her. He had to be going soon.

She rolled over and stretched. "Mmm. You made coffee," she murmured. "Aren't you sweet." Her eyes fluttered open. "I had another dream."

"Who were you this time?"

"Oh, I was me. I dreamed we made mad, passionate love all night long."

He laughed. "That wasn't a dream."

"Yes, it was." She took him by the shirt and brought his mouth to hers, kissing him. She tugged at his shirt. "Take this off. You don't need it this morning."

He took her hands. "I have a few good-byes—before I come in. I mentioned it last night." He tried to give her a cheerful smile.

She touched his mouth with her fingertips. "I'm sorry,

Nemo. I forgot. I just wasn't thinking. It must be terrible for you to leave your friends."

"It won't be so bad. They'll visit. I think Jonathan halfway wants me to come in."

She gave him a quick kiss. "Well, get going then, so you can hurry home to me."

"I like the sound of that. I'll be home by eleven at the latest. I'll meet you right here." He patted the bed beside her. "Shirtless."

NEMO'S MIND WAS A MILLION MILES AWAY AS HE TOOK THE Metro to Pentagon Station and stepped into a VIM, thinking about Justine and their new life together. He'd taken a few steps out of his coffin before he realized he wasn't where he was supposed to be. He was standing in a clearing in front of a rustic cabin, a stream running alongside it, the blue shadows of mountains in the distance.

An old man sat on the deck overlooking the stream. Nemo walked down to him and took the seat beside him. "Mr. Rogers," Nemo said. "We meet at last."

The old man smiled. "Yes, I wish we had more time. I'd rather you didn't call me *Mr. Rogers.* If you were as old as I am, you'd know why. Call me Newman, or Grandpa."

"I think I'll go with Newman."

"Wise choice. The other has to be earned, doesn't it? Like Daddy. I met Wade Donley once, crossed his path, quite on purpose. He had his little girl with him, your mother. She was no taller than this cane, clinging to her daddy's leg as we talked." He paused, remembering. Nemo had seen photographs like that. "I liked him a great deal. He was a good man. We talked about medical imaging techniques, I think. If he knew it was me that'd fathered the girl beside him, he didn't let it show. But he certainly knew she wasn't really his daughter and he never let that show either.

"Elizabeth adored her father, and rightly so. What good would it have done anyone for me to announce I was her father? By the time you were born, I was in here. I sent Lawrence to look after you."

"Did he know that?"

"Of course. I'm afraid I have to ask the Constructs to keep entirely too many secrets."

"You communicate with all of them, don't you? They're your spies."

The old man regarded him with his wrinkled eyes, nodding slightly. "I guess you could put it that way. That certainly wasn't my intention. They've become my friends, shared their world with me. They've kept me sane, I think. Completely devoted to me for reasons I can't begin to understand. They've taught me a great deal about love and humility, though I've often wondered why they don't hate me for creating them. It's not an easy life."

Nemo remembered history class—where he'd learned everything he knew about his grandfather. "But you didn't create them. You were opposed to the whole idea from the beginning."

He smiled. "That's true. But I created them, just the same." He waved his cane a few inches off the deck. "Oh, I didn't finish the work, but what was left undone, a fairly talented graduate student could've completed. Einstein was opposed to the atom bomb, too, but without him, there wouldn't have been one. That must've weighed on him from time to time. But unlike the atomic bomb, the Constructs have made the world a better place."

"Lawrence has been awfully good to me," Nemo said, staring at the rushing water, thinking about their years together. He looked up the stream to the woods beyond, the mountains at the horizon. "Where are we?"

"Foothills of the Blue Ridge. In my youth I preferred the Rockies. Now that I'm older I've come to appreciate older mountains. This is my retreat. I haven't spent near enough time here lately."

"How did you bring me here so fast?"

"As you've observed many times, the usual limits needn't apply in here. Place means nothing. I had to write it in. Some people go crazy without it. Time, on the other hand, is a different matter, so I must get to the point. I've brought you here to ask you a favor. You have an appointment with Gabriel at ten o'clock. I want you to keep it. I'm rather counting on it, actually."

Nemo felt a tingling at the base of his scalp. "You *want* me to convey this virus into the Bin?"

"Exactly."

Nemo was still basking in the relief he'd felt deciding he wasn't going to do it. The whole thing seemed like temporary insanity to him now. "I can't do it. It's just not right. Why would you, of all people, want to cut off the Bin?"

The old man sighed heavily. "Because it's time. You were right, you know. Gabriel *will* just find someone else. Or someone else as clever as Gabriel will find a pawn of his own. But when that happens, I won't know exactly when, and it won't be a pawn I can trust." His cane swept the horizon. "As we speak, there are thirty-four sects, cults, religions, and political organizations whose raison d'être is to destroy the Bin and everyone in it. I'm a clever fellow, Nemo, but I don't trust the odds. My most optimistic simulation says we've got seven years. Or it could be seven days. The only way to stop them is to convince them they've accomplished their glorious mission."

Nemo remembered Gabriel atop the pyramid, spewing his righteous venom. "Maybe the two worlds should be severed."

"Severed—I quite agree. But it's not just a matter of cutting the connection. The virus you're being asked to bring in isn't designed just to cut off the Bin, but to wipe it clean. Twelve billion lives in an instant. Gabriel has told you what you wanted to hear, and if things had gone according to his plan, you would've had no way of knowing that you'd been lied to."

Nemo felt as if he were falling as he imagined the horror of what he had almost done. "You're sure of this?"

"Of course I'm sure. I fed them the virus, most of it anyway. They were getting *very* close on their own. They're good, Nemo. Gabriel's a religious fanatic, but he's also brilliant. It had to be the real thing. He'd spot a fake. But what he doesn't know is that I've written a sister program to disarm the virus, and sever the Bin, at the precise moment you enter. The door will be closed, to be sure. That's absolutely essential, so that we may deceive them. But everyone inside won't be murdered in the process."

Nemo's mind was racing, trying to take all this in. But there was one thing that still made no sense to him. "How did they come to pick me as their messenger boy? I'm not even a Christian."

"I'm afraid that's my doing. At my request, Winston was deliberately careless arranging for the plot to lure you into the Bin. There was even an exchange of memos to the effect that you might pose a security risk, if the plan backfired. Gabriel hacked your file and thought he could make sure it did. Peter's visions were just a gift from God. Gabriel puts a great deal of stock in them."

Nemo could hardly believe what he was hearing. "So you handed them your own grandson, nudged me over the edge with Justine, thinking I'd charge in with the virus. It almost worked. But you hadn't bargained on her downloading herself, had you?"

"You've both surprised me, I'm proud to say."

"You had Lawrence introduce me to Elaine so that I'd stop Justine and come inside."

"Yes, I did. You didn't *want* to know what Justine was about to do?"

"Of course I did."

"Then what, exactly, are you accusing me of?"

"Of arranging this whole business, of using us, so that I would carry in this virus. Your own grandson—and a woman you supposedly loved."

He rested his chin on his cane, watching the stream cascade over the rocks. "Do you have any idea how many conflicting desires there are in the world at any given moment? Sometimes I have to kill twenty or thirty birds with a single stone, metaphorically of course. I haven't killed anyone yet. I don't have the luxury of pure, simple motives. Sometimes I wonder whether I used all this intrigue as an excuse to resurrect Angelina, or whether it's the other way around, and I've used her. I trust God knows. My motives are mixed, Nemo, but they're not evil, and you do have a choice, your own motives to consider.

"Before you give me your answer, I have to warn you that you could be in danger. I have to put the sister program into place before you come in. If they suspect what I'm doing, they'll want to keep you out—by any means necessary. Without access to the Bin, they can't destroy it."

"And the End of Days never comes."

Newman snorted his contempt. "As if God would wait on them to tell Him what to do!"

"You believe in God?"

"Oh yes, Nemo, most definitely. Will you do it?"

"I need to think about it."

"You have approximately five minutes. You still have

to catch a train to Richmond. I can't zap you around in the real world."

Nemo didn't know why he should trust this man. He'd hated him all his life without ever knowing him. What he was saying made perfect sense. Sooner or later, the Gabriels of the world would have their way, if something wasn't done to stop them. But the sense of it wasn't enough. Nemo'd have to trust him as irrationally as he'd hated him before. "I have to tell Justine. She's expecting me by eleven."

Newman Rogers smiled, the proud grandfather. "I'll tell Justine you'll be coming in at noon. And don't be late, by the way. If they're onto us, they'll take countermeasures to disable the sister program. But it will take them some time. Don't give it to them."

"So if I'm twenty minutes late, I could end up murdering everyone in the Bin just by uploading myself?"

"I'd say it'd be more like eighteen minutes, maybe nineteen. I must tell you, Nemo, that, according to my simulations, our chances for success are not very good. It's not a question of *if* something goes wrong. It almost certainly will. But Lawrence tells me you're quite resourceful."

"He taught me everything I know."

17

HOLLYWOOD CEMETERY LOOKED A LOT DIFFERENT in the daylight. The morning sun was burning off last night's rain, and a mist hung over everything. The birds were singing in the trees, pecking on the graves for worms. The rain had strewn the walkways with flower petals.

Nemo strolled past the iron dog, obviously harmless in the light of day. He turned slowly around in a circle, looking for any sign of human life. He hadn't seen a soul since he got on the train in D.C. but the whole time he had the feeling he was being watched.

He walked up to Monroe's black iron monument. It looked like an ornate cage. There was still no one around. He tried the gate, and it came open. At the foot of the sarcophagus, a grass-covered trapdoor stood open, and narrow steps led into the earth. He looked down the stairs and saw a light some thirty feet down. He couldn't tell how far the steps continued beyond that.

He passed three lights on the way down—bare bulbs, hanging from a conduit that ran along the ceiling of the concrete shaft. Someone had been very busy. Nemo's estimation of Gabriel went up several notches. He wondered what their power source was, especially when he got to the bottom. He was in a concrete room, at least thirty by thirty, with a twelve-foot ceiling, covered with banks of fluorescent lights shining down on a computer that took up most of the floor. He'd never seen anything like it.

Gabriel walked out from behind it, still in his robes. No. Clean, fresh ones. All dressed up for Judgment Day.

"Good morning, Nemo." He beckoned with his hand. "This way."

On the other side of the computer was a console and a chair atop a low pedestal. "Have a seat," he said. "This won't take long."

Nemo climbed into the chair, looking around at the array of electronics, the likes of which the world hadn't seen for twenty years at least. "Where did you get all this stuff?"

"We made it," he said. "Surprised? You shouldn't be. Faith can move mountains. I learned about computers at my father's knee. He was the man who fired Newman Rogers. He died humiliated and broken."

"Now you have the last laugh."

Gabriel grinned. "Something like that. Are you ready, or has your night in bed with your whore changed your mind?"

Nemo hung his head. He wanted to come up out of this chair and strangle Gabriel on the spot. But he couldn't just think about what he wanted to do. Besides, he'd spotted four lasers pointed at him. There were probably more. He remembered his shame, tried to feel it all over again. "That's why I'm doing this. I have to rid myself of her. As long as she's there, I'm not strong enough to stay away. But I have to. She's—" He looked Gabriel in the eye. "Never mind what she is. Let's just get this over with. I have to catch a train, remember?" He heard a slight ringing in his ears. This jumping in and out of the Bin apparently had him completely exhausted.

Gabriel smiled. "Sin is a bit too delicious, isn't it? You're doing the right thing, Nemo. While you're here, I can implant more than the virus." He gestured to the sprawling computer. "Anything you like. Isn't there something you'd like to know? A foreign language, or a dozen? A musical instrument perhaps? I believe you've heard Rick and Ian play. They couldn't play a note before they came to me. But you're an intelligent young man—how about the combined knowledge of all the civilizations that ever existed?"

Nemo had no doubt at all the man could do what he claimed. "No thanks. Just the virus."

Gabriel chuckled. "All for love—or nothing—eh? We're done here. You can go catch that train now."

Nemo almost panicked. Gabriel must be on to him, sending him on his way, with a stand-in probably waiting in the wings. "What about the virus and the download?"

Gabriel chuckled. "All done!" He gestured proudly at the equipment around them. "You could've stood on your head and recited the Song of Songs, and it would've downloaded you and implanted the virus flawlessly. Well, go on, get up. Party's over."

The ringing in Nemo's ears stopped. He carefully rose from the chair, as if he might leave part of himself behind if he moved too quickly, and stepped down from the pedestal.

"You'll need this, as well," Gabriel said, handing him a silver vial. "Drink it between 11:30 and 11:45. You did remember not to eat, didn't you?"

"Yeah, sure." Actually he'd forgotten to eat, which wasn't quite the same thing. Now he noticed how empty he was.

"The next thing you know, we'll be waking you up here. The last thing you'll remember is my saying, 'Party's over.' I hope you were thinking pleasant thoughts."

Actually, he'd been thinking that Gabriel was the biggest prick he'd ever met.

NEMO CAUGHT HIS TRAIN AND SLUMPED DOWN IN A SEAT UP front by the doors. His hands were shaking, and his heart wouldn't slow down. He wondered if it was the virus that made him feel this way. But he'd felt this before. It was fear, pure and simple. Fear of what he was about to do. Fear that he would fail.

He tried to imagine what it was like to be someone like Gabriel, so convinced of his righteousness that he could wipe out everyone in the Bin and feel no remorse, actually rejoice in it. Even in the midst of his greatest rage at the Bin, Nemo'd never wished it out of existence. He wondered, when the Bin was gone, whether Gabriel would find the release he sought, or whether he'd lose his own reason for being.

Either way, Nemo wouldn't be in a position to know, unless the Constructs somehow maintained their connection with the Bin. He hoped so. He hadn't had time for his good-byes. He'd never see Jonathan and Lawrence again. He hoped, somehow, they'd understand.

He was still clutching the silver vial in his hand. He opened up his hand and stared at it, nestled in his palm. If he took it, he could live in both places, two lives diverging, oblivious to each other. *Party's over*, he thought. It would begin just then, rising from that chair. And then what? Would this resurrected Nemo glory in being the great deliverer, or hang himself from the nearest tree? He slid open the window. It came down to instinct in the end. Which way you jumped when the lightning bolt strikes. He threw the vial out the window, and it vanished in a quick, silver arc.

The door at the back of the car opened and closed, and

someone came up the aisle, sliding into the seat behind him. Before Nemo could turn around, he felt cold metal press against the back of his neck. A gun barrel.

"That was a very valuable item you just threw away."

Nemo knew the voice. It was Rick. Ian must be somewhere close by. "Are you going to shoot me for littering? Gabriel might not like that."

The door at the front of the car slid open, and Ian stepped through. "What do you think you're doing?" he asked Rick. "He's no good to us dead." Rick withdrew his gun. Ian bent down and got in Nemo's face. He looked like a cherub with his ring of curls. "Why did you throw the antidote away?"

"Look Ian, we're on the same side here."

The back of Ian's fist came out of nowhere and caught Nemo just below the eye. "Why did you throw the antidote away?"

Nemo pretended the blow hurt more than it did, stalling for time to formulate an acceptable lie. He didn't figure he'd have many opportunities for revision. "Obviously, because I don't want to take it. I'm committing suicide, asshole. So why don't you just shoot me and get it over with."

Ian's eyes narrowed. "Suicide." He straightened up, rubbed the side of his nose with the fist he'd just hit Nemo with. "Why?"

"None of your business. I've done something horrible. I want to die."

"Suicide is a sin."

And murder isn't? Nemo thought. "I don't care. I told Gabriel from the beginning I was doing this for my own reasons. I'm sure he'll be glad to hear you shot me for being a sinner."

Rick stood up and came out in the aisle, the gun still in hand. It had a long barrel with a silencer on the end of it. "He's lying. He's going in to shack up with that whore. It's a setup."

Ian took a cellular phone out of his pocket and made a call. Nemo thought of all those damn things he'd tossed aside as so much junk, now that there weren't any phone companies. But these guys had their own phone company. He wondered what else they had, and what they intended to do with it.

"Gabriel," Ian said, "we've got a problem here." He walked to the back of the car so that Nemo couldn't hear him. Rick kept looking back at Ian, awaiting orders, probably hoping for the chance to shoot Nemo with his nice long gun. Ian walked back to Nemo and handed him the phone. "Gabriel wants to talk to you."

Nemo took the phone and put it to his ear. "Would you call off your dogs, Gabriel? I'm holding up my end of the bargain. Your virus will be delivered."

"Perhaps. You didn't tell me you intended to kill yourself."

"That's my business, isn't it?"

"If you're telling the truth. Why do you want to die?"

Nemo stared at the clock at the end of the car, counting off the seconds. The lives of billions of people all came down to his ability to lie. "If you found out you'd been fucking your grandmother, wouldn't you want to die?"

There was a long silence on the other end. "Let me speak with Ian."

Nemo handed Ian the phone and waited as Ian listened without saying a word. He folded up the phone and slipped it into his pocket.

"We'll just ride along with you for now, Nemo. Gabriel's checking on a few things."

They hurtled along. Ian drumming on the back of Nemo's seat with a pair of pens. Rick across the aisle, watching him, his finger on the trigger. Nemo figured he was a dead man. Pretty soon Gabriel would find the sister program, and Ian's little phone would ring. Would they shoot him right away, he wondered, or would they question him first? He considered making a jump for it, but the train was doing about two hundred miles an hour. He'd rather be shot.

And then he felt it—the train gradually slowing for Quantico. A familiar plume of smoke rose up into the sky at the horizon. The train would slow to about fifty or sixty through here before it went into a tunnel. He might make it. He eyed the door, right in front of him.

He could jump off the train, but then what? He'd never make it to D.C. on foot. He couldn't exactly flag down another train. His head snapped up. He could see the stacks now, gradually growing taller. That's exactly what he'd do—flag down another train.

The phone started bleating, and Ian walked to the back of the car and answered it. Rick stood up and drifted back a few paces so that he could hear. Nemo was trying to time it just right, wishing he had Rosalind here to make the call. He was going to jump immediately, as soon as the brakes kicked in, while Rick and Ian were being knocked on their butts. He figured it was his only chance not to get shot. He could feel Rick's eyes on the back of his neck. Nemo kept his eyes on the smokestacks, calculating the angle. Now.

He reached up and yanked on the emergency cord, rolling into the doors and out into the marsh, skidding at least fifty feet in the muck, sending a shower of water high into the air, like the wake from a power boat. He struggled to his feet and almost fell down again. There was a lot more water than there had been before. He was standing in mud up to his calves. He brought up his right foot, and his boot came off, trapped in the gook. The left boot was more stubborn, but after a few yards he decided it was slowing him down and took it off. He must've looked like a wounded bird trying to take flight, flapping and splashing.

The train was stopped a half mile down the tracks. He could see Rick and Ian standing beside it, deciding whether to follow him or not, possibly get stranded out here in this sea of mud, when all they had to do was keep him out of the Bin. The way he had it figured, they'd decide he'd already accomplished that for them when he jumped off the train. Nemo knew they had exactly three minutes to make up their minds before the train took off and left them there. Meanwhile, Nemo tried to run.

They were still standing by the train when the faint bong of the train's warning bell drifted across the marsh like a bird call, and Rick and Ian climbed on board. Nemo cheered silently, but he didn't slow his pace, such as it was. It would be a miracle if he made it to D.C. at all, much less by noon. As he approached the fence, the land sloped upward and became relatively dry. He didn't bother with trying to avoid being seen. If an alarm was raised, it would almost certainly be answered by a Construct, and he could use any help he could get. As he walked on the gravel up to the tracks, he realized he was going to need some shoes before he rode a train out of here. Unfortunately, he knew where he could get some.

He didn't have to wait long for a train to arrive. He studied it as it approached, and noticed rungs on the ends of the cars. He didn't have to hang underneath it like a bat. The train came to a stop at the gate, and he climbed onto the front. He remembered an old video set in San Francisco, a guy hanging off a streetcar singing a song.

The train moved toward the door more slowly than he recalled. Maybe a surveillance camera had tripped an alarm, and they were shutting down. But the train kept inching along, and the door opened seconds before he thought he was going to smash into it. Inside it was exactly as he remembered, every detail. He'd been here often enough in his dreams. Before the train had even come to a stop, the cold settled into his wet clothes and into his bones. He felt as if he were encased in ice.

He had to jump from the train to clear the tracks, stumbling to his hands and knees when he hit the concrete. He peeled his hands from the floor, leaving icy shadows where they'd been. He started to stand, but decided he was better off on his knees, putting off standing on his bare feet for as long as he could. "Open the damn thing," he muttered under his breath. "Please God, I'm freezing to death here."

The minute the doors started rising, he moved in. The robots stayed back until the doors stopped completely. He'd have a few seconds. When he had enough room, he scurried under the doors. The whir of the door motors echoed inside, amplifying it.

There weren't nearly as many bodies as there'd been before. The car was maybe a third full. As the door continued its ascent, he had more light, but he also had less time. He searched the shadows, but he couldn't find what he was looking for. It was late spring. Sandals, useless little loafers, moccasins. He had to dig deeper. He pushed a couple of bodies aside and spotted a heavy work boot, ankle high. But he could only see one, laced up to the top. The whir of the door motors stopped. He had plenty of light now as the robots' floodlights came on.

He wrapped his hands around the boot and the ankle inside it, and yanked. A man's body slid out of the pile far enough so he could see both the legs now, both boots. He glanced over his shoulder and saw the robot at his back moving in. He had to give it something to do. He grabbed the body of a young man about his age by the belt and dragged it to the floor between himself and the robot, and started working on the bootlaces.

He could hear the little motors in the robot's servo arms as it picked up the body from the floor, but he couldn't think about that. He had to unlace the boots with stiff clumsy fingers. He almost had the second boot off when the robot started moving again. He grabbed at the nearest body and rolled it to the floor without looking to see whether it was young or old or male or female. He was crying now. He didn't have time to think about why. It was just another sound. He freed the second boot, tied them together, and hung them around his neck. Now he needed clothes. He yanked on the man's ankles again and stripped off his jeans, but he couldn't get at his shirt, and it was light-weight cotton anyway.

The robot had both bodies now. Nemo moved to the side and let it roll in. He worked his way down the length of the car. The other robots had completed their duties and retreated to their resting positions. As he passed their jurisdictions, they started forward thinking he was another stray corpse. Finally, he found what he was looking for, a leather jacket several sizes too big for him. He stripped it off, struggling with the massive body, and stepped through the line of robots. Once he was behind them, it was as if he didn't exist. They all watched the cars roll into the fire.

He stripped off his wet clothes and put on the jeans and jacket. They both were huge. The sleeves hung down three or four inches below his wrists. He sat on the concrete and put on the boots. They were pretty tight, but it didn't matter. He could no longer feel his feet. The deafening roar of the fire started, and he limped to the door, hugging himself, stamping his feet, just waiting for a train.

It came as scheduled, the heat from it as inviting as a woodstove in the dead of winter. The cars closed themselves up—like birds folding in their wings. He draped his wet clothes over the rungs and climbed onto them, his hands inside the leather sleeves. The clothes sizzled and steamed but didn't burn through. He hung on tightly as the train quickly accelerated. The two-hundred-mile an hour wind cooled the metal down soon enough, dried his tears, and beat at him like a huge fist, until finally, with the Washington Monument peaking up over the horizon, the train began to slow and dove into the ground.

He came to a stop in a room that was the mirror image of the crematorium, only where the incinerator would be was a carousel fed by a chute sloping down from the wall above. Every once in a while, the flap at the top of the chute came open, and a body slid down to the carousel, where it was retrieved by a robot and placed on the waiting train.

To the left of the carousel was an elevator. As Nemo approached it, he saw there was no call button. Access was controlled by a retinal scan. You looked into a little green light shining down from above the doors. He says he's a clever fellow, Nemo thought. Let's see how clever. He walked up to the elevator and stared into the light. "Come on, Grandpa," he whispered. "Override the damn thing." The doors slid open, and he stepped inside. There were no buttons or controls of any kind. "Receiving," he said, and the elevator began to rise. He leaned back against the wall and heaved a sigh of relief. It was almost over.

The doors opened, and he was looking at Rick's back. He and Ian were waiting at the top of the escalator. The clock above the train platform said 12:16.

"Down," he said, and Rick turned around. He raised his gun and fired as the doors slid closed. Nemo rolled up into a ball as a bullet ricocheted inside the elevator, then clattered to the floor. The doors came open, and Nemo was back where he started, with the dead. He crawled out of the elevator on his hands and knees. The flap in the wall came open, and a body slid down the chute. An old woman, still holding her handbag. He didn't suppose she was carrying a gun.

But he didn't need a gun. He needed another way out of here. He eyed the flap at the top of the chute. It was a low-tech affair, a ramp covered with polished steel, like the slide in the playground when he was a kid.

He gathered his feet under him, ran past the robots, and vaulted onto the carousel. As he passed the bottom of the chute, about waist high, he jumped and grabbed hold of it on either side. His knees slipped on the slick metal, but he pulled himself up until his rubber soles caught and held. Still holding the sides, he started up the chute in a low crouch. It was much longer than it'd looked from the ground, and steeper. But if no one died in the next few minutes, he'd be okay.

As he reached the top, a bald head pushed through the flap. Nemo planted himself and ducked his head, let the body slide over his back and fall to the floor. One of the robots rolled over to pick it up. Nemo pulled open the flap and crawled through, shoving a robot out of the way. It fell over on its back like a turtle.

Nemo looked up to see the blue, glowing face of Victor. "Are you all right, Nemo?" he asked.

"Just great. You need to upload me immediately."

"We know. Come with us."

Nemo had always wondered what it looked like, the last glimpse of the real world people had before they went in. It was like a small chapel with no pews, only a single chair in the middle. As he sat down in the chair, he called to Victor, "Tell Lawrence good-bye for me."

Victor smiled, his feline fangs hanging over his lower lip. *Farewell*, he signed. *We are honored to have known you.*

Victor reached out and touched a console beside him,

and Nemo found himself moving through space, thick with stars, toward a point where they all seemed to come together in a blaze of light of every hue. As he approached, the individual stars disappeared, and the light enveloped him, consumed him, and filled him with joy.

And then, he was lying on his back in bed. He felt something touch his dirt-caked face, and he reached up and found Justine's hands. He opened his eyes, and her face was before him. "We love you, Nemo," she whispered. "Welcome home."

Epilogue

AT 12:21 ALL CONTACT WITH THE BIN CEASED. BY 12:45 the trains into D.C. were jammed. Lawrence and Jonathan rode silently, their eyes on the crowd. Some were wild-eyed with joy: The Rapture would come at any moment. They would see the face of God. Others just looked dazed. Something had changed, and they wanted to go see for themselves what it was, what it meant, if anything, in their lives.

Several of the zealots were carrying axes and sledgehammers in addition to the usual guns and knives, so no one noticed the pick and shovel Lawrence and Jonathan had brought along.

A guy all dressed up in camos, an automatic stuck in his belt, was pushing his way down the aisle when he spotted Lawrence. "Hey, green man," he shouted. "What're you doing out today? You a Christian?"

"Wouldn't be on this train 'less we were," Lawrence drawled.

"He's okay," Jonathan said. "He's with me."

The camo man squinted at Jonathan. "You're Harold's boy, ain't you? Good man, your father." He continued on down the aisle, looking for infidels.

"Why on earth would he bother to shoot anyone at this stage of the game?" Lawrence wondered aloud.

PENTAGON STATION WAS A MADHOUSE. THERE WASN'T enough that was fragile to go around. All the glass had been broken within minutes, and the mob found little satisfaction, after the first few strokes, in banging away at concrete walls with sledgehammers. A swarm of them had settled on the escalator up to Receiving and the VIMs, and were beating, prying, even shooting at it.

Lawrence led the way to an elevator at the end of the platform. A pair of men were there, contemplating beating down the polished steel doors with a claw hammer and a hatchet. "How are we going to get past them?" Jonathan asked.

"Follow established procedures, of course," Lawrence replied. He walked up behind the men. "Excuse me, gentlemen, this lift is reserved for authorized personnel."

They looked up at Lawrence, as big as a refrigerator, but talking like some damned fairy, and the one with the hatchet said, "We just got authorization, or haven't you heard? The Bin's been fried." He hefted the hatchet in his hand. "We're in charge now."

Lawrence laughed, and the man took a swipe with his hatchet, just to scare him a little. Lawrence reached out and plucked it from his hand, examined the blade, and handed it back to him. "Why don't you run along and bust up some kindling?" he said, talking differently now.

The man with the hatchet took a swing in earnest, aiming for the throat, but Lawrence snatched it out of his hand again. The man back-pedaled into the elevator doors, and his companion took off running. Smiling pleasantly, Lawrence held out the hatchet, handle first. "Apparently, your authority does not extend to this facility," he said. The man took his hatchet and ran.

As they rode up the elevator, Jonathan asked what Lawrence would've done if the men had had guns.

"Taken another elevator," he said.

VICTOR MET THEM AS THE ELEVATOR DOORS OPENED, AND led them through darkened rooms, to where Nemo's body lay, covered with a sheet. Lawrence pulled it off, and they were all silent for a moment.

"Shouldn't we clean him up?" Jonathan asked. "Where did he get these clothes?"

Lawrence said, "He worked hard for those clothes. We figure he'd be proud to be buried in them."

"The woman almost didn't make it," Victor said. "She came in late. She's over here." He pointed out Elaine's body, in a worn blue velvet dress, probably her finest.

"She's every bit as beautiful as you described," Jonathan said to Lawrence.

"Your train's waiting in the tunnel," Victor said. "We've programmed it to take you straight through to Oregon Hill, no stops."

"What about you?"

"As soon as you two leave, we're headed for the hills."

"See you there, tonight," Lawrence said. He bent down and carefully took Nemo's body in his arms. Victor carried Elaine's. Jonathan followed with the pick and shovel.

As the train got underway, Jonathan said, "I still think we ought to bury him at home. Hollywood'll be crawling with Gabriel's people."

"We won't have any trouble," Lawrence said.

*   *   *

AT THE GATES TO HOLLYWOOD CEMETERY, A GUARD stepped in front of them. "I don't know you," he said to Lawrence. His tone made it clear he didn't want to know any Constructs.

"We've come to bury our dead," Lawrence said quietly.

Beyond the gates, there were hundreds of people, scattered among the graves, sitting on blankets or standing in small groups. Children ran up and down the walks. Jonathan and Lawrence had attracted the attention of the men hanging around the gate, talking to the guards. One of the other guards, a tall black man, approached them.

"We've come to bury our dead," Lawrence repeated.

The black man bent over and looked into Nemo's face. "Let them through," he said to the first guard.

"Gabriel's not going to like this."

"I said, let them in."

The first guard stiffened. "Do you speak for them?" he asked.

The black man straightened up and looked into Lawrence's eyes. "Yes, I do," he said.

As they moved through the cemetery, people pointed, and they picked up a trail of kids, but no one tried to stop them. Perhaps because the guard walked along with them. They went past the Monroe Monument, topped a rise overlooking the river, and came to a pair of headstones for Wade Donley and Angelina Donley.

"We figure there's room on either side of them," Lawrence said as they laid the bodies on the ground.

IT TOOK ALL AFTERNOON TO DIG TWO GRAVES WITH A PICK and a shovel. The black guard stayed on, helped dig when Jonathan was worn out. Lawrence never stopped. Harold, Constance, and Matthew showed up, bringing food and water. Others came to watch, most leaving after a few minutes, a handful staying behind, sitting in a circle around the graves. As the sun was setting there were maybe a dozen who bowed their heads and prayed as Jonathan conducted the funeral service.

Lawrence didn't listen too closely to the exact words. They didn't matter that much. He'd never been very religious—an Easter Baptist, a punctual Anglican, a lazy Buddhist. But sometimes things happened to change your mind. He looked out over the river. What looked like the first star of the evening was hanging low over the silver ribbon of water. It wasn't really a star, its light merely a reflection from the sun, but it was just as bright as one, shining by the grace of God.